The Best Short Stories of Mark Twain

THE BEST SHORT STORIES OF MARK TWAIN

Edited, with a Preface and Notes,
by Lawrence I. Berkove

Introduction by Pete Hamill

THE MODERN LIBRARY
NEW YORK

2004 Modern Library Paperback Edition

 Published in the United States by Modern Library, an imprint of The Random House Publishing Group, a division of Random House, Inc., New York, and simultaneously in Canada by Random House of Canada Limited, Toronto.

Grateful acknowledgment is made to the following for permission to reprint previously published material:

HarperCollins Publishers Inc.: "The Great Dark" and "Letter to the Earth" from *Letters from the Earth* by Mark Twain, edited by Bernard DeVoto, copyright © 1938, 1944, 1946, 1959, 1962 by The Mark Twain Company, copyright © 1942 by The President and Fellows of Harvard College. Reprinted by permission of HarperCollins Publishers Inc.

University of California Press: "The Second Advent" from *Fables of Man* by Mark Twain, edited by John Tucker, copyright © 1972 by The Mark Twain Company; "Captain Stormfield" piece by Mark Twain from unpublished manuscripts and works in the Bancroft Library of the University of California, copyright © 2001 by Mark Twain Foundation. Reprinted by permission of the University of California Press.

LIBRARY OF CONGRESS CATALOGING-IN-PUBLICATION DATA

Twain, Mark, 1835–1910.
[Short stories. Selections]
The best short stories of Mark Twain / edited, with a preface and notes, by Lawrence I. Berkove; introduction by Pete Hamill.—Modern Library pbk. ed.
p. cm.
Includes bibliographical references.
ISBN 0-8129-7118-3
1. Humorous stories, American. I. Berkove, Lawrence I. II. Title.

PS1302.B47 2004
813'.4—dc22 2003066518

Modern Library website address: www.modernlibrary.com

Printed in the United States of America

4 6 8 9 7 5

Mark Twain

Mark Twain was born Samuel Langhorne Clemens on November 30, 1835, in Florida, Missouri. His family moved to the Mississippi River port town of Hannibal four years later. His father—who failed as a storekeeper, worked as a clerk, and was finally appointed justice of the peace—died when Sam was eleven. Soon afterward the boy began working as an apprentice printer, and by age sixteen he was occasionally writing newspaper sketches. He left Hannibal at eighteen to work as an itinerant printer in New York, Philadelphia, St. Louis, and Cincinnati. From 1857 to 1861 he worked on Mississippi River steamboats, advancing from cub pilot to licensed pilot.

When the Civil War interrupted river traffic, Sam headed west with his brother Orion, who had been appointed secretary of the Nevada Territory. Settling at first in Carson City, he left his brother's employ and tried his luck at prospecting at various mining sites. He was unsuccessful at mining, but his humorous contributions to various regional periodicals attracted notice, and in September 1862 he accepted an offer of employment on the *Virginia City Territorial Enterprise,* soon to be one of the West's outstanding newspapers. There he came under the influence of Sagebrush School writers, especially Joseph T. Goodman and Dan De Quille, and his writing career began.

At first he adopted the pen name of Josh, but in January 1863 he changed it to Mark Twain, originally a river term indicating safe water. He left Virginia City in May 1864 for San Francisco, from where he continued to send columns to the *Enterprise,* but he also wrote for several local newspapers, including the *San Francisco Call,* the *Alta California,* and the *Sacramento Union*. The *Union* sent him on a five-month trip to the Sandwich Islands (Hawaii) in 1866, from which he wrote articles that were soon adapted for a lecture tour that began on his return, and later for chapters of *Roughing It*. The *Alta California* paid for his passage in 1867 on an organized tour of Europe and the Near East. His growing fame as a humorous writer and lecturer was enhanced by *The Celebrated Jumping Frog of Calaveras County and Other Sketches* (1867).

After his marriage to Olivia Louis (Livy) Langdon in 1870, Twain settled first in Buffalo, New York, and then for two decades in Hartford, Connecticut. His newspaper sketches from his European trip were expanded into *The Innocents Abroad* (1869), and his Western and Sandwich Island adventures were transformed into *Roughing It* (1872), both financial successes. *The Gilded Age*, written in collaboration with Charles Dudley Warner, followed in 1873. Twain subsequently mined his childhood experiences for three of his masterpieces: *The Adventures of Tom Sawyer* (1876), *Life on the Mississippi* (1883), and, finally, *Adventures of Huckleberry Finn* (1884–85), on which he worked for nearly a decade. Another vein, historical fiction, resulted in *The Prince and the Pauper* (1882), *A Connecticut Yankee in King Arthur's Court* (1889), and *Personal Recollections of Joan of Arc* (1896). He continued his interest in travel writing with *A Tramp Abroad* (1880) and *Following the Equator* (1897). Literary associates during these years included such eminent authors as Bret Harte, George Washington Cable, Joel Chandler Harris, and the most important and longlasting of them all, William Dean Howells.

During these years, Twain embarked on numerous business ventures, most of them unsuccessful. A notable exception was his undertaking to publish the memoirs of the terminally ill Ulysses S. Grant in 1885, but this was more than balanced by his typical experiences. His most disastrous investment was in a typesetting machine designed by James W. Paige. Twain lost a fortune in that project, and its failure contributed to his declaration of bankruptcy in 1894.

Despite his public image as a humorist and the genial author of seemingly heartwarming tales of an idyllic American boyhood, Twain was at heart a serious and even gloomy thinker, particularly about religion. Even as early as *Roughing It*, but certainly from *Huckleberry Finn* onward, it is possible to find evidences in his writings of deepening pessimism increasingly thinly concealed by irony. The deaths of two of his daughters, Susy and Jean, added to the bitterness of his reflections. His novel *The Tragedy of Pudd'nhead Wilson* (1894), an indictment of slavery, was not artistically successful, and his late works, such as "To the

Person Sitting in Darkness"(1901), "The War Prayer" (1905), and "King Leopold's Soliloquy"(1905) are overtly critical of imperialism and colonialism. The privately published *What Is Man?* (1906) is an extremely bleak expression of determinism, and the posthumously published *Mysterious Stranger* fragments and *Letters from the Earth,* both criticisms of religious teachings, are among the darkest things he wrote. In his last years, his financial troubles finally resolved, but alone except for his daughter Clara, Twain settled near Redding, Connecticut, and died in his mansion, Stormfield, on April 21, 1910.

Contents

Biographical Note v
Introduction *by Pete Hamill* xi
Editor's Preface *by Lawrence I. Berkove* xix

THE BEST SHORT STORIES OF MARK TWAIN

Jim Smiley and His Jumping Frog 3
The Story of the Bad Little Boy Who Didn't Come to Grief 10
Cannibalism in the Cars 14
Journalism in Tennessee 22
The Story of the Good Little Boy Who Did Not Prosper 29
How I Edited an Agricultural Paper Once 34
Political Economy 40
A True Story, Repeated Word for Word as I Heard It 46
The Facts Concerning the Recent Carnival of Crime in Connecticut 51
Punch, Brothers, Punch! 67
Jim Baker's Blue-Jay Yarn 72
The Stolen White Elephant 77
The McWilliamses and the Burglar Alarm 95
The Private History of a Campaign That Failed 101
Extracts from Adam's Diary 120
The Man That Corrupted Hadleyburg 130
The $30,000 Bequest 172

Eve's Diary 198
Captain Stormfield's Visit to Heaven 213
Letter from the Recording Angel 264
The Great Dark 269
The Second Advent 309

Appendix
War Times 327
Private History of the "Jumping Frog" Story 331
How to Tell a Story 339
Notes 345
Selected Bibliography 363

INTRODUCTION

Pete Hamill

At Christmas of 1946, a great box filled with treasure arrived at our tenement flat in Brooklyn. There were four of us kids at the time. I was eleven, the oldest. The box, we learned, came from a well-off family that had employed my mother as a domestic after her arrival from Ireland in 1929. After she married they remained friends, and the box was as much for her as it was for us. The wrapping was torn off, the box sliced open. And there was the treasure: the collected works of Mark Twain.

Those green books with their imitation-leather bindings became part of childhood itself. We read them, absorbed them, unconsciously made them part of our own American past. At first, my own favorite was the thrilling chronicle of Tom Sawyer. We went with him into the caves near the Mississippi the way we went into the smaller caves of Prospect Park, a few blocks from where we lived in the metropolis. Perhaps a Brooklyn version of Injun Joe waited within. Perhaps our courage would collapse. Perhaps we would enter the darkness and never return, never again see home, never again glimpse the sunny loveliness of Becky Thatcher. *The Adventures of Tom Sawyer* was not simply a wonderful story; it was, if you were eleven, a guide to conduct.

But there was more awaiting us on that green shelf. We wandered the true West in *Roughing It.* We traveled on magical steamboats in *Life on the Mississippi,* learning the secrets of the river art, understanding that each of us must serve an apprenticeship in life if we hoped for mastery, whether it was in baseball or drawing comic strips. We were Brooklyn Yankees in King Arthur's Court. We wondered which of our friends was Pudd'nhead Wilson and whether he had a secret twin.

At eleven or twelve, only *Adventures of Huckleberry Finn* made me uneasy. My father was a drinker. He always worked, and in that hard-drinking, blue-collar neighborhood he bore no resemblance to Huck's father, the isolated and notorious town drunk. But Finn was an Irish name. In some disturbing way, Twain's novel made me understand, for the first time, that what seemed normal among the people of our own little Brooklyn hamlet was considered shameful in other places. Particularly in that mysterious America beyond the frontier of New York. In the journey of Huck and the Nigger Jim, where the black man was the instructor of the boy, the goal was not to get home but to flee its illusory safety and imprisoning hypocrisy. In my first reading I couldn't articulate any of this, but I was unsettled by the injustices of race. We knew almost nothing about race in our neighborhood until Jackie Robinson came to play for the Brooklyn Dodgers in 1947, forcing all of us into the first moral discussions of our young lives. The horrors of the Holocaust seemed far away, but race was on the other side of the park, in Ebbets Field. Even within that context, I could read about Huck and Jim on their great distant American river and not truly understand them. The tale of Tom Sawyer did not disturb me in any way at all.

Then in 1953, as a young would-be sailor in the United States Navy, I was assigned to Ellyson Field in Pensacola, Florida, culturally a Southern town, and in the superb little library on the base fell under the spell of Ernest Hemingway, F. Scott Fitzgerald, and John Dos Passos. Hemingway led me back to Huck and Jim by stating in *Green Hills of Africa:* "All modern American literature comes from one book by Mark Twain called *Huckleberry Finn.*" He did not elaborate, although the remark has been often repeated. In part, he surely meant that Twain wrote in the American language and not some imitation of the prose styles of England. I read *Huckleberry Finn* again just short of my eighteenth birthday, six years after the box of treasure came to Brooklyn, and knew that it was a great novel. In the decades that followed, I read the book more than a dozen times. I've never read *Tom Sawyer* again.

The tales, sketches, and stories in this collection were not then part of my understanding of Samuel L. Clemens, the man who was Mark Twain. In my memory, they were not in any volume of those now vanished green books in Brooklyn. Some had not yet even been published. Over the years, I've read most of them, in stray collections, in anthologies. Many are not short stories, in the sense that Guy de Maupassant wrote short stories, or Anton Chekhov, Alphonse Daudet, or Henry James, writers that Clemens might have read in his lifetime (he died in

1910, at age seventy-five). None offer that moment of epiphany that James Joyce gave us in the stories of *Dubliners.* None present the sometimes brutal, and always indirect, ironies of Hemingway.

In Twain's short fictions there is always for me an echo of another master: the great Irish clergyman Jonathan Swift. Like Twain in the nineteenth and early twentieth centuries, Swift in the eighteenth century often used exaggerated, savage satire to make a contemporary point. In "A Modest Proposal" (1729), the great Irishman suggested, with a straight face, that the starving Irish should be encouraged to eat their children. His masterpiece, of course, was *Gulliver's Travels* (1726), which could be read as a kind of children's tale of fantastic voyages, or as a critique of the idiocies of Eurocentrism, human hypocrisy, and mindless political cruelty. He later said his purpose was "to mend the world," a motive that could have been proposed a century and a half later by Mark Twain. Like Sam Clemens, who adopted the name Mark Twain in his late twenties, Swift used a variety of pseudonyms, my favorite being Isaac Bickerstaff. Like Clemens, he lived into his seventies. Like Clemens, he became bitterly disillusioned with most of the human race.

Sam Clemens knew *Gulliver's Travels* well enough to apologize to his wife, Livy, for giving her the book shortly after their 1870 marriage without first cutting out the "indelicate" parts. In "Captain Stormfield's Visit to Heaven" (this edition includes the full, expanded story first published in 1995, but "Extract from Captain Stormfield's Visit to Heaven" was published in 1909), Twain is more direct about his appreciation of Swift. This tale is sometimes called science fiction, but it contains very little science. It's the fictional narrative of the captain, in a voice borrowed from a cherished Clemens friend named Captain Ned Wakefield, who was obscene, daring, and brave. Stormfield dies at the beginning of the story, but he remains conscious and, as he travels through space, is certain he is bound for Hell. For a while he shares the company of a Jew, a black man, and a Presbyterian, like the setup for a hoary barroom joke. But they vanish from the tale, and Stormfield makes it, to his surprise, to Heaven, where he is swiftly admitted by the kind of bureaucratic gatekeepers who administered to immigrants at Castle Garden.

Stormfield quickly discovers that Heaven is much larger and more inclusive than the one advertised by fire-and-brimstone preachers and other ecclesiastical frauds on earth. But its very size eventually urges him to see something smaller, and his friend Sandy takes him to visit an asteroid (which he calls an "asterisk"). Here everything is a miniature version of the earth, including the people.

"Nice little dollies, they were, and not bigger than Gulliver's Lilliput people," Stormfield recalls, and goes on to make observations that in 1909 applied to the British Empire and could be applied today to the United States. "They were not afraid of us; in fact they held us in rather frank contempt, because we were giants. Giants have never been respected, in any world."

But the size of the people of the asterisk—"they were no bigger than a banana"—did not save them from the endless folly and deceptions of other humans. "These little animals were having wars all the time, and raising armies and building navies, and striving after the approval of God every way they could. And wherever there was a savage country that needed civilizing, they went there and took it, and divided it up among the several enlightened monarchs, and civilized it—each monarch in his own way, but generally with Bibles and bullets and taxes. And the way they did whoop-up Morals, and Patriotism, and Religion, and the Brotherhood of Man was noble to see."

Alas, Twain's Swiftian tale of Heaven doesn't truly end; it merely stops. In 1907 the seventy-two-year-old Twain was a tired writer. But the attitude the story expresses is consistent with many other Twain tales. He is opposed to self-righteousness, to unearned authority, to false piety, to hypocrisy, to the wooly language of sermons. He despises the wormy oratory of the professional patriot. To puncture such fraudulence, he uses dark laughter as the point of his spear. Some of his moral tales are slight, with the weight of hurried newspaper columns. Two examples in this collection are "The Story of the Bad Little Boy Who Didn't Come to Grief" (1865) and its later variation, "The Story of the Good Little Boy Who Did Not Prosper" (1870). Both are attacks on the bogus visions of Sunday-school pamphlets, with their crude promises that virtue will be rewarded and vice punished. Twain contrasts their porous narratives with the harder certainties of the real world. Good little boys can get wrecked by the world, says Twain; bad little boys can succeed. Twain knows this to be true, because as a boy named Sam Clemens, living in a two-room shack in Hannibal, Missouri, forced by his father's death to go to work at twelve, he knew more about the real world than the authors of the pamphlets he was satirizing. The world was tougher than any Sunday school. And dark laughter was the best way to deal with moral absurdity.

Sometimes in those early stories he goes on too long, not trusting the reader to get his point. In that way his early work resembles the first stories of Chekhov, who was also considered a "mere" humorist, offering his own takes on harmless topical matters. Both writers learned to leave off the tedious setups and get into the story directly; both eventually knew that the story could end without underlining the point.

Every writer, of course, should be judged on his best work, not his weakest, and Twain wrote some extraordinary stories. Many involved the corrupting illusions that came with visions of instant wealth. In this collection, the densest, most accomplished example is "The Man That Corrupted Hadleyburg" (1899). It is a story with various layers of ambiguity, one that evokes empathy for some of the corrupted and contempt for others, as all enter the crucible of need or greed. Religion offers them no true armor against sin, as conventional pieties collapse in the face of a possible fortune in gold.

The theme is more disturbingly treated in "The $30,000 Bequest." This is about the growing illusions that grip the imaginations of a married couple as they begin to imagine alternative lives made possible by the promise of thirty thousand dollars from a distant relative. This is to come to them after the relative dies, and he has stated in his letter that such an event was imminent. The catch: They must not come to his town to inquire about his death. That is, they must wait. As they wait, for weeks, months, and then years, there's a role reversal, as the husband, nicknamed "Sally," takes over most domestic chores, and the wife, whose name is contracted to "Aleck," becomes the manager of the imagined fortune. She invests the promised money on paper, consults business journals, works at her desk on projected profits from Wall Street and land speculation. She creates for herself and her husband an imaginary world of great houses, lavish parties, the marriages of their daughters to aristocrats or monarchs. These visions of castles in air have an almost sensual reality. But there isn't a hint of the sexual in the tale.

This is not surprising. As Justin Kaplan wrote in his prizewinning 1967 biography, *Mr. Clemens and Mark Twain:* "The loss of sexual innocence, by Mark Twain's standards, was the equivalent of a total collapse of morality; by a process of displacement, money plays the role of sex in his work. He was notoriously reticent about depicting mature sexual and emotional relationships, but he did write a kind of pornography of the dollar."

Pornography is, of course, primarily concerned with the imagining of sex; its actual practice is not always part of the deal. Millions of Americans, including Sam Clemens, were driven by gaudy fantasies of immense wealth. Only a few ever attained it. In mature reflection, Clemens believed that an earlier American innocence ended with the 1849 California gold rush, when the get-rich-quick mentality took over the American imagination. This culminated in the excesses and vast new fortunes that marked post–Civil War America. He labeled the epoch "The Gilded Age," the title of the clumsy 1873 novel he wrote with his Hartford neighbor, the writer Charles Dudley Warner. One point: Base metal can be painted gold, but it remains base metal. Clemens had gone from an impoverished youth to work on the Mississippi riverboats, learned to be a printer and a newspaperman, and in his late twenties lived as a devil-may-care bohemian in San Francisco. But he was himself susceptible to the lurid temptations of big money and to social acceptance by some of the newly rich mountebanks he satirized. When temptation became more concrete, he succumbed. He was, after all, an American.

In the rush of his first literary success (*The Innocents Abroad* of 1869), he married a rich woman named Olivia ("Livy") Langdon, made small fortunes as a "humorist" on the lecture circuit, commanded large fees for his magazine articles. He loved being famous almost as much as he loved being rich. After assorted sorrows in Buffalo, New York, he established his family in Hartford, Connecticut, and built one of those preposterous multiturreted Victorian houses, packed with stuffed junk and many servants, a house that might have evoked laughter from a less successful Mark Twain. That house, and its accompanying lifestyle, was a symbol of the era's appetites and Clemens's endless personal hungers. Writing alone could not sustain it, and Twain became an entrepreneur, too. He published and distributed his own books. He edited and published the superb memoirs of Ulysses S. Grant. He squandered many thousands in a failed attempt to invent (with a partner) a form of Linotype machine. These activities ate up time and money. They would eventually lead Clemens to an eight-year exile in Europe (where he and his family could live well on less money) and culminate in his bankruptcy in 1894. As the son of a man who had gone bankrupt and wrecked his family's prospects, Samuel Clemens, upon the collapse of his own gaudy dream, was filled with shame, impotence, and terror.

The contradictions of his life often indirectly permeated his fictions. His "dream tales" often express feelings of self-loathing and a split personality, as can be seen in "The Facts Concerning the Recent Carnival of Crime in Connecticut" (1876) or "The Great Dark" (1898/1962). Some could be straight-out hilarious: "Journalism in Tennessee" (1869), "How I Edited an Agricultural Paper Once" (1870), or that glorious parody of dime-novel detective stories, "The Stolen White Elephant" (1882). Only a few come from the great artist who would write *Huckleberry Finn.* One such is "The Private History of a Campaign That Failed" (1885). This account of his brief service in a volunteer secessionist unit during the early days of the Civil War is sometimes comic, sketching the amateurish incompetence of Clemens and his young confederates. But it has a darker, more ambiguous side, too, as Twain describes the killing of a stranger by the panicky young soldiers, a man who was not involved in the war at all. The piece is antiwar in the best sense, not a screed but a story about futility and fear, observed from the ground, where the rain never stops and the earth is always pasty with mud. It also helps explain why young Sam Clemens soon deserted and lit out for the Territory.

Another is "A True Story" (1874), in which an old black woman tells her story (written in dialect that is never comic or racist). She describes how she lost her son during the height of slavery, and how, after twenty years, she found him again. There isn't a sentence of empty rhetoric in the story. In its simplicity and purity, its sorrow and its joy, it says more about the antihuman horrors of slavery than a thousand tracts. It also helps explain why America was soon to be given the gift of the blues.

This collection is, in the end, a celebration of the many sides of Mark Twain. Here is the American heir of Jonathan Swift. Here is the pure entertainer. Here are the rebel and the conformist. Here is the troubled man struggling to eradicate (or explore) the dark side of the moon, his own fears, his own gigantic contradictions, his own weaknesses. Here, too, is the great artist, the poet of his own childhood and ours.

For years, Samuel Langhorne Clemens struggled against the image of himself as Mark Twain the Humorist, a mere entertainer, and yet he persistently used that image to make money. He was not, after all, the last American for whom the mask became the man. But in 1885, with *Huckleberry Finn,* he produced a great work of art, one that remains in print all over the world almost a century after his death. After Twain's passing, other American writers would attain great celebrity before vanishing like shooting stars. Other writers would dissipate their talents with hack work to maintain absurd lifestyles. But the pieces in this collection demonstrate that even the minor work of a great artist can throb with vitality, and reading them, I saw Clemens on a stage in a packed hall, shuffling a bit, pausing for effect, and then unleashing the laughter. They prove one thing: Mark Twain lives on, as does Samuel Langhorne Clemens.

—

PETE HAMILL, journalist, screenwriter, novelist, and short-story writer, is the author of *A Drinking Life: A Memoir* and *Why Sinatra Matters.* His ten novels include *Snow in August* and *Forever.* He lives in New York City.

Editor's Preface

Lawrence I. Berkove

"Lord, how we are made—how strangely we are made!" says Mrs. Richards in "The Man That Corrupted Hadleyburg." Written in the latter years of Twain's life, that short and simple comment is as good a capsule summary of Twain's philosophy as anything he ever wrote. It applies equally well to the human race and to its Maker. Twain variously—and sometimes simultaneously—found humanity to be funny, ridiculous, exasperating, disgusting, and damned but seldom sensible and never stable. It supplied him with endless opportunities to express humor, pity, anger, and despair. Twain found its Maker sublime, mysterious, sinister, terrible, and hateful. God created everything good and could have kept it so; instead He allowed—or directed—the first couple to sin once and then visited an awful and ongoing punishment upon them, all their descendants, and all the world forever. All of this Twain found passing strange. In his early writing career he contented himself with emphasizing the humor of what he saw. Increasingly, however, his resentment forced its way to the forefront and humor receded to become only a contributing element in bittersweet.

Several generations of scholarship have been devoted to penetrating the depths and subtleties of Twain's most famous works, his novels and travel books, but his short stories have only recently begun to be examined as extensively. It is the purpose of this anthology to collect the best of these short stories, including some that presently are relatively unknown, and let them add their evidence to what we know about the range and depth of this incomparable writer.

Twain's reputation has been established on his humor. He was one of the funniest and most gifted authors who ever lived. His book *Roughing It* (1872) is practically a compendium of nineteenth-century American humor, and passages of his most famous books, *Innocents Abroad* (1869), *The Gilded Age* (1873), *Tom Sawyer* (1876), *Huckleberry Finn* (1885), *A Connecticut Yankee in King Arthur's Court* (1889), *Pudd'nhead Wilson* (1894), and *Following the Equator* (1897), have become classic comic set pieces. Not surprisingly, this penchant for humor also informs his short stories. His first nationally famous story, "Jim Smiley and His Jumping Frog" (1865), is a magnificent achievement of the humorous storyteller's art and lends itself especially well to oral interpretation. The misleadingly named "Political Economy" (1870) and "The McWilliamses and the Burglar Alarm" (1882) are choice works of absurd humor, capitalizing on the contrast between modern scientific technology and stubborn and unreconstructed human nature. Late works, such as "The Man That Corrupted Hadleyburg" (1899) and even "The Great Dark" (1898/1962), and "The Second Advent" (1881/1972) have moments of humor but of the grim kind one finds in *Hamlet* and *Macbeth,* where the audience, spellbound by the unrolling tragedy, is forced to smile or snicker against its will by incongruous sallies of jesting or ridiculousness. Here humor intensifies the sense of tragedy.

In reality few of Twain's stories are purely funny. Most, carefully read, have a bittersweet quality that is at least as much a part of Mark Twain as his humor. Twain himself recognized this most eloquently in one of the aphorisms in *Following the Equator:* "Every one is a moon, and has a dark side which he never shows to anybody." Twain's public persona remained that of a humorist throughout his life, but with the hindsight that comes from knowing more about his personal life than all but his closest family and friends did in his lifetime, of having collected as many of his works and letters as is humanly possible, and of reading them in modern and sophisticated ways, we now know that he had a dark side and we know how to recognize it. Accordingly, the main difference between the early and late stories is the relative proportions of bitter to sweet. In his early works, the sweet predominates; in his late, the bitter. Both qualities, however, are addressed to the same phenomena: the ridiculousness of human nature, life, and creation.

A main source of Twain's humor was his Calvinist upbringing. The frontier Calvinism of his early years was gloomy and harsh. It taught that human nature was so spoiled by original sin that it was corrupt, and that the great majority of the race was damned to hell. It taught that everything was predestined, including most humans to damnation and a very few to salvation. This meant that there was no such thing as free will, and that freedom as it was generally understood did not exist. Further, it taught the doctrine of double damnation, that is, that even if most humans were not already predestined to Hell, their natures were so corrupt that they would end up damned anyhow. And it taught that a benevolent Deity created this order of things. Twain was never comfortable with the teachings of this religion and considered it not only patently cruel and unfair but also ridiculous. Sly digs at its teachings and not-so-sly digs at its believers occur early in his literature, and the satire becomes only sharper and eventually more obvious in his late writings.

Although Twain attempted to distance himself from Calvinism in his young manhood after he read Tom Paine and adopted his deistic arguments, and in his early married years when he strove to accept liberal evangelistic Protestantism, and again in his later years when he considered himself a secular determinist, the truth is that he could never completely shake off his belief in the teachings of his youth. It was not just a matter of ridding himself of a laughable conception of Deity; the trouble was that for Twain it made sense. Every day he observed fresh reasons to consider the human race damned and its "freedom" an illusion. His uncomfortable recognition of this fact is documented in an 1884 letter to his friend William Dean Howells: "A but-little considered fact in human nature: that the religious folly you are born in you will *die* in, no matter what apparently reasonabler religious folly may seem to have taken its place meanwhile, & abolished & obliterated it." What Twain was willing to say directly to a close friend like Howells he was most unwilling to say publicly. After all, he wanted to sell his books and stories, and a religious public such as America had in the nineteenth century was unlikely to buy his writings and attend his lectures if it identified them as harangues and him as a heretic. Humor, especially what looked like good-humored satire, allowed him to so sugarcoat his bitter ideas that few readers of his day even detected them.

A method of combining entertainment with the expression of his convictions occurred to him after he moved to Nevada in 1861 and began absorbing selected aspects of its culture, particularly its fondness for the hoax. The hoax is essentially a put-on, a deception. In the almost lawless mining country of Nevada Territory, hoaxes—frauds or swindles—were everyday occurrences. The early Nevada authors and journalists who comprised what is known as the Sagebrush School not surprisingly incorporated hoaxes into their literature, both as subject matter and technique, and Twain quickly assimilated the ironic Sagebrush style, which both used and exposed hoaxes. It was particularly congenial to his mind not only because it showed him how to mask a serious purpose with humorous deception, but also because it could be applied to Calvinism. The concept of the hoax was peculiarly apt for a trickster Deity passing Himself off as benevolent although He created a world of illusion and a human race that was intended to be defective; that felt free but was predestined; that was so corrupt it could only fail in its efforts to follow impossible laws and standards; that was damned even as it tried to merit salvation by living virtuously. Twain quickly saw the possibilities of using hoaxes to satirize a situation in which religion dangled Heaven and salvation before a doomed and damned race. His satires were never intended to be entirely funny, though they were usually received as such. Inspired by bitter reflections, they seldom lacked bite.

Religious satire tends to fade when the specific religious outlook that inspired it is either lost or transformed by time into something future generations do not respond to. Twain's specific satires, however, remain fresh because they are usually linked to broader aspects of humor. For example, in "The Story of the Bad Little Boy Who Didn't Come to Grief" and "The Story of the Good Little Boy Who Did Not Prosper," both satires of Sunday-school fiction, Twain's use of exaggeration is so patent and hilarious that no reader is likely to take them seriously. Likewise, Twain's control of tone to create a narrator who affects surprise that events in the real world could be so different from how they are depicted in religious books turns readers into complicit sophisticates who laugh at the narrator's credulous naïveté even as they recognize his belief in religious propaganda as a pose. Although the serious motive in each of these works may be minor by itself, when the works are collected in chronological order and studied as a whole, then the serious purposes behind the recurring religious satire become threads or themes that tie them together.

Stories like "Cannibalism in the Cars" and "Journalism in Tennessee" continue the technique of exaggeration to the point of absurdity, although both stories had some real-life antecedents: in the former case, the well-known account of the 1846 Donner party's resort to cannibalism, and in the latter, the precarious status of outspoken journalists in Nevada and California, which Twain had observed firsthand. With this in mind, it is not difficult to see that the core of these stories is an exposé of the potential savagery of human nature usually veneered, often thinly, with gentility. What is ridiculous in the first story, therefore, is not so much the capacity for cannibalism as the witty way and cheerful tone in which it is "confessed."

As Twain matured, it is apparent that he gave considerable thought to the subjects of God and man, and that he progressed beyond simple black-or-white positions. A more complex view of human nature, for example, occurs in "A True Story" with its stark depiction of the cruelty of slavery outweighed by its inspiring view of a deep humanity that triumphs over the pain and suffering caused by oppression. "The Carnival of Crime" also treats its subject with ambivalence. It opens by developing sympathy in readers for the way conscience relentlessly rags its victims, and then suddenly reveals the sympathy to be misplaced when the narrator, mild-mannered and genteel at the beginning of the story, first works himself into a literally murderous rage and then turns into a moral monster as soon as he breaks "free" of his conscience. Although later in his life Twain argued that consciences are the product of training, in this story they are innate, "appointed by authority." The issue of what sort of "authority" it is that permits conscience to torment its victims beyond reason is not explored but is buried by the humor of the story's extreme and seemingly absurd conclusion.

A muted criticism of the Deity characterizes the Adam and Eve diaries. Adam, wanting only to enjoy Eden within the framework of law, does not question why animals that subsist on a vegetarian diet have teeth designed for killing one another, or why buzzards appear to be adapted to eating decayed flesh. It is Eve who notices these ominous signs and wonders about them. Twain quietly portrays Eden as a fool's paradise and its two human inhabitants as victims of a scenario that was predestined from the beginning and that had fixed roles for them, roles they could not evade or alter. Situational humor derives from Adam's denseness and his exasperation at Eve's astute perceptions and her proficiency at domesticating him, organizing their lives, and naming, yet beyond that humor Twain turns both diaries into love stories, all the more poignant and tender for having occurred even as God stripped Adam and Eve of their immortality for a single and predestined infraction and drove them out of Eden into a harsh, disappointing, and now deadly world. These two works are important for recognizing that despite Twain's frequent ridiculing of the human race—its folly, moral faults, and viciousness—at root he had compassion for it. He considered it as mainly guilty of acting no better than God made it, but it is significant that he chose our first parents to show that even fallen human beings remained capable of achieving nobility and love.

"The $30,000 Bequest" and "The Man That Corrupted Hadleyburg" both depict the corrupting power of money—even the *expectation* of money—and the susceptibility of human nature to corrupting temptation. There is general agreement that "The Man That Corrupted Hadleyburg" is one of Twain's finest, boldest, and most pessimistic works. As a product of his late years, it is often related to the bleak deterministic philosophy of *What Is Man?* (1906) and its core idea, the "master impulse" of the craving for self-approval that is embedded in human nature. While determinism and classical Calvinism have in common unflattering views of human nature and beliefs that human beings are not free, the story at least implies an idea of God and semi-indirectly posits the existence of a resourceful but evil Tempter ("appointed by authority"?) in the form of a mysterious stranger who seeks out Hadleyburg's weaknesses in order to corrupt it. Godless determinism regards man as a machine; notions of right and wrong are superfluous to it. The idea of a Devil, on the other hand, is very much within the scope of Calvinism, and the word *corrupt* is its distinctive take on the state of human nature after the Fall. Twain might have intellectually convinced himself of determinism, but in his heart and in his art, Calvinism still reigned.

In the spirit of revisionism that prompted him to retell the stories of Adam and Eve, Twain in "Captain Stormfield's Visit to Heaven" offers up his view of what an improved God and Heaven might be like. It is a delightful tale, narrated in the colorful vernacular of its namesake protagonist, whom Twain based upon Edgar "Ned" Wakeman, the captain of the ship on which Twain sailed in 1866 from San Francisco to Nicaragua. He is rough around the edges, but malice is not part of his nature and his prejudices do not have deep roots. Heaven, he discovers, is infinitely larger and more accommodating than the biblical place, and its Lord is a benevolent and liberal but not completely effective deistic God. It is not necessary, in this conception, to be a Calvinist, Christian, or even a human being to merit Heaven; portions of it are assigned to every creed under the sun, and even to beings raised under different suns in distant galaxies. All that is necessary, apparently, is to be a basically good individual.

The final story selections are all posthumous publications and all reflect Twain's rage and despair at the hoaxes of existence. His bitter reflections were undoubtedly intensified by the frustrations and personal tragedies that attended his last years. Although "Letter from the Recording Angel" eviscerates a cheap hypocrite, part of the piece's humor also derives from Andrew Langdon's status as one of the elect, destined to Heaven regardless of his dismal earthly record. This parody distorts Calvinistic doctrine, but Twain was too angry at it to be accurate about details. Even in its incomplete form, "The Great Dark" is one of Twain's major fictional explorations of theological issues, equivalent in importance to the *Mysterious Stranger* fragments. Classical Christianity teaches that this life is transient and illusory, and Twain in this story blurs the boundaries between reality and dream and contemplates hoaxing levels of existence that are all dreams—nightmares. "The Second Advent" is plainly heretical, but the story is more complicated than it may appear at first glance. It seems to mock the biblical account of the virgin birth, but the miracles that occur later in the story undercut the earlier irony. The idea of a second advent implies a cyclical pattern to history, an idea that Twain pursued from at least as early as *Connecticut Yankee* (1889), but it is a history that is predestined. As the heretical Calvinist Twain saw it, human history is, not surprisingly, a record of failure because the human race is corrupt and damned; its institutions are no better than it; and the miracles of religion, if accurately reported, would record unforeseen but adverse consequences that disadvantaged many more than they benefited. In theory, religion sounds fine, as does the notion of a second advent, but both turn out to be hoaxes because they are offered to a race incapable of rising to them.

Somewhere deep in Twain's stories, therefore, are common elements of themes that unite the humorous with the tragic and resolve the apparent contradictions between them as different approaches to the same ideas and values. There is, in short, an intellectual and moral aspect to Twain that is absolutely distinctive and of powerful effect. Enhancing that is the brilliance of his artistry. Both considerations have played a part in the selection of individual works for this anthology.

The Best Short Stories of Mark Twain

Jim Smiley and His Jumping Frog

Mr. A. Ward,[1]

Dear Sir:—Well, I called on good-natured, garrulous old Simon Wheeler, and I inquired after your friend Leonidas W. Smiley, as you requested me to do, and I hereunto append the result. If you can get any information out of it you are cordially welcome to it. I have a lurking suspicion that your Leonidas W. Smiley is a myth—that you never knew such a personage, and that you only conjectured that if I asked old Wheeler about him it would remind him of his infamous *Jim* Smiley, and he would go to work and bore me nearly to death with some infernal reminiscence of him as long and tedious as it should be useless to me. If that was your design, Mr. Ward, it will gratify you to know that it succeeded.

I found Simon Wheeler dozing comfortably by the bar-room stove of the little old dilapidated tavern in the ancient mining camp of Boomerang, and I noticed that he was fat and bald-headed, and had an expression of winning gentleness and simplicity upon his tranquil countenance. He roused up and gave me good-day. I told him a friend of mine had commissioned me to make some inquiries about a cherished companion of his boyhood named Leonidas W. Smiley—Rev. Leonidas W. Smiley—a young minister of the gospel, who he had heard was at one time a resident of this village of Boomerang. I added that if Mr. Wheeler could tell me anything about this Rev. Leonidas W. Smiley, I would feel under many obligations to him.

Simon Wheeler backed me into a corner and blockaded me there with his chair—and then sat down and reeled off the monotonous narrative which follows this paragraph. He never smiled, he never frowned, he never changed his voice from the quiet, gently-flowing key to which he tuned[2] the initial sentence, he never betrayed the slightest suspicion of enthusiasm—but all through the interminable narrative there ran a vein of impressive earnestness and sincerity, which showed me plainly that so far from his imagining that there was anything ridiculous or funny about his story, he regarded it as a really important matter, and admired its two heroes as men of transcendent genius in finesse. To me, the spectacle of a man drifting serenely along through such a queer yarn without ever smiling was exquisitely absurd. As I said before, I asked him to tell me what he knew of Rev. Leonidas W. Smiley, and he replied as follows. I let him go on in his own way, and never interrupted him once:

—

There was a feller here once by the name of *Jim* Smiley, in the winter of '49—or maybe it was the spring of '50—I don't recollect exactly, some how, though what makes me think it was one or the other is because I remember the big flume wasn't finished when he first come to the camp; but anyway, he was the curiosest man about always betting on anything that turned up you ever see, if he could get anybody to bet on the other side, and if he couldn't he'd change sides—any way that suited the other man would suit *him*—any way just so's he got a bet, *he* was satisfied. But still, he was lucky—uncommon lucky; he most always come out winner. He was always ready and laying for a chance; there couldn't be no solitry thing mentioned but what that feller'd offer to bet on it—and take any side you please, as I was just telling you: if there was a horse race, you'd find him flush or you find him busted at the end of it; if there was a dog-fight, he'd bet on it; if there was a cat-fight, he'd bet on it; if there was a chicken-fight, he'd bet on it; why if there was two birds setting on a fence, he would bet you which one would fly first—or if there was a camp-meeting he would be there reglar to bet on parson Walker, which he judged to be the best exhorter about here, and so he was, too, and a good man; if he even see a straddle-bug start to go any wheres, he would bet you how long it would take him to get wherever he was going to, and if you took him up he would foller that straddle-bug to Mexico but what he would find out where he was bound for and how long he was on the road. Lots of the boys here has seen that Smiley and can tell you about him. Why, it never made no difference to *him*—he would bet on *anything*—the dangdest feller. Parson Walker's wife laid very sick, once, for a good while, and it seemed as if they warn't going to save her; but one morning he come in and Smiley asked him how she was, and he said she was considerable better—thank the Lord for his inf'nit mercy—and coming on so smart that with the blessing of Providence she'd get well yet—and Smiley, before he thought, says, "Well, I'll resk two-and-a-half that she don't, anyway."

Thish-yer Smiley had a mare—the boys called her the fifteen-minute nag, but that was only in fun, you know, because, of course, she was faster than that—and he used to win money on that horse, for all she was so slow and always had the asthma, or the distemper, or the consumption, or something of that kind. They used to give her two or three hundred yards' start, and then pass her under way; but always at the fag-end of the race she'd get excited and desperate-like, and come cavorting and spraddling up, and scattering her legs around limber, sometimes in the air, and sometimes out to one side amongst the fences, and kicking up m-o-r-e dust, and raising m-o-r-e racket with her coughing and sneezing and blowing her nose—and always fetch up at the stand just about a neck ahead, as near as you could cipher it down.

And he had a little small bull-pup, that to look at him you'd think he warn't worth a cent, but to set around and look ornery, and lay for a chance to steal something. But as soon as money was up on him he was a different dog—his under-jaw'd begin to stick out like the for'castle of a steamboat, and his teeth would uncover, and shine savage like the furnaces. And a dog might tackle him, and bully-rag him, and bite him, and throw him over his shoulder two or three times, and Andrew Jackson—which was the name of the pup—Andrew Jackson would never let on but what he was satisfied, and hadn't expected nothing else—and the bets being doubled and doubled on the other side all the time, till the money was all up—and then all of a sudden he would grab that other dog just by the joint of his hind legs and freeze to it—not chaw, you understand, but only just grip and hang on till they throwed up the sponge, if it was a year. Smiley always came out winner on that pup till he harnessed a dog once that didn't have no hind legs, because they'd been sawed off in a circular saw, and when the thing had gone along far enough, and the money was all up, and he came to make a snatch for his pet holt, he saw in a minute how he'd been imposed on, and how the other dog had him in the door, so to speak, and he 'peared surprised, and then he looked sorter discouraged like, and didn't try no more to win the fight, and so he got shucked out bad. He gave Smiley a look as much as to say his heart was broke, and it was *his* fault, for putting up a dog that hadn't no hind legs for him to take holt of, which was his main dependence in a fight, and then he limped off a piece, and laid down and died. It was a good pup, was that Andrew Jackson, and would have made a name for hisself if he'd lived, for the stuff was in him, and he had genius—I know it, because he hadn't had no opportunities to speak of, and it don't stand to reason that a dog could make such a fight as he could under them circumstances, if he hadn't no talent. It always makes me feel sorry when I think of that last fight of his'on, and the way it turned out.

Well, thish-yer Smiley had rat-terriers and chicken cocks, and tomcats, and all them kind of things, till you couldn't rest, and you couldn't fetch nothing for him to bet on but he'd match you. He ketched a frog one day and took him home and said he cal'lated to educate him; and so he never done nothing for three months but set in his back yard and learn that frog to jump. And you bet you he *did* learn him, too. He'd give him a little hunch behind, and the next minute you'd see that frog whirling in the air like a doughnut—see him turn one summerset, or maybe a couple, if he got a good start, and come down flat-footed and all right, like a cat. He got him up so in the matter of ketching flies, and kept him in practice so constant, that he'd nail a fly every time as far as he could see him. Smiley said all a frog wanted was education, and he could do most anything—and I believe him. Why, I've seen him set Dan'l Webster down here on this floor—Dan'l Webster was the name of the frog—and sing out, "Flies! Dan'l, flies," and quicker'n you could wink, he'd spring straight up, and snake a fly off'n the counter there, and flop down on the floor again as solid as a gob of mud, and fall to scratching the side of his head with his hind foot as indifferent as if he hadn't no idea he'd done any more'n any frog might do. You never see a frog so modest and straightfor'ard as he was, for all he was so gifted. And when it come to fair-and-square jumping on a dead level, he could get over more ground at one straddle than any animal of his breed you ever see. Jumping on a dead level was his strong suit, you understand, and when it come to that, Smiley would ante up money on him as long as he had a red. Smiley was monstrous proud of his frog, and well he might be, for fellers that had travelled and ben everywheres all said he laid over any frog that ever *they* see.

Well, Smiley kept the beast in a little lattice box, and he used to fetch him down town sometimes and lay for a bet. One day a feller—a stranger in the camp, he was—come across him with his box, and says:

"What might it be that you've got in the box?"

And Smiley says, sorter indifferent like, "It might be a parrot, or it might be a canary, maybe, but it ain't—it's only just a frog."

And the feller took it, and looked at it careful, and turned it round this way and that, and says, "H'm—so 'tis. Well, what's *he* good for?"

"Well," Smiley says, easy and careless, "He's good enough for *one* thing I should judge—he can out-jump ary frog in Calaveras county."

The feller took the box again, and took another long, particular look, and give it back to Smiley and says, very deliberate, "Well—I don't see no points about that frog that's any better'n any other frog."

"Maybe you don't," Smiley says. "Maybe you understand frogs, and maybe you don't understand 'em; maybe you've had experience, and maybe you ain't only a amature, as it were. Anyways, I've got *my* opinion, and I'll resk forty dollars that he can out-jump ary frog in Calaveras county."

And the feller studied a minute, and then says, kinder sad, like, "Well—I'm only a stranger here, and I ain't got no frog—but if I had a frog I'd bet you."

And then Smiley says, "That's all right—that's all right—if you'll hold my box a minute I'll go and get you a frog;" and so the feller took the box, and put up his forty dollars along with Smiley's, and set down to wait.

So he set there a good while thinking and thinking to hisself, and then he got the frog out and prized his mouth open and took a teaspoon and filled him full of quail-shot—filled him pretty near up to his chin—and set him on the floor. Smiley he went out to the swamp and slopped around in the mud for a long time, and finally he ketched a frog and fetched him in and give him to this feller and says:

"Now if you're ready, set him alongside of Dan'l, with his forepaws just even with Dan'l's, and I'll give the word." Then he says, "one—two—three—jump!" and him and the feller touched up the frogs from behind, and the new frog hopped off lively, but Dan'l give a heave, and hysted up his shoulders—so—like a Frenchman, but it wasn't no use—he couldn't budge; he was planted as solid as a anvil, and he couldn't no more stir than if he was anchored out. Smiley was a good deal surprised, and he was disgusted too, but he didn't have no idea what the matter was, of course.

The feller took the money and started away, and when he was going out at the door he sorter jerked his thumb over his shoulder—this way—at Dan'l, and says again, very deliberate, "Well—*I* don't see no points about that frog that's any better'n any other frog."

Smiley he stood scratching his head and looking down at Dan'l a long time, and at last he says, "I do wonder what in the nation that frog throwed off for—I wonder if there ain't something the matter with him—he 'pears to look might baggy, somehow"—and he ketched Dan'l by the nap of the neck, and lifted him up and says, "Why blame my cats if he don't weigh five pound"—and turned him upside down, and he belched out about a double-handful of shot. And then he see how it was, and he was the maddest man—he set the frog down and took out after that feller, but he never ketched him. And——

[Here Simon Wheeler heard his name called from the front-yard, and got up to go and see what was wanted.] And turning to me as he moved away, he said: "Just sit where you are, stranger, and rest easy—I ain't going to be gone a second."

But by your leave, I did not think that a continuation of the history of the enterprising vagabond Jim Smiley would be likely to afford me much information concerning the Rev. Leonidas W. Smiley, and so I started away.

At the door I met the sociable Wheeler returning, and he buttonholed me and recommenced:

"Well, thish-yer Smiley had a yaller one-eyed cow that didn't have no tail only just a short stump like a bannanner, and——"

"O, curse Smiley and his afflicted cow!" I muttered, good-naturedly, and bidding the old gentleman good-day, I departed.

Yours, truly,
MARK TWAIN
[1865]

The Story of the Bad Little Boy Who Didn't Come to Grief

Once there was a bad little boy, whose name was Jim—though, if you will notice, you will find that bad little boys are nearly always called James in your Sunday-school books. It was very strange, but still it was true, that this one was called Jim.

He didn't have any sick mother, either—a sick mother who was pious and had the consumption, and would be glad to lie down in the grave and be at rest, but for the strong love she bore her boy, and the anxiety she felt that the world would be harsh and cold towards him when she was gone. Most bad boys in the Sunday books are named James, and have sick mothers, who teach them to say, "Now I lay me down," etc., and sing them to sleep with sweet plaintive voices, and then kiss them goodnight, and kneel down by the bedside and weep. But it was different with this fellow. He was named Jim, and there wasn't any thing the matter with his mother—no consumption, nor any thing of that kind. She was rather stout than otherwise, and she was not pious; moreover, she was not anxious on Jim's account. She said if he were to break his neck, it wouldn't be much loss. She always spanked Jim to sleep, and she never kissed him goodnight; on the contrary, she boxed his ears when she was ready to leave him.

Once this little bad boy stole the key of the pantry and slipped in there and helped himself to some jam, and filled up the vessel with tar, so that his mother would never know the difference; but all at once a terrible feeling didn't come over him, and something didn't seem to whisper to him, "Is it right to disobey my mother? Isn't it sinful to do this? Where do bad little boys go who gobble up their good kind mother's jam?" and then he didn't kneel down all alone and promise never to be wicked any more, and rise up with a light, happy heart, and go and tell his mother all about it, and beg her forgiveness, and be blessed by her with tears of pride and thankfulness in her eyes. No; that is the way with all other bad boys in the books; but it happened otherwise with this Jim, strangely enough. He ate that jam, and said it was bully, in his sinful, vulgar way; and he put in the tar, and said that was bully also, and laughed, and observed that "the old woman would get up and snort" when she found it out; and when she did find it out, he denied knowing any thing about it, and she whipped him severely, and he did the crying himself. Every thing about this boy was curious—every thing turned out differently with him from the way it does to the bad Jameses in the books.

Once he climbed up in Farmer Acorn's apple-tree to steal apples, and the limb didn't break, and he didn't fall and break his arm, and get torn by the farmer's great dog, and then languish on a sick bed for weeks, and repent and become good. Oh! no; he stole as many apples as he wanted, and came down all right; and he was all ready for the dog, too, and knocked him endways with a brick when he came to tear him. It was very strange—nothing like it ever happened in those mild little books with marbled backs, and with pictures in them of men with swallow-tailed coats, and bell-crowned hats, and pantaloons that are short in the legs, and women with the waists of their dresses under their arms and no hoops on. Nothing like it in any of the Sunday-school books.

Once he stole the teacher's penknife, and when he was afraid it would be found out, and he would get whipped, he slipped it into George Wilson's cap—poor Widow Wilson's son, the moral boy, the good little boy of the village, who always obeyed his mother, and never told an untruth, and was fond of his lessons and infatuated with Sunday-school. And when the knife dropped from the cap, and poor George hung his head and blushed, as if in conscious guilt, and the grieved teacher charged the theft upon him, and was just in the very act of bringing the switch down upon his trembling shoulders, a white-haired improbable justice of the peace did not suddenly appear in their midst and strike an attitude and say, "spare this noble boy—there stands the cowering culprit! I was passing the school-door at recess, and, unseen myself, I saw the theft committed!" And then Jim didn't get whaled, and the venerable justice didn't read the tearful school a homily, and take George by the hand and say such a boy deserved to be exalted, and then tell him to come and make his home with him, and sweep out the office, and make fires, and run errands, and chop wood, and study law, and help his wife do household labors, and have all the balance of the time to play, and get forty cents a month, and be happy. No; it would have happened that way in the books, but it didn't happen that way to Jim. No meddling old clam of a justice dropped in to make trouble, and so the model boy George got thrashed, and Jim was glad of it; because, you know, Jim hated moral boys. Jim said he was "down on them milksops." Such was the coarse language of this bad, neglected boy.

But the strangest thing that ever happened to Jim was the time he went boating on Sunday and didn't get drowned, and that other time that he got caught out in the storm when he was fishing on Sunday, and didn't get struck by lightning. Why, you might look, and look, all through the Sunday-school books, from now till next Christmas, and you would never come across any thing like this. Oh! no; you would find that all the bad boys who go boating on Sunday invariably get drowned; and all the bad boys who get caught out in storms, when they are fishing on Sunday, infallibly get struck by lightning. Boats with bad boys in them always upset on Sunday, and it always storms when bad boys go fishing on the Sabbath. How this Jim ever escaped is a mystery to me.

This Jim bore a charmed life—that must have been the way of it. Nothing could hurt him. He even gave the elephant in the menagerie a plug of tobacco, and the elephant didn't knock the top of his head off with his trunk. He browsed around the cupboard after essence of peppermint, and didn't make a mistake and drink aqua fortis. He stole his father's gun and went hunting on the Sabbath, and didn't shoot three or four of his fingers off. He struck his little sister on the temple with his fist when he was angry, and she didn't linger in pain through long summer days, and die with sweet words of forgiveness upon her lips that redoubled the anguish of his breaking heart. No; she got over it. He ran off and went to sea at last, and didn't come back and find himself sad and alone in the world, his loved ones sleeping in the quiet churchyard, and the vine-embowered home of his boyhood tumbled down and gone to decay. Ah! no; he came home drunk as a piper, and got into the station-house the first thing.

And he grew up, and married, and raised a large family, and brained them all with an ax one night, and got wealthy by all manner of cheating and rascality, and now he is the infernalest wickedest scoundrel in his native village, and is universally respected, and belongs to the Legislature.

So you see there never was a bad James in the Sunday-school books that had such a streak of luck as this sinful Jim with the charmed life.

[1865]

CANNIBALISM IN THE CARS.

I visited St. Louis lately, and on my way west, after changing cars at Terre Haute, Indiana, a mild, benevolent-looking gentleman of about forty-five, or may be fifty, came in at one of the way-stations and sat down beside me. We talked together pleasantly on various subjects for an hour, perhaps, and I found him exceedingly intelligent and entertaining. When he learned that I was from Washington, he immediately began to ask questions about various public men, and about Congressional affairs; and I saw very shortly that I was conversing with a man who was perfectly familiar with the ins and outs of political life at the Capital, even to the ways and manners, and customs of procedure of Senators and Representatives in the Chambers of the National Legislature. Presently two men halted near us for a single moment, and one said to the other:

"Harris, if you'll do that for me, I'll never forget you, my boy."

My new comrade's eyes lighted pleasantly. The words had touched upon a happy memory, I thought. Then his face settled into thoughtfulness—almost into gloom. He turned to me and said, "Let me tell you a story; let me give you a secret chapter of my life—a chapter that has never been referred to by me since its events transpired. Listen patiently, and promise that you will not interrupt me."

I said I would not, and he related the following strange adventure, speaking sometimes with animation, sometimes with melancholy, but always with feeling and earnestness.

THE STRANGER'S NARRATIVE

On the 19th December, 1853, I started from St. Louis in the evening train, bound for Chicago. There were only twenty-four passengers, all told. There were no ladies and no children. We were in excellent spirits, and pleasant acquaintanceships were soon formed. The journey bade fair to be a happy one, and no individual in the party, I think, had even the vaguest presentiment of the horrors we were soon to undergo.

At 11 P.M. it began to snow hard. Shortly after leaving the small village of Weldon, we entered upon that tremendous prairie solitude that stretches its leagues on leagues of houseless dreariness far away towards the Jubilee Settlements. The winds unobstructed by trees or hills, or even vagrant rocks, whistled fiercely across the level desert, driving the falling snow before it like spray from the crested waves of a stormy sea. The snow was deepening fast, and we knew, by the diminished speed of the train, that the engine was ploughing through it with steadily increasing difficulty. Indeed it almost came to a dead halt sometimes, in the midst of great drifts that piled themselves like colossal graves across the track. Conversation began to flag. Cheerfulness gave place to grave concern. The possibility of being imprisoned in the snow, on the bleak prairie, fifty miles from any house, presented itself to every mind, and extended its depressing influence over every spirit.

At two o'clock in the morning I was aroused out of an uneasy slumber by the ceasing of all motion about me. The appalling truth flashed upon me instantly—we were captives in a snow-drift! "All hands to the rescue!" Every man sprang to obey. Out into the wild night, the pitchy darkness, the billowing snow, the driving storm, every soul leaped, with the consciousness that a moment lost now might bring destruction to us all. Shovels, hands, boards—anything, everything that could displace snow, was brought into instant requisition. It was a weird picture, that small company of frantic men fighting the banking snows, half in the blackest shadow and half in the angry light of the locomotive's reflector.

One short hour sufficed to prove the utter uselessness of our efforts. The storm barricaded the track with a dozen drifts while we dug one away. And worse than this, it was discovered that the last grand charge the engine had made upon the enemy had broken the fore-and-aft shaft of the driving-wheel! With a free track before us we should still have been helpless. We entered the car wearied with labor, and very sorrowful. We gathered about the stoves, and gravely canvassed our situation. We had no provisions whatever—in this lay our chief distress. We could not freeze, for there was a good supply of wood in the tender. This was our only comfort. The discussion ended at last in accepting the disheartening decision of the conductor,—viz.: That it would be death for any man to attempt to travel fifty miles on foot through snow like that. We could not send for help, and even if we could, it could not come. We must submit and await, as patiently as we might, succor or starvation! I think the stoutest heart there felt a momentary chill when those words were uttered.

Within the hour conversation subsided to a low murmur here and there about the car, caught fitfully between the rising and falling of the blast; the lamps grew dim; and the majority of the castaways settled themselves among the flickering shadows to think—to forget the present if they could—to sleep, if they might.

The eternal night—it surely seemed eternal to us—wore its lagging hours away at last, and the cold grey dawn broke in the east. As the light grew stronger the passengers began to stir and give signs of life, one after another, and each in turn pushed his slouched hat up from his forehead, stretched his stiffened limbs, and glanced out at the windows upon the cheerless prospect. It was cheerless indeed!—not a living thing visible anywhere, not a human habitation; nothing but a vast white desert; uplifted sheets of snow drifting hither and thither before the wind—a world of eddying flakes shutting out the firmament above.

All day we moped about the cars, saying little, thinking much. Another lingering, dreary night—and hunger.

Another dawning—another day of silence, sadness, wasting hunger, hopeless watching for succor that could not come. A night of restless slumber, filled with dreams of feasting—wakings distressed with the gnawings of hunger.

The fourth day came and went—and the fifth! Five days of dreadful imprisonment! A savage hunger looked out at every eye. There was in it a sign of awful import—the foreshadowing of a something that was vaguely shaping itself in every heart—a something which no tongue dared yet to frame into words.

The sixth day passed—the seventh dawned upon as gaunt and haggard and hopeless a company of men as ever stood in the shadow of death. It must out now! That thing which had been growing up in every heart was ready to leap from every lip at last! Nature had been taxed to the utmost—she must yield. RICHARD H. GASTON, of Minnesota, tall, cadaverous, and pale, rose up. All knew what was coming. All prepared—every emotion, every semblance of excitement was smothered—only a calm, thoughtful seriousness appeared in the eyes that were lately so wild.

"Gentlemen,—It cannot be delayed longer! The time is at hand! We must determine which of us shall die to furnish food for the rest!"

Mr. JOHN J. WILLIAMS, of Illinois, rose and said: "Gentlemen,—I nominate the Rev. James Sawyer, of Tennessee."

Mr. WM. R. ADAMS, of Indiana, said: "I nominate Mr. Daniel Slote, of New York."

Mr. CHARLES J. LANGDON: "I nominate Mr. Samuel A. Bowen, of St. Louis."

Mr. SLOTE: "Gentlemen,—I desire to decline in favor of Mr. John A. Van Nostrand, jun., of New Jersey."

Mr. GASTON: "If there be no objection, the gentleman's desire will be acceded to."

Mr. VAN NOSTRAND objecting, the resignation of Mr. Slote was rejected. The resignations of Messrs. Sawyer and Bowen were also offered, and refused upon the same grounds.

Mr. A. L. BASCOM, of Ohio: "I move that the nominations now close, and that the House proceed to an election by ballot."

Mr. SAWYER: "Gentlemen,—I protest earnestly against these proceedings. They are, in every way, irregular and unbecoming. I must beg to move that they be dropped at once, and that we elect a chairman of the meeting and proper officers to assist him, and then we can go on with the business before us understandingly."

Mr. BELKNAP, of Iowa: "Gentlemen,—I object. This is no time to stand upon forms and ceremonious observances. For more than seven days we have been without food. Every moment we lose in idle discussion increases our distress. I am satisfied with the nominations that have been made—every gentleman present is, I believe—and I, for one, do not see why we should not proceed at once to elect one or more of them. I wish to offer a resolution——"

Mr. GASTON: "It would be objected to, and have to lie over one day under the rules, thus bringing about the very delay you wish to avoid. The gentleman from New Jersey——"

MR. VAN NOSTRAND: "Gentlemen, I am a stranger among you; I have not sought the distinction that has been conferred upon me, and I feel a delicacy."

MR. MORGAN, of Alabama: "I move the previous question."

The motion was carried, and further debate shut off, of course. The motion to elect officers was passed, and under it Mr. Gaston was chosen Chairman, Mr. Blake, Secretary, Messrs. Holcomb, Dyer, and Baldwin, a Committee on nominations, and Mr. R. M. Howland, Purveyor, to assist the committee in making selections.

A recess of half an hour was then taken, and some little caucusing followed. At the sound of the gavel the meeting reassembled, and the committee reported in favor of Messrs. George Ferguson, of Kentucky, Lucien Hermann, of Louisiana, and W. Messick, of Colorado, as candidates. The report was accepted.

MR. ROGERS, of Missouri: "Mr. President,—The report being properly before the House now, I move to amend it by substituting for the name of Mr. Hermann that of Mr. Lucius Harris, of St. Louis, who is well and honorably known to us all. I do not wish to be understood as casting the least reflection upon the high character and standing of the gentleman from Louisiana—far from it. I respect and esteem him as much as any gentleman here present possibly can; but none of us can be blind to the fact that he has lost more flesh during the week that we have lain here than any among you—none of us can be blind to the fact that the committee has been derelict in its duty, either through negligence or a graver fault, in thus offering for our suffrages a gentleman who, however pure his own motives may be, has really less nutriment in him——"

THE CHAIR: "The gentleman from Missouri will take his seat. The Chair cannot allow the integrity of the Committee to be questioned save by the regular course, under the rules. What action will the House take upon the gentleman's motion?"

MR. HALLIDAY, of Virginia: "I move to further amend the report by substituting Mr. Harvey Davis, of Oregon, for Mr. Messick. It may be urged by gentlemen that the hardships and privations of a frontier life have rendered Mr. Davis tough; but, gentlemen, is this a time to cavil at toughness? is this a time to be fastidious concerning trifles? is this a time to dispute about matters of paltry significance? No, gentlemen, bulk is what we desire—substance, weight, bulk—these are the supreme requisites now—not talent, not genius, not education. I insist upon my motion."

Mr. Morgan (excitedly): "Mr. Chairman,—I do most strenuously object to this amendment. The gentleman from Oregon is old, and furthermore is bulky only in bone—not in flesh. I ask the gentleman from Virginia if it is soup we want instead of solid sustenance? if he would delude us with shadows? if he would mock our suffering with an Oregonian spectre? I ask him if he can look upon the anxious faces around him, if he can gaze into our sad eyes, if he can listen to the beating of our expectant hearts, and still thrust this famine-stricken fraud upon us? I ask him if he can think of our desolate state, of our past sorrows, of our dark future, and still unpityingly foist upon us this wreck, this ruin, this tottering swindle, this gnarled and blighted and sapless vagabond from Oregon's inhospitable shores? Never!" (Applause.)

The amendment was put to vote, after a fiery debate, and lost. Mr. Harris was substituted on the first amendment. The balloting then began. Five ballots were held without a choice. On the sixth, Mr. Harris was elected, all voting for him but himself. It was then moved that his election should be ratified by acclamation, which was lost, in consequence of his again voting against himself.

Mr. Radway moved that the House now take up the remaining candidates, and go into an election for breakfast. This was carried.

On the first ballot there was a tie, half the members favoring one candidate on account of his youth, and half favoring the other on account of his superior size. The President gave the casting vote for the latter, Mr. Messick. This decision created considerable dissatisfaction among the friends of Mr. Ferguson, the defeated candidate, and there was some talk of demanding a new ballot; but in the midst of it, a motion to adjourn was carried, and the meeting broke up at once.

The preparations for supper diverted the attention of the Ferguson faction from the discussion of their grievance for a long time, and then, when they would have taken it up again, the happy announcement that Mr. Harris was ready, drove all thought of it to the winds.

We improvised tables by propping up the backs of car-seats, and sat down with hearts full of gratitude to the finest supper that had blessed our vision for seven torturing days. How changed we were from what we had been a few short hours before! Hopeless, sad-eyed misery, hunger, feverish anxiety, desperation, then—thankfulness, serenity, joy too deep for utterance now. That I know was the cheeriest hour of my eventful life. The wind howled, and blew the snow wildly about our prison-house, but they were powerless to distress us any more. I liked Harris. He might have been better done, perhaps, but I am free to say that no man ever agreed with me better than Harris, or afforded me so large a degree of satisfaction. Messick was very well, though rather high-flavored, but for genuine nutritiousness and delicacy of fibre, give me Harris. Messick had his good points—I will not attempt to deny it, nor do I wish to do it—but he was no more fitted for breakfast than a mummy would be, sir—not a bit. Lean?—why, bless me!—and tough? Ah, he was very tough! You could not imagine it,—you could never imagine anything like it.

"Do you mean to tell me that——"

Do not interrupt me, please. After breakfast we elected a man by the name of Walker, from Detroit, for supper. He was very good. I wrote his wife so afterwards. He was worthy of all praise. I shall always remember Walker. He was a little rare, but very good. And then the next morning we had Morgan, of Alabama, for breakfast. He was one of the finest men I ever sat down to,—handsome, educated, refined, spoke several languages fluently—a perfect gentleman—he was a perfect gentleman, and singularly juicy. For supper we had that Oregon patriarch, and he *was* a fraud, there is no question about it—old, scraggy, tough—nobody can picture the reality. I finally said, gentlemen, you can do as you like, but *I* will wait for another election. And Grimes, of Illinois, said, "Gentlemen, *I* will wait also. When you elect a man that has *something* to recommend him, I shall be glad to join you again." It soon became evident that there was general dissatisfaction with Davis, of Oregon, and so, to preserve the good-will that had prevailed so pleasantly since we had had Harris, an election was called, and the result of it was that Baker, of Georgia, was chosen. He was splendid! Well, well—after that we had Doolittle, and Hawkins, and McElroy (there was some complaint about McElroy, because he was uncommonly short and thin), and Penrod, and two Smiths, and Bailey (Bailey had a wooden leg, which was clear loss, but he was otherwise good), and an Indian boy, and an organ-grinder, and a gentleman by the name of Buckminster—a poor stick of a vagabond that wasn't any good for company and no account for breakfast. We were glad we got him elected before relief came.

"And so the blessed relief *did* come at last?"

Yes, it came one bright sunny morning, just after election. John Murphy was the choice, and there never was a better, I am willing to testify; but John Murphy came home with us, in the train that came to succor us, and lived to marry the widow Harris——

"Relict[1] of——"

Relict of our first choice. He married her, and is happy and respected and prosperous yet. Ah, it was like a novel, sir—it was like a romance. This is my stopping-place, sir; I must bid you good-bye. Any time that you can make it convenient to tarry a day or two with me, I shall be glad to have you. I like you, sir; I have conceived an affection for you. I could like you as well as I liked Harris himself, sir. Good day, sir, and a pleasant journey.

He was gone. I never felt so stunned, so distressed, so bewildered in my life. But in my soul I was glad he was gone. With all his gentleness of manner and his soft voice, I shuddered whenever he turned his hungry eye upon me; and when I heard that I had achieved his perilous affection, and that I stood almost with the late Harris in his esteem, my heart fairly stood still!

I was bewildered beyond description. I did not doubt his word; I could not question a single item in a statement so stamped with the earnestness of truth as his; but its dreadful details overpowered me, and threw my thoughts into hopeless confusion.

I saw the conductor looking at me. I said, "Who is that man?"

"He was a member of Congress once, and a good one. But he got caught in a snowdrift in the cars, and like to been starved to death. He got so frost-bitten and frozen up generally, and used up for want of something to eat, that he was sick and out of his head two or three months afterwards. He is all right now, only he is a monomaniac, and when he gets on that old subject he never stops till he has eat up that whole car-load of people he talks about. He would have finished the crowd by this time, only he had to get out here. He has got their names as pat as A, B, C. When he gets them all eat up but himself, he always says:—'Then the hour for the usual election for breakfast having arrived, and there being no opposition, I was duly elected, after which, there being no objections offered, I resigned. Thus I am here.' "

I felt inexpressibly relieved to know that I had only been listening to the harmless vagaries of a madman, instead of the genuine experiences of a bloodthirsty cannibal.

[1868]

Journalism in Tennessee

The editor of the Memphis *Avalanche* swoops thus mildly down upon a correspondent who posted him as a Radical: "While he was writing the first word, the middle word, dotting his i's, crossing his t's, and punching his period, he knew he was concocting a sentence that was saturated with infamy and reeking with falsehood."

—*Exchange*

I was told by the physician that a Southern climate would improve my health, and so I went down to Tennessee and got a berth on the *Morning Glory and Johnson County War-Whoop,* as associate editor. When I went on duty I found the chief editor sitting tilted back in a three-legged chair with his feet on a pine table. There was another pine table in the room, and another afflicted chair, and both were half buried under newspapers and scraps and sheets of manuscript. There was a wooden box of sand, sprinkled with cigar stubs and "old soldiers,"[1] and a stove with a door hanging by its upper hinge.

The chief editor had a long-tailed black cloth frock coat on, and white linen pants. His boots were small and neatly blacked. He wore a ruffled shirt, a large seal ring, a standing collar of obsolete pattern and a checkered neckerchief with the ends hanging down. Date of costume, about 1848. He was smoking a cigar and trying to think of a word. And in trying to think of a word, and in pawing his hair for it, he had rumpled his locks a good deal. He was scowling fearfully, and I judged that he was concocting a particularly knotty editorial. He told me to take the exchanges and skim through them and write up the "Spirit of the Tennessee Press," condensing into the article all of their contents that seemed of interest.

I wrote as follows:

"SPIRIT OF THE TENNESSEE PRESS

"The editors of the *Semi-Weekly Earthquake* evidently labor under a misapprehension with regard to the Ballyhack railroad. It is not the object of the company to leave Buzzardville off to one side. On the contrary they consider it one of the most important points along the line, and consequently can have no desire to slight it. The gentlemen of the *Earthquake* will of course take pleasure in making the correction.

"John W. Blossom, Esq., the able editor of the Higginsville *Thunderbolt and Battle-Cry of Freedom,* arrived in the city yesterday. He is stopping at the Van Buren House.

"We observe that our cotemporary of the Mud Springs *Morning Howl* has fallen into the error of supposing that the election of Van Werter is not an established fact, but he will have discovered his mistake before this reminder reaches him, no doubt. He was doubtless misled by incomplete election returns.

"It is pleasant to note that the city of Blathersville is endeavoring to contract with some New York gentlemen to pave its well nigh impassable streets with the Nicholson pavement.[2] But it is difficult to accomplish a desire like this since Memphis got some New Yorkers to do a like service for her and then declined to pay for it. However the *Daily Hurrah* still urges the measure with ability, and seems confident of ultimate success.

"We are pained to learn that Col. Bascom, chief editor of the *Dying Shriek for Liberty,* fell in the street a few evenings since and broke his leg. He has lately been suffering with debility, caused by overwork and anxiety on account of sickness in his family, and it is supposed that he fainted from the exertion of walking too much in the sun."

I passed my manuscript over to the chief editor for acceptance, alteration or destruction. He glanced at it and his face clouded. He ran his eye down the pages, and his countenance grew portentous. It was easy to see that something was wrong. Presently he sprang up and said:

"Thunder and lightning! Do you suppose I am going to speak of those cattle that way? Do you suppose my subscribers are going to stand such gruel as that? Give me the pen!"

I never saw a pen scrape and scratch its way so viciously, or plough through another man's verbs and adjectives so relentlessly. While he was in the midst of his work somebody shot at him through the open window and marred the symmetry of his ear.

"Ah," said he, "that is that scoundrel Smith, of the *Moral Volcano*—he was due yesterday." And he snatched a navy revolver from his belt and fired. Smith dropped, shot in the thigh. The shot spoiled Smith's aim, who was just taking a second chance, and he crippled a stranger. It was me. Merely a finger shot off.

Then the chief editor went on with his erasures and interlineations. Just as he finished them a hand-grenade came down the stove-pipe, and the explosion shivered the stove into a thousand fragments. However, it did no further damage, except that a vagrant piece knocked a couple of my teeth out.

"That stove is utterly ruined," said the chief editor.

I said I believed it was.

"Well, no matter—don't want it this kind of weather. I know the man that did it. I'll get him. Now *here* is the way this stuff ought to be written."

I took the manuscript. It was scarred with erasures and interlineations till its mother wouldn't have known it, if it had had one. It now read as follows:

"SPIRIT OF THE TENNESSEE PRESS.

"The inveterate liars of the *Semi-Weekly Earthquake* are evidently endeavoring to palm off upon a noble and chivalrous people another of their vile and brutal falsehoods with regard to that most glorious conception of the nineteenth century, the Ballyhack railroad. The idea that Buzzardville was to be left off at one side originated in their own fulsome brains—or rather in the settlings which *they* regard as brains. They had better swallow this lie, and not stop to chew it, either, if they want to save their abandoned, reptile carcasses the cowhiding they so richly deserve.

"That ass, Blossom of the Higginsville *Thunderbolt and Battle-Cry of Freedom,* is down here again, bumming his board at the Van Buren.

"We observe that the besotted blackguard of the Mud Springs *Morning Howl* is giving out, with his usual propensity for lying, that Van Werter is not elected. The heaven-born mission of journalism is to disseminate truth—to eradicate error—to educate, refine and elevate the tone of public morals and manners; and make all men more gentle, more virtuous, more charitable, and in all ways better, and holier and happier—and yet this black-hearted villain, this hell-spawned miscreant, prostitutes his great office persistently to the dissemination of falsehood, calumny, vituperation and degrading vulgarity. His paper is notoriously unfit to take into the people's homes, and ought to be banished to the gambling hells and brothels where the mass of reeking pollution which does duty as its editor, lives and moves, and has his being.

"Blathersville wants a Nicholson pavement—it wants a jail and a poorhouse more. The idea of a pavement in a one-horse town with two gin-mills and a blacksmith shop in it, and that mustard-plaster of a newspaper, the *Daily Hurrah*! Better borrow of Memphis, where the article is cheap. The crawling insect, Buckner, who edits the *Hurrah*, is braying about this pavement business with his customary loud-mouthed imbecility, and imagining that he is talking sense. Such foul, mephitic scum as this verminous Buckner, are a disgrace to journalism.

"That degraded ruffian Bascom, of the *Dying Shriek for Liberty*, fell down and broke his leg yesterday—pity it wasn't his neck. He says it was 'debility caused by overwork and anxiety!' It was debility caused by trying to lug six gallons of forty-rod whisky around town when his hide is only gauged for four, and anxiety about where he was going to bum another six. He 'fainted from the exertion of walking too much in the sun!' And well he might say that—but if he would walk *straight* he would get just as far and not have to walk half as much. For years the pure air of this town has been rendered perilous by the deadly breath of this perambulating pestilence, this pulpy bloat, this steaming, animated tank of mendacity, gin and profanity, this Bascom! Perish all such from out the sacred and majestic mission of journalism!"

"Now *that* is the way to write—peppery and to the point. Mush-and-milk journalism gives me the fan-tods."[3]

About this time a brick came through the window with a splintering crash, and gave me a considerable of a jolt in the middle of the back. I moved out of range—I began to feel in the way. The chief said:

"That was the Colonel, likely, I've been expecting him for two days. He will be up, now, right away."

He was correct. The "Colonel" appeared in the door a moment afterward, with a dragoon revolver in his hand. He said:

"Sir, have I the honor of addressing the white-livered poltroon who edits this mangy sheet?"

"You have—be seated, Sir—be careful of the chair, one of the legs is gone. I believe I have the pleasure of addressing the blatant, black-hearted scoundrel, Col. Blatherskite Tecumseh?"

"The same. I have a little account to settle with you. If you are at leisure, we will begin."

"I have an article on the 'Encouraging Progress of Moral and Intellectual Development in America,' to finish, but there is no hurry. Begin."

Both pistols rang out their fierce clamor at the same instant. The chief lost a lock of hair, and the Colonel's bullet ended its career in the fleshy part of my thigh. The Colonel's left shoulder was clipped a little. They fired again. Both missed their men this time, but I got my share, a shot in the arm. At the third fire both gentlemen were wounded slightly, and I had a knuckle chipped. I then said I believed I would go out and take a walk, as this was a private matter and I had a delicacy about participating in it further. But both gentlemen begged me to keep my seat and assured me that I was not in the way. I had thought differently, up to this time.

They then talked about the elections and the crops a while, and I fell to tying up my wounds. But presently they opened fire again with animation, and every shot took effect—but it is proper to remark that five out of the six fell to my share. The sixth one mortally wounded the Colonel, who remarked, with fine humor, that he would have to say good morning, now, as he had business up town. He then inquired the way to the undertaker's and left. The chief turned to me and said:

"I am expecting company to dinner and shall have to get ready. It will be a favor to me if you will read proof and attend to the customers."

I winced a little at the idea of attending to the customers, but I was too bewildered by the fusillade that was still ringing in my ears to think of anything to say. He continued:

"Jones will be here at 3. Cowhide him. Gillespie will call earlier, perhaps—throw him out of the window. Ferguson will be along about 4—kill him. That is all for to-day, I believe. If you have any odd time, you may write a blistering article on the police—give the Chief Inspector rats. The cowhides are under the table; weapons in the drawer—ammunition there in the corner—lint and bandages up there in the pigeonholes. In case of accident, go to Lancet, the surgeon, down stairs. He advertises—we take it out in trade."

He was gone. I shuddered. At the end of the next three hours I had been through perils so awful that all peace of mind and all cheerfulness had gone from me. Gillespie had called, and thrown *me* out of the window. Jones arrived promptly, and when I got ready to do the cowhiding, he took the job off my hands. In an encounter with a stranger, not in the bill of fare, I had lost my scalp. Another stranger, by the name of Thompson, left me a mere wreck and ruin of chaotic rags. And at last, at bay in the corner, and beset by an infuriated mob of editors, blacklegs,[4] politicians and desperadoes, who raved and swore and flourished their weapons about my head till the air shimmered with glancing flashes of steel, I was in the act of resigning my berth on the paper when the chief arrived, and with him a rabble of charmed and enthusiastic friends. Then ensued a scene of riot and carnage such as no human pen, or steel one either, could describe. People were shot, probed, dismembered, blown up, thrown out of the window. There was a brief tornado of murky blasphemy, with a confused and frantic war-dance glimmering through it, and then all was over. In five minutes there was silence, and the gory chief and I sat alone and surveyed the sanguinary ruin that strewed the floor around us. He said:

"You'll like this place when you get used to it." I said:

"I'll have to get you to excuse me. I think maybe I might write to suit you, after a while, as soon as I had had some practice and learned the language—I am confident I could. But to speak the plain truth, that sort of energy of expression has its inconveniences, and a man is liable to interruption. You see that, yourself. Vigorous writing is calculated to elevate the public, no doubt, but then I do not like to attract so much attention as it calls forth. I can't write with comfort when I am interrupted so much as I have been to-day. I like this berth well enough, but I don't like to be left here to wait on the customers. The experiences are novel, I grant you, and entertaining, too, after a fashion, but they are not judiciously distributed. A gentleman shoots at you, through the window, and cripples *me;* a bomb-shell comes down the stove-pipe for your gratification, and sends the stove door down *my* throat; a friend drops in to swap compliments with you, and freckles *me* with bullet holes till my skin won't hold my principles; you go to dinner, and Jones comes with his cowhide, Gillespie throws me out of the window, Thompson tears all my clothes off, and an entire stranger takes my scalp with the easy freedom of an old acquaintance; and in less than five minutes all the blackguards in the country arrive in their war paint and proceed to scare the rest of me to death with their tomahawks. Take it altogether, I never have had such a spirited time in all my life as I have had to-day. No. I like you, and I like your calm, unruffled way of explaining things to the customers, but you see I am not used to it. The Southern heart is too impulsive—Southern hospitality is too lavish with the stranger. The paragraphs which I have written to-day, and into whose cold sentences your masterly hand has infused the fervent spirit of Tennesseean journalism, will wake up another nest of hornets. All that mob of editors will come—and they will come hungry, too, and want somebody for breakfast. I shall have to bid you adieu. I decline to be present at these festivities. I came South for my health—I will go back on the same errand, and suddenly. Tennessee journalism is too stirring for me." After which, we parted, with mutual regret, and I took apartments at the hospital.

[1869]

The Story of the Good Little Boy Who Did Not Prosper

[The following has been written at the instance of several literary friends, who thought that if the history of "The Bad Little Boy who Did not Come to Grief" (a moral sketch which I published five or six years ago) was worthy of preservation several weeks in print, a fair and unprejudiced companion-piece to it would deserve a similar immortality.—EDITOR MEMORANDA.]

Once there was a good little boy by the name of Jacob Blivens. He always obeyed his parents, no matter how absurd and unreasonable their demands were; and he always learned his book, and never was late at Sabbath school. He would not play hookey, even when his sober judgment told him it was the most profitable thing he could do. None of the other boys could ever make that boy out, he acted so strangely. He wouldn't lie, no matter how convenient it was. He just said it was wrong to lie, and that was sufficient for him. And he was so honest that he was simply ridiculous. The curious ways that that Jacob had surpassed everything. He wouldn't play marbles on Sunday, he wouldn't rob birds' nests, he wouldn't give hot pennies to organ-grinders' monkeys; he didn't seem to take any interest in any kind of rational amusement. So the other boys used to try to reason it out and come to an understanding of him, but they couldn't arrive at any satisfactory conclusion; as I said before, they could only figure out a sort of vague idea that he was "afflicted," and so they took him under their protection, and never allowed any harm to come to him.

This good little boy read all the Sunday-school books; they were his greatest delight. This was the whole secret of it. He believed in the good little boys they put in the Sunday-school books; he had every confidence in them. He longed to come across one of them alive, once; but he never did. They all died before his time, maybe. Whenever he read about a particularly good one, he turned over quickly to the end to see what became of him, because he wanted to travel thousands of miles and gaze on him; but it wasn't any use; that good little boy always died in the last chapter, and there was a picture of the funeral, with all his relations and the Sunday-school children standing around the grave in pantaloons that were too short, and bonnets that were too large, and everybody crying into handkerchiefs that had as much as a yard and a half of stuff in them. He was always headed off in this way. He never could see one of those good little boys, on account of his always dying in the last chapter.

Jacob had a noble ambition to be put in a Sunday-school book. He wanted to be put in, with pictures representing him gloriously declining to lie to his mother, and she weeping for joy about it; and pictures representing him standing on the doorstep giving a penny to a poor beggar-woman with six children, and telling her to spend it freely, but not to be extravagant, because extravagance is a sin; and pictures of him magnanimously refusing to tell on the bad boy who always lay in wait for him around the corner, as he came from school, and welted him over the head with a lath, and then chased him home, saying "Hi! hi!" as he proceeded. That was the ambition of young Jacob Blivens. He wished to be put in a Sunday-school book. It made him feel a little uncomfortable sometimes when he reflected that the good little boys always died. He loved to live, you know, and this was the most unpleasant feature about being a Sunday-school-book boy. He knew it was not healthy to be good. He knew it was more fatal than consumption to be so supernaturally good as the boys in the books were; he knew that none of them had ever been able to stand it long, and it pained him to think that if they put him in a book he wouldn't ever see it, or even if they did get the book out before he died, it wouldn't be popular without any picture of his funeral in the back part of it. It couldn't be much of a Sunday-school book that couldn't tell about the advice he gave to the community when he was dying. So, at last, of course he had to make up his mind to do the best he could under the circumstances—to live right, and hang on as long as he could, and have his dying speech all ready when his time came.

But somehow, nothing ever went right with this good little boy; nothing ever turned out with him the way it turned out with the good little boys in the books. They always had a good time, and the bad boys had the broken legs; but in his case there was a screw loose somewhere, and it all happened just the other way. When he found Jim Blake stealing apples, and went under the tree to read to him about the bad little boy who fell out of a neighbor's apple tree, and broke his arm, Jim fell out of the tree too, but he fell on *him,* and broke *his* arm, and Jim wasn't hurt at all. Jacob couldn't understand that. There wasn't anything in the books like it.

And once, when some bad boys pushed a blind man over in the mud, and Jacob ran to help him up and receive his blessing, the blind man did not give him any blessing at all, but whacked him over the head with his stick and said he would like to catch him shoving *him* again and then pretending to help him up. This was not in accordance with any of the books. Jacob looked them all over to see.

One thing that Jacob wanted to do was to find a lame dog that hadn't any place to stay, and was hungry and persecuted, and bring him home and pet him and have that dog's imperishable gratitude. And at last he found one, and was happy; and he brought him home and fed him, but when he was going to pet him the dog flew at him and tore all the clothes off him except those that were in front, and made a spectacle of him that was astonishing. He examined authorities, but he could not understand the matter. It was of the same breed of dogs that was in the books, but it acted very differently. Whatever this boy did, he got into trouble. The very things the boys in the books got rewarded for turned out to be about the most unprofitable things he could invest in.

Once when he was on his way to Sunday school he saw some bad boys starting off pleasuring in a sail-boat. He was filled with consternation, because he knew from his reading that boys who went sailing on Sunday invariably got drowned. So he ran out on a raft to warn them, but a log turned with him and slid him into the river. A man got him out pretty soon, and the doctor pumped the water out of him and gave him a fresh start with his bellows, but he caught cold and lay sick abed nine weeks. But the most unaccountable thing about it was that the bad boys in the boat had a good time all day, and then reached home alive and well, in the most surprising manner. Jacob Blivens said there was nothing like these things in the books. He was perfectly dumbfounded.

When he got well he was a little discouraged, but he resolved to keep on trying, anyhow. He knew that so far his experiences wouldn't do to go in a book, but he hadn't yet reached the allotted term of life for good little boys, and he hoped to be able to make a record yet, if he could hold on till his time was fully up. If everything else failed, he had his dying speech to fall back on.

He examined his authorities, and found that it was now time for him to go to sea as a cabin boy. He called on a ship captain and made his application, and when the captain asked for his recommendations he proudly drew out a tract and pointed to the words: "To Jacob Blivens, from his affectionate teacher." But the captain was a coarse, vulgar man, and he said, "Oh, that be blowed! *that* wasn't any proof that he knew how to wash dishes or handle a slush-bucket, and he guessed he didn't want him." This was altogether the most extraordinary thing that ever had happened to Jacob in all his life. A compliment from a teacher, on a tract, had never failed to move the tenderest of emotions of ship captains and open the way to all offices of honor and profit in their gift—it never had in any book that ever *he* had read. He could hardly believe his senses.

This boy always had a hard time of it. Nothing ever came out according to the authorities with him. At last, one day, when he was around hunting up bad little boys to admonish, he found a lot of them in the old iron foundry fixing up a little joke on fourteen or fifteen dogs, which they had tied together in long procession and were going to ornament with empty nitro-glycerine cans made fast to their tails. Jacob's heart was touched. He sat down on one of those cans—for he never minded grease when duty was before him—and he took hold of the foremost dog by the collar, and turned his reproving eye upon wicked Tom Jones. But just at that moment Alderman McWelter, full of wrath, stepped in. All the bad boys ran away; but Jacob Blivens rose in conscious innocence and began one of those stately little Sunday-school-book speeches which always commence with "Oh, Sir!" in dead opposition to the fact that no boy, good or bad, ever starts a remark with "Oh, Sir!" But the Alderman never waited to hear the rest. He took Jacob Blivens by the ear and turned him around, and hit him a whack in the rear with the flat of his hand; and in an instant that good little boy shot out through the roof and soared away toward the sun, with the fragments of those fifteen dogs stringing after him like the tail of a kite. And there wasn't a sign of that Alderman or that old iron foundry left on the face of the earth; and as for young Jacob Blivens, he never got a chance to make his last dying speech after all his trouble fixing it up, unless he made it to the birds; because, although the bulk of him came down all right in a tree-top in an adjoining county, the rest of him was apportioned around among four townships, and so they had to hold five inquests on him to find out whether he was dead or not, and how it occurred. You never saw a boy scattered so.*

*This catastrophe is borrowed (without the unknown but most ingenious owner's permission) from a stray newspaper item, and trimmed up and altered to fit Jacob Blivens, who stood sadly in need of a doom that would send him out of the world with *éclat*—EDITOR MEMORANDA.

Thus perished the good little boy who did the best he could, but didn't come out according to the books. Every boy who ever did as he did prospered, except him. His case is truly remarkable. It will probably never be accounted for.

[1870]

How I Edited an Agricultural Paper Once

I did not take the temporary editorship of an agricultural paper without misgivings. Neither would a landsman take command of a ship without misgivings. But I was in circumstances that made the salary an object. The regular editor of the paper was going off for a holiday, and I accepted the terms he offered, and took his place.

The sensation of being at work again was luxurious, and I wrought all the week with unflagging pleasure. We went to press, and I waited a day with some solicitude to see whether my effort was going to attract any notice. As I left the office, toward sundown, a group of men and boys at the foot of the stairs dispersed with one impulse, and gave me passageway, and I heard one or two of them say: "That's him!" I was naturally pleased by this incident. The next morning I found a similar group at the foot of the stairs, and scattering couples and individuals standing here and there in the street, and over the way, watching me with interest. The group separated and fell back as I approached, and I heard a man say: "Look at his eye!" I pretended not to observe the notice I was attracting, but secretly I was pleased with it, and was purposing to write an account of it to my aunt. I went up the short flight of stairs, and heard cheery voices and a ringing laugh as I drew near the door, which I opened, and caught a glimpse of two young, rural-looking men, whose faces blanched and lengthened when they saw me, and then they both plunged through the window, with a great crash. I was surprised.

In about half an hour an old gentleman, with a flowing beard and a fine but rather austere face, entered, and sat down at my invitation. He seemed to have something on his mind. He took off his hat and set it on the floor, and got out of it a red silk handkerchief and a copy of our paper. He put the paper on his lap, and, while he polished his spectacles with his handkerchief, he said:

"Are you the new editor?"

I said I was.

"Have you ever edited an agricultural paper before?"

"No," I said; "this is my first attempt."

"Very likely. Have you had any experience in agriculture, practically?"

"No, I believe I have not."

"Some instinct told me so," said the old gentleman, putting on his spectacles and looking over them at me with asperity, while he folded his paper into a convenient shape. "I wish to read you what must have made me have that instinct. It was this editorial. Listen, and see if it was you that wrote it:

"Turnips should never be pulled—it injures them. It is much better to send a boy up and let him shake the tree.

"Now, what do you think of that?—for I really suppose you wrote it?"

"Think of it? Why, I think it is good. I think it is sense. I have no doubt that, every year, millions and millions of bushels of turnips are spoiled in this township alone by being pulled in a half-ripe condition, when, if they had sent a boy up to shake the tree——"

"Shake your grandmother! Turnips don't grow on trees!"

"Oh, they don't, don't they? Well, who said they did? The language was intended to be figurative, wholly figurative. Anybody, that knows anything, will know that I meant that the boy should shake the vine."

Then this old person got up and tore his paper all into small shreds, and stamped on them, and broke several things with his cane, and said I did not know as much as a cow; and then went out, and banged the door after him, and, in short, acted in such a way that I fancied he was displeased about something. But, not knowing what the trouble was, I could not be any help to him.

Pretty soon after this a long, cadaverous creature, with lanky locks hanging down to his shoulders and a week's stubble bristling from the hills and valleys of his face, darted within the door, and halted, motionless, with finger on lip, and head and body bent in listening attitude. No sound was heard. Still he listened. No sound. Then he turned the key in the door, and came elaborately tip-toeing toward me, till he was within long reaching distance of me, when he stopped, and, after scanning my face with intense interest for a while, drew a folded copy of our paper from his bosom, and said:

"There—you wrote that. Read it to me, quick! Relieve me—I suffer."

I read as follows—and as the sentences fell from my lips I could see the relief come—I could see the drawn muscles relax, and the anxiety go out of the face, and rest and peace steal over the features like the merciful moonlight over a desolate landscape:

> The guano is a fine bird, but great care is necessary in rearing it. It should not be imported earlier than June nor later than September. In the winter it should be kept in a warm place, where it can hatch out its young.
>
> It is evident that we are to have a backward season for grain. Therefore, it will be well for the farmer to begin setting out his corn-stalks and planting his buckwheat cakes in July instead of August.
>
> Concerning the Pumpkin.—This berry is a favorite with the natives of the interior of New England, who prefer it to the gooseberry for the making of fruit cake, and who likewise give it the preference over the raspberry for feeding cows, as being more filling and fully as satisfying. The pumpkin is the only esculent of the orange family that will thrive in the North, except the gourd and one or two varieties of the squash. But the custom of planting it in the front yard with the shrubbery is fast going out of vogue, for it is now generally conceded that the pumpkin, as a shade tree, is a failure.
>
> Now, as the warm weather approaches, and the ganders begin to spawn——

The excited listener sprang toward me, to shake hands, and said:

"There, there—that will do! I know I am all right now, because you have read it just as I did, word for word. But, stranger, when I first read it this morning I said to myself, I never, never believed it before, notwithstanding my friends kept me under watch so strict, but now I believe I *am* crazy; and with that I fetched a howl that you might have heard two miles, and started out to kill somebody—because, you know, I knew it would come to that sooner or later, and so I might as well begin. I read one of them paragraphs over again, so as to be certain, and then I burned my house down and started. I have crippled several people, and have got one fellow up a tree, where I can get him if I want him. But I thought I would call in here as I passed along, and make the thing perfectly certain; and now it *is* certain, and I tell you it is lucky for the chap that is in the tree. I should have killed him, sure, as I went back. Good-by, sir, good-by—you have taken a great load off my mind. My reason has stood the strain of one of your agricultural articles, and I know that nothing can ever unseat it now. *Good*-by, sir."

I felt a little uncomfortable about the cripplings and arsons this person had been entertaining himself with, for I could not help feeling remotely accessory to them; but these thoughts were quickly banished, for the regular editor walked in! [I thought to myself, Now if you had gone to Egypt, as I recommended you to, I might have had a chance to get my hand in; but you wouldn't do it, and here you are. I sort of expected you.]

The editor was looking sad, and perplexed, and dejected. He surveyed the wreck which that old rioter and these two young farmers had made, and then said:

"This is a sad business—a very sad business. There is the mucilage bottle broken, and six panes of glass, and a spittoon and two candlesticks. But that is not the worst. The reputation of the paper is injured, and permanently, I fear. True, there never was such a call for the paper before, and it never sold such a large edition or soared to such celebrity; but does one want to be famous for lunacy, and prosper upon the infirmities of his mind? My friend, as I am an honest man, the street out here is full of people, and others are roosting on the fences, waiting to get a glimpse of you, because they think you are crazy. And well they might, after reading your editorials. They are a disgrace to journalism. Why, what put it into your head that you could edit a paper of this nature? You do not seem to know the first rudiments of agriculture. You speak of a furrow and a harrow as being the same thing; you talk of the moulting season for cows; and you recommend the domestication of the pole-cat on account of its playfulness and its excellence as a ratter. Your remark that clams will lie quiet if music be played to them, was superfluous—entirely superfluous. Nothing disturbs clams. Clams *always* lie quiet. Clams care nothing whatever about music. Ah, heavens and earth, friend, if you had made the acquiring of ignorance the study of your life, you could not have graduated with higher honor than you could to-day. I never saw anything like it. Your observation that the horse-chestnut, as an article of commerce, is steadily gaining in favor, is simply calculated to destroy this journal. I want you to throw up your situation and go. I want no more holiday—I could not enjoy it if I had it. Certainly not with you in my chair. I would always stand in dread of what you might be going to recommend next. It makes me lose all patience every time I think of your discussing oyster-beds under the head of 'Landscape Gardening.' I want you to go. Nothing on earth could persuade me to take another holiday. Oh, why didn't you *tell* me you didn't know anything about agriculture?"

"*Tell* you, you cornstalk, you cabbage, you son of a cauliflower! It's the first time I ever heard such an unfeeling remark. I tell you I have been in the editorial business going on fourteen years, and it is the first time I ever heard of a man's having to know anything in order to edit a newspaper. You turnip! Who write the dramatic critiques for the second-rate papers? Why, a parcel of promoted shoemakers and apprentice apothecaries, who know just as much about good acting as I do about good farming and no more. Who review the books? People who never wrote one. Who do up the heavy leaders on finance? Parties who have had the largest opportunities for knowing nothing about it. Who criticise the Indian campaigns? Gentlemen who do not know a war-whoop from a wigwam, and who never have had to run a foot-race with a tomahawk or pluck arrows out of the several members of their families to build the evening camp-fire with. Who write the temperance appeals and clamor about the flowing bowl? Folks who will never draw another sober breath till they do it in the grave. Who edit the agricultural papers, you—yam? Men, as a general thing, who fail in the poetry line, yellow-covered novel line, sensation-drama line, city-editor line, and finally fall back on agriculture as a temporary reprieve from the poor-house. *You* try to tell *me* anything about the newspaper business! Sir, I have been through it from Alpha to Omaha, and I tell you that the less a man knows the bigger noise he makes and the higher the salary he commands. Heaven knows if I had but been ignorant instead of cultivated, and impudent instead of diffident, I could have made a name for myself in this cold, selfish world. I take my leave, sir. Since I have been treated as you have treated me, I am perfectly willing to go. But I have done my duty. I have fulfilled my contract, as far as I was permitted to do it. I said I could make your paper of interest to all classes, and I have. I said I could run your circulation up to twenty thousand copies, and if I had had two more weeks I'd have done it. And I'd have given you the best class of readers that ever an agricultural paper had—not a farmer in it, nor a solitary individual who could tell a watermelon from a peach-vine to save his life. *You* are the loser by this rupture, not me, Pie-plant. Adios."

I then left.

[1870]

POLITICAL ECONOMY.

Political economy is the basis of all good government. The wisest men of all ages have brought to bear upon this subject the——

[Here I was interrupted and informed that a stranger wished to see me down at the door. I went and confronted him, and asked to know his business, struggling all the time to keep a tight rein on my seething political economy ideas, and not let them break away from me or get tangled in their harness. And privately I wished the stranger was in the bottom of the canal with a cargo of wheat on top of him. I was all in a fever, but he was cool. He said he was sorry to disturb me, but as he was passing he noticed that I needed some lightning-rods. I said, "Yes, yes—go on—what about it?" He said there was nothing about it, in particular—nothing except he would like to put them up for me. I am new to housekeeping; have been used to hotels and boarding-houses all my life. Like anybody else of similar experience, I try to appear (to strangers) to be an old housekeeper; consequently I said in an off-hand way that I had been intending for some time to have six or eight lightning-rods put up, but——The stranger started, and looked inquiringly at me, but I was serene. I thought that if I chanced to make any mistakes he would not catch me by my countenance. He said he would rather have my custom than any man's in town. I said all right, and started off to wrestle with my great subject again, when he called me back and said it would be necessary to know exactly how many "points" I wanted put up, what parts of the house I wanted them on, and what quality of rod I preferred. It was close quarters for a man not used to the exigencies of housekeeping, but I went through creditably, and he probably never suspected that I was a novice. I told him to put up eight "points," and put them all on the roof, and use the best quality of rod. He said he could furnish the "plain" article, at 20 cents a foot; "coppered," 25 cents; "zinc-plated, spiral-twist," at 30 cents, that would stop a streak of lightning any time, no matter where it was bound, and "render its errand harmless and its further progress apocryphal." I said apocryphal was no slouch of a word, emanating from the source it did, but philology aside I liked the spiral-twist and would take that brand. Then he said he *could* make two hundred and fifty feet answer, but to do it right, and make the best job in town of it, and attract the admiration of the just and the unjust alike, and compel all parties to say they never saw a more symmetrical and hypothetical display of lightning-rods since they were born, he supposed he really couldn't get along without four hundred, though he was not vindictive and trusted he was willing to try. I said go ahead and use four hundred and make any kind of a job he pleased out of it, but let me get back to my work. So I got rid of him at last, and now, after half an hour spent in getting my train of political economy thoughts coupled together again, I am ready to go on once more.]

richest treasures of their genius, their experience of life, and their learning. The great lights of commercial jurisprudence, international confraternity, and biological deviation, of all ages, all civilizations, and all nationalities, from Zoroaster down to Horace Greeley, have——

[Here I was interrupted again and required to go down and confer further with that lightning-rod man. I hurried off, boiling and surging with prodigious thoughts wombed in words of such majesty that each one of them was in itself a straggling procession of syllables that might be fifteen minutes passing a given point, and once more I confronted him—he so calm and sweet, I so hot and frenzied. He was standing in the contemplative attitude of the Colossus of Rhodes, with one foot on my infant tuberose and the other among my pansies, his hands on his hips, his hat-brim tilted forward, one eye shut and the other gazing critically and admiringly in the direction of my principal chimney. He said now *there* was a state of things to make a man glad to be alive; and added, "I leave it to *you* if you ever saw anything more deliriously picturesque than eight lightning-rods on one chimney?" I said I had no present recollection of anything that transcended it. He said that in his opinion nothing on this earth but Niagara Falls was superior to it in the way of natural scenery. All that was needed now, he verily believed, to make my house a perfect balm to the eye, was to kind of touch up the other chimneys a little and thus "add to the generous *coup d'œil* a soothing uniformity of achievement which would allay the excitement naturally consequent upon the first *coup d'état*."[1] I asked him if he learned to talk out of a book, and if I could borrow it anywhere. He smiled pleasantly, and said that his manner of speaking was not taught in books, and that nothing but familiarity with lightning could enable a man to handle his conversational style with impunity. He then figured up an estimate, and said that about eight more rods scattered about my roof would about fix me right, and he guessed five hundred feet of stuff would do it; and added that the first eight had got a little the start of him, so to speak, and used up a mere trifle of material more than he had calculated on—a hundred feet or along there. I said I was in a dreadful hurry, and I wished we could get this business permanently mapped out so that I could go on with my work. He said: "I *could* have put up those eight rods, and marched off about my business—some men *would* have done it. But no, I said to myself, this man is a stranger to me and I will die before I'll wrong him; there ain't lightning-rods enough on that house, and for one I'll never stir out of my tracks till I've done as I would be done by, and told him so. Stranger, my duty is accomplished; if the recalcitrant and dephlogistic[2] messenger of heaven strikes your——" "There, now, there," I said, "put on the other eight—add five hundred feet of spiral-twist—do anything and everything you want to do; but calm your sufferings and try to keep your feelings where you can reach them with the dictionary. Meanwhile, if we understand each other now, I will go to work again." I think I have been sitting here a full hour, this time, trying to get back to where I was when my train of thought was broken up by the last interruption, but I believe I have accomplished it at last and may venture to proceed again.]

wrestled with this great subject, and the greatest among them have found it a worthy adversary and one that always comes up fresh and smiling after every throw. The great Confucius said that he would rather be a profound political economist than chief of police; Cicero frequently said that political economy was the grandest consummation that the human mind was capable of consuming; and even our own Greeley has said vaguely but forcibly that——

[Here the lightning-rod man sent up another call for me. I went down in a state of mind bordering on impatience. He said he would rather have died than interrupt me, but when he was employed to do a job, and that job was expected to be done in a clean, workmanlike manner, and when it was finished and fatigue urged him to seek the rest and recreation he stood so much in need of, and he was about to do it, but looked up and saw at a glance that all the calculations had been a little out, and if a thunder storm were to come up and that house which he felt a personal interest in stood there with nothing on earth to protect it but sixteen lightning-rods—— "Let us have peace!" I shrieked. "Put up a hundred and fifty! Put some on the kitchen! Put a dozen on the barn! Put a couple on the cow!—put one on the cook!—scatter them all over the persecuted place till it looks like a zinc-plated, spiral-twisted, silver-mounted cane-brake! Move! Use up all the material you can get your hands on, and when you run out of lightning-rods put up ram-rods, cam-rods, stair-rods, piston-rods—*anything* that will pander to your dismal appetite for artificial scenery and bring respite to my raging brain and healing to my lacerated soul!" Wholly unmoved—further than to smile sweetly—this iron being simply turned back his wristbands daintily and said he would now "proceed to hump himself." Well, all that was nearly three hours ago. It is questionable whether I am calm enough yet to write on the noble theme of political economy, but I cannot resist the desire to try, for it is the one subject that is nearest to my heart and dearest to my brain of all this world's philosophy.]

"Political economy is heaven's best boon to man." When the loose but gifted Byron lay in his Venetian exile, he observed that if it could be granted him to go back and live his misspent life over again, he would give his lucid and unintoxicated intervals to the composition, not of frivolous rhymes, but of essays upon political economy. Washington loved this exquisite science; such names as Baker, Beckwith, Judson, Smith, are imperishably linked with it; and even imperial Homer, in the ninth book of the Iliad, has said:

Fiat justitia, ruat cœlum,
Post mortem unum, ante bellum,
Hic jacet hoc, ex-parte res,
Politicum e-conomico est.[3]

The grandeur of these conceptions of the old poet, together with the felicity of the wording which clothes them and the sublimity of the imagery whereby they are illustrated, have singled out that stanza and made it more celebrated than any that ever——

["Now, not a word out of you—not a single word. Just state your bill and relapse into impenetrable silence for ever and ever on these premises. Nine hundred dollars? Is that all? This check for the amount will be honored at any respectable bank in America. What is that multitude of people gathered in the street for? How?—'looking at the lightning-rods!' Bless my life, did they never see any lightning-rods before? Never saw 'such a stack of them on one establishment,' did I understand you to say? I will step down and critically observe this popular ebullition of ignorance."]

THREE DAYS LATER—We are all about worn out. For four-and-twenty hours our bristling premises were the talk and wonder of the town. The theatres languished, for their happiest scenic inventions were tame and commonplace compared with my lightning-rods. Our street was blocked night and day with spectators, and among them were many who came from the country to see. It was a blessed relief, on the second day, when a thunder storm came up and the lightning began to "go for" my house, as the historian Josephus quaintly phrases it. It cleared the galleries, so to speak. In five minutes there was not a spectator within half a mile of my place; but all the high houses about that distance away were full, windows, roof, and all. And well they might be, for all the falling

stars and Fourth of July fireworks of a generation put together and rained down simultaneously out of heaven in one brilliant shower upon one helpless roof, would not have any advantage of the pyrotechnic display that was making my house so magnificently conspicuous in the general gloom of the storm. By actual count the lightning struck at my establishment seven hundred and sixty-four times in forty minutes, but tripped on one of those faithful rods every time and slid down the spiral-twist and shot into the earth before it probably had time to be surprised at the way the thing was done. And through all that bombardment only one patch of slates was ripped up, and that was because for a single instant the rods in the vicinity were transporting all the lightning they could possibly accommodate. Well, nothing was ever seen like it since the world began. For one whole day and night not a member of my family stuck his head out of the window but he got the hair snatched off it as smooth as a billiard-ball, and if the reader will believe me not one of us ever dreamt of stirring abroad. But at last the awful siege came to an end—because there was absolutely no more electricity left in the clouds above us within grappling distance of my insatiable rods. *Then* I sallied forth, and gathered daring workmen together, and not a bite or a nap did we take till the premises were utterly stripped of all their terrific armament except just three rods on the house, one on the kitchen, and one on the barn—and behold these remain there even unto this day. And then, and not till then, the people ventured to use our street again. I will remark here, in passing, that during that fearful time I did not continue my essay upon political economy. I am not even yet settled enough in nerve and brain to resume it.

To Whom it May Concern—Parties having need of three thousand two hundred and eleven feet of best quality zinc-plated spiral-twist lightning-rod stuff, and sixteen hundred and thirty-one silver-tipped points, all in tolerable repair (and, although much worn by use, still equal to any ordinary emergency), can hear of a bargain by addressing the publishers of this magazine.

[1870]

A True Story, Repeated Word for Word as I Heard It

It was summer time, and twilight. We were sitting on the porch of the farm-house, on the summit of the hill, and "Aunt Rachel"[1] was sitting respectfully below our level, on the steps,—for she was our servant, and colored. She was of mighty frame and stature; she was sixty years old, but her eye was undimmed and her strength unabated. She was a cheerful, hearty soul, and it was no more trouble for her to laugh than it is for a bird to sing. She was under fire, now, as usual when the day was done. That is to say, she was being chaffed without mercy, and was enjoying it. She would let off peal after peal of laughter, and then sit with her face in her hands and shake with throes of enjoyment which she could no longer get breath enough to express. At such a moment as this a thought occurred to me, and I said:—

"Aunt Rachel, how is it that you've lived sixty years and never had any trouble?"

She stopped quaking. She paused, and there was a moment of silence. She turned her face over her shoulder toward me, and said, without even a smile in her voice:—

"Misto C——,[2] is you in 'arnest?"

It surprised me a good deal; and it sobered my manner and my speech, too. I said:—

"Why, I thought—that is, I meant—why, you *can't* have had any trouble. I've never heard you sigh, and never seen your eye when there wasn't a laugh in it."

She faced fairly around, now, and was full of earnestness.

"Has I had any trouble? Misto C——, I's gwyne to tell you, den I leave it to you. I was bawn down 'mongst de slaves; I knows all 'bout slavery, 'case I ben one of 'em my own se'f. Well, sah, my ole man—dat's my husban'—he was lovin' an' kind to me, jist as kind as you is to yo' own wife. An' we had chil'en—seven chil'en—an' we loved dem chil'en jist de same as you loves yo' chil'en. Dey was black, but de Lord can't make no chil'en so black but what dey mother loves 'em an' wouldn't give 'em up, no, not for anything dat's in dis whole world.

"Well, sah, I was raised in ole Fo'ginny, but my mother she was raised in Maryland; an' my *souls*! she was turrible when she'd git started! My *lan'*! but she'd make de fur fly! When she'd git into dem tantrums, she always had one word dat she said. She'd straighten herse'f up an' put her fists in her hips an' say, 'I want you to understan' dat I wa'n't bawn in de mash to be fool' by trash! I's one o' de ole Blue Hen's Chickens, *I* is!' 'Ca'se, you see, dat's what folks dat's bawn in Maryland calls deyselves, an' dey's proud of it. Well, dat was her word. I don't ever forgit it, beca'se she said it so much, an' beca'se she said it one day when my little Henry tore his wris' awful, an' most busted his head, right up at de top of his forehead, an' de niggers didn't fly aroun' fas' enough to 'tend to him. An' when dey talk' back at her, she up an' she says, 'Look-a-heah!' she says, 'I want you niggers to understan' dat I wa'n't bawn in de mash to be fool' by trash! I's one o' de ole Blue Hen's Chickens, *I* is!' an' den she clar' dat kitchen an' bandage' up de chile herse'f. So I says dat word, too, when I's riled.

"Well, bymeby my ole mistis say she's broke, an' she got to sell all de niggers on de place. An' when I heah dat dey gwyne to sell us all off at oction in Richmon', oh de good gracious! I know what dat mean!"

Aunt Rachel had gradually risen, while she warmed to her subject, and now she towered above us, black against the stars.

"Dey put chains on us an' put us on a stan' as high as dis po'ch,—twenty foot high,—an' all de people stood aroun', crowds an' crowds. An' dey 'd come up dah an' look at us all roun', an' squeeze our arm, an' make us git up an' walk, an' den say, 'Dis one too ole,' or 'Dis one lame,' or 'Dis one don't 'mount to much.' An' dey sole my ole man, an' took him away, an' dey begin to sell my chil'en an' take *dem* away, an' I begin to cry; an' de man say, 'Shet up yo' dam blubberin',' an' hit me on de mouf wid his han'. An' when de las' one was gone but my little Henry, I grab' *him* clost up to my breas' so, an' I ris up an' says, 'You shan't take him away,' I says; 'I'll kill de man dat tetches him!' I says. But my little Henry whisper an' say, 'I gwyne to run away, an' den I work an' buy yo' freedom.' Oh, bless de chile, he always so good! But dey got him—dey got him, de men did; but I took and tear de clo'es mos' off of 'em, an' beat 'em over de head wid my chain; an' *dey* give it to *me,* too, but I didn't mine dat.

"Well, dah was my ole man gone, an' all my chil'en, all my seven chil'en—an' six of 'em I hain't set eyes on ag'in to dis day, an' dat's twenty-two year ago las' Easter. De man dat bought me b'long' in New-bern, an' he took me dah. Well, bymeby de years roll on an' de waw come. My marster he was a Confedrit colonel, an' I was his family's cook. So when de Unions took dat town, dey all run away an' lef' me all by myse'f wid de other niggers in dat mons'us big house. So de big Union officers move in dah, an' dey ask me would I cook for *dem.* 'Lord bless you,' says I, 'dat's what I's *for.*'

"Dey wa'n't no small-fry officers, mine you, dey was de biggest dey *is;* an' de way dey made dem sojers mosey roun'! De Gen'l he tole me to boss dat kitchen; an' he say, 'If anybody come meddlin' wid you, you jist make 'em walk chalk; don't you be afeard,' he say; 'you's 'mong frens, now.'

"Well, I thinks to myse'f, if my little Henry ever got a chance to run away, he'd make to de Norf, o' course. So one day I comes in dah whah de big officers was, in de parlor, an' I drops a kurtchy, so, an' I up an' tole 'em 'bout my Henry, dey a-listenin' to my troubles jist de same as if I was white folks; an' I says, 'What I come for is beca'se if he got away and got up Norf whah you gemmen comes from, you might 'a' seen him, maybe, an' could tell me so as I could fine him ag'in; he was very little, an' he had a sk-yar on his lef' wris', an' at de top of his forehead.' Den dey look mournful, an' de Gen'l say, 'How long sence you los' him?' an' I say, 'Thirteen year.' Den de Gen'l say, 'He wouldn't be little no mo', now—he's a man!'

"I never thought o' dat befo'! He was only dat little feller to *me,* yit. I never thought 'bout him growin' up an' bein' big. But I see it den. None o' de gemmen had run acrost him, so dey couldn't do nothin' for me. But all dat time, do' *I* didn't know it, my Henry *was* run off to de Norf, years an' years, an' he was a barber, too, an' worked for hisse'f. An' bymeby, when de waw come, he ups an' he says, 'I's done barberin',' he says; 'I's gwyne to fine my ole mammy, less'n she's dead.' So he sole out an' went to whah dey was recruitin', an' hired hisse'f out to de colonel for his ser-vant; an' den he went all froo de battles everywhah, huntin' for his ole mammy; yes indeedy, he'd hire to fust one officer an' den another, tell he'd ransacked de whole Souf; but you see *I* didn't know nuffin 'bout *dis.* How was *I* gwyne to know it?

"Well, one night we had a big sojer ball; de sojers dah at Newbern was always havin' balls an' carryin' on. Dey had 'em in my kitchen, heaps o' times, 'ca'se it was so big. Mine you, I was *down* on sich doin's; beca'se my place was wid de officers, an' it rasp' me to have dem common sojers cavortin' roun' my kitchen like dat. But I alway' stood aroun' an' kep' things straight, I did; an' sometimes dey'd git my dander up, an' den I'd make 'em clar dat kitchen, mine I *tell* you!

"Well, one night—it was a Friday night—dey comes a whole plattoon f'm a *nigger* ridgment dat was on guard at de house,—de house was head-quarters, you know,—an' den I was jist a-*bilin'*! Mad? I was jist a-*boomin'*! I swelled aroun', an' swelled aroun'; I jist was a-itchin' for 'em to do somefin for to start me. *An'* dey was a-waltzin' an a-dancin'! *my*! but dey was havin' a time! an' I jist a-swellin' an' a-swellin' up! Pooty soon, 'long comes *sich* a spruce young nigger a-sailin' down de room wid a yaller wench roun' de wais'; an' roun' an' roun' an' roun' dey went, enough to make a body drunk to look at 'em; an' when dey got abreas' o' me, dey went to kin' o' balancin' aroun', fust on one leg an' den on t'other, an' smilin' at my big red turban, an' makin' fun, an' I ups an' says, '*Git* along wid you!—rubbage!' De young man's face kin' o' changed, all of a sudden, for 'bout a second, but den he went to smilin' ag'in, same as he was befo'. Well, 'bout dis time, in comes some niggers dat played music an' b'long' to de ban', an' dey *never* could git along widout puttin' on airs. An' de very fust air dey put on dat night, I lit into 'em! Dey laughed, an' dat made me wuss. De res' o' de niggers got to laughin', an' den my soul *alive* but I was hot! My eye was jist a-blazin'! I jist straightened myself up, so,—jist as I is now, plum to de ceilin', mos',—an' I digs my fists into my hips, an' I says, 'Look-a-heah!' I says, 'I want you niggers to understan' dat I wa'n't bawn in de mash to be fool' by trash! I's one o' de ole Blue Hen's Chickens, *I* is!' an' den I see dat young man stan' a-starin' an' stiff, lookin' kin' o' up at de ceilin' like he fo'got somefin, an' couldn't 'member it no mo'. Well, I jist march' on dem niggers,—so, lookin' like a gen'l,—an' dey jist cave' away befo' me an' out at de do'. An' as dis young man was a-goin' out, I heah him say to another nigger, 'Jim,' he says, 'you go 'long an' tell de cap'n I be on han' 'bout eight o'clock in de mawnin'; dey's somefin on my mine,' he says; 'I don't sleep no mo' dis night. You go 'long,' he says, 'an' leave me by my own se'f.'

"Dis was 'bout one o'clock in de mawnin'. Well, 'bout seven, I was up an' on han', gittin' de officers' breakfast. I was a-stoopin' down by de stove,—jist so, same as if yo' foot was de stove,—an' I'd opened de stove do' wid my right han',—so, pushin' it back, jist as I pushes yo' foot,—an' I'd jist got de pan o' hot biscuits in my han' an' was 'bout to raise up, when I see a black face come aroun' under mine, an' de eyes a-lookin' up into mine, jist as I's a-lookin' up clost under yo' face now; an' I jist stopped *right dah,* an' never budged! jist gazed, an' gazed, so; an' de pan begin to tremble, an' all of a sudden I *knowed*! De pan drop' on de flo' an' I grab his lef' han' an' shove back his sleeve,—jist so, as I's doin' to you,—an' den I goes for his forehead an' push de hair back, so, an' 'Boy!' I says, 'if you an't my Henry, what is you doin' wid dis welt on yo' wris' an' dat sk-yar on yo' forehead? De Lord God ob heaven be praise', I got my own ag'in!'

"Oh, no, Misto C——, *I* hain't had no trouble. An' no *joy*!"

[1874]

The Facts Concerning the Recent Carnival of Crime in Connecticut

I was feeling blithe, almost jocund. I put a match to my cigar, and just then the morning's mail was handed in. The first superscription I glanced at was in a handwriting that sent a thrill of pleasure through and through me. It was aunt Mary's; and she was the person I loved and honored most in all the world, outside of my own household. She had been my boyhood's idol; maturity, which is fatal to so many enchantments, had not been able to dislodge her from her pedestal; no, it had only justified her right to be there, and placed her dethronement permanently among the impossibilities. To show how strong her influence over me was, I will observe that long after everybody else's "*do*-stop-smoking" had ceased to affect me in the slightest degree, aunt Mary could still stir my torpid conscience into faint signs of life when she touched upon the matter. But all things have their limit, in this world. A happy day came at last, when even aunt Mary's words could no longer move me. I was not merely glad to see that day arrive; I was more than glad—I was grateful; for when its sun had set, the one alloy that was able to mar my enjoyment of my aunt's society was gone. The remainder of her stay with us that winter was in every way a delight. Of course she pleaded with me just as earnestly as ever, after that blessed day, to quit my pernicious habit, but to no purpose whatever; the moment she opened the subject I at once became calmly, peacefully, contentedly indifferent—absolutely, adamantinely indifferent. Consequently the closing weeks of that memorable visit melted away as pleasantly as a dream, they were so freighted, for me, with tranquil satisfaction. I could not have enjoyed my pet vice more if my gentle tormentor had been a smoker herself, and an advocate of the practice. Well, the sight of her handwriting reminded me that I was getting very hungry to see her again. I easily guessed what I should find in her letter. I opened it. Good! just as I expected; she was coming! Coming this very day, too, and by the morning train; I might expect her any moment.

I said to myself, "I am thoroughly happy and content, now. If my most pitiless enemy could appear before me at this moment, I would freely right any wrong I may have done him."

Straightway the door opened, and a shriveled, shabby dwarf entered. He was not more than two feet high. He seemed to be about forty years old. Every feature and every inch of him was a trifle out of shape; and so, while one could not put his finger upon any particular part and say, "This is a conspicuous deformity," the spectator perceived that this little person was a deformity as a whole—a vague, general, evenly-blended, nicely-adjusted deformity. There was a fox-like cunning in the face and the sharp little eyes, and also alertness and malice. And yet, this vile bit of human rubbish seemed to bear a sort of remote and ill-defined resemblance to me! It was dully perceptible in the mean form, the countenance, and even the clothes, gestures, manner, and attitudes of the creature. He was a far-fetched, dim suggestion of a burlesque upon me, a caricature of me in little. One thing about him struck me forcibly, and most unpleasantly: he was covered all over with a fuzzy, greenish mold, such as one sometimes sees upon mildewed bread. The sight of it was nauseating.

He stepped along with a chipper air, and flung himself into a doll's chair in a very free and easy way, without waiting to be asked. He tossed his hat into the waste basket. He picked up my old chalk pipe from the floor, gave the stem a wipe or two on his knee, filled the bowl from the tobacco-box at his side, and said to me in a tone of pert command,—

"Gimme a match!"

I blushed to the roots of my hair; partly with indignation, but mainly because it somehow seemed to me that this whole performance was very like an exaggeration of conduct which I myself had sometimes been guilty of in my intercourse with familiar friends;—but never, never with strangers, I observed to myself. I wanted to kick the pygmy into the fire, but some incomprehensible sense of being legally and legitimately under his authority forced me to obey his order. He applied the match to the pipe, took a contemplative whiff or two, and remarked, in an irritatingly familiar way,—

"Seems to me it's devilish odd weather for this time of year."

I flushed again, and in anger and humiliation as before; for the language was hardly an exaggeration of some that I have uttered in my day, and moreover was delivered in a tone of voice and with an exasperating drawl that had the seeming of a deliberate travesty of my style. Now there is nothing I am quite so sensitive about as a mocking imitation of my drawling infirmity of speech. I spoke up sharply and said,—

"Look here, you miserable ash-cat! you will have to give a little more attention to your manners, or I will throw you out of the window!"

The manikin smiled a smile of malicious content and security, puffed a whiff of smoke contemptuously toward me, and said, with a still more elaborate drawl,—

"Come—go gently, now; don't put on *too* many airs with your betters."

This cool snub rasped me all over, but it seemed to subjugate me, too, for a moment. The pygmy contemplated me a while with his weasel eyes, and then said, in a peculiarly sneering way,—

"You turned a tramp away from your door this morning."

I said crustily,—

"Perhaps I did, perhaps I didn't. How do *you* know?"

"Well, I know. It isn't any matter *how* I know."

"Very well. Suppose I *did* turn a tramp away from the door—what of it?"

"Oh, nothing; nothing in particular. Only you lied to him."

"I *didn't*! That is, I"—

"Yes, but you did; you lied to him."

I felt a guilty pang,—in truth I had felt it forty times before that tramp had traveled a block from my door,—but still I resolved to make a show of feeling slandered; so I said,—

"This is a baseless impertinence. I said to the tramp"—

"There—wait. You were about to lie again. *I* know what you said to him. You said the cook was gone down town and there was nothing left from breakfast. Two lies. You knew the cook was behind the door, and plenty of provisions behind *her*."

This astonishing accuracy silenced me; and it filled me with wondering speculations, too, as to how this cub could have got his information. Of course he could have culled the conversation from the tramp, but by what sort of magic had he contrived to find out about the concealed cook? Now the dwarf spoke again:—

"It was rather pitiful, rather small, in you to refuse to read that poor young woman's manuscript the other day, and give her an opinion as to its literary value; and she had come so far, too, and *so* hopefully. Now *wasn't* it?"

I felt like a cur! And I had felt so every time the thing had recurred to my mind, I may as well confess. I flushed hotly and said,—

"Look here, have you nothing better to do than prowl around prying into other people's business? Did that girl tell you that?"

"Never mind whether she did or not. The main thing is, you did that contemptible thing. And you felt ashamed of it afterwards. Aha! you feel ashamed of it *now*!"

This with a sort of devilish glee. With fiery earnestness I responded,—

"I told that girl, in the kindest, gentlest way, that I could not consent to deliver judgment upon *any* one's manuscript, because an individual's verdict was worthless. It might underrate a work of high merit and lose it to the world, or it might overrate a trashy production and so open the way for its infliction upon the world. I said that the great public was the only tribunal competent to sit in judgment upon a literary effort, and therefore it must be best to lay it before that tribunal in the outset, since in the end it must stand or fall by that mighty court's decision any way."

"Yes, you said all that. So you did, you juggling, small-souled shuffler! And yet when the happy hopefulness faded out of that poor girl's face, when you saw her furtively slip beneath her shawl the scroll she had so patiently and honestly scribbled at,—so ashamed of her darling now, so proud of it before,—when you saw the gladness go out of her eyes and the tears come there, when she crept away so humbly who had come so"—

"Oh, peace! peace! peace! Blister your merciless tongue, haven't all these thoughts tortured me enough, without *your* coming here to fetch them back again?"

Remorse! remorse! It seemed to me that it would eat the very heart out of me! And yet that small fiend only sat there leering at me with joy and contempt, and placidly chuckling. Presently he began to speak again. Every sentence was an accusation, and every accusation a truth. Every clause was freighted with sarcasm and derision, every slow-dropping word burned like vitriol. The dwarf reminded me of times when I had flown at my children in anger and punished them for faults which a little inquiry would have taught me that others, and not they, had committed. He reminded me of how I had disloyally allowed old friends to be traduced in my hearing, and been too craven to utter a word in their defense. He reminded me of many dishonest things which

I had done; of many which I had procured to be done by children and other irresponsible persons; of some which I had planned, thought upon, and longed to do, and been kept from the performance by fear of consequences only. With exquisite cruelty he recalled to my mind, item by item, wrongs and unkindnesses I had inflicted and humiliations I had put upon friends since dead, "who died thinking of those injuries, maybe, and grieving over them," he added, by way of poison to the stab.

"For instance," said he, "take the case of your younger brother, when you two were boys together, many a long year ago. He always lovingly trusted in you with a fidelity that your manifold treacheries were not able to shake. He followed you about like a dog, content to suffer wrong and abuse if he might only be with you; patient under these injuries so long as it was your hand that inflicted them. The latest picture you have of him in health and strength must be such a comfort to you! You pledged your honor that if he would let you blindfold him no harm should come to him; and then, giggling and choking over the rare fun of the joke, you led him to a brook thinly glazed with ice, and pushed him in; and how you did laugh! Man, you will never forget the gentle, reproachful look he gave you as he struggled shivering out, if you live a thousand years! Oho! you see it now, you see it *now*!"

"Beast, I have seen it a million times, and shall see it a million more! and may you rot away piecemeal, and suffer till doomsday what I suffer now, for bringing it back to me again!"

The dwarf chuckled contentedly, and went on with his accusing history of my career. I dropped into a moody, vengeful state, and suffered in silence under the merciless lash. At last this remark of his gave me a sudden rouse:—

"Two months ago, on a Tuesday, you woke up, away in the night, and fell to thinking, with shame, about a peculiarly mean and pitiful act of yours toward a poor ignorant Indian in the wilds of the Rocky Mountains in the winter of eighteen hundred and"—

"Stop a moment, devil! Stop! Do you mean to tell me that even my very *thoughts* are not hidden from you?"

"It seems to look like that. Didn't you think the thoughts I have just mentioned?"

"If I didn't, I wish I may never breathe again! Look here, friend—look me in the eye. Who *are* you?"

"Well, who do you think?"

"I think you are Satan himself. I think you are the devil."

"No."

"No? Then who *can* you be?"

"Would you really like to know?"

"*Indeed* I would."

"Well, I am your *Conscience*!"

In an instant I was in a blaze of joy and exultation. I sprang at the creature, roaring,—

"Curse you, I have wished a hundred million times that you were tangible, and that I could get my hands on your throat once! Oh, but I will wreak a deadly vengeance on"—

Folly! Lightning does not move more quickly than my Conscience did! He darted aloft so suddenly that in the moment my fingers clutched the empty air he was already perched on the top of the high book-case, with his thumb at his nose in token of derision. I flung the poker at him, and missed. I fired the boot-jack. In a blind rage I flew from place to place, and snatched and hurled any missile that came handy; the storm of books, inkstands, and chunks of coal gloomed the air and beat about the manikin's perch relentlessly, but all to no purpose; the nimble figure dodged every shot; and not only that, but burst into a cackle of sarcastic and triumphant laughter as I sat down exhausted. While I puffed and gasped with fatigue and excitement, my Conscience talked to this effect:—

"My good slave, you are curiously witless—no, I mean characteristically so. In truth, you are always consistent, always yourself, always an ass. Otherwise it must have occurred to you that if you attempted this murder with a sad heart and a heavy conscience, I would droop under the burdening influence instantly. Fool, I should have weighed a ton, and could not have budged from the floor; but instead, you are so cheerfully anxious to kill me that your Conscience is as light as a feather; hence I am away up here out of your reach. I can almost respect a mere ordinary sort of fool; but *you*—pah!"

I would have given anything, then, to be heavy-hearted, so that I could get this person down from there and take his life, but I could no more be heavy-hearted over such a desire than I could have sorrowed over its accomplishment. So I could only look longingly up at my master, and rave at the ill-luck that denied me a heavy conscience the one only time that I had ever wanted such a thing in my life. By and by I got to musing over the hour's strange adventure, and of course my human curiosity began to work. I set myself to framing in my mind some questions for this fiend to answer. Just then one of my boys entered, leaving the door open behind him, and exclaimed,—

"My! what *has* been going on, here! The book-case is all one riddle of"—

I sprang up in consternation, and shouted,—

"Out of this! Hurry! Jump! Fly! Shut the door! Quick, or my Conscience will get away!"

The door slammed to, and I locked it. I glanced up and was grateful, to the bottom of my heart, to see that my owner was still my prisoner. I said,—

"Hang you, I might have lost you! Children are the heedlessest creatures. But look here, friend, the boy did not seem to notice you at all; how is that?"

"For a very good reason. I am invisible to all but you."

I made mental note of that piece of information with a good deal of satisfaction. I could kill this miscreant now, if I got a chance, and no one would know it. But this very reflection made me so light-hearted that my Conscience could hardly keep his seat, but was like to float aloft toward the ceiling like a toy balloon. I said, presently,—

"Come, my Conscience, let us be friendly. Let us fly a flag of truce for a while. I am suffering to ask you some questions."

"Very well. Begin."

"Well, then, in the first place, why were you never visible to me before?"

"Because you never asked to see me before; that is, you never asked in the right spirit and the proper form before. You were just in the right spirit this time, and when you called for your most pitiless enemy I was that person by a very large majority, though you did not suspect it."

"Well, did that remark of mine turn you into flesh and blood?"

"No. It only made me visible to you. I am unsubstantial, just as other spirits are."

This remark prodded me with a sharp misgiving. If he was unsubstantial, how was I going to kill him? But I dissembled, and said persuasively,—

"Conscience, it isn't sociable of you to keep at such a distance. Come down and take another smoke."

This was answered with a look that was full of derision, and with this observation added:—

"Come where you can get at me and kill me? The invitation is declined with thanks."

"All right," said I to myself; "so it seems a spirit *can* be killed, after all; there will be one spirit lacking in this world, presently, or I lose my guess." Then I said aloud,—

"Friend"—

"There; wait a bit. I am not your friend, I am your enemy; I am not your equal, I am your master. Call me 'my lord,' if you please. You are too familiar."

"I don't like such titles. I am willing to call you *sir*. That is as far as"—

"We will have no argument about this. Just obey; that is all. Go on with your chatter."

"Very well, my lord,—since nothing but my lord will suit you,—I was going to ask you how long you will be visible to me?"

"Always!"

I broke out with strong indignation: "This is simply an outrage. That is what I think of it. You have dogged, and dogged, and *dogged* me, all the days of my life, invisible. That was misery enough; now to have such a looking thing as you tagging after me like another shadow all the rest of my days is an intolerable prospect. You have my opinion, my lord; make the most of it."

"My lad, there was never so pleased a conscience in this world as I was when you made me visible. It gives me an inconceivable advantage. *Now,* I can look you straight in the eye, and call you names, and leer at you, jeer at you, sneer at you; and *you* know what eloquence there is in visible gesture and expression, more especially when the effect is heightened by audible speech. I shall always address you henceforth in your o-w-n s-n-i-v-e-l-i-n-g d-r-a-w-l—baby!"

I let fly with the coal-hod. No result. My lord said,—

"Come, come! Remember the flag of truce!"

"Ah, I forgot that. I will try to be civil; and *you* try it, too, for a novelty. The idea of a *civil* conscience! It is a good joke; an excellent joke. All the consciences *I* have ever heard of were nagging, badgering, fault-finding, execrable savages! Yes; and always in a sweat about some poor little insignificant trifle or other—destruction catch the lot of them, *I* say! I would trade mine for the small-pox and seven kinds of consumption, and be glad of the chance. Now tell me, why *is* it that a conscience can't haul a man over the coals once, for an offense, and then let him alone? Why is it that it wants to keep on pegging at him, day and night and night and day, week in and week out, forever and ever, about the same old thing? There is no sense in that, and no reason in it. I think a conscience that will act like that is meaner than the very dirt itself."

"Well, *we* like it; that suffices."

"Do you do it with the honest intent to improve a man?"

That question produced a sarcastic smile, and this reply:—

"No, sir. Excuse me. We do it simply because it is 'business.' It is our trade. The *purpose* of it *is* to improve the man, but *we* are merely disinterested agents. We are appointed by authority, and haven't anything to say in the matter. We obey orders and leave the consequences where they belong. But I am willing to admit this much: we *do* crowd the orders a trifle when we get a chance, which is most of the time. We enjoy it. We are instructed to remind a man a few times of an error; and I don't mind acknowledging that we try to give pretty good measure. And when we get hold of a man of a peculiarly sensitive nature, oh, but we do haze him! I have known consciences to come all the way from China and Russia to see a person of that kind put through his paces, on a special occasion. Why, I knew a man of that sort who had accidentally crippled a mulatto baby; the news went abroad, and I wish you may never commit another sin if the consciences didn't flock from all over the earth to enjoy the fun and help his master exercise him. That man walked the floor in torture for forty-eight hours, without eating or sleeping, and then blew his brains out. The child was perfectly well again in three weeks."

"Well, you are a precious crew, not to put it too strong. I think I begin to see, now, why you have always been a trifle inconsistent with me. In your anxiety to get all the juice you can out of a sin, you make a man repent of it in three or four different ways. For instance, you found fault with me for lying to that tramp, and I suffered over that. But it was only yesterday that I told a tramp the square truth, to wit, that, it being regarded as bad citizenship to encourage vagrancy, I would give him nothing. What did you do *then*? Why, you made me say to myself, 'Ah, it would have been so much kinder and more blameless to ease him off with a little white lie, and send him away feeling that if he could not have bread, the gentle treatment was at least something to be grateful for!' Well, I suffered all day about *that.* Three days before, I had fed a tramp, and fed him freely, supposing it a virtuous act. Straight off you said, 'O false citizen, to have fed a tramp!' and I suffered as usual. I gave a tramp work; you objected to it,—*after* the contract was made, of course; you never speak up beforehand. Next, I *refused* a tramp work; you objected to *that.* Next, I proposed to kill a tramp; you kept me awake all night, oozing remorse at every pore. Sure I was going to be right *this* time, I sent the next tramp away with my benediction; and I wish you may live as long as I do, if you didn't make me smart all night again because I didn't kill him. Is there *any* way of satisfying that malignant invention which is called a conscience?"

"Ha, ha! this is luxury! Go on!"

"But come, now, answer me that question. *Is* there any way?"

"Well, none that I propose to tell *you,* my son. Ass! I don't care *what* act you may turn your hand to, I can straightway whisper a word in your ear and make you think you have committed a dreadful meanness. It is my *business*—and my joy—to make you repent of *every*thing you do. If I have fooled away any opportunities it was not intentional; I beg to assure you it was not intentional."

"Don't worry; you haven't missed a trick that *I* know of. I never did a thing in all my life, virtuous or otherwise, that I didn't repent of within twenty-four hours. In church last Sunday I listened to a charity sermon. My first impulse was to give three hundred and fifty dollars; I repented of that and reduced it a hundred; repented of that and reduced it another hundred; repented of that and reduced it another hundred; repented of that and reduced the remaining fifty to twenty-five; repented of that and came down to fifteen; repented of that and dropped to two dollars and a half; when the plate came around at last, I repented once more and contributed ten cents. Well, when I got home, I did wish to goodness I had that ten cents back again! You never *did* let me get through a charity sermon without having something to sweat about."

"Oh, and I never shall, I never shall. You can always depend on me."

"I think so. Many and many's the restless night I've wanted to take you by the neck. If I could only get hold of you now!"

"Yes, no doubt. But I am not an ass; I am only the saddle of an ass. But go on, go on. You entertain me more than I like to confess."

"I am glad of that. (You will not mind my lying a little, to keep in practice.) Look here; not to be too personal, I think you are about the shabbiest and most contemptible little shriveled-up reptile that can be imagined. I am grateful enough that you are invisible to other people, for I should die with shame to be seen with such a mildewed monkey of a conscience as *you* are. Now if you were five or six feet high, and"—

"Oh, come! who is to blame?"

"*I* don't know."

"Why, you are; nobody else."

"Confound you, I wasn't consulted about your personal appearance."

"I don't care, you had a good deal to do with it, nevertheless. When you were eight or nine years old, I was seven feet high and as pretty as a picture."

"I wish you had died young! So you have grown the wrong way, have you?"

"Some of us grow one way and some the other. You had a large conscience once; if you've a small conscience now, I reckon there are reasons for it. However, both of us are to blame, you and I. You see, you used to be conscientious about a great many things; morbidly so, I may say. It was a great many years ago. You probably do not remember it, now. Well, I took a great interest in my work, and I so enjoyed the anguish which certain pet sins of yours afflicted you with, that I kept pelting at you until I rather overdid the matter. You began to rebel. Of course I began to lose ground, then, and shrivel a little,—diminish in stature, get moldy, and grow deformed. The more I weakened, the more stubbornly you fastened on to those particular sins; till at last the places on my person that represent those vices became as callous as shark skin. Take smoking, for instance. I played that card a little too long, and I lost. When people plead with you at this late day to quit that vice, that old callous place seems to enlarge and cover me all over like a shirt of mail. It exerts a mysterious, smothering effect; and presently I, your faithful hater, your devoted Conscience, go sound asleep! Sound? It is no name for it. I couldn't hear it thunder at such a time. You have some few other vices—perhaps eighty, or maybe ninety—that affect me in much the same way."

"This is flattering; you must be asleep a good part of your time."

"Yes, of late years. I should be asleep *all* the time, but for the help I get."

"Who helps you?"

"Other consciences. Whenever a person whose conscience I am acquainted with tries to plead with you about the vices you are callous to, I get my friend to give his client a pang concerning some villainy of his own, and that shuts off his meddling and starts him off to hunt personal consolation. My field of usefulness is about trimmed down to tramps, budding authoresses, and that line of goods, now; but don't you worry—I'll harry you on *them* while they last! Just you put your trust in me."

"I think I can. But if you had only been good enough to mention these facts some thirty years ago, I should have turned my particular attention to sin, and I think that by this time I should not only have had you pretty permanently asleep on the entire list of human vices, but reduced to the size of a homœopathic pill, at that. That is about the style of conscience *I* am pining for. If I only had you shrunk down to a homœopathic pill, and could get my hands on you, would I put you in a glass case for a keepsake? No, sir. I would give you to a yellow dog! That is where *you* ought to be—you and all your tribe. You are not fit to be in society, in my opinion. Now another question. Do you know a good many consciences in this section?"

"Plenty of them."

"I would give anything to see some of them! Could you bring them here? And would they be visible to me?"

"Certainly not."

"I suppose I ought to have known that, without asking. But no matter, you can describe them. Tell me about my neighbor Thompson's conscience, please."

"Very well. I know him intimately; have known him many years. I knew him when he was eleven feet high and of a faultless figure. But he is very rusty and tough and misshapen, now, and hardly ever interests himself about anything. As to his present size—well, he sleeps in a cigar box."

"Likely enough. There are few smaller, meaner men in this region than Hugh Thompson. Do you know Robinson's conscience?"

"Yes. He is a shade under four and a half feet high; used to be a blonde; is a brunette, now, but still shapely and comely."

"Well, Robinson is a good fellow. Do you know Tom Smith's conscience?"

"I have known him from childhood. He was thirteen inches high, and rather sluggish, when he was two years old—as nearly all of us are, at that age. He is thirty-seven feet high, now, and the stateliest figure in America. His legs are still racked with growing-pains, but he has a good time, nevertheless. Never sleeps. He is the most active and energetic member of the New England Conscience Club; is president of it. Night and day you can find him pegging away at Smith, panting with his labor, sleeves rolled up, countenance all alive with enjoyment. He has got his victim splendidly dragooned, now. He can make poor Smith imagine that the most innocent little thing he does is an odious sin; and then he sets to work and almost tortures the soul out of him about it."

"Smith is the noblest man in all this section, and the purest; and yet is always breaking his heart because he cannot be good! Only a conscience *could* find pleasure in heaping agony upon a spirit like that. Do you know my aunt Mary's conscience?"

"I have seen her at a distance, but am not acquainted with her. She lives in the open air altogether, because no door is large enough to admit her."

"I can believe that. Let me see. Do you know the conscience of that publisher who once stole some sketches of mine for a 'series' of his, and then left me to pay the law expenses I had to incur in order to choke him off?"

"Yes. He has a wide fame. He was exhibited, a month ago, with some other antiquities, for the benefit of a recent Member of the Cabinet's conscience, that was starving in exile. Tickets and fares were high, but I traveled for nothing by pretending to be the conscience of an editor, and got in for half price by representing myself to be the conscience of a clergyman. However, the publisher's conscience, which was to have been the main feature of the entertainment, was a failure—as an exhibition. He was there, but what of that? The management had provided a microscope with a magnifying power of only thirty thousand diameters, and so nobody got to see him, after all. There was great and general dissatisfaction, of course, but"—

Just here there was an eager footstep on the stair; I opened the door, and my aunt Mary burst into the room. It was a joyful meeting, and a cheery bombardment of questions and answers concerning family matters ensued. By and by my aunt said,—

"But I am going to abuse you a little now. You promised me, the day I saw you last, that you would look after the needs of the poor family around the corner as faithfully as I had done it myself. Well, I found out by accident that you failed of your promise. *Was* that right?"

In simple truth, I never had thought of that family a second time! And now such a splintering pang of guilt shot through me! I glanced up at my Conscience. Plainly, my heavy heart was affecting him. His body was drooping forward; he seemed about to fall from the book-case. My aunt continued:—

"And think how you have neglected my poor *protégée* at the almshouse, you dear, hard-hearted promise-breaker!" I blushed scarlet, and my tongue was tied. As the sense of my guilty negligence waxed sharper and stronger, my Conscience began to sway heavily back and forth; and when my aunt, after a little pause, said in a grieved tone, "Since you never once went to see her, maybe it will not distress you now to know that that poor child died, months ago, utterly friendless and forsaken!" my Conscience could no longer bear up under the weight of my sufferings, but tumbled headlong from his high perch and struck the floor with a dull, leaden thump. He lay there writhing with pain and quaking with apprehension, but straining every muscle in frantic efforts to get up. In a fever of expectancy I sprang to the door, locked it, placed my back against it, and bent a watchful gaze upon my struggling master. Already my fingers were itching to begin their murderous work.

"Oh, what *can* be the matter!" exclaimed my aunt, shrinking from me, and following with her frightened eyes the direction of mine. My breath was coming in short, quick gasps now, and my excitement was almost uncontrollable. My aunt cried out,—

"Oh, do not look so! You appall me! Oh, what can the matter be? What is it you see? Why do you stare so? Why do you work your fingers like that?"

"Peace, woman!" I said, in a hoarse whisper. "Look elsewhere; pay no attention to me; it is nothing—nothing. I am often this way. It will pass in a moment. It comes from smoking too much."

My injured lord was up, wild-eyed with terror, and trying to hobble toward the door. I could hardly breathe, I was so wrought up. My aunt wrung her hands, and said,—

"Oh, I knew how it would be; I knew it would come to this at last! Oh, I implore you to crush out that fatal habit while it may yet be time! You must not, you shall not be deaf to my supplications longer!" My struggling Conscience showed sudden signs of weariness! "Oh, promise me you will throw off this hateful slavery of tobacco!" My Conscience began to reel drowsily, and grope with his hands—enchanting spectacle! "I beg you, I beseech you, I implore you! Your reason is deserting you! There is madness in your eye! It flames with frenzy! Oh, hear me, hear me, and be saved! See, I plead with you on my very knees!" As she sank before me my Conscience reeled again, and then drooped languidly to the floor, blinking toward me a last supplication for mercy, with heavy eyes. "Oh, promise, or you are lost! Promise, and be redeemed! Promise! Promise and live!" With a long-drawn sigh my conquered Conscience closed his eyes and fell fast asleep!

With an exultant shout I sprang past my aunt, and in an instant I had my life-long foe by the throat. After so many years of waiting and longing, he was mine at last. I tore him to shreds and fragments. I rent the fragments to bits. I cast the bleeding rubbish into the fire, and drew into my nostrils the grateful incense of my burnt-offering. At last, and forever, my Conscience was dead!

I was a free man! I turned upon my poor aunt, who was almost petrified with terror, and shouted,—

"Out of this with your paupers, your charities, your reforms, your pestilent morals! You behold before you a man whose life-conflict is done, whose soul is at peace; a man whose heart is dead to sorrow, dead to suffering, dead to remorse; a man WITHOUT A CONSCIENCE! In my joy I spare you, though I could throttle you and never feel a pang! Fly!"

She fled. Since that day my life is all bliss. Bliss, unalloyed bliss. Nothing in all the world could persuade me to have a conscience again. I settled all my old outstanding scores, and began the world anew. I killed thirty-eight persons during the first two weeks—all of them on account of ancient grudges. I burned a dwelling that interrupted my view. I swindled a widow and some orphans out of their last cow, which is a very good one, though not thoroughbred, I believe. I have also committed scores of crimes, of various kinds, and have enjoyed my work exceedingly, whereas it would formerly have broken my heart and turned my hair gray, I have no doubt.

In conclusion I wish to state, by way of advertisement, that medical colleges desiring assorted tramps for scientific purposes, either by the gross, by cord measurement, or per ton, will do well to examine the lot in my cellar before purchasing elsewhere, as these were all selected and prepared by myself, and can be had at a low rate, because I wish to clear out my stock and get ready for the spring trade.

[1876]

Punch, Brothers, Punch!

Will the reader please to cast his eye over the following verses, and see if he can discover anything harmful in them?

> "Conductor, when you receive a fare,
> Punch in the presence of the passenjare!
> A blue trip slip for an eight-cent fare,
> A buff trip slip for a six-cent fare,
> A pink trip slip for a three-cent fare,
> Punch in the presence of the passenjare!
>
> CHORUS
>
> Punch, brothers! punch with care!
> Punch in the presence of the passenjare!"

I came across these jingling rhymes in a newspaper, a little while ago, and read them a couple of times. They took instant and entire possession of me. All through breakfast they went waltzing through my brain; and when, at last, I rolled up my napkin, I could not tell whether I had eaten anything or not. I had carefully laid out my day's work the day before—a thrilling tragedy in the novel which I am writing. I went to my den to begin my deed of blood. I took up my pen, but all I could get it to say was, "Punch in the presence of the passenjare." I fought hard for an hour, but it was useless. My head kept humming, "A blue trip slip for an eight-cent fare, a buff trip slip for a six-cent fare," and so on and so on, without peace or respite. The day's work was ruined—I could see that plainly enough. I gave up and drifted down town, and presently discovered that my feet were keeping time to that relentless jingle. When I could stand it no longer I altered my step. But it did no good; those rhymes accommodated themselves to the new step and went on harassing me just as before. I returned home, and suffered all the afternoon; suffered all through an unconscious and unrefreshing dinner; suffered, and cried, and jingled all through the evening; went to bed and rolled, tossed, and jingled right along, the same as ever; got up at midnight frantic, and tried to read; but there was nothing visible upon the whirling page except "Punch! punch in the presence of the passenjare." By sunrise I was out of my mind, and everybody marveled and was distressed at the idiotic burden of my ravings,—"Punch! oh, punch! punch in the presence of the passenjare!"

Two days later, on Saturday morning, I arose, a tottering wreck, and went forth to fulfill an engagement with a valued friend, the Rev. Mr. ——, to walk to the Talcott Tower, ten miles distant. He stared at me, but asked no questions. We started. Mr. —— talked, talked, talked—as is his wont. I said nothing; I heard nothing. At the end of a mile, Mr. —— said,—

"Mark, are you sick? I never saw a man look so haggard and worn and absent-minded. Say something; do!"

Drearily, without enthusiasm, I said: "Punch, brothers, punch with care! Punch in the presence of the passenjare!"

My friend eyed me blankly, looked perplexed, then said,—

"I do not think I get your drift, Mark. There does not seem to be any relevancy in what you have said, certainly nothing sad; and yet—maybe it was the way you *said* the words—I never heard anything that sounded so pathetic. What is"—

But I heard no more. I was already far away with my pitiless, heartbreaking "blue trip slip for an eight-cent fare, buff trip slip for a six-cent fare, pink trip slip for a three-cent fare; punch in the presence of the passenjare." I do not know what occurred during the other nine miles. However, all of a sudden Mr. —— laid his hand on my shoulder and shouted,—

"Oh, wake up! wake up! wake up! Don't sleep all day! Here we are at the Tower, man! I have talked myself deaf and dumb and blind, and never got a response. Just look at this magnificent autumn landscape! Look at it! look at it! Feast your eyes on it! You have traveled; you have seen boasted landscapes elsewhere. Come, now, deliver an honest opinion. What do you say to this?"

I sighed wearily, and murmured,—

"A buff trip slip for a six-cent fare, a pink trip slip for a three-cent fare, punch in the presence of the passenjare."

Rev. Mr. —— stood there, very grave, full of concern, apparently, and looked long at me; then he said,—

"Mark, there is something about this that I cannot understand. Those are about the same words you said before; there does not seem to be anything in them, and yet they nearly break my heart when you say them. Punch in the—how is it they go?"

I began at the beginning and repeated all the lines. My friend's face lighted with interest. He said,—

"Why, what a captivating jingle it is! It is almost music. It flows along so nicely. I have nearly caught the rhymes myself. Say them over just once more, and then I'll have them, sure."

I said them over. Then Mr. —— said them. He made one little mistake, which I corrected. The next time and the next he got them right. Now a great burden seemed to tumble from my shoulders. That torturing jingle departed out of my brain, and a grateful sense of rest and peace descended upon me. I was light-hearted enough to sing; and I did sing for half an hour, straight along, as we went jogging homeward. Then my freed tongue found blessed speech again, and the pent talk of many a weary hour began to gush and flow. It flowed on and on, joyously, jubilantly, until the fountain was empty and dry. As I wrung my friend's hand at parting, I said,—

"Have n't we had a royal good time! But now I remember, you have n't said a word for two hours. Come, come, out with something!"

The Rev. Mr. —— turned a lacklustre eye upon me, drew a deep sigh, and said, without animation, without apparent consciousness,—

"Punch, brothers, punch with care! Punch in the presence of the passenjare!"

A pang shot through me as I said to myself, "Poor fellow, poor fellow! *he* has got it, now."

I did not see Mr. —— for two or three days after that. Then, on Tuesday evening, he staggered into my presence and sank dejectedly into a seat. He was pale, worn; he was a wreck. He lifted his faded eyes to my face and said,—

"Ah, Mark, it was a ruinous investment that I made in those heartless rhymes. They have ridden me like a nightmare, day and night, hour after hour, to this very moment. Since I saw you I have suffered the torments of the lost. Saturday evening I had a sudden call, by telegraph, and took the night train for Boston. The occasion was the death of a valued old friend who had requested that I should preach his funeral sermon. I took my seat in the cars and set myself to framing the discourse. But I never got beyond the opening paragraph; for then the train started and the car-wheels began their 'clack-clack-clack-clack! clack-clack-clack-clack!' and right away those odious rhymes fitted themselves to that accompaniment. For an hour I sat there and set a syllable of those rhymes to every separate and distinct clack the car-wheels made. Why, I was as fagged out, then, as if I had been chopping wood all day. My skull was splitting with headache. It seemed to me that I must go mad if I sat there any longer; so I undressed and went to bed. I stretched myself out in my berth, and—well, you know what the result was. The thing went right along, just the same. 'Clack-clack-clack, a blue trip slip, clack-clack-clack, for an eight-cent fare; clack-clack-clack, a buff trip slip, clack-clack-clack, for a six-cent fare, and so on, and so on, and so on—*punch,* in the presence of the passenjare!' Sleep? Not a single wink! I was almost a lunatic when I got to Boston. Don't ask me about the funeral. I did the best I could, but every solemn individual sentence was meshed and tangled and woven in and out with 'Punch, brothers, punch with care, punch in the presence of the passenjare.' And the most distressing thing was that my *delivery* dropped into the undulating rhythm of those pulsing rhymes, and I could actually catch absent-minded people nodding *time* to the swing of it with their stupid heads. And, Mark, you may believe it or not, but before I got through, the entire assemblage were placidly bobbing their heads in solemn unison, mourners, undertaker, and all. The moment I had finished, I fled to the anteroom in a state bordering on frenzy. Of course it would be my luck to find a sorrowing and aged maiden aunt of the deceased there, who had arrived from Springfield too late to get into the church. She began to sob, and said,—

" 'Oh, oh, he is gone, he is gone, and I did n't see him before he died!'

" 'Yes!' I said, 'he *is* gone, he *is* gone, he *is* gone—oh, *will* this suffering never cease!'

" '*You* loved him, then! Oh, you too loved him!'

" 'Loved him! Loved *who*?'

" 'Why, my poor George! my poor nephew!'

" 'Oh—*him!* Yes—oh, yes, yes. Certainly—certainly. Punch—punch—oh, this misery will kill me!'

" 'Bless you! bless you, sir, for these sweet words! *I,* too, suffer in this dear loss. Were you present during his last moments?'

" 'Yes! I—*whose* last moments?'

" '*His.* The dear departed's.'

" 'Yes! Oh, yes—yes—*yes!* I suppose so, I think so, *I* don't know! Oh, certainly—I was there—*I* was there!'

" 'Oh, what a privilege! what a precious privilege! And his last words—oh, tell me, tell me his last words! What did he say?'

" 'He said—he said—oh, my head, my head, my head! He said—he said—he never said *any*thing but Punch, punch, *punch* in the presence of the passenjare! Oh, leave me, madam! In the name of all that is generous, leave me to my madness, my misery, my despair!—a buff trip slip for a six-cent fare, a pink trip slip for a three-cent fare—endu-rance *can* no fur-ther go!—PUNCH in the presence of the passenjare!' "

My friend's hopeless eyes rested upon mine a pregnant minute, and then he said impressively,—

"Mark, you do not say anything. You do not offer me any hope. But, ah me, it is just as well—it is just as well. You could not do me any good. The time has long gone by when words could comfort me. Something tells me that my tongue is doomed to wag forever to the jigger of that remorseless jingle. There—there it is coming on me again: a blue trip slip for an eight-cent fare, a buff trip slip for a"—

Thus murmuring faint and fainter, my friend sank into a peaceful trance and forgot his sufferings in a blessed respite.

How did I finally save him from the asylum? I took him to a neighboring university and made him discharge the burden of his persecuting rhymes into the eager ears of the poor, unthinking students. How is it with *them,* now? The result is too sad to tell. Why did I write this article? It was for a worthy, even a noble, purpose. It was to warn you, reader, if you should come across those merciless rhymes, to avoid them—avoid them as you would a pestilence!

[1876]

Jim Baker's Blue-Jay Yarn

Animals talk to each other, of course. There can be no question about that; but I suppose there are very few people who can understand them. I never knew but one man who could. I knew he could, however, because he told me so himself. He was a middle-aged, simple-hearted miner who had lived in a lonely corner of California, among the woods and mountains, a good many years, and had studied the ways of his only neighbors, the beasts and the birds, until he believed he could accurately translate any remark which they made. This was Jim Baker. According to Jim Baker, some animals have only a limited education, and use only very simple words, and scarcely ever a comparison or a flowery figure; whereas, certain other animals have a large vocabulary, a fine command of language and a ready and fluent delivery; consequently these latter talk a great deal; they like it; they are conscious of their talent, and they enjoy "showing off." Baker said, that after long and careful observation, he had come to the conclusion that the blue-jays were the best talkers he had found among birds and beasts. Said he:—

"There's more *to* a blue-jay than any other creature. He has got more moods, and more different kinds of feelings than other creature; and mind you, whatever a blue-jay feels, he can put into language. And no mere commonplace language, either, but rattling, out-and-out book-talk—and bristling with metaphor, too—just bristling! And as for command of language—why *you* never see a blue-jay get stuck for a word. No man ever did. They just boil out of him! And another thing: I've noticed a good deal, and there's no bird, or cow, or anything that uses as good grammar as a blue-jay. You may say a cat uses good grammar. Well, a cat does—but you let a cat get excited, once; you let a cat get to pulling fur with another cat on a shed, nights, and you'll hear grammar that will give you the lockjaw. Ignorant people think it's the *noise* which fighting cats make that is so aggravating, but it ain't so; it's the sickening grammar they use. Now I've never heard a jay use bad grammar but very seldom; and when they do, they are as ashamed as a human; they shut right down and leave.

"You may call a jay a bird. Well, so he is, in a measure—because he's got feathers on him, and don't belong to no church, perhaps; but otherwise he is just as much a human as you be. And I'll tell you for why. A jay's gifts, and instincts, and feelings, and interests, cover the whole ground. A jay hasn't got any more principle than a Congressman. A jay will lie, a jay will steal, a jay will deceive, a jay will betray; and four times out of five, a jay will go back on his solemnest promise. The sacredness of an obligation is a thing which you can't cram into no blue-jay's head. Now on top of all this, there's another thing: a jay can out-swear any gentleman in the mines. You think a cat can swear. Well, a cat can; but you give a blue-jay a subject that calls for his reserve-powers, and where is your cat? Don't talk to *me*—I know too much about this thing. And there's yet another thing: in the one little particular of scolding—just good, clean, out-and-out scolding—a blue-jay can lay over anything, human or divine. Yes, sir, a jay is everything that a man is. A jay can cry, a jay can laugh, a jay can feel shame, a jay can reason and plan and discuss, a jay likes gossip and scandal, a jay has got a sense of humor, a jay knows when he is an ass just as well as you do—maybe better. If a jay ain't human, he better take in his sign, that's all. Now I'm going to tell you a perfectly true fact about some blue-jays."

"When I first begun to understand jay language correctly, there was a little incident happened here. Seven years ago, the last man in this region but me, moved away. There stands his house,—been empty ever since; a log house, with a plank roof—just one big room, and no more; no ceiling—nothing between the rafters and the floor. Well, one Sunday morning I was sitting out here in front of my cabin, with my cat, taking the sun, and looking at the blue hills, and listening to the leaves rustling so lonely in the trees, and thinking of the home away yonder in the States, that I hadn't heard from in thirteen years, when a blue-jay lit on that house, with an acorn in his mouth, and says, 'Hello, I reckon I've struck something.' When he spoke, the acorn dropped out of his mouth and rolled down the roof, of course, but he didn't care; his mind was all on the thing he had struck. It was a knot-hole in the roof. He cocked his head to one side, shut one eye and put the other one to the hole, like a 'possum looking down a jug; then he glanced up with his bright eyes, gave a wink or two with his wings—which signifies gratification, you understand,—and says, 'It looks like a hole, it's located like a hole,—blamed if I don't believe it *is* a hole!'

"Then he cocked his head down and took another look; he glances up perfectly joyful, this time; winks his wings and his tail both, and says, 'O, no, this ain't no fat thing, I reckon! If I ain't in luck!—why it's a perfectly elegant hole!' So he flew down and got that acorn, and fetched it up and dropped it in, and was just tilting his head back, with the heavenliest smile on his face, when all of a sudden he was paralyzed into a listening attitude and that smile faded gradually out of his countenance like breath off'n a razor, and the queerest look of surprise took its place. Then he says, 'Why I didn't hear it fall!' He cocked his eye at the hole again, and took a long look; raised up and shook his head; stepped around to the other side of the hole and took another look from that side; shook his head again. He studied a while, then he just went into the *de*tails—walked round and round the hole and spied into it from every point of the compass. No use. Now he took a thinking attitude on the comb of the roof and scratched the back of his head with his right foot a minute, and finally says, 'Well, it's too many for *me,* that's certain; must be a mighty long hole; however, I ain't got no time to fool around here, I got to 'tend to business; I reckon it's all right—chance it, anyway.'

"So he flew off and fetched another acorn and dropped it in, and tried to flirt his eye to the hole quick enough to see what become of it, but he was too late. He held his eye there as much as a minute; then he raised up and sighed, and says, 'Consound it, I don't seem to understand this thing, no way; however, I'll tackle her again.' He fetched another acorn, and done his level best to see what become of it, but he couldn't. He says, 'Well, *I* never struck no such a hole as this, before; I'm of the opinion it's a totally new kind of a hole.' Then he begun to get mad. He held in for a spell, walking up and down the comb of the roof and shaking his head and muttering to himself; but his feelings got the upper hand of him, presently, and he broke loose and cussed himself black in the face. I never see a bird take on so about a little thing. When he got through he walks to the hole and looks in again for half a minute; then he says, 'Well, you're a long hole, and a deep hole, and a mighty singular hole altogether—but I've started in to fill you, and I'm d—d if I *don't* fill you, if it takes a hundred years!'

"And with that, away he went. You never see a bird work so since you was born. He laid into his work like a nigger, and the way he hove acorns into that hole for about two hours and a half was one of the most exciting and astonishing spectacles I ever struck. He never stopped to take a look any more—he just hove 'em in and went for more. Well at last he could hardly flop his wings, he was so tuckered out. He comes a-drooping down, once more, sweating like an ice-pitcher, drops his acorn in and says, '*Now* I guess I've got the bulge on you by this time!' So he bent down for a look. If you'll believe me, when his head come up again he was just pale with rage. He says, 'I've shoveled acorns enough in there to keep the family thirty years, and if I can see a sign of one of 'em I wish I may land in a museum with a belly full of sawdust in two minutes!'

"He just had strength enough to crawl up on to the comb and lean his back agin the chimbly, and then he collected his impressions and begun to free his mind. I see in a second that what I had mistook for profanity in the mines was only just the rudiments, as you may say.

"Another jay was going by, and heard him doing his devotions, and stops to inquire what was up. The sufferer told him the whole circumstance, and says, 'Now yonder's the hole, and if you don't believe me, go and look for yourself.' So this fellow went and looked, and comes back and says, 'How many did you say you put in there?' 'Not any less than two tons,' says the sufferer. The other jay went and looked again. He couldn't seem to make it out, so he raised a yell, and three more jays come. They all examined the hole, they all made the sufferer tell it over again, then they all discussed it, and got off as many leather-headed opinions about it as an average crowd of humans could have done.

"They called in more jays; then more and more, till pretty soon this whole region 'peared to have a blue flush about it. There must have been five thousand of them; and such another jawing and disputing and ripping and cussing, you never heard. Every jay in the whole lot put his eye to the hole and delivered a more chuckle-headed opinion about the mystery than the jay that went there before him. They examined the house all over, too. The door was standing half open, and at last one old jay happened to go and light on it and look in. Of course that knocked the mystery galley-west in a second. There lay the acorns, scattered all over the floor. He flopped his wings and raised a whoop. 'Come here!' he says, 'Come here, everybody; hang'd if this fool hasn't been trying to fill up a house with acorns!' They all came a-swooping down like a blue cloud, and as each fellow lit on the door and took a glance, the whole absurdity of the contract that that first jay had tackled hit him home and he fell over backwards suffocating with laughter, and the next jay took his place and done the same.

"Well, sir, they roosted around here on the house-top and the trees for an hour, and guffawed over that thing like human beings. It ain't any use to tell me a blue-jay hasn't got a sense of humor, because I know better. And memory, too. They brought jays here from all over the United States to look down that hole, every summer for three years. Other birds too. And they could all see the point, except an owl that come from Nova Scotia to visit the Yo Semite, and he took this thing in on his way back. He said he couldn't see anything funny in it. But then he was a good deal disappointed about Yo Semite, too."

[1880]

The Stolen White Elephant*

I

The following curious history was related to me by a chance railway acquaintance. He was a gentleman more than seventy years of age, and his thoroughly good and gentle face and earnest and sincere manner imprinted the unmistakable stamp of truth upon every statement which fell from his lips. He said:—

You know in what reverence the royal white elephant of Siam is held by the people of that country. You know it is sacred to kings, only kings may possess it, and that it is indeed in a measure even superior to kings, since it receives not merely honor but worship. Very well; five years ago, when the troubles concerning the frontier line arose between Great Britain and Siam, it was presently manifest that Siam had been in the wrong.[1] Therefore every reparation was quickly made, and the British representative stated that he was satisfied and the past should be forgotten. This greatly relieved the King of Siam, and partly as a token of gratitude, but partly also, perhaps, to wipe out any little remaining vestige of unpleasantness which England might feel toward him, he wished to send the Queen a present,—the sole sure way of propitiating an enemy, according to Oriental ideas. This present ought not only to be a royal one, but transcendently royal. Wherefore, what offering could be so meet as that of a white elephant? My position in the Indian civil service was such

*Left out of "A Tramp Abroad," because it was feared that some of the particulars had been exaggerated, and that others were not true. Before these suspicions had been proven groundless, the book had gone to press.—M.T.

that I was deemed peculiarly worthy of the honor of conveying the present to her Majesty. A ship was fitted out for me and my servants and the officers and attendants of the elephant, and in due time I arrived in New York harbor and placed my royal charge in admirable quarters in Jersey City. It was necessary to remain awhile in order to recruit the animal's health before resuming the voyage.

All went well during a fortnight,—then my calamities began. The white elephant was stolen! I was called up at dead of night and informed of this fearful misfortune. For some moments I was beside myself with terror and anxiety; I was helpless. Then I grew calmer and collected my faculties. I soon saw my course,—for indeed there was but the one course for an intelligent man to pursue. Late as it was, I flew to New York and got a policeman to conduct me to the headquarters of the detective force. Fortunately I arrived in time, though the chief of the force, the celebrated Inspector Blunt, was just on the point of leaving for his home. He was a man of middle size and compact frame, and when he was thinking deeply he had a way of knitting his brows and tapping his forehead reflectively with his finger, which impressed you at once with the conviction that you stood in the presence of a person of no common order. The very sight of him gave me confidence and made me hopeful. I stated my errand. It did not flurry him in the least; it had no more visible effect upon his iron self-possession than if I had told him somebody had stolen my dog. He motioned me to a seat, and said calmly,—

"Allow me to think a moment, please."

So saying, he sat down at his office table and leaned his head upon his hand. Several clerks were at work at the other end of the room; the scratching of their pens was all the sound I heard during the next six or seven minutes. Meantime the inspector sat there, buried in thought. Finally he raised his head, and there was that in the firm lines of his face which showed me that his brain had done its work and his plan was made. Said he,—and his voice was low and impressive,—

"This is no ordinary case. Every step must be warily taken; each step must be made sure before the next is ventured. And secrecy must be observed,—secrecy profound and absolute. Speak to no one about the matter, not even the reporters. I will take care of *them;* I will see that they get only what it may suit my ends to let them know." He touched a bell; a youth appeared. "Alaric, tell the reporters to remain for the present." The boy retired. "Now let us proceed to business,—and systematically. Nothing can be accomplished in this trade of mine without strict and minute method."

He took a pen and some paper. "Now—name of the elephant?"

"Hassan Ben Ali Ben Selim Abdallah Mohammed Moisé Alhammal Jamsetjejeebhoy Dhuleep Sultan Ebu Bhudpoor."

"Very well. Given name?"

"Jumbo."[2]

"Very well. Place of birth?"

"The capital city of Siam."

"Parents living?"

"No,—dead."

"Had they any other issue besides this one?"

"None. He was an only child."

"Very well. These matters are sufficient under that head. Now please describe the elephant, and leave out no particular, however insignificant,—that is, insignificant from *your* point of view. To men in my profession there *are* no insignificant particulars; they do not exist."

I described,—he wrote. When I was done, he said,—

"Now listen. If I have made any mistakes, correct me."

He read as follows:—

"Height, 19 feet; length from apex of forehead to insertion of tail, 26 feet; length of trunk, 16 feet; length of tail, 6 feet; total length, including trunk and tail, 48 feet; length of tusks, 9½ feet; ears in keeping with these dimensions; footprint resembles the mark left when one up-ends a barrel in the snow; color of the elephant, a dull white; has a hole the size of a plate in each ear for the insertion of jewelry, and possesses the habit in a remarkable degree of squirting water upon spectators and of maltreating with his trunk not only such persons as he is acquainted with, but even entire strangers; limps slightly with his right hind leg, and has a small scar in his left armpit caused by a former boil; had on, when stolen, a castle containing seats for fifteen persons, and a gold-cloth saddle-blanket the size of an ordinary carpet."

There were no mistakes. The inspector touched the bell, handed the description to Alaric, and said,—

"Have fifty thousand copies of this printed at once and mailed to every detective office and pawnbroker's shop on the continent." Alaric retired. "There,—so far, so good. Next, I must have a photograph of the property."

I gave him one. He examined it critically, and said,—

"It must do, since we can do no better; but he has his trunk curled up and tucked into his mouth. That is unfortunate, and is calculated to mislead, for of course he does not usually have it in that position." He touched his bell.

"Alaric, have fifty thousand copies of this photograph made, the first thing in the morning, and mail them with the descriptive circulars."

Alaric retired to execute his orders. The inspector said,—

"It will be necessary to offer a reward, of course. Now as to the amount?"

"What sum would you suggest?"

"To *begin* with, I should say,—well, twenty-five thousand dollars. It is an intricate and difficult business; there are a thousand avenues of escape and opportunities of concealment. These thieves have friends and pals everywhere—"

"Bless me, do you know who they are?"

The wary face, practised in concealing the thoughts and feelings within, gave me no token, nor yet the replying words, so quietly uttered:—

"Never mind about that. I may, and I may not. We generally gather a pretty shrewd inkling of who our man is by the manner of his work and the size of the game he goes after. We are not dealing with a pickpocket or a hall thief, now, make up your mind to that. This property was not 'lifted' by a novice. But, as I was saying, considering the amount of travel which will have to be done, and the diligence with which the thieves will cover up their traces as they move along, twenty-five thousand may be too small a sum to offer, yet I think it worth while to start with that."

So we determined upon that figure, as a beginning. Then this man, whom nothing escaped which could by any possibility be made to serve as a clew, said:—

"There are cases in detective history to show that criminals have been detected through peculiarities in their appetites. Now, what does this elephant eat, and how much?"

"Well, as to *what* he eats,—he will eat *anything*. He will eat a man, he will eat a Bible,—he will eat anything *between* a man and a Bible."

"Good,—very good indeed, but too general. Details are necessary,—details are the only valuable things in our trade. Very well,—as to men. At one meal,—or, if you prefer, during one day,—how many men will he eat, if fresh?"

"He would not care whether they were fresh or not; at a single meal he would eat five ordinary men."

"Very good; five men; we will put that down. What nationalities would he prefer?"

"He is indifferent about nationalities. He prefers acquaintances, but is not prejudiced against strangers."

"Very good. Now, as to Bibles. How many Bibles would he eat at a meal?"

"He would eat an entire edition."

"It is hardly succinct enough. Do you mean the ordinary octavo, or the family illustrated?"

"I think he would be indifferent to illustrations; that is, I think he would not value illustrations above simple letterpress."

"No, you do not get my idea. I refer to bulk. The ordinary octavo Bible weighs about two pounds and a half, while the great quarto with the illustrations weighs ten or twelve. How many Doré Bibles[3] would he eat at a meal?"

"If you knew this elephant, you could not ask. He would take what they had."

"Well, put it in dollars and cents, then. We must get at it somehow. The Doré costs a hundred dollars a copy, Russia leather, bevelled."

"He would require about fifty thousand dollars' worth,—say an edition of five hundred copies."

"Now that is more exact. I will put that down. Very well; he likes men and Bibles; so far, so good. What else will he eat? I want particulars."

"He will leave Bibles to eat bricks, he will leave bricks to eat bottles, he will leave bottles to eat clothing, he will leave clothing to eat cats, he will leave cats to eat oysters, he will leave oysters to eat ham, he will leave ham to eat sugar, he will leave sugar to eat pie, he will leave pie to eat potatoes, he will leave potatoes to eat bran, he will leave bran to eat hay, he will leave hay to eat oats, he will leave oats to eat rice, for he was mainly raised on it. There is nothing whatever that he will not eat but European butter, and he would eat that if he could taste it."

"Very good. General quantity at a meal,—say about—"

"Well, anywhere from a quarter to half a ton."

"And he drinks—"

"Everything that is fluid. Milk, water, whiskey, molasses, castor oil, camphene, carbolic acid,—it is no use to go into particulars; whatever fluid occurs to you set it down. He will drink anything that is fluid, except European coffee."

"Very good. As to quantity?"

"Put it down five to fifteen barrels,—his thirst varies; his other appetites do not."

"These things are unusual. They ought to furnish quite good clews toward tracing him."

He touched the bell.

"Alaric, summon Captain Burns."

Burns appeared. Inspector Blunt unfolded the whole matter to him, detail by detail. Then he said in the clear, decisive tones of a man whose plans are clearly defined in his head, and who is accustomed to command,—

"Captain Burns, detail Detectives Jones, Davis, Halsey, Bates, and Hackett to shadow the elephant."

"Yes, sir."

"Detail Detectives Moses, Dakin, Murphy, Rogers, Tupper, Higgins, and Bartholomew to shadow the thieves."

"Yes, sir."

"Place a strong guard—a guard of thirty picked men, with a relief of thirty—over the place from whence the elephant was stolen, to keep strict watch there night and day, and allow none to approach—except reporters—without written authority from me."

"Yes, sir."

"Place detectives in plain clothes in the railway, steamship, and ferry depots, and upon all roadways leading out of Jersey City, with orders to search all suspicious persons."

"Yes, sir."

"Furnish all these men with photograph and accompanying description of the elephant, and instruct them to search all trains and outgoing ferry-boats and other vessels."

"Yes, sir."

"If the elephant should be found, let him be seized, and the information forwarded to me by telegraph."

"Yes, sir."

"Let me be informed at once if any clews should be found,—footprints of the animal, or anything of that kind."

"Yes, sir."

"Get an order commanding the harbor police to patrol the frontages vigilantly."

"Yes, sir."

"Despatch detectives in plain clothes over all the railways, north as far as Canada, west as far as Ohio, south as far as Washington."

"Yes, sir."

"Place experts in all the telegraph offices to listen to all messages; and let them require that all cipher despatches be interpreted to them."

"Yes, sir."

"Let all these things be done with the utmost secrecy,—mind, the most impenetrable secrecy."

"Yes, sir."

"Report to me promptly at the usual hour."

"Yes, sir."

"Go!"

"Yes, sir."

He was gone.

Inspector Blunt was silent and thoughtful a moment, while the fire in his eye cooled down and faded out. Then he turned to me and said in a placid voice,—

"I am not given to boasting, it is not my habit; but—we shall find the elephant."

I shook him warmly by the hand and thanked him; and I *felt* my thanks, too. The more I had seen of the man the more I liked him, and the more I admired him and marvelled over the mysterious wonders of his profession. Then we parted for the night, and I went home with a far happier heart than I had carried with me to his office.

II

Next morning it was all in the newspapers, in the minutest detail. It even had additions,—consisting of Detective This, Detective That, and Detective The Other's "Theory" as to how the robbery was done, who the robbers were, and whither they had flown with their booty. There were eleven of these theories, and they covered all the possibilities; and this single fact shows what independent thinkers detectives are. No two theories were alike, or even much resembled each other, save in one striking particular, and in that one all the eleven theories were absolutely agreed. That was, that although the rear of my building was torn out and the only door remained locked, the elephant had not been removed through the rent, but by some other (undiscovered) outlet. All agreed that the robbers had made that rent only to mislead the detectives. That never would have occurred to me or to any other layman, perhaps, but it had not deceived the detectives for a moment. Thus, what I had supposed was the only thing that had no mystery about it was in fact the very thing I had gone furthest astray in. The eleven theories all named the supposed robbers, but no two named the same robbers; the total number of suspected persons was thirty-seven. The various newspaper accounts all closed with the most important opinion of all,—that of Chief Inspector Blunt. A portion of this statement read as follows:—

"The chief knows who the two principals are, namely, 'Brick' Duffy and 'Red' McFadden. Ten days before the robbery was achieved he was already aware that it was to be attempted, and had quietly proceeded to shadow these two noted villains; but unfortunately on the night in question their track was lost, and before it could be found again the bird was flown,—that is, the elephant.

"Duffy and McFadden are the boldest scoundrels in the profession; the chief has reasons for believing that they are the men who stole the stove out of the detective headquarters on a bitter night last winter,—in consequence of which the chief and every detective present were in the hands of the physicians before morning, some with frozen feet, others with frozen fingers, ears, and other members."

When I read the first half of that I was more astonished than ever at the wonderful sagacity of this strange man. He not only saw everything in the present with a clear eye, but even the future could not be hidden from him. I was soon at his office, and said I could not help wishing he had had those men arrested, and so prevented the trouble and loss; but his reply was simple and unanswerable:—

"It is not our province to prevent crime, but to punish it. We cannot punish it until it is committed."

I remarked that the secrecy with which we had begun had been marred by the newspapers; not only all our facts but all our plans and purposes had been revealed; even all the suspected persons had been named; these would doubtless disguise themselves now, or go into hiding.

"Let them. They will find that when I am ready for them my hand will descend upon them, in their secret places, as unerringly as the hand of fate. As to the newspapers, we *must* keep in with them. Fame, reputation, constant public mention,—these are the detective's bread and butter. He must publish his facts, else he will be supposed to have none; he must publish his theory, for nothing is so strange or striking as a detective's theory, or brings him so much wondering respect; we must publish our plans, for these the journals insist upon having, and we could not deny them without offending. We must constantly show the public what we are doing, or they will believe we are doing nothing. It is much pleasanter to have a newspaper say, 'Inspector Blunt's ingenious and extraordinary theory is as follows,' than to have it say some harsh thing, or, worse still, some sarcastic one."

"I see the force of what you say. But I noticed that in one part of your remarks in the papers this morning you refused to reveal your opinion upon a certain minor point."

"Yes, we always do that; it has a good effect. Besides, I had not formed any opinion on that point, any way."

I deposited a considerable sum of money with the inspector, to meet current expenses, and sat down to wait for news. We were expecting the telegrams to begin to arrive at any moment now. Meantime I reread the newspapers and also our descriptive circular, and observed that our $25,000 reward seemed to be offered only to detectives. I said I thought it ought to be offered to anybody who would catch the elephant. The inspector said:—

"It is the detectives who will find the elephant, hence the reward will go to the right place. If other people found the animal, it would only be by watching the detectives and taking advantage of clews and indications stolen from them, and that would entitle the detectives to the reward, after all. The proper office of a reward is to stimulate the men who deliver up their time and their trained sagacities to this sort of work, and not to confer benefits upon chance citizens who stumble upon a capture without having earned the benefits by their own merits and labors."

This was reasonable enough, certainly. Now the telegraphic machine in the corner began to click, and the following despatch was the result:—

FLOWER STATION, N.Y., 7.30 A.M.

Have got a clew. Found a succession of deep tracks across a farm near here. Followed them two miles east without result; think elephant went west. Shall now shadow him in that direction.

DARLEY, *Detective*

"Darley's one of the best men on the force," said the inspector. "We shall hear from him again before long."

Telegram No. 2 came:—

BARKER'S, N.J., 7.40 A.M.

Just arrived. Glass factory broken open here during night, and eight hundred bottles taken. Only water in large quantity near here is five miles distant. Shall strike for there. Elephant will be thirsty. Bottles were empty.

BAKER, *Detective*

"That promises well, too," said the inspector. "I told you the creature's appetites would not be bad clews."

Telegram No. 3:—

TAYLORVILLE, L.I., 8.15 A.M.

A haystack near here disappeared during night. Probably eaten. Have got a clew, and am off.

HUBBARD, *Detective*

"How he does move around!" said the inspector. "I knew we had a difficult job on hand, but we shall catch him yet."

FLOWER STATION, N.Y., 9 A.M.

> Shadowed the tracks three miles westward. Large, deep, and ragged. Have just met a farmer who says they are not elephant tracks. Says they are holes where he dug up saplings for shade-trees when ground was frozen last winter. Give me orders how to proceed.

DARLEY, *Detective*

"Aha! a confederate of the thieves! The thing grows warm," said the inspector.

He dictated the following telegram to Darley:—

> Arrest the man and force him to name his pals. Continue to follow the tracks,—to the Pacific, if necessary.

Chief BLUNT

Next telegram:—

CONEY POINT, PA., 8.45 A.M.

> Gas office broken open here during night and three months' unpaid gas bills taken. Have got a clew and am away.

MURPHY, *Detective*

"Heavens!" said the inspector; "would he eat gas bills?"

"Through ignorance,—yes; but they cannot support life. At least, unassisted."

Now came this exciting telegram:—

IRONVILLE, N.Y., 9.30 A.M.

> Just arrived. This village in consternation. Elephant passed through here at five this morning. Some say he went east, some say west, some north, some south,—but all say they did not wait to notice particularly. He killed a horse; have secured a piece of it for a clew. Killed it with his trunk; from style of blow, think he struck it left-handed. From position in which horse lies, think elephant travelled northward along line of Berkley railway. Has four and a half hours' start, but I move on his track at once.

HAWES, *Detective*

I uttered exclamations of joy. The inspector was as self-contained as a graven image. He calmly touched his bell.

"Alaric, send Captain Burns here."

Burns appeared.

"How many men are ready for instant orders?"

"Ninety-six, sir."

"Send them north at once. Let them concentrate along the line of the Berkley road north of Ironville."

"Yes, sir."

"Let them conduct their movements with the utmost secrecy. As fast as others are at liberty, hold them for orders."

"Yes, sir."

"Go!"

"Yes, sir."

Presently came another telegram:—

SAGE CORNERS, N.Y., 10.30

Just arrived. Elephant passed through here at 8.15. All escaped from the town but a policeman. Apparently elephant did not strike at policeman, but at the lamp-post, Got both. I have secured a portion of the policeman as clew.

STUMM, *Detective*

"So the elephant has turned westward," said the inspector. "However, he will not escape, for my men are scattered all over that region."

The next telegram said:—

GLOVER'S, 11.15

Just arrived. Village deserted, except sick and aged. Elephant passed through three quarters of an hour ago. The anti-temperance mass meeting was in session; he put his trunk in at a window and washed it out with water from cistern. Some swallowed it—since dead; several drowned. Detectives Cross and O'Shaughnessy were passing through town, but going south,—so missed elephant. Whole region for many miles around in terror,—people flying from their homes. Wherever they turn they meet elephant, and many are killed.

BRANT, *Detective*

I could have shed tears, this havoc so distressed me. But the inspector only said,—

"You see,—we are closing in on him. He feels our presence; he has turned eastward again."

Yet further troublous news was in store for us. The telegraph brought this:—

HOGANPORT, 12.19

Just arrived. Elephant passed through half an hour ago, creating wildest fright and excitement. Elephant raged around streets; two plumbers going by, killed one—other escaped. Regret general.

O'FLAHERTY, *Detective*

"Now he is right in the midst of my men," said the inspector. "Nothing can save him."

A succession of telegrams came from detectives who were scattered through New Jersey and Pennsylvania, and who were following clews consisting of ravaged barns, factories, and Sunday school libraries, with high hopes,—hopes amounting to certainties, indeed. The inspector said,—

"I wish I could communicate with them and order them north, but that is impossible. A detective only visits a telegraph office to send his report; then he is off again, and you don't know where to put your hand on him."

Now came this despatch:—

BRIDGEPORT, CT., 12.15

Barnum offers rate of $4,000 a year for exclusive privilege of using elephant as travelling advertising medium from now till detectives find him. Wants to paste circus-posters on him. Desires immediate answer.

BOGGS, *Detective*

"That is perfectly absurd!" I exclaimed.

"Of course it is," said the inspector. "Evidently Mr. Barnum, who thinks he is so sharp, does not know me,—but I know him."

Then he dictated this answer to the despatch:—

Mr. Barnum's offer declined. Make it $7,000 or nothing.

Chief BLUNT

"There. We shall not have to wait long for an answer. Mr. Barnum is not at home; he is in the telegraph office,—it is his way when he has business on hand. Inside of three—"

Done.—P. T. Barnum.

So interrupted the clicking telegraphic instrument. Before I could make a comment upon this extraordinary episode, the following despatch carried my thoughts into another and very distressing channel:—

BOLIVIA, N.Y., 12.50

Elephant arrived here from the south and passed through toward the forest at 11.50, dispersing a funeral on the way, and diminishing the mourners by two. Citizens fired some small cannon-balls into him, and then fled. Detective Burke and I arrived ten minutes later, from the north, but mistook some excavations for footprints, and so lost a good deal of time; but at last we struck the right trail and followed it to the woods. We then got down on our hands and knees and continued to keep a sharp eye on the track, and so shadowed it into the brush. Burke was in advance. Unfortunately the animal had stopped to rest; therefore, Burke having his head down, intent upon the track, butted up against the elephant's hind legs before he was aware of his vicinity. Burke instantly rose to his feet, seized the tail, and exclaimed joyfully, "I claim the re——" but got no further, for a single blow of the huge trunk laid the brave fellow's fragments low in death. I fled rearward, and the elephant turned and shadowed me to the edge of the wood, making tremendous speed, and I should inevitably have been lost, but that the remains of the funeral providentially intervened again and diverted his attention. I have just learned that nothing of that funeral is now left; but this is no loss, for there is an abundance of material for another. Meantime, the elephant has disappeared again.

MULROONEY, *Detective*

We heard no news except from the diligent and confident detectives scattered about New Jersey, Pennsylvania, Delaware, and Virginia—who were all following fresh and encouraging clews—until shortly after 2 P.M., when this telegram came:—

BAXTER CENTRE, 2.15

Elephant been here, plastered over with circus-bills, and broke up a revival, striking down and damaging many who were on the point of entering upon a better life. Citizens penned him up, and established a guard. When Detective Brown and I arrived, some time after, we entered enclosure and proceeded to identify elephant by photograph and description. All marks tallied exactly except one, which we could not see,—the boil-scar under armpit. To make sure, Brown crept under to look, and was immediately brained,—that is, head crushed and destroyed, though nothing issued from debris. All fled; so did elephant, striking right and left with much effect. Has escaped, but left bold blood-track from cannon-wounds. Rediscovery certain. He broke southward, through a dense forest.

BRENT, *Detective*

That was the last telegram. At nightfall a fog shut down which was so dense that objects but three feet away could not be discerned. This lasted all night. The ferry-boats and even the omnibuses had to stop running.

III

Next morning the papers were as full of detective theories as before; they had all our tragic facts in detail also, and a great many more which they had received from their telegraphic correspondents. Column after column was occupied, a third of its way down, with glaring head-lines, which it made my heart sick to read. Their general tone was like this:—

"THE WHITE ELEPHANT AT LARGE! HE MOVES UPON HIS FATAL MARCH! WHOLE VILLAGES DESERTED BY THEIR FRIGHT-STRICKEN OCCUPANTS! PALE TERROR GOES BEFORE HIM, DEATH AND DEVASTATION FOLLOW AFTER! AFTER THESE, THE DETECTIVES. BARNS DESTROYED, FACTORIES GUTTED, HARVESTS DEVOURED, PUBLIC ASSEMBLAGES DISPERSED, ACCOMPANIED BY SCENES OF CARNAGE IMPOSSIBLE TO DESCRIBE! THEORIES OF THIRTY-FOUR OF THE MOST DISTINGUISHED DETECTIVES ON THE FORCE! THEORY OF CHIEF BLUNT!"

"There!" said Inspector Blunt, almost betrayed into excitement, "this is magnificent! This is the greatest windfall that any detective organization ever had. The fame of it will travel to the ends of the earth, and endure to the end of time, and my name with it."

But there was no joy for me. I felt as if I had committed all those red crimes, and that the elephant was only my irresponsible agent. And how the list had grown! In one place he had "interfered with an election and killed five repeaters."[4] He had followed this act with the destruction of two poor fellows, named O'Donohue and McFlannigan, who had "found a refuge in the home of the oppressed of all lands only the day before, and were in the act of exercising for the first time the noble right of American citizens[5] at the polls, when stricken down by the relentless hand of the Scourge of Siam." In another, he had "found a crazy sensation-preacher preparing his next season's heroic attacks on the dance, the theatre, and other things which can't strike back, and had stepped on him." And in still another place he had "killed a lightning-rod agent." And so the list went on, growing redder and redder, and more and more heart-breaking. Sixty persons had been killed, and two hundred and forty wounded. All the accounts bore just testimony to the activity and devotion of the detectives, and all closed with the remark that "three hundred thousand citizens and four detectives saw the dread creature, and two of the latter he destroyed."

I dreaded to hear the telegraphic instrument begin to click again. By and by the messages began to pour in, but I was happily disappointed in their nature. It was soon apparent that all trace of the elephant was lost. The fog had enabled him to search out a good hiding-place unobserved. Telegrams from the most absurdly distant points reported that a dim vast mass had been glimpsed there through the fog at such and such an hour, and was "undoubtedly the elephant." This dim vast mass had been glimpsed in New Haven, in New Jersey, in Pennsylvania, in interior New York, in Brooklyn, and even in the city of New York itself! But in all cases the dim vast mass had vanished quickly and left no trace. Every detective of the large force scattered over this huge extent of country sent his hourly report, and each and every one of them had a clew, and was shadowing something, and was hot upon the heels of it.

But the day passed without other result.

The next day the same.

The next just the same.

The newspaper reports began to grow monotonous with facts that amounted to nothing, clews which led to nothing, and theories which had nearly exhausted the elements which surprise and delight and dazzle.

By advice of the inspector I doubled the reward.

Four more dull days followed. Then came a bitter blow to the poor, hard-working detectives,—the journalists declined to print their theories, and coldly said, "Give us a rest."

Two weeks after the elephant's disappearance I raised the reward to $75,000 by the inspector's advice. It was a great sum, but I felt that I would rather sacrifice my whole private fortune than lose my credit with my government. Now that the detectives were in adversity, the newspapers turned upon them, and began to fling the most stinging sarcasms at them. This gave the minstrels an idea, and they dressed themselves as detectives and hunted the elephant on the stage in the most extravagant way. The caricaturists made pictures of detectives scanning the country with spy-glasses, while the elephant, at their backs, stole apples out of their pockets. And they made all sorts of ridiculous pictures of the detective badge,—you have seen that badge printed in gold on the back of detective novels, no doubt,—it is a wide-staring eye, with the legend, "WE NEVER SLEEP."[6] When detectives called for a drink, the would-be facetious bar-keeper resurrected an obsolete form of expression and said, "Will you have an eye-opener?" All the air was thick with sarcasms.

But there was one man who moved calm, untouched, unaffected, through it all. It was that heart of oak, the Chief Inspector. His brave eye never drooped, his serene confidence never wavered. He always said,—

"Let them rail on; he laughs best who laughs last."

My admiration for the man grew into a species of worship. I was at his side always. His office had become an unpleasant place to me, and now became daily more and more so. Yet if he could endure it I meant to do so also; at least, as long as I could. So I came regularly, and stayed,—the only outsider who seemed to be capable of it. Everybody wondered how I could; and often it seemed to me that I must desert, but at such times I looked into that calm and apparently unconscious face, and held my ground.

About three weeks after the elephant's disappearance I was about to say, one morning, that I should *have* to strike my colors and retire, when the great detective arrested the thought by proposing one more superb and masterly move.

This was to compromise with the robbers. The fertility of this man's invention exceeded anything I have ever seen, and I have had a wide intercourse with the world's finest minds. He said he was confident he could compromise for $100,000 and recover the elephant. I said I believed I could scrape the amount together, but what would become of the poor detectives who had worked so faithfully? He said,—

"In compromises they always get half."

This removed my only objection. So the inspector wrote two notes, in this form:—

DEAR MADAM,—Your husband can make a large sum of money (and be entirely protected from the law) by making an immediate appointment with me.

Chief BLUNT

He sent one of these by his confidential messenger to the "reputed wife" of Brick Duffy, and the other to the reputed wife of Red McFadden.

Within the hour these offensive answers came:—

YE OWLD FOOL: brick McDuffys bin ded 2 yere.

BRIDGET MAHONEY

CHIEF BAT,—Red McFadden is hung and in heving 18 month. Any Ass but a detective knose that.

MARY O'HOOLIGAN

"I had long suspected these facts," said the inspector; "this testimony proves the unerring accuracy of my instinct."

The moment one resource failed him he was ready with another. He immediately wrote an advertisement for the morning papers, and I kept a copy of it:—

A.—xwblv. 242 N. Tjnd—fz328wmlg. Ozpo,—; 2 m! ogw. Mum.

He said that if the thief was alive this would bring him to the usual rendezvous. He further explained that the usual rendezvous was a place where all business affairs between detectives and criminals were conducted. This meeting would take place at twelve the next night.

We could do nothing till then, and I lost no time in getting out of the office, and was grateful indeed for the privilege.

At 11 the next night I brought $100,000 in bank-notes and put them into the chief's hands, and shortly afterward he took his leave, with the brave old undimmed confidence in his eye. An almost intolerable hour dragged to a close; then I heard his welcome tread, and rose gasping and tottered to meet him. How his fine eyes flamed with triumph! He said,—

"We've compromised! The jokers will sing a different tune to-morrow! Follow me!"

He took a lighted candle and strode down into the vast vaulted basement where sixty detectives always slept, and where a score were now playing cards to while the time. I followed close after him. He walked swiftly down to the dim remote end of the place, and just as I succumbed to the pangs of suffocation and was swooning away he stumbled and fell over the outlying members of a mighty object, and I heard him exclaim as he went down,—

"Our noble profession is vindicated. Here is your elephant!"

I was carried to the office above and restored with carbolic acid. The whole detective force swarmed in, and such another season of triumphant rejoicing ensued as I had never witnessed before. The reporters were called, baskets of champagne were opened, toasts were drunk, the hand-shakings and congratulations were continuous and enthusiastic. Naturally the chief was the hero of the hour, and his happiness was so complete and had been so patiently and worthily and bravely won that it made me happy to see it, though I stood there a homeless beggar, my priceless charge dead, and my position in my country's service lost to me through what would always seem my fatally careless execution of a great trust. Many an eloquent eye testified its deep admiration for the chief, and many a detective's voice murmured, "Look at him,—just the king of the profession,—only give him a clew, it's all he wants, and there ain't anything hid that he can't find." The dividing of the $50,000 made great pleasure; when it was finished the chief made a little speech while he put his share in his pocket, in which he said, "Enjoy it, boys, for you've earned it; and more than that you've earned for the detective profession undying fame."

A telegram arrived, which read:—

MONROE, MICH., 10 P.M.

First time I've struck a telegraph office in over three weeks. Have followed those footprints, horseback, through the woods, a thousand miles to here, and they get stronger and bigger and fresher every day. Don't worry—inside of another week I'll have the elephant. This is dead sure.

DARLEY, *Detective*

The chief ordered three cheers for "Darley, one of the finest minds on the force," and then commanded that he be telegraphed to come home and receive his share of the reward.

So ended that marvellous episode of the stolen elephant. The newspapers were pleasant with praises once more, the next day, with one contemptible exception. This sheet said, "Great is the detective! He may be a little slow in finding a little thing like a mislaid elephant,—he may hunt him all day and sleep with his rotting carcass all night for three weeks, but he will find him at last—if he can get the man who mislaid him to show him the place!"

Poor Hassan was lost to me forever. The cannon-shots had wounded him fatally, he had crept to that unfriendly place in the fog, and there, surrounded by his enemies and in constant danger of detection, he had wasted away with hunger and suffering till death gave him peace.

The compromise cost me $100,000; my detective expenses were $42,000 more; I never applied for a place again under my government; I am a ruined man and a wanderer in the earth,—but my admiration for that man, whom I believe to be the greatest detective the world has ever produced, remains undimmed to this day, and will so remain unto the end.

[1882]

The McWilliamses and the Burglar Alarm

The conversation drifted smoothly and pleasantly along from weather to crops, from crops to literature, from literature to scandal, from scandal to religion; then took a random jump, and landed on the subject of burglar alarms. And now for the first time Mr. McWilliams showed feeling. Whenever I perceive this sign on this man's dial, I comprehend it, and lapse into silence, and give him opportunity to unload his heart. Said he, with but ill-controlled emotion:

"I do not go one single cent on burglar alarms, Mr. Twain—not a single cent—and I will tell you why. When we were finishing our house, we found we had a little cash left over, on account of the plumber not knowing it. I was for enlightening the heathen[1] with it, for I was always unaccountably down on the heathen somehow; but Mrs. McWilliams said no, let's have a burglar alarm. I agreed to this compromise. I will explain that whenever I want a thing, and Mrs. McWilliams wants another thing, and we decide upon the thing that Mrs. McWilliams wants—as we always do—she calls that a compromise. Very well: the man came up from New York and put in the alarm, and charged three hundred and twenty-five dollars for it, and said we could sleep without uneasiness now. So we did for a while—say a month. Then one night we smelled smoke, and I was advised to get up and see what the matter was. I lit a candle, and started toward the stairs, and met a burglar coming out of a room with a basket of tinware, which he had mistaken for solid silver in the dark. He was smoking a pipe. I said, 'My friend, we do not allow smoking in this room.' He said he was a stranger, and could not be expected to know the rules of the house; said he had been in many houses just as good as this one, and it had never been objected to before. He added that as far as his experience went, such rules had never been considered to apply to burglars, anyway.

"I said: 'Smoke along, then, if it is the custom, though I think that the conceding of a privilege to a burglar which is denied to a bishop is a conspicuous sign of the looseness of the times. But waiving all that, what business have you to be entering this house in this furtive and clandestine way, without ringing the burglar alarm?'

"He looked confused and ashamed, and said, with embarrassment: 'I beg a thousand pardons. I did not know you had a burglar alarm, else I would have rung it. I beg you will not mention it where my parents may hear of it, for they are old and feeble, and such a seemingly wanton breach of the hallowed conventionalities of our Christian civilization might all too rudely sunder the frail bridge which hangs darkling between the pale and evanescent present and the solemn great deeps of the eternities. May I trouble you for a match?'

"I said: 'Your sentiments do you honor, but if you will allow me to say it, metaphor is not your best hold. Spare your thigh; this kind light only on the box, and seldom there, in fact, if my experience may be trusted. But to return to business; how did you get in here?'

" 'Through a second-story window.'

"It was even so. I redeemed the tinware at pawnbroker's rates, less cost of advertising, bade the burglar good-night, closed the window after him, and retired to headquarters to report. Next morning we sent for the burglar-alarm man, and he came up and explained that the reason the alarm did not 'go off' was that no part of the house but the first floor was attached to the alarm. This was simply idiotic: one might as well have no armor at all in battle as to have it only on his legs. The expert now put the whole second story on the alarm, charged three hundred dollars for it, and went his way. By-and-by, one night, I found a burglar in the third story, about to start down a ladder with a lot of miscellaneous property. My first impulse was to crack his head with a billiard cue; but my second was to refrain from this attention, because he was between me and the cue rack. The second impulse was plainly the soundest, so I refrained, and proceeded to compromise. I redeemed the property at former rates, after deducting ten per cent. for use of ladder, it being my ladder, and next day we sent down for the expert once more, and had the third story attached to the alarm, for three hundred dollars.

"By this time the 'annunciator' had grown to formidable dimensions. It had forty-seven tags on it, marked with the names of the various rooms and chimneys, and it occupied the space of an ordinary wardrobe. The gong was the size of a wash-bowl, and was placed above the head of our bed. There was a wire from the house to the coachman's quarters in the stable, and a noble gong alongside his pillow.

"We should have been comfortable now but for one defect. Every morning at five the cook opened the kitchen door, in the way of business, and rip went that gong! The first time this happened I thought the last day was come sure. I didn't think it *in* bed—no, but out of it—for the first effect of that frightful gong is to hurl you across the house, and slam you against the wall, and then curl you up, and squirm you like a spider on a stove lid, till somebody shuts that kitchen door. In solid fact, there is no clamor that is even remotely comparable to the dire clamor which that gong makes. Well, this catastrophe happened every morning regularly at five o'clock, and lost us three hours' sleep; for, mind you, when that thing wakes you, it doesn't merely wake you in spots; it wakes you all over, conscience and all, and you are good for eighteen hours of wide-awakedness subsequently—eighteen hours of the very most inconceivable wide-awakedness that you ever experienced in your life. A stranger died on our hands one time, and we vacated and left him in our room overnight. Did that stranger wait for the general judgment? *No,* sir; he got up at five the next morning in the most prompt and unostentatious way. I knew he would; I knew it mighty well. He collected his life-insurance, and lived happy ever after, for there was plenty of proof as to the perfect squareness of his death.

"Well, we were gradually fading away toward a better land, on account of our daily loss of sleep; so we finally had the expert up again, and he ran a wire to the outside of our door, and placed a switch there, whereby Thomas, the butler, could take off and put on the alarm; but Thomas always made one little mistake—he switched the alarm off at night when he went to bed, and switched it on again at daybreak in the morning, just in time for the cook to open the kitchen door, and enable that gong to slam us across the house, sometimes breaking a window with one or the other of us. At the end of a week we recognized that this switch business was a delusion and a snare. We also discovered that a band of burglars had been lodging in the house the whole time—not exactly to steal, for there wasn't much left now, but to hide from the police, for they were hot pressed, and they shrewdly judged that the detectives would never think of a tribe of burglars taking sanctuary in a house notoriously protected by the most imposing and elaborate burglar alarm in America.

"Sent down for the expert again, and this time he struck a most dazzling idea—he fixed the thing so that opening the kitchen door would take off the alarm. It was a noble idea, and he charged accordingly. But you already foresee the result. I switched on the alarm every night at bedtime, no longer trusting to Thomas's frail memory; and as soon as the lights were out the burglars walked in at the kitchen door, thus taking the alarm off without waiting for the cook to do it in the morning. You see how aggravatingly we were situated. For months we couldn't have any company. Not a spare bed in the house; all occupied by burglars.

"Finally, I got up a cure of my own. The expert answered the call, and ran another under-ground wire to the stable, and established a switch there, so that the coachman could put on and take off the alarm. That worked first-rate, and a season of peace ensued, during which we got to inviting company once more and enjoying life.

"But by-and-by the irrepressible alarm invented a new kink. One winter's night we were flung out of bed by the sudden music of that awful gong, and when we hobbled to the annunciator, turned up the gas, and saw the word 'Nursery' exposed, Mrs. McWilliams fainted dead away, and I came precious near doing the same thing myself. I seized my shot-gun, and stood timing the coachman whilst that appalling buzzing went on. I knew that his gong had flung him out too, and that he would be along with his gun as soon as he could jump into his clothes. When I judged that the time was ripe, I crept to the room next the nursery, glanced through the window, and saw the dim outline of the coachman in the yard below, standing at a present-arms and waiting for a chance. Then I hopped into the nursery and fired, and in the same instant the coachman fired at the red flash of my gun. Both of us were successful: I crippled a nurse, and he shot off all my back hair. We turned up the gas, and telephoned for a surgeon. There was not a sign of a burglar, and no window had been raised. One glass was absent, but that was where the coachman's charge had come through. Here was a fine mystery—a burglar alarm 'going off' at midnight of its own accord, and not a burglar in the neighborhood!

"The expert answered the usual call, and explained that it was a 'false alarm.' Said it was easily fixed. So he overhauled the nursery window, charged a remunerative figure for it, and departed.

"What we suffered from false alarms for the next three years no stylographic pen can describe. During the first few months I always flew with my gun to the room indicated, and the coachman always sallied forth with his battery to support me. But there was never anything to shoot at—windows all tight and secure. We always sent down for the expert next day, and he fixed those particular windows so they would keep quiet a week or so, and always remembered to send us a bill about like this:

Wire	$2.15
Nipple	.75
Two hours' labor	1.50
Wax	.47
Tape	.34
Screws	.15
Recharging battery	.98
Three hours' labor	2.25
String	.02
Lard	.66
Pond's Extract	1.25
Springs, 4 @ .50	2.00
Railroad fares	7.25
	$19.77

"At length a perfectly natural thing came about—after we had answered three or four hundred false alarms—to wit, we stopped answering them. Yes, I simply rose up calmly, when slammed across the house by the alarm, calmly inspected the annunciator, took note of the room indicated, and then calmly disconnected that room from the alarm, and went back to bed as if nothing had happened. Moreover, I left that room off permanently, and did not send for the expert. Well, it goes without saying that in the course of time *all* the rooms were taken off, and the entire machine was out of service.

"It was at this unprotected time that the heaviest calamity of all happened. The burglars walked in one night and carried off the burglar alarm! yes, sir, every hide and hair of it; ripped it out, tooth and toe-nail; springs, bells, gongs, battery, and all; they took a hundred and fifty miles of copper wire; they just cleaned her out, bag and baggage, and never left us a vestige of her to swear at—swear by, I mean.

"We had a time of it to get her back; but we accomplished it finally, for money. Then the alarm firm said that what we needed now was to have her put in right—with their new patent springs in the windows to make false alarms impossible, and their new patent clock attachment to take off and put on the alarm morning and night without human assistance. That seemed a good scheme. They promised to have the whole thing finished in ten days. They began work, and we left for the summer. They worked a couple of days; then *they* left for the summer. After which the burglars moved in, and began *their* summer vacation. When we returned in the fall, the house was as empty as a beer closet in premises where painters have been at work. We refurnished, and then sent down to hurry up the expert. He came up and finished the job, and said: 'Now this clock is set to put on the alarm every night at 10, and take it off every morning at 5.45. All you've got to do is to wind her up every week, and then leave her alone—she will take care of the alarm herself.'

"After that we had a most tranquil season during three months. The bill was prodigious, of course, and I had said I would not pay it until the new machinery had proved itself to be flawless. The time stipulated was three months. So I paid the bill, and the very next day the alarm went to buzzing like ten thousand bee swarms at ten o'clock in the morning. I turned the hands around twelve hours, according to instructions, and this took off the alarm; but there was another hitch at night, and I had to set her ahead twelve hours once more to get her to put the alarm on again. That sort of nonsense went on a week or two; then the expert came up and put in a new clock. He came up every three months during the next three years, and put in a new clock. But it was always a failure. His clocks all had the same perverse defect: they *would* put the alarm on in the daytime, and they would *not* put it on at night; and if you forced it on yourself, they would take it off again the minute your back was turned.

"Now there is the history of that burglar alarm—everything just as it happened; nothing extenuated, and naught set down in malice. Yes, sir; and when I had slept nine years with burglars, and maintained an expensive burglar alarm the whole time, for their protection, not mine, and at my sole cost—for not a d——d cent could I ever get *them* to contribute—I just said to Mrs. McWilliams that I had had enough of that kind of pie; so with her full consent I took the whole thing out and traded it off for a dog, and shot the dog. I don't know what *you* think about it, Mr. Twain; but *I* think those things are made solely in the interest of the burglars. Yes, sir, a burglar alarm combines in its person all that is objectionable about a fire, a riot, and a harem, and at the same time has none of the compensating advantages, of one sort or another, that customarily belong with that combination. Good-by; I get off here."

So saying, Mr. McWilliams gathered up his satchel and umbrella, and bowed himself out of the train.

[1882]

The Private History of a Campaign That Failed

You have heard from a great many people who did something in the war; is it not fair and right that you listen a little moment to one who started out to do something in it, but didn't? Thousands entered the war, got just a taste of it, and then stepped out again, permanently. These, by their very numbers, are respectable, and are therefore entitled to a sort of voice,—not a loud one, but a modest one; not a boastful one, but an apologetic one. They ought not to be allowed much space among better people—people who did something—I grant that; but they ought at least to be allowed to state why they didn't do anything, and also to explain the process by which they didn't do anything. Surely this kind of light must have a sort of value.

Out West there was a good deal of confusion in men's minds during the first months of the great trouble—a good deal of unsettledness, of leaning first this way, then that, then the other way. It was hard for us to get our bearings. I call to mind an instance of this. I was piloting on the Mississippi when the news came that South Carolina had gone out of the Union on the 20th of December, 1860. My pilot-mate was a New Yorker. He was strong for the Union; so was I. But he would not listen to me with any patience; my loyalty was smirched, to his eye, because my father had owned slaves. I said, in palliation of this dark fact, that I had heard my father say, some years before he died, that slavery was a great wrong, and that he would free the solitary negro he then owned if he could think it right to give away the property of the family when he was so straitened in means. My mate retorted that a mere impulse was nothing—anybody could pretend to a good impulse; and went on decrying my Unionism and libeling my ancestry. A month later the secession atmosphere had considerably thickened on the Lower Mississippi, and I became a rebel; so did he. We were together in New Orleans, the 26th of January, when Louisiana went out of the Union. He did his full share of the rebel shouting, but was bitterly opposed to letting me do mine. He said that I came of bad stock—of a father who had been willing to set slaves free. In the following summer he was piloting a Federal gun-boat and shouting for the Union again, and I was in the Confederate army. I held his note for some borrowed money. He was one of the most upright men I ever knew; but he repudiated that note without hesitation, because I was a rebel, and the son of a man who owned slaves.

In that summer—of 1861—the first wash of the wave of war broke upon the shores of Missouri. Our State was invaded by the Union forces. They took possession of St. Louis, Jefferson Barracks, and some other points. The Governor, Claib Jackson, issued his proclamation calling out fifty thousand militia to repel the invader.

I was visiting in the small town where my boyhood had been spent—Hannibal, Marion County. Several of us got together in a secret place by night and formed ourselves into a military company. One Tom Lyman, a young fellow of a good deal of spirit but of no military experience, was made captain; I was made second lieutenant. We had no first lieutenant; I do not know why; it was long ago. There were fifteen of us. By the advice of an innocent connected with the organization, we called ourselves the Marion Rangers. I do not remember that any one found fault with the name. I did not; I thought it sounded quite well. The young fellow who proposed this title was perhaps a fair sample of the kind of stuff we were made of. He was young, ignorant, good-natured, well-meaning, trivial, full of romance, and given to reading chivalric novels

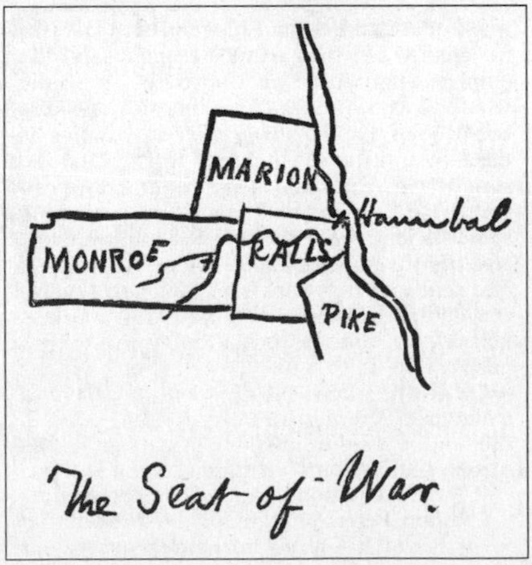

and singing forlorn love-ditties. He had some pathetic little nickel-plated aristocratic instincts, and detested his name, which was Dunlap; detested it, partly because it was nearly as common in that region as Smith, but mainly because it had a plebeian sound to his ear. So he tried to ennoble it by writing it in this way: *d' Unlap.* That contented his eye, but left his ear unsatisfied, for people gave the new name the same old pronunciation—emphasis on the front end of it. He then did the bravest thing that can be imagined,—a thing to make one shiver when one remembers how the world is given to resenting shams and affectations; he began to write his name so: *d'Un Lap.* And he waited patiently through the long storm of mud that was flung at this work of art, and he had his reward at last; for he lived to see that name accepted, and the emphasis put where he wanted it, by people who had known him all his life, and to whom the tribe of Dunlaps had been as familiar as the rain and the sunshine for forty years. So sure of victory at last is the courage that can wait. He said he had found, by consulting some ancient French chronicles, that the name was rightly and originally written d'Un Lap; and said that if it were translated into English it would mean Peterson: *Lap,* Latin or Greek, he said, for stone or rock, same as the French *pierre,* that is to say, Peter; *d',* of or from; *un,* a or one; hence, d'Un Lap, of or from a stone or a Peter; that is to say, one who is the son of a stone, the son of a Peter—Peterson. Our militia company were not learned, and the explanation confused them; so they called him Peterson Dunlap. He proved useful to us in his way; he named our camps for us, and he generally struck a name that was "no slouch," as the boys said.

That is one sample of us. Another was Ed Stevens, son of the town jeweler,—trim-built, handsome, graceful, neat as a cat; bright, educated, but given over entirely to fun. There was nothing serious in life to him. As far as he was concerned, this military expedition of ours was simply a holiday. I should say that about half of us looked upon it in the same way; not consciously, perhaps, but unconsciously. We did not think; we were not capable of it. As for myself, I was full of unreasoning joy to be done with turning out of bed at midnight and four in the morning, for a while; grateful to have a change, new scenes, new occupations, a new interest. In my thoughts that was as far as I went; I did not go into the details; as a rule one doesn't at twenty-four.

Another sample was Smith, the blacksmith's apprentice. This vast donkey had some pluck, of a slow and sluggish nature, but a soft heart; at one time he would knock a horse down for some impropriety, and at another he would get homesick and cry. However, he had one ultimate credit to his account which some of us hadn't: he stuck to the war, and was killed in battle at last.

Jo Bowers, another sample, was a huge, good-natured, flax-headed lubber; lazy, sentimental, full of harmless brag, a grumbler by nature; an experienced, industrious, ambitious, and often quite picturesque liar, and yet not a successful one, for he had had no intelligent training, but was allowed to come up just any way. This life was serious enough to him, and seldom satisfactory. But he was a good fellow anyway, and the boys all liked him. He was made orderly sergeant; Stevens was made corporal.

These samples will answer—and they are quite fair ones. Well, this herd of cattle started for the war. What could you expect of them? They did as well as they knew how, but really what was justly to be expected of them? Nothing, I should say. That is what they did.

We waited for a dark night, for caution and secrecy were necessary; then, toward midnight, we stole in couples and from various directions to the Griffith place, beyond the town; from that point we set out together on foot. Hannibal lies at the extreme southeastern corner of Marion County, on the Mississippi River; our objective point was the hamlet of New London, ten miles away, in Ralls County.

The first hour was all fun, all idle nonsense and laughter. But that could not be kept up. The steady trudging came to be like work; the play had somehow oozed out of it; the stillness of the woods and the somberness of the night began to throw a depressing influence over the spirits of the boys, and presently the talking died out and each person shut himself up in his own thoughts. During the last half of the second hour nobody said a word.

Now we approached a log farm-house where, according to report, there was a guard of five Union soldiers. Lyman called a halt; and there, in the deep gloom of the overhanging branches, he began to whisper a plan of assault upon that house, which made the gloom more depressing than it was before. It was a crucial moment; we realized, with a cold suddenness, that here was no jest—we were standing face to face with actual war. We were equal to the occasion. In our response there was no hesitation, no indecision: we said that if Lyman wanted to meddle with those soldiers, he could go ahead and do it; but if he waited for us to follow him, he would wait a long time.

Lyman urged, pleaded, tried to shame us, but it had no effect. Our course was plain, our minds were made up: we would flank the farm-house—go out around. And that is what we did.

We struck into the woods and entered upon a rough time, stumbling over roots, getting tangled in vines, and torn by briers. At last we reached an open place in a safe region, and sat down, blown and hot, to cool off and nurse our scratches and bruises. Lyman was annoyed, but the rest of us were cheerful; we had flanked the farm-house, we had made our first military movement, and it was a success; we had nothing to fret about, we were feeling just the other way. Horse-play and laughing began again; the expedition was become a holiday frolic once more.

Then we had two more hours of dull trudging and ultimate silence and depression; then, about dawn, we straggled into New London, soiled, heel-blistered, fagged with our little march, and all of us except Stevens in a sour and raspy humor and privately down on the war. We stacked our shabby old shot-guns in Colonel Ralls's barn, and then went in a body and breakfasted with that veteran of the Mexican war. Afterwards he took us to a distant meadow, and there in the shade of a tree we listened to an old-fashioned speech from him, full of gunpowder and glory, full of that adjective-piling, mixed metaphor, and windy declamation which was regarded as eloquence in that ancient time and that remote region; and then he swore us on the Bible to be faithful to the State of Missouri and drive all invaders from her soil, no matter whence they might come or under what flag they might march. This mixed us considerably, and we could not make out just what service we were embarked in; but Colonel Ralls, the practiced politician and phrase-juggler, was not similarly in doubt; he knew quite clearly that he had invested us in the cause of the Southern Confederacy. He closed the solemnities by belting around me the sword which his neighbor, Colonel Brown, had worn at Buena Vista and Molino del Rey;[1] and he accompanied this act with another impressive blast.

Then we formed in line of battle and marched four miles to a shady and pleasant piece of woods on the border of the far-reaching expanses of a flowery prairie. It was an enchanting region for war—our kind of war.

We pierced the forest about half a mile, and took up a strong position, with some low, rocky, and wooded hills behind us, and a purling, limpid creek in front. Straightway half the command were in swimming, and the other half fishing. The ass with the French name gave this position a romantic title, but it was too long, so the boys shortened and simplified it to Camp Ralls.

We occupied an old maple-sugar camp, whose half-rotted troughs were still propped against the trees. A long corn-crib served for sleeping

The Sword of Buena Vista and Molino del Rey

quarters for the battalion. On our left, half a mile away, was Mason's farm and house; and he was a friend to the cause. Shortly after noon the farmers began to arrive from several directions, with mules and horses for our use, and these they lent us for as long as the war might last, which they judged would be about three months.[2] The animals were of all sizes, all colors, and all breeds. They were mainly young and frisky, and nobody in the command could stay on them long at a time; for we were town boys, and ignorant of horsemanship. The creature that fell to my share was a very small mule, and yet so quick and active that it could throw me without difficulty; and it did this whenever I got on it. Then it would bray—stretching its neck out, laying its ears back, and spreading its jaws till you could see down to its works. It was a disagreeable animal, in every way. If I took it by the bridle and tried to lead it off the grounds, it would sit down and brace back, and no one could budge it. However, I was not entirely destitute of military resources, and I did presently manage to spoil this game; for I had seen many a steamboat aground in my time, and knew a trick or two which even a grounded mule would be obliged to respect. There was a well by the corn-crib; so I substituted thirty fathom of rope for the bridle, and fetched him home with the windlass.

I will anticipate here sufficiently to say that we did learn to ride, after some days' practice, but never well. We could not learn to like our animals; they were not choice ones, and most of them had annoying peculiarities of one kind or another. Stevens's horse would carry him, when he was not noticing, under the huge excrescences which form on the trunks of oak-trees, and wipe him out of the saddle; in this way Stevens got several bad hurts. Sergeant Bowers's horse was very large and tall, with slim, long legs, and looked like a railroad bridge. His size enabled him to reach all about, and as far as he wanted to, with his head; so he was always biting Bowers's legs. On the march, in the sun, Bowers slept a good deal; and as soon as the horse recognized that he was asleep he would reach around and bite him on the leg. His legs were black and blue with bites. This was the only thing that could ever make him swear, but this always did; whenever the horse bit him he always swore, and of course Stevens, who laughed at everything, laughed at this, and would even get into such convulsions over it as to lose his balance and fall off his horse; and then Bowers, already irritated by the pain of the horse-bite, would resent the laughter with hard language, and there would be a quarrel; so that horse made no end of trouble and bad blood in the command.

However, I will get back to where I was—our first afternoon in the sugar-camp. The sugar-troughs came very handy as horsetroughs, and we had plenty of corn to fill them with. I ordered Sergeant Bowers to feed my mule; but he said that if I reckoned he went to war to be dry-nurse to a mule, it wouldn't take me very long to find out my mistake. I believed that this was insubordination, but I was full of uncertainties about everything military, and so I let the thing pass, and went and ordered Smith, the blacksmith's apprentice, to feed the mule; but he merely gave me a large, cold, sarcastic grin, such as an ostensibly seven-year-old horse gives you when you lift his lip and find he is fourteen, and turned his back on me. I then went to the captain, and asked if it was not right and proper and military for me to have an orderly. He said it was, but as there was only one orderly in the corps, it was but right that he himself should have Bowers on his staff. Bowers said he wouldn't serve on anybody's staff; and if anybody thought he could make him, let him try it. So, of course, the thing had to be dropped; there was no other way.

Next, nobody would cook; it was considered a degradation; so we had no dinner. We lazied the rest of the pleasant afternoon away, some dozing under the trees, some smoking cob-pipes and talking sweethearts and war, some playing games. By late suppertime all hands were famished; and to meet the difficulty all hands turned to, on an equal footing, and gathered wood, built fires, and cooked the meal. Afterward everything was smooth for a while; then trouble broke out between the corporal and the sergeant, each claiming to rank the other. Nobody knew which was the higher office; so Lyman had to settle the matter by making the rank of both officers equal. The commander of an ignorant crew

"It was a disagreeable animal, in every way."

like that has many troubles and vexations which probably do not occur in the regular army at all. However, with the song-singing and yarn-spinning around the camp-fire, everything presently became serene again; and by and by we raked the corn down level in one end of the crib, and all went to bed on it, tying a horse to the door, so that he would neigh if any one tried to get in.*

We had some horsemanship drill every forenoon; then, afternoons, we rode off here and there in squads a few miles, and visited the farmers' girls, and had a youthful good time, and got an honest good dinner or supper, and then home again to camp, happy and content.

For a time, life was idly delicious, it was perfect; there was nothing to mar it. Then came some farmers with an alarm one day. They said it was rumored that the enemy were advancing in our direction, from over Hyde's prairie. The result was a sharp stir among us, and general consternation. It was a rude awakening from our pleasant trance. The rumor was but a rumor—nothing definite about it; so, in the confusion, we did not know which way to retreat. Lyman was for not retreating at all, in these uncertain circumstances; but he found that if he tried to maintain that attitude he would fare badly, for the command were in no humor to put up with insubordination. So he yielded the point and called a council of war—to consist of himself and the three other officers; but the privates made such a fuss about being left out, that we had to allow them to be present. I mean we had to allow them to remain, for they were already present, and doing the most of the talking too. The question was, which way to retreat; but all were so flurried that nobody seemed to have even a guess to offer. Except Lyman. He explained in a few calm words, that inasmuch as the enemy were approaching from over Hyde's prairie, our course was simple: all we had to do was not to retreat *toward* him; any other direction would answer our needs perfectly. Everybody saw in a moment how true this was, and how wise; so Lyman got a great many compliments. It was now decided that we should fall back on Mason's farm.

*It was always my impression that that was what the horse was there for, and I know that it was also the impression of at least one other of the command, for we talked about it at the time, and admired the military ingenuity of the device; but when I was out West three years ago I was told by Mr. A. G. Fuqua, a member of our company, that the horse was his, that the leaving him tied at the door was a matter of mere forgetfulness, and that to attribute it to intelligent invention was to give him quite too much credit. In support of his position, he called my attention to the suggestive fact that the artifice was not employed again. I had not thought of that before.

It was after dark by this time, and as we could not know how soon the enemy might arrive, it did not seem best to try to take the horses and things with us; so we only took the guns and ammunition, and started at once. The route was very rough and hilly and rocky, and presently the night grew very black and rain began to fall; so we had a troublesome time of it, struggling and stumbling along in the dark; and soon some person slipped and fell, and then the next person behind stumbled over him and fell, and so did the rest, one after the other; and then Bowers came with the keg of powder in his arms, whilst the command were all mixed together, arms and legs, on the muddy slope; and so he fell, of course, with the keg, and this started the whole detachment down the hill in a body, and they landed in the brook at the bottom in a pile, and each that was undermost pulling the hair and scratching and biting those that were on top of him; and those that were being scratched and bitten scratching and biting the rest in their turn, and all saying they would die before they would ever go to war again if they ever got out of this brook this time, and the invader might rot for all they cared, and the country along with him—and all such talk as that, which was dismal to hear and take part in, in such smothered, low voices, and such a grisly dark place and so wet, and the enemy may be coming any moment.

The keg of powder was lost, and the guns too; so the growling and complaining continued straight along whilst the brigade pawed around the pasty hillside and slopped around in the brook hunting for these things; consequently we lost considerable time at this; and then we heard a sound, and held our breath and listened, and it seemed to be the enemy coming, though it could have been a cow, for it had a cough like a cow; but we did not wait, but left a couple of guns behind and struck out for Mason's again as briskly as we could scramble along in the dark. But we got lost presently among the rugged little ravines, and wasted a deal of time finding the way again, so it was after nine when we reached Mason's stile at last; and then before we could open our mouths to give the countersign, several dogs came bounding over the fence, with great riot and noise, and each of them took a soldier by the slack of his trousers and began to back away with him. We could not shoot the dogs without endangering the persons they were attached to; so we had to look on, helpless, at what was perhaps the most mortifying spectacle of the civil war. There was light enough, and to spare, for the Masons had now run out on the porch with candles in their hands. The old man and his son came and undid the dogs without difficulty, all but Bowers's; but they couldn't undo his dog, they didn't know his combination; he was of the bull kind, and seemed to be set with a Yale time-lock; but they got him loose at last with some scalding water, of which Bowers got his share and returned thanks. Peterson Dunlap afterwards made up a fine name for this engagement, and also for the night march which preceded it, but both have long ago faded out of my memory.

We now went into the house, and they began to ask us a world of questions, whereby it presently came out that we did not know anything concerning who or what we were running from; so the old gentleman made himself very frank, and said we were a curious breed of soldiers, and guessed we could be depended on to end up the war in time, because no government could stand the expense of the shoe-leather we should cost it trying to follow us around. "Marion *Rangers*! good name, b'gosh!" said he. And wanted to know why we hadn't had a picket-guard at the place where the road entered the prairie, and why we hadn't sent out a scouting party to spy out the enemy and bring us an account of his strength, and so on, before jumping up and stampeding out of a strong position upon a mere vague rumor—and so on and so forth, till he made us all feel shabbier than the dogs had done, not half so enthusiastically welcome. So we went to bed shamed and low-spirited; except Stevens. Soon Stevens began to devise a garment for Bowers which could be made to automatically display his battle-scars to the grateful, or conceal them from the envious, according to his occasions; but Bowers was in no humor for this, so there was a fight, and when it was over Stevens had some battle-scars of his own to think about.

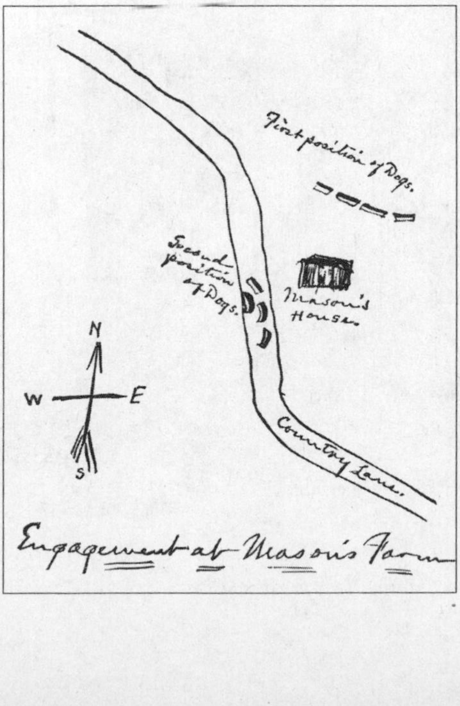

Then we got a little sleep. But after all we had gone through, our activities were not over for the night; for about two o'clock in the morning we heard a shout of warning from down the lane, accompanied by a chorus from all the dogs, and in a moment everybody was up and flying around to find out what the alarm was about. The alarmist was a horseman who gave notice that a detachment of Union soldiers was on its way from Hannibal with orders to capture and hang any bands like ours which it could find, and said we had no time to lose. Farmer Mason was in a flurry this time, himself. He hurried us out of the house with all haste, and sent one of his negroes with us to show us where to hide ourselves and our tell-tale guns among the ravines half a mile away. It was raining heavily.

We struck down the lane, then across some rocky pasture-land which offered good advantages for stumbling; consequently we were down in the mud most of the time, and every time a man went down he blackguarded the war, and the people that started it, and everybody connected with it, and gave himself the master dose of all for being so foolish as to go into it. At last we reached the wooded mouth of a ravine, and there we huddled ourselves under the streaming trees, and sent the negro back home. It was a dismal and heart-breaking time. We were like to be drowned with the rain, deafened with the howling wind and the

Farmer Mason explaining the principles of war.

booming thunder, and blinded by the lightning. It was indeed a wild night. The drenching we were getting was misery enough, but a deeper misery still was the reflection that the halter might end us before we were a day older. A death of this shameful sort had not occurred to us as being among the possibilities of war. It took the romance all out of the campaign, and turned our dreams of glory into a repulsive nightmare. As for doubting that so barbarous an order had been given, not one of us did that.

The long night wore itself out at last, and then the negro came to us with the news that the alarm had manifestly been a false one, and that breakfast would soon be ready. Straightway we were lighted-hearted again, and the world was bright, and life as full of hope and promise as ever—for we were young then. How long ago that was! Twenty-four years.

The mongrel child of philology named the night's refuge Camp Devastation, and no soul objected. The Masons gave us a Missouri country breakfast, in Missourian abundance, and we needed it: hot biscuits; hot "wheat bread" prettily criss-crossed in a lattice pattern on top; hot corn pone; fried chicken; bacon, coffee, eggs, milk, buttermilk, etc.;—and the world may be confidently challenged to furnish the equal to such a breakfast, as it is cooked in the South.

We staid several days at Mason's; and after all these years the memory of the dullness, the stillness and lifelessness of that slumberous farm-house still oppresses my spirit as with a sense of the presence of death and mourning. There was nothing to do, nothing to think about; there was no interest in life. The male part of the household were away in the fields all day, the women were busy and out of our sight; there was no sound but the plaintive wailing of a spinning-wheel, forever moaning out from some distant room,—the most lonesome sound in nature, a sound steeped and sodden with homesickness and the emptiness of life. The family went to bed about dark every night, and as we were not invited to intrude any new customs, we naturally followed theirs. Those nights were a hundred years long to youths accustomed to being up till twelve. We lay awake and miserable till that hour every time, and grew old and decrepit waiting through the still eternities for the clock-strikes. This was no place for town boys. So at last it was with something very like joy that we received news that the enemy were on our track again. With a new birth of the old warrior spirit, we sprang to our places in line of battle and fell back on Camp Ralls.

Captain Lyman had taken a hint from Mason's talk, and he now gave orders that our camp should be guarded against surprise by the posting of pickets. I was ordered to place a picket at the forks of the road in Hyde's prairie. Night shut down black and threatening. I told Sergeant Bowers to go out to that place and stay till midnight; and, just as I was expecting, he said he wouldn't do it. I tried to get others to go, but all refused. Some excused themselves on account of the weather; but the rest were frank enough to say they wouldn't go in any kind of weather. This kind of thing sounds odd now, and impossible, but there was no surprise in it at the time. On the contrary, it seemed a perfectly natural thing to do. There were scores of little camps scattered over Missouri where the same thing was happening. These camps were composed of young men who had been born and reared to a sturdy independence, and who did not know what it meant to be ordered around by Tom, Dick, and Harry, whom they had known familiarly all their lives, in the village or on the farm. It is quite within the probabilities that this same thing was happening all over the South. James Redpath recognized the justice of this assumption, and furnished the following instance in support of it. During a short stay in East Tennessee he was in a citizen colonel's tent one day, talking, when a big private appeared at the door, and without salute or other circumlocution said to the colonel:

"Say, Jim, I'm a-goin' home for a few days."

"What for?"

"Well, I hain't b'en there for a right smart while, and I'd like to see how things is comin' on."

"How long are you going to be gone?"

" 'Bout two weeks."

"Well, don't be gone longer than that; and get back sooner if you can."

That was all, and the citizen officer resumed his conversation where the private had broken it off. This was in the first months of the war, of course. The camps in our part of Missouri were under Brigadier-General Thomas H. Harris. He was a townsman of ours, a first-rate fellow, and well liked; but we had all familiarly known him as the sole and modest-salaried operator in our telegraph office, where he had to send about one dispatch a week in ordinary times, and two when there was a rush of business; consequently, when he appeared in our midst one day, on the wing, and delivered a military command of some sort, in a large military fashion, nobody was surprised at the response which he got from the assembled soldiery:

"Oh, now, what'll you take to *don't,* Tom Harris!"

It was quite the natural thing. One might justly imagine that we were hopeless material for war. And so we seemed, in our ignorant state; but there were those among us who afterward learned the grim trade; learned to obey like machines; became valuable soldiers; fought all through the war, and came out at the end with excellent records. One of the very boys who refused to go out on picket duty that night, and called me an ass for thinking he would expose himself to danger in such a foolhardy way, had become distinguished for intrepidity before he was a year older.

I did secure my picket that night—not by authority, but by diplomacy. I got Bowers to go, by agreeing to exchange ranks with him for the time being, and go along and stand the watch with him as his subordinate. We staid out there a couple of dreary hours in the pitchy darkness and the rain, with nothing to modify the dreariness but Bowers's monotonous growlings at the war and the weather; then we began to nod, and presently found it next to impossible to stay in the saddle; so we gave up the tedious job, and went back to the camp without waiting for the relief guard. We rode into camp without interruption or objection from anybody, and the enemy could have done the same, for there were no sentries. Everybody was asleep; at midnight there was nobody to send out another picket, so none was sent. We never tried to establish a watch at night again, as far as I remember, but we generally kept a picket out in the daytime.

In that camp the whole command slept on the corn in the big corncrib; and there was usually a general row before morning, for the place was full of rats, and they would scramble over the boys' bodies and faces, annoying and irritating everybody; and now and then they would bite some one's toe, and the person who owned the toe would start up and magnify his English and begin to throw corn in the dark. The ears were half as heavy as bricks, and when they struck they hurt. The persons struck would respond, and inside of five minutes every man would be locked in a death-grip with his neighbor. There was a grievous deal of blood shed in the corn-crib, but this was all that was spilt while I was in the war. No, that is not quite true. But for one circumstance it would have been all. I will come to that now.

Our scares were frequent. Every few days rumors would come that the enemy were approaching. In these cases we always fell back on some other camp of ours; we never staid where we were. But the rumors always turned out to be false; so at last even we began to grow indifferent to them. One night a negro was sent to our corn-crib with the same old warning: the enemy was hovering in our neighborhood. We all said let him hover. We resolved to stay still and be comfortable. It was a fine warlike resolution, and no doubt we all felt the stir of it in our veins—for a moment. We had been having a very jolly time, that was full of horseplay and school-boy hilarity; but that cooled down now, and presently the fast-waning fire of forced jokes and forced laughs died out altogether, and the company became silent. Silent and nervous. And soon uneasy—worried—apprehensive. We had said we would stay, and we were committed. We could have been persuaded to go, but there was nobody brave enough to suggest it. An almost noiseless movement presently began in the dark, by a general but unvoiced impulse. When the movement was completed, each man knew that he was not the only person who had crept to the front wall and had his eye at a crack between the logs. No, we were all there; all there with our hearts in our throats, and staring out toward the sugar-troughs where the forest footpath came through. It was late, and there was a deep woodsy stillness everywhere. There was a veiled moonlight, which was only just strong enough to enable us to mark the general shape of objects. Presently a muffled sound caught our ears, and we recognized it as the hoof-beats of a horse or horses. And right away a figure appeared in the forest path; it could have been made of smoke, its mass had so little sharpness of outline. It was a man on horseback; and it seemed to me that there were others behind him. I got hold of a gun in the dark, and pushed it through a crack between the logs, hardly knowing what I was doing, I was so dazed with fright. Somebody said "Fire!" I pulled the trigger. I seemed to see a hundred flashes and hear a hundred reports, then I saw the man fall down out of the saddle. My first feeling was of surprised gratification; my first impulse was an apprentice-sportsman's impulse to run and pick up his game. Somebody said, hardly audibly, "Good—we've got him!—wait for the rest." But the rest did not come. We waited—listened—still no more came. There was not a sound, not the whisper of a leaf; just perfect stillness; an uncanny kind of stillness, which was all the more uncanny on account of the damp, earthy, late-night smells now rising and pervading it. Then, wondering, we crept stealthily out, and approached the man. When we got to him the moon revealed him distinctly. He was lying on his back, with his arms abroad; his mouth was open and his chest heaving with long gasps, and his white shirt-front was all splashed with blood. The thought shot through me that I was a murderer; that I had killed a man—a man who had never done me any harm. That was the coldest sensation that ever went through my marrow. I was down by him in a moment, helplessly stroking his forehead; and I would have given anything then—my own life freely—to make him again what he had been five minutes before. And all the boys seemed to be feeling in the same way; they hung over him, full of pitying interest, and tried all they could to help him, and said all sorts of regretful things. They had forgotten all about the enemy; they thought only of this one forlorn unit of the foe. Once my imagination persuaded me that the dying man gave me a reproachful look out of his shadowy eyes, and it seemed to me that I could rather he had stabbed me than done that. He muttered and mumbled like a dreamer in his sleep, about his wife and his child; and I thought with a new despair, "This thing that I have done does not end with him; it falls upon *them* too, and they never did me any harm, any more than he."

In a little while the man was dead. He was killed in war; killed in fair and legitimate war; killed in battle, as you may say; and yet he was as sincerely mourned by the opposing force as if he had been their brother. The boys stood there a half hour sorrowing over him, and recalling the details of the tragedy, and wondering who he might be, and if he were a spy, and saying that if it were to do over again they would not hurt him unless he attacked them first. It soon came out that mine was not the only shot fired; there were five others,—a division of the guilt which was a grateful relief to me, since it in some degree lightened and diminished the burden I was carrying. There were six shots fired at once; but I was not in my right mind at the time, and my heated imagination had magnified my one shot into a volley.

The man was not in uniform, and was not armed. He was a stranger in the country; that was all we ever found out about him. The thought of him got to preying upon me every night; I could not get rid of it. I could not drive it away, the taking of that unoffending life seemed such a wanton thing. And it seemed an epitome of war; that all war must be just that—the killing of strangers against whom you feel no personal animosity; strangers whom, in other circumstances, you would help if you found them in trouble, and who would help you if you needed it. My campaign was spoiled. It seemed to me that I was not rightly equipped for this awful business; that war was intended for men, and I for a child's nurse. I resolved to retire from this avocation of sham soldiership while I could save some remnant of my self-respect. These morbid thoughts clung to me against reason; for at bottom I did not believe I had touched that man. The law of probabilities decreed me guiltless of his blood; for in all my small experience with guns I had never hit anything I had tried to hit, and I knew I had done my best to hit him. Yet there was no solace in the thought. Against a diseased imagination, demonstration goes for nothing.

The rest of my war experience was of a piece with what I have already told of it. We kept monotonously falling back upon one camp or another, and eating up the country. I marvel now at the patience of the farmers and their families. They ought to have shot us; on the contrary, they were as hospitably kind and courteous to us as if we had deserved it. In one of these camps we found Ab Grimes, an Upper Mississippi pilot, who afterwards became famous as a dare-devil rebel spy, whose career bristled with desperate adventures. The look and style of his comrades suggested that they had not come into the war to play, and their deeds made good the conjecture later. They were fine horsemen and good revolver-shots; but their favorite arm was the lasso. Each had one at his pommel, and could snatch a man out of the saddle with it every time, on a full gallop, at any reasonable distance.

In another camp the chief was a fierce and profane old blacksmith of sixty, and he had furnished his twenty recruits with gigantic home-made bowie-knives, to be swung with the two hands, like the *machetes* of the Isthmus. It was a grisly spectacle to see that earnest band practicing their murderous cuts and slashes under the eye of that remorseless old fanatic.

The last camp which we fell back upon was in a hollow near the village of Florida, where I was born—in Monroe County. Here we were warned, one day, that a Union colonel was sweeping down on us with a whole regiment at his heels. This looked decidedly serious. Our boys went apart and consulted; then we went back and told the other companies present that the war was a disappointment to us and we were going to disband. They were getting ready, themselves, to fall back on some place or other, and were only waiting for General Tom Harris, who was expected to arrive at any moment; so they tried to persuade us to wait a little while, but the majority of us said no, we were accustomed to falling back, and didn't need any of Tom Harris's help; we could get along perfectly well without him—and save time too. So about half of our fifteen, including myself, mounted and left on the instant; the others yielded to persuasion and staid—staid through the war.

An hour later we met General Harris on the road, with two or three people in his company—his staff, probably, but we could not tell; none of them were in uniform; uniforms had not come into vogue among us yet. Harris ordered us back; but we told him there was a Union colonel coming with a whole regiment in his wake, and it looked as if there was going to be a disturbance; so we had concluded to go home. He raged a little, but it was of no use; our minds were made up. We had done our share; had killed one man, exterminated one army, such as it was; let him go and kill the rest, and that would end the war. I did not see that brisk young general again until last year; then he was wearing white hair and whiskers.

In time I came to know that Union colonel whose coming frightened me out of the war and crippled the Southern cause to that extent—General Grant. I came within a few hours of seeing him[3] when he was as unknown as I was myself; at a time when anybody could have said, "Grant?—Ulysses S. Grant? I do not remember hearing the name before." It seems difficult to realize that there was once a time when such a remark could be rationally made; but there *was*, and I was within a few miles of the place and the occasion too, though proceeding in the other direction.

The thoughtful will not throw this war-paper of mine lightly aside as being valueless. It has this value: it is a not unfair picture of what went on in many and many a militia camp in the first months of the rebellion, when the green recruits were without discipline, without the steadying and heartening influence of trained leaders; when all their circumstances were new and strange, and charged with exaggerated terrors, and before the invaluable experience of actual collision in the field had turned them from rabbits into soldiers. If this side of the picture of that early day has not before been put into history, then history has been to that degree incomplete, for it had and has its rightful place there. There was more Bull Run material scattered through the early camps of this country than exhibited itself at Bull Run. And yet it learned its trade presently, and helped to fight the great battles later. I could have become a soldier myself, if I had waited. I had got part of it learned; I knew more about retreating than the man that invented retreating.

[1885]

Extracts from Adam's Diary

TRANSLATED FROM THE ORIGINAL MS.

MONDAY—This new creature with the long hair is a good deal in the way. It is always hanging around and following me about. I don't like this; I am not used to company. I wish it would stay with the other animals. . . . . Cloudy to-day, wind in the east; think we shall have rain. . . . . *We?* Where did I get that word? . . . . I remember now,—the new creature uses it.

TUESDAY—Been examining the great waterfall. It is the finest thing on the estate, I think. The new creature calls it Niagara Falls[1]—why, I am sure I do not know. Says it *looks* like Niagara Falls. That is not a reason, it is mere waywardness and imbecility. I get no chance to name anything myself. The new creature names everything that comes along, before I can get in a protest.[2] And always that same pretext is offered—it *looks* like the thing. There is the dodo, for instance. Says the moment one looks at it one sees at a glance that it "looks like a dodo." It will have to keep that name, no doubt. It wearies me to fret about it, but it does no good, anyway. Dodo! It looks no more like a dodo than I do.

WEDNESDAY—Built me a shelter against the rain, but could not have it to myself in peace. The new creature intruded. When I tried to put it out it shed water out of the holes it looks with, and wiped it away with the back of its paws, and made a noise such as some of the other animals make when they are in distress. I wish it would not talk; it is always talking. That sounds like a cheap fling at the poor creature, a slur; but I do not mean it so. I have never heard the human voice before, and any new and strange sound intruding itself here upon the solemn hush of these dreaming solitudes offends my ear and seems a false note. And this new sound is so close to me; it is right at my shoulder, right at my ear, first on one side and then on the other, and I am used only to sounds that are more or less distant from me.

FRIDAY—The naming goes recklessly on, in spite of anything I can do. I had a very good name for the estate, and it was musical and pretty—GARDEN-OF-EDEN. Privately, I continue to call it that, but not any longer publicly. The new creature says it is all woods and rocks and scenery, and therefore has no resemblance to a garden. Says it *looks* like a park, and does not look like anything *but* a park. Consequently, without consulting me it has been new named—NIAGARA FALLS PARK. This is sufficiently high-handed, it seems to me. And already there is a sign up:

KEEP OFF THE GRASS

My life is not as happy as it was.

SATURDAY—The new creature eats too much fruit. We are going to run short, most likely. "We" again—that is *its* word; mine, too, now, from hearing it so much. Good deal of fog this morning. I do not go out in the fog, myself. The new creature does. It goes out in all weathers, and stumps right in with its muddy feet. And talks. It used to be so pleasant and quiet here.

SUNDAY—Pulled through. This day is getting to be more and more trying. It was selected and set apart last November[3] as a day of rest. I already had six of them per week before. This is another of those unaccountable things. There seems to be too much legislation, too much fussing, and fixing, and tidying-up, and not enough of the better-let-well-enough-alone policy. [*Mem.*—Must keep that sort of opinions to myself.] This morning found the new creature trying to clod apples out of that forbidden tree.

MONDAY—The new creature says its name is Eve. That is all right, I have no objections. Says it is to call it by when I want it to come. I said it was superfluous, then. The word evidently raised me in its respect; and indeed it is a large, good word and will bear repetition. It says it is not an It, it is a She. This is probably doubtful; yet it is all one to me; what she is were nothing to me if she would but go by herself and not talk.

TUESDAY—She has littered the whole estate with execrable names and offensive signs:

☞THIS WAY TO THE WHIRLPOOL.
☞THIS WAY TO GOAT ISLAND.
☞CAVE OF THE WINDS THIS WAY.

She says this park would make a tidy summer resort, if there were any custom for it. Summer resort—another invention of hers—just words, without any meaning. What is a summer resort? But it is best not to ask her, she has such a rage for explaining.

FRIDAY—She has taken to begging and imploring me to stop going over the Falls. What harm does it do? Says it makes her shudder. I wonder why; I have always done it—always liked the plunge, and the excitement and the coolness. I supposed it was what the Falls were for. They have no other use that I can see, and they must have been made for something. She says they were only made for scenery—like the rhinoceros and the mastodon.

I went over the Falls in a barrel—not satisfactory to her. Went over in a tub—still not satisfactory. Swam the Whirlpool and the Rapids in a fig-leaf suit. It got much damaged. Hence, tedious complaints about my extravagance. I am too much hampered here. What I need is change of scene.

SATURDAY—I escaped last Tuesday night, and traveled two days, and built me another shelter, in a secluded place, and obliterated my tracks as well as I could, but she hunted me out by means of a beast which she has tamed and calls a wolf, and came making that pitiful noise again, and shedding that water out of the places she looks with. I was obliged to return with her, but will presently emigrate again, when occasion offers. She engages herself in many foolish things: among others, trying to study out why the animals called lions and tigers live on grass and flowers, when, as she says, the sort of teeth they wear would indicate that they were intended to eat each other.[4] This is foolish, because to do that would be to kill each other, and that would introduce what, as I understand it, is called "death"; and death, as I have been told, has not yet entered the Park. Which is a pity, on some accounts.

SUNDAY—Pulled through.

MONDAY—I believe I see what the week is for: it is to give time to rest up from the weariness of Sunday. It seems a good idea, in a region where good ideas are rather conspicuously scarce. [*Mem.*—Must keep this sort of remarks private.] .... She has been climbing that tree again. Clodded her out of it. She said nobody was looking. Seems to consider that a sufficient justification for chancing any dangerous thing. Told her that. The word justification moved her admiration—and envy, too, I thought. It is a good word.

THURSDAY—She told me she was made out of a rib taken from my body. This is at least doubtful, if not more than that. I have not missed any rib.... She is in much trouble about the buzzard; says grass does not agree with it; is afraid she can't raise it; thinks it was intended to live on decayed flesh. The buzzard must get along the best it can with what is provided. We cannot overturn the whole scheme to accommodate the buzzard.

SATURDAY—She fell in the pond yesterday, when she was looking at herself in it, which she is always doing. She nearly strangled, and said it was most uncomfortable. This made her sorry for the creatures which live in there, which she calls fish, for she continues to fasten names on to things that don't need them and don't come when they are called by them, which is a matter of no consequence to her, she is such a fool anyway; so she got a lot of them out and brought them in and put them in my bed to keep warm, but I have noticed them now and then all day and I don't see that they are any happier there than they were before. When night comes I shall throw them outdoors. I will not sleep with them, for I find them clammy and unpleasant to lie among when a person hasn't anything on.

SUNDAY—Pulled through.

TUESDAY—She has taken up with a snake now. The other animals are glad, for she was always experimenting with them and bothering them; and I am glad, because the snake talks, and this enables me to get a rest.

FRIDAY—She says the snake advises her to try the fruit of that tree, and says the result will be a great and fine and noble education. I told her there would be another result, too—it would introduce death into the world. That was a mistake—it had been better to keep the remark to myself; it only gave her an idea—she could save the sick buzzard, and furnish fresh meat to the despondent lions and tigers. I advised her to keep away from the tree. She said she wouldn't. I foresee trouble. Will emigrate.

WEDNESDAY—I have had a variegated time. I escaped that night, and rode a horse all night as fast as he could go, hoping to get clear out of the Garden and hide in some other country before the trouble should begin; but it was not to be. About an hour after sun-up, as I was riding through a flowery plain where thousands of animals were grazing, slumbering, or playing with each other, according to their common wont, all of a sudden they broke into a tempest of frightful noises, and in one moment the plain was a frantic commotion and every beast was destroying its neighbor. I knew what it meant—Eve had eaten that fruit, and death was come into the world. . . . . The tigers ate my horse, paying no attention when I ordered them to desist, and they would even have eaten me if I had stayed—which I didn't, but went away in much haste. . . . . I found this place, outside the Garden, and was fairly comfortable for a few days, but she has found me out. Found me out, and has named the place Tonawanda—says it *looks* like that. In fact I was not sorry she came, for there are but meagre pickings here, and she brought some of those apples. I was obliged to eat them, I was so hungry. It was against my principles, but I find that principles have no real force except when one is well fed. . . . She came curtained in boughs and bunches of leaves, and when I asked her what she meant by such nonsense, and snatched them away and threw them down, she tittered and blushed. I had never seen a person titter and blush before, and to me it seemed unbecoming and idiotic. She said I would soon know how it was myself. This was correct. Hungry as I was, I laid down the apple half eaten—certainly the best one I ever saw, considering the lateness of the season—and arrayed myself in the discarded boughs and branches, and then spoke to her with some severity and ordered her to go and get some more and not make such a spectacle of herself. She did it, and after this we crept down to where the wild-beast battle had been, and collected some skins, and I made her patch together a couple of suits proper for public occasions. They are uncomfortable, it is true, but stylish, and that is the main point about clothes.... I find she is a good deal of a companion. I see I should be lonesome and depressed without her, now that I have lost my property. Another thing, she says it is ordered that we work for our living hereafter. She will be useful. I will superintend.

TEN DAYS LATER—She accuses *me* of being the cause of our disaster! She says, with apparent sincerity and truth, that the Serpent assured her that the forbidden fruit was not apples, it was chestnuts. I said I was innocent, then, for I had not eaten any chestnuts. She said the Serpent informed her that "chestnut" was a figurative term meaning an aged and mouldy joke. I turned pale at that, for I have made many jokes to pass the weary time, and some of them could have been of that sort, though I had honestly supposed they were new when I made them. She asked me if I had made one just at the time of the catastrophe. I was obliged to admit that I had made one to myself, though not aloud. It was this. I was thinking about the Falls, and I said to myself, "How wonderful it is to see that vast body of water tumble down there!" Then in an instant a bright thought flashed into my head, and I let it fly, saying, "It would be a deal more wonderful to see it tumble *up* there!"—and I was just about to kill myself with laughing at it when all nature broke loose in war and death and I had to flee for my life. "There," she said, with triumph, "that is just it; the Serpent mentioned that very jest, and called it the First Chestnut, and said it was coeval with the creation." Alas, I am indeed to blame. Would that I were not witty; oh, would that I had never had that radiant thought!

NEXT YEAR—We have named it Cain. She caught it while I was up country trapping on the North Shore of the Erie; caught it in the timber a couple of miles from our dug-out—or it might have been four, she isn't certain which. It resembles us in some ways, and may be a relation. That is what she thinks, but this is an error, in my judgment. The difference in size warrants the conclusion that it is a different and new kind of animal—a fish, perhaps, though when I put it in the water to see, it sank, and she plunged in and snatched it out before there was opportunity for the experiment to determine the matter. I still think it is a fish, but she is indifferent about what it is, and will not let me have it to try. I do not understand this. The coming of the creature seems to have changed her whole nature and made her unreasonable about experiments. She thinks more of it than she does of any of the other animals, but is not able to explain why. Her mind is disordered—everything shows it. Sometimes she carries the fish in her arms half the night when it complains and wants to get to the water. At such times the water comes out of the places in her face that she looks out of, and she pats the fish on the back and makes soft sounds with her mouth to soothe it, and betrays sorrow and solicitude in a hundred ways. I have never seen her do like this with any other fish, and it troubles me greatly. She used to carry the young tigers around so, and play with them, before we lost our property, but it was only play; she never took on about them like this when their dinner disagreed with them.

SUNDAY—She don't work, Sundays, but lies around all tired out, and likes to have the fish wallow over her; and she makes fool noises to amuse it, and pretends to chew its paws, and that makes it laugh. I have not seen a fish before that could laugh. This makes me doubt.... I have come to like Sunday myself. Superintending all the week tires a body so. There ought to be more Sundays. In the old days they were tough, but now they come handy.

WEDNESDAY—It isn't a fish. I cannot quite make out what it is. It makes curious devilish noises when not satisfied, and says "goo-goo" when it is. It is not one of us, for it doesn't walk; it is not a bird, for it doesn't fly; it is not a frog, for it doesn't hop; it is not a snake, for it doesn't crawl; I feel sure it is not a fish, though I cannot get a chance to find out whether it can swim or not. It merely lies around, and mostly on its back, with its feet up. I have not seen any other animal do that before. I said I believed it was an enigma; but she only admired the word without understanding it. In my judgment it is either an enigma or some kind of a bug. If it dies, I will take it apart and see what its arrangements are. I never had a thing perplex me so.

THREE MONTHS LATER—The perplexity merely augments instead of diminishing. I sleep but little. It has ceased from lying around, and goes about on its four legs, now. Yet it differs from the other four-legged animals, in that its front legs are unusually short, consequently this causes the main part of its person to stick up uncomfortably high in the air, and this is not attractive. It is built much as we are, but its method of traveling shows that it is not of our breed. The short front legs and long hind ones indicate that it is of the kangaroo family, but it is a marked variation of the species, since the true kangaroo hops, whereas this one never does. Still it is a curious and interesting variety, and has not been catalogued before. As I discovered it, I have felt justified in securing the credit of the discovery by attaching my name to it, and hence have called it *Kangaroorum Adamiensis.* .... It must have been a young one when it came, for it has grown exceedingly since. It must be five times as big, now, as it was then, and when discontented is able to make from twenty-two to thirty-eight times the noise it made at first. Coercion does not modify this, but has the contrary effect. For this reason I discontinued the system. She reconciles it by persuasion, and by giving it things which she had told it she wouldn't give it before. As observed previously, I was not at home when it first came, and she told me she found it in the woods. It seems odd that it should be the only one, yet it must be so, for I have worn myself out these many weeks trying to find another one to add to my collection, and for this one to play with; for surely then it would be quieter and we could tame it more easily. But I find none, nor any vestige of any; and strangest of all, no tracks. It has to live on the ground, it cannot help itself; therefore, how does it get about without leaving a track? I have set a dozen traps, but they do no good. I catch all small animals except that one; animals that merely go into the trap out of curiosity, I think, to see what the milk is there for. They never drink it.

THREE MONTHS LATER—The Kangaroo still continues to grow, which is very strange and perplexing. I never knew one to be so long getting its growth. It has fur on its head now; not like kangaroo fur, but exactly like our hair except that it is much finer and softer, and instead of being black is red. I am like to lose my mind over the capricious and harassing developments of this unclassifiable zoological freak. If I could catch another one—but that is hopeless; it is a new variety, and the only sample; this is plain. But I caught a true kangaroo and brought it in, thinking that this one, being lonesome, would rather have that for company than have no kin at all, or any animal it could feel a nearness to or get sympathy from in its forlorn condition here among strangers who do not know its ways or habits, or what to do to make it feel that it is among friends; but it was a mistake—it went into such fits at the sight of the kangaroo that I was convinced it had never seen one before. I pity the poor noisy little animal, but there is nothing I can do to make it happy. If I could tame it—but that is out of the question; the more I try the worse I seem to make it. It grieves me to the heart to see it in its little storms of sorrow and passion. I wanted to let it go, but she wouldn't hear of it. That seemed cruel and not like her; and yet she may be right. It might be lonelier than ever; for since I cannot find another one, how could *it*?

FIVE MONTHS LATER—It is not a kangaroo. No, for it supports itself by holding to her finger, and thus goes a few steps on its hind legs, and then falls down. It is probably some kind of a bear; and yet it has no tail—as yet—and no fur, except on its head. It still keeps on growing—that is a curious circumstance, for bears get their growth earlier than this. Bears are dangerous—since our catastrophe—and I shall not be satisfied to have this one prowling about the place much longer without a muzzle on. I have offered to get her a kangaroo if she would let this one go, but it did no good—she is determined to run us into all sorts of foolish risks, I think. She was not like this before she lost her mind.

A FORTNIGHT LATER—I examined its mouth. There is no danger yet; it has only one tooth. It has no tail yet. It makes more noise now than it ever did before—and mainly at night. I have moved out. But I shall go over, mornings, to breakfast, and to see if it has more teeth. If it gets a mouthful of teeth it will be time for it to go, tail or no tail, for a bear does not need a tail in order to be dangerous.

FOUR MONTHS LATER—I have been off hunting and fishing a month, up in the region that she calls Buffalo; I don't know why, unless it is because there are not any buffalos there. Meantime the bear has learned to paddle around all by itself on its hind legs, and says "poppa" and "momma." It is certainly a new species. This resemblance to words may be purely accidental, of course, and may have no purpose or meaning; but even in that case it is still extraordinary, and is a thing which no other bear can do. This imitation of speech, taken together with general absence of fur and entire absence of tail, sufficiently indicates that this is a new kind of bear. The further study of it will be exceedingly interesting. Meantime I will go off on a far expedition among the forests of the north and make an exhaustive search. There must certainly be another one somewhere, and this one will be less dangerous when it has company of its own species. I will go straightway; but I will muzzle this one first.

THREE MONTHS LATER—It has been a weary, weary hunt, yet I have had no success. In the meantime, without stirring from the home-estate, she has caught another one! I never saw such luck. I might have hunted these woods a hundred years, I never would have run across that thing.

NEXT DAY—I have been comparing the new one with the old one, and it is perfectly plain that they are the same breed. I was going to stuff one of them for my collection, but she is prejudiced against it for some reason or other; so I have relinquished the idea, though I think it is a mistake. It would be an irreparable loss to science if they should get away. The old one is tamer than it was, and can laugh and talk like the parrot, having learned this, no doubt, from being with the parrot so much, and having the imitative faculty in a highly developed degree. I shall be astonished if it turns out to be a new kind of parrot; and yet I ought not to be astonished, for it has already been everything else it could think of, since those first days when it was a fish. The new one is as ugly now as the old one was at first; has the same sulphur-and-raw-meat complexion and the same singular head without any fur on it. She calls it Abel.

TEN YEARS LATER—They are boys; we found it out long ago. It was their coming in that small, immature shape that fooled us; we were not used to it. There are some girls now. Abel is a good boy, but if Cain had stayed a bear it would have improved him. After all these years, I see that I was mistaken about Eve in the beginning; it is better to live outside the Garden with her than inside it without her. At first I thought she talked too much; but now I should be sorry to have that voice fall silent and pass out of my life. Blessed be the chestnut that brought us near together and taught me to know the goodness of her heart and the sweetness of her spirit![5]

[1893]

The Man That Corrupted Hadleyburg

I

It was many years ago. Hadleyburg was the most honest and upright town in all the region round about. It had kept that reputation unsmirched during three generations, and was prouder of it than of any other of its possessions. It was so proud of it, and so anxious to insure its perpetuation, that it began to teach the principles of honest dealing to its babies in the cradle, and made the like teachings the staple of their culture thenceforward through all the years devoted to their education. Also, throughout the formative years temptations were kept out of the way of the young people, so that their honesty could have every chance to harden and solidify, and become a part of their very bone. The neighboring towns were jealous of this honorable supremacy, and affected to sneer at Hadleyburg's pride in it and call it vanity; but all the same they were obliged to acknowledge that Hadleyburg was in reality an incorruptible town; and if pressed they would also acknowledge that the mere fact that a young man hailed from Hadleyburg was all the recommendation he needed when he went forth from his natal town to seek for responsible employment.

But at last, in the drift of time, Hadleyburg had the ill luck to offend a passing stranger—possibly without knowing it, certainly without caring, for Hadleyburg was sufficient unto itself, and cared not a rap for strangers or their opinions. Still, it would have been well to make an ex-

"It lit up his whole head with an evil joy."

ception in this one's case, for he was a bitter man and revengeful. All through his wanderings during a whole year he kept his injury in mind, and gave all his leisure moments to trying to invent a compensating satisfaction for it. He contrived many plans, and all of them were good, but none of them was quite sweeping enough; the poorest of them would hurt a great many individuals, but what he wanted was a plan which would comprehend the entire town, and not let so much as one person escape unhurt. At last he had a fortunate idea, and when it fell into his brain it lit up his whole head with an evil joy. He began to form a plan at once, saying to himself, "That is the thing to do—I will corrupt the town."

Six months later he went to Hadleyburg, and arrived in a buggy at the house of the old cashier of the bank about ten at night. He got a sack out of the buggy, shouldered it, and staggered with it through the cottage yard, and knocked at the door. A woman's voice said "Come in," and he entered, and set his sack behind the stove in the parlor, saying politely to the old lady who sat reading the *Missionary Herald*[1] by the lamp:

"Pray keep your seat, madam, I will not disturb you. There—now it is pretty well concealed; one would hardly know it was there. Can I see your husband a moment, madam?"

No, he was gone to Brixton, and might not return before morning.

"Very well, madam, it is no matter. I merely wanted to leave that sack in his care, to be delivered to the rightful owner when he shall be found. I am a stranger; he does not know me; I am merely passing through the town to-night to discharge a matter which has been long in my mind. My errand is now completed, and I go pleased and a little proud, and you will never see me again. There is a paper attached to the sack which will explain everything. Good-night, madam."

The old lady was afraid of the mysterious big stranger, and was glad to see him go. But her curiosity was roused, and she went straight to the sack and brought away the paper. It began as follows:

> "TO BE PUBLISHED; or, the right man sought out by private inquiry—either will answer. This sack contains gold coin weighing a hundred and sixty pounds four ounces—"

"Mercy on us, and the door not locked!"

Mrs. Richards flew to it all in a tremble and locked it, then pulled down the window-shades and stood frightened, worried, and wondering if there was anything else she could do toward making herself and the money more safe. She listened awhile for burglars, then surrendered to curiosity and went back to the lamp and finished reading the paper:

> "I am a foreigner, and am presently going back to my own country, to remain there permanently. I am grateful to America for what I have received at her hands during my long stay under her flag; and to one of her citizens—a citizen of Hadleyburg—I am especially grateful for a great kindness done me a year or two ago. Two great kindnesses, in fact. I will explain. I was a gambler. I say I *was.* I was a ruined gambler. I arrived in this village at night, hungry and without a penny. I asked for help—in the dark; I was ashamed to beg in the light. I begged of the right man. He gave me twenty dollars—that is to say, he gave me life, as I considered it. He also gave me fortune; for out of that money I have made myself rich at the gaming-table. And finally, a remark which he made to me has remained with me to this day, and has at last conquered me; and in conquering has saved the remnant of my morals: I shall gamble no more. Now I have no idea who that man was, but I want him found, and I want him to have this money, to give away, throw away, or keep, as he pleases. It is merely my way of testifying my gratitude to him. If I could stay, I would find him myself; but no matter, he will be found. This is an honest town, an incorruptible town, and I know I can trust it without fear. This man can be identified by the remark which he made to me; I feel persuaded that he will remember it.
>
> "And now my plan is this: If you prefer to conduct the inquiry privately, do so. Tell the contents of this present writing to any one who is likely to be the right man. If he shall answer, 'I am the man; the remark I made was so-and-so,' apply the test—to wit: open the sack, and in it you will find a

sealed envelope containing that remark. If the remark mentioned by the candidate tallies with it, give him the money, and ask no further questions, for he is certainly the right man.

"But if you shall prefer a public inquiry, then publish this present writing in the local paper—with these instructions added, to wit: Thirty days from now, let the candidate appear at the town-hall at eight in the evening (Friday), and hand his remark, in a sealed envelope, to the Rev. Mr. Burgess (if he will be kind enough to act); and let Mr. Burgess there and then destroy the seals of the sack, open it, and see if the remark is correct; if correct, let the money be delivered, with my sincere gratitude, to my benefactor thus identified."

Mrs. Richards sat down, gently quivering with excitement, and was soon lost in thinkings—after this pattern: "What a strange thing it is! .... And what a fortune for that kind man who set his bread afloat upon the waters![2] .... If it had only been my husband that did it!—for we are so poor, so old and poor! ...." Then, with a sigh—"But it was not my Edward; no, it was not he that gave a stranger twenty dollars. It is a pity too; I see it now...." Then, with a shudder—"But it is *gambler's* money! the wages of sin; we couldn't take it; we couldn't touch it. I don't like to be near it; it seems a defilement." She moved to a farther chair.... "I wish Edward would come, and take it to the bank; a burglar might come at any moment; it is dreadful to be here all alone with it."

At eleven Mr. Richards arrived, and while his wife was saying, "I am *so* glad you've come!" he was saying, "I'm so tired—tired clear out; it is dreadful to be poor, and have to make these dismal journeys at my time of life. Always at the grind, grind, grind, on a salary—another man's slave, and he sitting at home in his slippers, rich and comfortable."

"I am so sorry for you, Edward, you know that; but be comforted; we have our livelihood; we have our good name—"

"Yes, Mary, and that is everything. Don't mind my talk—it's just a moment's irritation and doesn't mean anything. Kiss me—there, it's all gone now, and I am not complaining any more. What have you been getting? What's in the sack?"

Then his wife told him the great secret. It dazed him for a moment; then he said:

"It weighs a hundred and sixty pounds? Why, Mary, it's for-ty thousand dollars—think of it—a whole fortune! Not ten men in this village are worth that much. Give me the paper."

He skimmed through it and said:

"Isn't it an adventure! Why, it's a romance; it's like the impossible things one reads about in books, and never sees in life." He was well stirred up now; cheerful, even gleeful. He tapped his old wife on the cheek, and said, humorously, "Why, we're rich, Mary, rich; all we've got to do is to bury the money and burn the papers. If the gambler ever comes to inquire, we'll merely look coldly upon him and say: 'What is this nonsense you are talking? We have never heard of you and your sack of gold before'; and then he would look foolish, and—"

"And in the mean time, while you are running on with your jokes, the money is still here, and it is fast getting along toward burglar-time."

"True. Very well, what shall we do—make the inquiry private? No, not that; it would spoil the romance. The public method is better. Think what a noise it will make! And it will make all the other towns jealous; for no stranger would trust such a thing to any town but Hadleyburg, and they know it. It's a great card for us. I must get to the printing-office now, or I shall be too late."

"But stop—stop—don't leave me here alone with it, Edward!"

But he was gone. For only a little while, however. Not far from his own house he met the editor-proprietor of the paper, and gave him the document, and said, "Here is a good thing for you, Cox—put it in."

"It may be too late, Mr. Richards, but I'll see."

At home again he and his wife sat down to talk the charming mystery over; they were in no condition for sleep. The first question was, Who could the citizen have been who gave the stranger the twenty dollars? It seemed a simple one; both answered it in the same breath—

"Barclay Goodson."

"Yes," said Richards, "he could have done it, and it would have been like him, but there's not another in the town."

"Everybody will grant that, Edward—grant it privately, anyway. For six months, now, the village has been its own proper self once more—honest, narrow, self-righteous, and stingy."

"It is what he always called it, to the day of his death—said it right out publicly, too."

"Yes, and he was hated for it."

"Oh, of course; but he didn't care. I reckon he was the best-hated man among us, except the Reverend Burgess."

"Well, Burgess deserves it—he will never get another congregation here. Mean as the town is, it knows how to estimate *him.* Edward, doesn't it seem odd that the stranger should appoint Burgess to deliver the money?"

"Well, yes—it does. That is—that is—"

"Why so much that-*is*-ing? Would *you* select him?"

"Mary, maybe the stranger knows him better than this village does."

"Much *that* would help Burgess!"

The husband seemed perplexed for an answer; the wife kept a steady eye upon him, and waited. Finally Richards said, with the hesitancy of one who is making a statement which is likely to encounter doubt,

"Mary, Burgess is not a bad man."

His wife was certainly surprised.

"Nonsense!" she exclaimed.

"He is not a bad man. I know. The whole of his unpopularity had its foundation in that one thing—the thing that made so much noise."

"That 'one thing,' indeed! As if that 'one thing' wasn't enough, all by itself."

"Plenty. Plenty. Only he wasn't guilty of it."

"How you talk! Not guilty of it! Everybody knows he *was* guilty."

"Mary, I give you my word—he was innocent."

"I can't believe it, and I don't. How do you know?"

"It is a confession. I am ashamed, but I will make it. I was the only man who knew he was innocent. I could have saved him, and—and—well, you know how the town was wrought up—I hadn't the pluck to do it. It would have turned everybody against me. I felt mean, ever so mean; but I didn't dare; I hadn't the manliness to face that."

Mary looked troubled, and for a while was silent. Then she said, stammeringly:

"I—I don't think it would have done for you to—to—One mustn't—er—public opinion—one has to be so careful—so—" It was a difficult road, and she got mired; but after a little she got started again. "It was a great pity, but—Why, we couldn't afford it, Edward—we couldn't indeed. Oh, I wouldn't have had you do it for anything!"

"It would have lost us the good-will of so many people, Mary; and then—and then—"

"What troubles me now is, what *he* thinks of us, Edward."

"He? *He* doesn't suspect that I could have saved him."

"Oh," exclaimed the wife, in a tone of relief, "I am glad of that. As long as he doesn't know that you could have saved him, he—he—well, that makes it a great deal better. Why, I might have known he didn't know, because he is always trying to be friendly with us, as little encouragement as we give him. More than once people have twitted me with it. There's the Wilsons, and the Wilcoxes, and the Harknesses, they take a mean pleasure in saying, '*Your friend* Burgess,' because they know it pesters me. I wish he wouldn't persist in liking us so; I can't think why he keeps it up."

"I can explain it. It's another confession. When the thing was new and hot, and the town made a plan to ride him on a rail, my conscience hurt me so that I couldn't stand it, and I went privately and gave him notice, and he got out of the town and staid out till it was safe to come back."

"Edward! If the town had found it out—"

"*Don't!* It scares me yet, to think of it. I repented of it the minute it was done; and I was even afraid to tell you, lest your face might betray it to somebody. I didn't sleep any that night, for worrying. But after a few days I saw that no one was going to suspect me, and after that I got to feeling glad I did it. And I feel glad yet, Mary—glad through and through."

"So do I, now, for it would have been a dreadful way to treat him. Yes, I'm glad; for really you did owe him that, you know. But, Edward, suppose it should come out yet, some day!"

"It won't."

"Why?"

"Because everybody thinks it was Goodson."

"Of course they would!"

"Certainly. And of course *he* didn't care. They persuaded poor old Sawlsberry to go and charge it on him, and he went blustering over there and did it. Goodson looked him over, like as if he was hunting for a place on him that he could despise the most, then he says, 'So you are the Committee of Inquiry, are you?' Sawlsberry said that was about what he was. 'Hm. Do they require particulars, or do you reckon a kind of a *general* answer will do?' 'If they require particulars, I will come back, Mr. Goodson; I will take the general answer first.' 'Very well, then, tell them to go to hell—I reckon that's general enough. And I'll give you some advice, Sawlsberry: when you come back for the particulars, fetch a basket to carry the relics of yourself home in.' "

"Just like Goodson; it's got all the marks. He had only one vanity; he thought he could give advice better than any other person."

"It settled the business, and saved us, Mary. The subject was dropped."

"Bless you, I'm not doubting *that.*"

Then they took up the gold-sack mystery again, with strong interest. Soon the conversation began to suffer breaks—interruptions caused by absorbed thinkings. The breaks grew more and more frequent. At last Richards lost himself wholly in thought. He sat long, gazing vacantly at the floor, and by-and-by he began to punctuate his thoughts with little nervous movements of his hands that seemed to indicate vexation. Meantime his wife too had relapsed into a thoughtful silence, and her movements were beginning to show a troubled discomfort. Finally Richards got up and strode aimlessly about the room, ploughing his hands through his hair, much as a somnambulist might do who was having a bad dream. Then he seemed to arrive at a definite purpose; and without a word he put on his hat and passed quickly out of the house. His wife sat brooding, with a drawn face, and did not seem to be aware that she was alone. Now and then she murmured, "Lead us not into t.... but—but—we are so poor, so poor! .... Lead us not into.... Ah, who would be hurt by it?—and no one would ever know.... Lead us...." The voice died out in mumblings. After a little she glanced up and muttered in a half-frightened, half-glad way—

"He is gone! But, oh dear, he may be too late—too late.... Maybe not—maybe there is still time." She rose and stood thinking, nervously clasping and unclasping her hands. A slight shudder shook her frame, and she said, out of a dry throat, "God forgive me—it's awful to think such things—but.... Lord, how we are made—how strangely we are made!"

She turned the light low, and slipped stealthily over and kneeled down by the sack and felt of its ridgy sides with her hands, and fondled them lovingly; and there was a gloating light in her poor old eyes. She fell into fits of absence; and came half out of them at times to mutter, "If we had only waited!—oh, if we had only waited a little, and not been in such a hurry!"

Meantime Cox had gone home from his office and told his wife all about the strange thing that had happened, and they had talked it over eagerly, and guessed that the late Goodson was the only man in the town who could have helped a suffering stranger with so noble a sum as twenty dollars. Then there was a pause, and the two became thoughtful and silent. And by-and-by nervous and fidgety. At last the wife said, as if to herself,

"Nobody knows this secret but the Richardses.... and us.... nobody."

The husband came out of his thinkings with a slight start, and gazed wistfully at his wife, whose face was become very pale; then he hesitatingly rose, and glanced furtively at his hat, then at his wife—a sort of mute inquiry. Mrs. Cox swallowed once or twice, with her hand at her throat, then in place of speech she nodded her head. In a moment she was alone, and mumbling to herself.

And now Richards and Cox were hurrying through the deserted streets, from opposite directions. They met, panting, at the foot of the printing-office stairs; by the night-light there they read each other's face. Cox whispered,

"Nobody knows about this but us?"

The whispered answer was,

"Not a soul—on honor, not a soul!"

"If it isn't too late to—"

The men were starting up stairs; at this moment they were overtaken by a boy, and Cox asked,

"Is that you, Johnny?"

"Yes, sir."

"You needn't ship the early mail—nor *any* mail; wait till I tell you."

"It's already gone, sir."

"Gone?" It had the sound of an unspeakable disappointment in it.

"Yes, sir. Time-table for Brixton and all the towns beyond changed to-day, sir—had to get the papers in twenty minutes earlier than common. I had to rush; if I had been two minutes later—"

The men turned and walked slowly away, not waiting to hear the rest. Neither of them spoke during ten minutes; then Cox said, in a vexed tone,

"What possessed you to be in such a hurry, *I* can't make out."

The answer was humble enough:

"I see it now, but somehow I never thought, you know, until it was too late. But the next time—"

"Next time be hanged! It won't come in a thousand years."

Then the friends separated without a good-night, and dragged themselves home with the gait of mortally stricken men. At their homes their wives sprang up with an eager "Well?"—then saw the answer with their eyes and sank down sorrowing, without waiting for it to come in words. In both houses a discussion followed of a heated sort—a new thing; there had been discussions before, but not heated ones, not ungentle ones. The discussions to-night were a sort of seeming plagiarisms of each other. Mrs. Richards said,

"If you had only waited, Edward—if you had only stopped to think; but no, you must run straight to the printing-office and spread it all over the world."

"It *said* publish it."

"That is nothing; it also said do it privately, if you liked. There, now—is that true, or not?"

"Why, yes—yes, it is true; but when I thought what a stir it would make, and what a compliment it was to Hadleyburg that a stranger should trust it so—"

"Oh, certainly, I know all that; but if you had only stopped to think, you would have seen that you *couldn't* find the right man, because he is in his grave, and hasn't left chick nor child nor relation behind him; and as long as the money went to somebody that awfully needed it, and nobody would be hurt by it, and—and—"

She broke down, crying. Her husband tried to think of some comforting thing to say, and presently came out with this:

"But after all, Mary, it must be for the best—it *must* be; we know that. And we must remember that it was so ordered—"

"Ordered! Oh, everything's *ordered,* when a person has to find some way out when he has been stupid. Just the same, it was *ordered* that the money should come to us in this special way, and it was you that must take it on yourself to go meddling with the designs of Providence—and who gave you the right. It was wicked, that is what it was—just blasphemous presumption, and no more becoming to a meek and humble professor of—"

"But, Mary, you know how we have been trained all our lives long, like the whole village, till it is absolutely second nature to us to stop not a single moment to think when there's an honest thing to be done—"

"Oh, I know it, I know it—it's been one everlasting training and training and training in honesty—honesty shielded, from the very cradle, against every possible temptation, and so it's *artificial* honesty, and weak as water when temptation comes, as we have seen this night. God knows I never had shade nor shadow of a doubt of my petrified and indestructible honesty until now—and now, under the very first big and real temptation, I—Edward, it is my belief that this town's honesty is as rotten as mine is; as rotten as yours is. It is a mean town, a hard, stingy town, and hasn't a virtue in the world but this honesty it is so celebrated for and so conceited about; and so help me, I do believe that if ever the day comes that its honesty falls under great temptation, its grand reputation will go to ruin like a house of cards. There, now, I've made confession, and I feel better; I am a humbug, and I've been one all my life, without knowing it. Let no man call me honest again—I will not have it."

"I— Well, Mary, I feel a good deal as you do; I certainly do. It seems strange, too, so strange. I never could have believed it—never."

A long silence followed; both were sunk in thought. At last the wife looked up and said,

"I know what you are thinking, Edward."

Richards had the embarrassed look of a person who is caught.

"I am ashamed to confess it, Mary, but—"

"It's no matter, Edward, I was thinking the same question myself."

"I hope so. State it."

"You were thinking, if a body could only guess out *what the remark was* that Goodson made to the stranger."

"It's perfectly true. I feel guilty and ashamed. And you?"

"I'm past it. Let us make a pallet here; we've got to stand watch till the bank vault opens in the morning and admits the sack.... Oh, dear, oh, dear—if we hadn't made the mistake!"

The pallet was made, and Mary said:

"The open sesame—what could it have been? I do wonder what that remark could have been? But come; we will get to bed now."

"And sleep?"

"No; think."

"Yes, think."

By this time the Coxes too had completed their spat and their reconciliation, and were turning in—to think, to think, and toss, and fret, and worry over what the remark could possibly have been which Goodson made to the stranded derelict: that golden remark; that remark worth forty thousand dollars, cash.

The reason that the village telegraph-office was open later than usual that night was this: The foreman of Cox's paper was the local representative of the Associated Press. One might say its honorary representative, for it wasn't four times a year that he could furnish thirty words that would be accepted. But this time it was different. His despatch stating what he had caught got an instant answer:

"Send the whole thing—all the details—twelve hundred words."

A colossal order! The foreman filled the bill; and he was the proudest man in the State. By breakfast-time the next morning the name of Hadleyburg the Incorruptible was on every lip in America, from Montreal to the Gulf, from the glaciers of Alaska to the orange-groves of Florida; and millions and millions of people were discussing the stranger and his money-sack, and wondering if the right man would be found, and hoping some more news about the matter would come soon—right away.

II

Hadleyburg village woke up world-celebrated—astonished—happy—vain. Vain beyond imagination. Its nineteen principal citizens[3] and their wives went about shaking hands with each other, and beaming, and smiling; and congratulating, and saying *this* thing adds a new word to the dictionary—*Hadleyburg,* synonym for *incorruptible*—destined to live in dictionaries forever! And the minor and unimportant citizens and their wives went around acting in much the same way. Everybody ran to the bank to see the gold-sack; and before noon grieved and envious crowds began to flock in from Brixton and all neighboring towns; and that afternoon and next day reporters began to arrive from everywhere to verify the sack and its history and write the whole thing up anew, and make dashing free-hand pictures of the sack, and of Richards's house, and the bank, and the Presbyterian church, and the Baptist church, and the public square, and the town-hall where the test would be applied and the money delivered; and damnable portraits of the Richardses, and Pinkerton the banker, and Cox, and the foreman, and Reverend Burgess, and the postmaster—and even of Jack Halliday, who was the loafing, good-natured, no-account, irreverent fisherman, hunter, boys' friend, stray-dogs' friend, typical "Sam Lawson"[4] of the town. The little mean, smirking, oily Pinkerton showed the sack to all comers, and rubbed his sleek palms together pleasantly, and enlarged upon the town's fine old reputation for honesty and upon this wonderful endorsement of it, and hoped and believed that the example would now spread far and wide over the American world, and be epoch-making in the matter of moral regeneration. And so on, and so on.

By the end of a week things had quieted down again; the wild intoxication of pride and joy had sobered to a soft, sweet, silent delight—a sort of deep, nameless, unutterable content. All faces bore a look of peaceful, holy happiness.

Then a change came. It was a gradual change: so gradual that its beginnings were hardly noticed; maybe were not noticed at all, except by Jack Halliday, who always noticed everything; and always made fun of it, too, no matter what it was. He began to throw out chaffing remarks about people not looking quite so happy as they did a day or two ago; and next he claimed that the new aspect was deepening to positive sadness; next, that it was taking on a sick look; and finally he said that everybody was become so moody, thoughtful, and absent-minded that he could rob the meanest man in town of a cent out of the bottom of his breeches pocket and not disturb his revery.

At this stage—or at about this stage—a saying like this was dropped at bedtime—with a sigh, usually—by the head of each of the nineteen principal households:

"Ah, what *could* have been the remark that Goodson made!"

And straightway—with a shudder—came this, from the man's wife:

"Oh, *don't*! What horrible thing are you mulling in your mind? Put it away from you, for God's sake!"

But that question was wrung from those men again the next night—and got the same retort. But weaker.

And the third night the men uttered the question yet again—with anguish, and absently. This time—and the following night—the wives fidgeted feebly, and tried to say something. But didn't.

And the night after that they found their tongues and responded—longingly,

"Oh, if we *could* only guess!"

Halliday's comments grew daily more and more sparklingly disagreeable and disparaging. He went diligently about, laughing at the town, individually and in mass. But his laugh was the only one left in the village: it fell upon a hollow and mournful vacancy and emptiness. Not even a smile was findable anywhere. Halliday carried a cigar-box around on a tripod, playing that it was a camera, and halted all passers and aimed the thing and said, "Ready!—now look pleasant, please," but not even this capital joke could surprise the dreary faces into any softening.

So three weeks passed—one week was left. It was Saturday evening—after supper. Instead of the aforetime Saturday-evening flutter and bustle and shopping and larking, the streets were empty and desolate. Richards and his old wife sat apart in their little parlor—miserable and thinking. This was become their evening habit now: the life-long habit which had preceded it, of reading, knitting, and contented chat, or receiving or paying neighborly calls, was dead and gone and forgotten, ages ago—two or three weeks ago; nobody talked now, nobody read, nobody visited—the whole village sat at home, sighing, worrying, silent. Trying to guess out that remark.

The postman left a letter. Richards glanced listlessly at the superscription and the post-mark—unfamiliar, both—and tossed the letter on the table and resumed his might-have-beens and his hopeless dull miseries where he had left them off. Two or three hours later his wife got wearily up and was going away to bed without a good-night—custom now—but she stopped near the letter and eyed it awhile with a dead interest, then broke it open, and began to skim it over. Richards, sitting there with his chair tilted back against the wall and his chin between his knees, heard something fall. It was his wife. He sprang to her side, but she cried out:

"Leave me alone, I am too happy. Read the letter—read it!"

He did. He devoured it, his brain reeling. The letter was from a distant State, and it said:

"I am a stranger to you, but no matter: I have something to tell. I have just arrived home from Mexico, and learned about that episode. Of course you do not know who made that remark, but I know, and I am the only person living who does know. It was *Goodson.* I knew him well, many years ago. I passed through your village that very night, and was his guest till the midnight train came along. I overheard him make that remark to the stranger in the dark—it was in Hale Alley. He and I talked of it the rest of the way home, and while smoking in his house. He mentioned many of your villagers in the course of his talk—most of them in a very uncomplimentary way, but two or three favorably: among these latter yourself. I say 'favorably'—nothing stronger. I remember his saying he did not actually *like* any person in the town—not one; but that you—I *think* he said you—am almost sure—had done him a very great service once, possibly without knowing the full value of it, and he wished he had a fortune, he would leave it to you when he died, and a curse apiece for the rest of the citizens. Now, then, if it was you that did him that service, you are his legitimate heir, and entitled to the sack of gold. I know that I can trust to your honor and honesty, for in a citizen of Hadleyburg these virtues are an unfailing inheritance, and so I am going to reveal to you the remark, well satisfied that if you are not the right man you will seek and find the right one and see that poor Goodson's debt of gratitude for the service referred to is paid. This is the remark: '*You are far from being a bad man: go, and reform.*'

HOWARD L. STEPHENSON"

"Oh, Edward, the money is ours, and I am so grateful, *oh,* so grateful—kiss me, dear, it's forever since we kissed—and we needed it so—the money—and now you are free of Pinkerton and his bank, and nobody's slave any more; it seems to me I could fly for joy."

It was a happy half-hour that the couple spent there on the settee caressing each other; it was the old days come again—days that had begun with their courtship and lasted without a break till the stranger brought the deadly money. By-and-by the wife said:

"Oh, Edward, how lucky it was you did him that grand service, poor Goodson! I never liked him, but I love him now. And it was fine and beautiful of you never to mention it or brag about it." Then, with a touch of reproach, "But you ought to have told *me,* Edward, you ought to have told your wife, you know."

"Well, I—er—well, Mary, you see—"

"Now stop hemming and hawing, and tell me about it, Edward. I always loved you, and now I'm proud of you. Everybody believes there was only one good generous soul in this village, and now it turns out that you—Edward, why don't you tell me?"

"Well—er—er—Why, Mary, I can't!"

"You *can't*? *Why* can't you?"

"You see, he—well, he—he made me promise I wouldn't."

The wife looked him over, and said, very slowly,

"Made—you—promise? Edward, what do you tell me that for?"

"Mary, do you think I would lie?"

She was troubled and silent for a moment, then she laid her hand within his and said:

"No.... no. We have wandered far enough from our bearings—God spare us that! In all your life you have never uttered a lie. But now—now that the foundations of things seem to be crumbling from under us, we—we—" She lost her voice for a moment, then said, brokenly, "Lead us not into temptation.... I think you made the promise, Edward. Let it rest so. Let us keep away from that ground. Now—that is all gone by; let us be happy again; it is no time for clouds."

Edward found it something of an effort to comply, for his mind kept wandering—trying to remember what the service was that he had done Goodson.

The couple lay awake the most of the night, Mary happy and busy, Edward busy, but not so happy. Mary was planning what she would do with the money. Edward was trying to recall that service. At first his conscience was sore on account of the lie he had told Mary—if it was a lie. After much reflection—suppose it *was* a lie? What then? Was it such a great matter? Aren't we always *acting* lies? Then why not *tell* them? Look at Mary—look what she had done. While he was hurrying off on his honest errand, what was she doing? Lamenting because the papers hadn't been destroyed and the money kept! Is theft better than lying?

That point lost its sting—the lie dropped into the background and left comfort behind it. The next point came to the front: *had* he rendered that service? Well, here was Goodson's own evidence as reported in Stephenson's letter; there could be no better evidence than that—it was even *proof* that he had rendered it. Of course. So that point was settled.... No, not quite. He recalled with a wince that this unknown Mr. Stephenson was just a trifle unsure as to whether the performer of it was Richards or some other—and, oh dear, he had put Richards on his honor! He must himself decide whither that money must go—and Mr.

Stephenson was not doubting that if he was the wrong man he would go honorably and find the right one. Oh, it was odious to put a man in such a situation—ah, why couldn't Stephenson have left out that doubt! What did he want to intrude that for?

Further reflection. How did it happen that *Richards's* name remained in Stephenson's mind as indicating the right man, and not some other man's name? That looked good. Yes, that looked very good. In fact, it went on looking better and better, straight along—until by-and-by it grew into positive *proof.* And then Richards put the matter at once out of his mind, for he had a private instinct that a proof once established is better left so.

He was feeling reasonably comfortable now, but there was still one other detail that kept pushing itself on his notice: of course he had done that service—that was settled; but what *was* that service? He must recall it—he would not go to sleep till he had recalled it; it would make his peace of mind perfect. And so he thought and thought. He thought of a dozen things—possible services, even probable services—but none of them seemed adequate, none of them seemed large enough, none of them seemed worth the money—worth the fortune Goodson had wished he could leave in his will. And besides, he couldn't remember having done them, anyway. Now, then—now, then—what *kind* of a service would it be that would make a man so inordinately grateful? Ah—the saving of his soul! That must be it. Yes, he could remember, now, how he once set himself the task of converting Goodson, and labored at it as much as—he was going to say three months; but upon closer examination it shrunk to a month, then to a week, then to a day, then to nothing. Yes, he remembered, now, and with unwelcome vividness, that Goodson had told him to go to thunder and mind his own business—*he* wasn't hankering to follow Hadleyburg to heaven!

So that solution was a failure—he hadn't saved Goodson's soul. Richards was discouraged. Then after a little came another idea: had he saved Goodson's property? No, that wouldn't do—he hadn't any. His life? That is it! Of course. Why, he might have thought of it before. This time he was on the right track, sure. His imagination-mill was hard at work in a minute, now.

Thereafter during a stretch of two exhausting hours he was busy saving Goodson's life. He saved it in all kinds of difficult and perilous ways. In every case he got it saved satisfactorily up to a certain point; then, just as he was beginning to get well persuaded that it had really happened, a troublesome detail would turn up which made the whole thing impossible. As in the matter of drowning, for instance. In that case he had swum out and tugged Goodson ashore in an unconscious state with a great crowd looking on and applauding, but when he had got it all thought out and was just beginning to remember all about it a whole swarm of disqualifying details arrived on the ground: the town would have known of the circumstance, Mary would have known of it, it would glare like a limelight in his own memory instead of being an inconspicuous service which he had possibly rendered "without knowing its full value." And at this point he remembered that he couldn't swim, anyway.

Ah—*there* was a point which he had been overlooking from the start: it had to be a service which he had rendered "possibly without knowing the full value of it." Why, really, that ought to be an easy hunt—much easier than those others. And sure enough, by-and-by he found it. Goodson, years and years ago, came near marrying a very sweet and pretty girl, named Nancy Hewitt, but in some way or other the match had been broken off; the girl died, Goodson remained a bachelor, and by-and-by became a soured one and a frank despiser of the human species. Soon after the girl's death the village found out, or thought it had found out, that she carried a spoonful of negro blood in her veins. Richards worked at these details a good while, and in the end he thought he remembered things concerning them which must have gotten mislaid in his memory through long neglect. He seemed to dimly remember that it was *he* that found out about the negro blood; that it was he that told the village; that the village told Goodson where they got it; that he thus saved Goodson from marrying the tainted girl; that he had done him this great service "without knowing the full value of it," in fact without knowing that he *was* doing it; but that Goodson knew the value of it, and what a narrow escape he had had, and so went to his grave grateful to his benefactor and wishing he had a fortune to leave him. It was all clear and simple now, and the more he went over it the more luminous and certain it grew; and at last, when he nestled to sleep satisfied and happy, he remembered the whole thing just as if it had been yesterday. In fact, he dimly remembered Goodson's *telling* him his gratitude once. Meantime Mary had spent six thousand dollars on a new house for herself and a pair of slippers for her pastor, and then had fallen peacefully to rest.

That same Saturday evening the postman had delivered a letter to each of the other principal citizens—nineteen letters in all. No two of the envelopes were alike, and no two of the superscriptions were in the same hand, but the letters inside were just like each other in every detail but one. They were exact copies of the letter received by Richards—

handwriting and all—and were all signed by Stephenson, but in place of Richards's name each receiver's own name appeared.

All night long eighteen principal citizens did what their caste-brother Richards was doing at the same time—they put in their energies trying to remember what notable service it was that they had unconsciously done Barclay Goodson. In no case was it a holiday job; still they succeeded.

And while they were at this work, which was difficult, their wives put in the night spending the money, which was easy. During that one night the nineteen wives spent an average of seven thousand dollars each out of the forty thousand in the sack—a hundred and thirty-three thousand altogether.

Next day there was a surprise for Jack Halliday. He noticed that the faces of the nineteen chief citizens and their wives bore that expression of peaceful and holy happiness again. He could not understand it, neither was he able to invent any remarks about it that could damage it or disturb it. And so it was his turn to be dissatisfied with life. His private guesses at the reasons for the happiness failed in all instances, upon examination. When he met Mrs. Wilcox and noticed the placid ecstasy in her face, he said to himself, "Her cat has had kittens"—and went and asked the cook; it was not so; the cook had detected the happiness, but did not know the cause. When Halliday found the duplicate ecstasy in the face of "Shadbelly" Billson (village nickname), he was sure some neighbor of Billson's had broken his leg, but inquiry showed that this had not happened. The subdued ecstasy in Gregory Yates's face could mean but one thing—he was a mother-in-law short; it was another mistake. "And Pinkerton—Pinkerton—he has collected ten cents that he thought he was going to lose." And so on, and so on. In some cases the guesses had to remain in doubt, in the others they proved distinct errors. In the end Halliday said to himself, "Anyway it foots up that there's nineteen Hadleyburg families temporarily in heaven; I don't know how it happened; I only know Providence is off duty to-day."

An architect and builder from the next State had lately ventured to set up a small business in this unpromising village, and his sign had now been hanging out a week. Not a customer yet; he was a discouraged man, and sorry he had come. But his weather changed suddenly now. First one and then another chief citizen's wife said to him privately:

"Come to my house Monday week—but say nothing about it for the present. We think of building."

He got eleven invitations that day. That night he wrote his daughter and broke off her match with her student. He said she could marry a mile higher than that.

Pinkerton the banker and two or three other well-to-do men planned country-seats—but waited. That kind don't count their chickens until they are hatched.

The Wilsons devised a grand new thing—a fancy-dress ball. They made no actual promises, but told all their acquaintanceship in confidence that they were thinking the matter over and thought they should give it—"and if we do, you will be invited, of course." People were surprised, and said, one to another, "Why, they are crazy, those poor Wilsons, they can't afford it." Several among the nineteen said privately to their husbands, "It is a good idea; we will keep still till their cheap thing is over, then *we* will give one that will make it sick."

The days drifted along, and the bill of future squanderings rose higher and higher, wilder and wilder, more and more foolish and reckless. It began to look as if every member of the nineteen would not only spend his whole forty thousand dollars before receiving-day, but be actually in debt by the time he got the money. In some cases light-headed people did not stop with planning to spend, they really spent—on credit. They bought land, mortgages, farms, speculative stocks, fine clothes, horses, and various other things, paid down the bonus, and made themselves liable for the rest—at ten days. Presently the sober second thought came, and Halliday noticed that a ghastly anxiety was beginning to show up in a good many faces. Again he was puzzled, and didn't know what to make of it. "The Wilcox kittens aren't dead, for they weren't born; nobody's broken a leg; there's no shrinkage in mother-in-laws; *nothing* has happened—it is an insolvable mystery."

There was another puzzled man, too—the Rev. Mr. Burgess. For days, wherever he went, people seemed to follow him or to be watching out for him; and if he ever found himself in a retired spot, a member of the nineteen would be sure to appear, thrust an envelope privately into his hand, whisper "To be opened at the town-hall Friday evening," then vanish away like a guilty thing. He was expecting that there might be one claimant for the sack—doubtful, however, Goodson being dead—but it never occurred to him that all this crowd might be claimants. When the great Friday came at last, he found that he had nineteen envelopes.

III

The town-hall had never looked finer. The platform at the end of it was backed by a showy draping of flags; at intervals along the walls were festoons of flags; the gallery fronts were clothed in flags; the supporting columns were swathed in flags; all this was to impress the stranger, for he would be there in considerable force, and in a large degree he would be connected with the press. The house was full. The 412 fixed seats were occupied; also the 68 extra chairs which had been packed into the aisles; the steps of the platform were occupied; some distinguished strangers were given seats on the platform; at the horseshoe of tables which fenced the front and sides of the platform sat a strong force of special correspondents who had come from everywhere. It was the best-dressed house the town had ever produced. There were some tolerably expensive toilets there, and in several cases the ladies who wore them had the look of being unfamiliar with that kind of clothes. At least the town thought they had that look, but the notion could have arisen from the town's knowledge of the fact that these ladies had never inhabited such clothes before.

The gold-sack stood on a little table at the front of the platform where all the house could see it. The bulk of the house gazed at it with a burning interest, a mouth-watering interest, a wistful and pathetic interest; a minority of nineteen couples gazed at it tenderly, lovingly, proprietarily, and the male half of this minority kept saying over to themselves the moving little impromptu speeches of thankfulness for the audience's applause and congratulations which they were presently going to get up and deliver. Every now and then one of these got a piece of paper out of his vest pocket and privately glanced at it to refresh his memory.

Of course there was a buzz of conversation going on—there always is; but at last when the Rev. Mr. Burgess rose and laid his hand on the sack he could hear his microbes gnaw, the place was so still. He related the curious history of the sack, then went on to speak in warm terms of Hadleyburg's old and well-earned reputation for spotless honesty, and of the town's just pride in this reputation. He said that this reputation was a treasure of priceless value; that under Providence its value had now become inestimably enhanced, for the recent episode had spread this fame far and wide, and thus had focused the eyes of the American world upon this village, and made its name for all time, as he hoped and believed, a synonym for commercial incorruptibility. (*Applause.*) "And who is to be the guardian of this noble treasure—the community as a whole? No! The responsibility is individual, not communal. From this day forth each and every one of you is in his own person its special guardian, and individually responsible that no harm shall come to it. Do you—does each of you—accept this great trust? [*Tumultuous assent.*]

Then all is well. Transmit it to your children and to your children's children. To-day your purity is beyond reproach—see to it that it shall remain so. To-day there is not a person in your community who could be beguiled to touch a penny not his own—see to it that you abide in this grace. [*"We will! we will!"*] This is not the place to make comparisons between ourselves and other communities—some of them ungracious toward us; they have their ways, we have ours; let us be content. [*Applause.*] I am done. Under my hand, my friends, rests a stranger's eloquent recognition of what we are; through him the world will always henceforth know what we are. We do not know who he is, but in your name I utter your gratitude, and ask you to raise your voices in indorsement."

The house rose in a body and made the walls quake with the thunders of its thankfulness for the space of a long minute. Then it sat down, and Mr. Burgess took an envelope out of his pocket. The house held its breath while he slit the envelope open and took from it a slip of paper. He read its contents—slowly and impressively—the audience listening with tranced attention to this magic document, each of whose words stood for an ingot of gold:

" '*The remark which I made to the distressed stranger was this: "You are very far from being a bad man; go, and reform."*' "Then he continued: "We shall know in a moment now whether the remark here quoted corresponds with the one concealed in the sack; and if that shall prove to be so—and it undoubtedly will—this sack of gold belongs to a fellow-citizen who will henceforth stand before the nation as the symbol of the special virtue which has made our town famous throughout the land—Mr. Billson!"

The house had gotten itself all ready to burst into the proper tornado of applause; but instead of doing it, it seemed stricken with a paralysis; there was a deep hush for a moment or two, then a wave of whispered murmurs swept the place—of about this tenor: "*Billson!* oh, come, this is *too* thin! Twenty dollars to a stranger—or *anybody*—*Billson!* Tell it to the marines!" And now at this point the house caught its breath all of a sudden in a new access of astonishment, for it discovered that whereas in one part of the hall Deacon Billson was standing up with his head meekly bowed, in another part of it Lawyer Wilson was doing the same. There was a wondering silence now for a while. Everybody was puzzled, and nineteen couples were surprised and indignant.

Billson and Wilson turned and stared at each other. Billson asked, bitingly,

"Why do *you* rise, Mr. Wilson?"

"Because I have a right to. Perhaps you will be good enough to explain to the house why *you* rise?"

"With great pleasure. Because I wrote that paper."

"It is an impudent falsity! I wrote it myself."

It was Burgess's turn to be paralyzed. He stood looking vacantly at first one of the men and then the other, and did not seem to know what to do. The house was stupefied. Lawyer Wilson spoke up, now, and said,

"I ask the Chair to read the name signed to that paper."

That brought the Chair to itself, and it read out the name;

" 'John Wharton *Billson*.' "

"There!" shouted Billson, "what have you got to say for yourself, now? And what kind of apology are you going to make to me and to this insulted house for the imposture which you have attempted to play here?"

"No apologies are due, sir; and as for the rest of it, I publicly charge you with pilfering my note from Mr. Burgess and substituting a copy of it signed with your own name. There is no other way by which you could have gotten hold of the test-remark; I alone, of living men, possessed the secret of its wording."

There was likely to be a scandalous state of things if this went on; everybody noticed with distress that the short-hand scribes were scribbling like mad; many people were crying "Chair, Chair! Order! order!" Burgess rapped with his gavel, and said:

"Let us not forget the proprieties due. There has evidently been a mistake somewhere, but surely that is all. If Mr. Wilson gave me an envelope—and I remember now that he did—I still have it."

He took one out of his pocket, opened it, glanced at it, looked surprised and worried, and stood silent a few moments. Then he waved his hand in a wandering and mechanical way, and made an effort or two to say something, then gave it up, despondently. Several voices cried out:

"Read it! read it! What is it?"

So he began in a dazed and sleep-walker fashion:

" '*The remark which I made to the unhappy stranger was this: "You are far from being a bad man.* [The house gazed at him, marvelling.] *Go, and reform."* ' [*Murmurs:* "Amazing! what can this mean?"] This one," said the Chair, "is signed Thurlow G. Wilson."

"There!" cried Wilson, "I reckon that settles it! I knew perfectly well my note was purloined."

"Purloined!" retorted Billson. "I'll let you know that neither you nor any man of your kidney must venture to—"

The Chair. "Order, gentlemen, order! Take your seats, both of you, please."

They obeyed, shaking their heads and grumbling angrily. The house was profoundly puzzled; it did not know what to do with this curious emergency. Presently Thompson got up. Thompson was the hatter. He would have liked to be a Nineteener; but such was not for him; his stock of hats was not considerable enough for the position. He said:

"Mr. Chairman, if I may be permitted to make a suggestion, can both of these gentlemen be right? I put it to you, sir, can both have happened to say the very same words to the stranger? It seems to me—"

The tanner got up and interrupted him. The tanner was a disgruntled man; he believed himself entitled to be a Nineteener, but he couldn't get recognition. It made him a little unpleasant in his ways and speech. Said he:

"Sho, *that's* not the point! *That* could happen—twice in a hundred years—but not the other thing. *Neither* of them gave the twenty dollars!" (*A ripple of applause.*)

Billson. "*I* did!"

Wilson. "*I* did!"

Then each accused the other of pilfering.

The Chair. "Order! Sit down, if you please—both of you. Neither of the notes has been out of my possession at any moment."

A Voice. "Good—that settles *that*!"

The Tanner. "Mr. Chairman, one thing is now plain: one of these men has been eavesdropping under the other one's bed, and filching family secrets. If it is not unparliamentary to suggest it, I will remark that both are equal to it. [*The Chair.* "Order! order!"] I withdraw the remark, sir, and will confine myself to suggesting that *if* one of them has overheard the other reveal the test-remark to his wife, we shall catch him now."

A Voice. "How?"

The Tanner. "Easily. The two have not quoted the remark in exactly the same words. You would have noticed that, if there hadn't been a considerable stretch of time and an exciting quarrel inserted between the two readings."

A Voice. "Name the difference."

The Tanner. "The word *very* is in Billson's note, and not in the other."

Many Voices. "That's so—he's right!"

The Tanner. "And so, if the Chair will examine the test-remark in the sack, we shall know which of these two frauds—[*The Chair.* "Order!"]—which of these two adventurers—[*The Chair.* "Order! order!"]—which of these two gentlemen—[*laughter and applause*]—is entitled to wear the belt as being the first dishonest blatherskite ever bred in this town—which he has dishonored, and which will be a sultry place for him from now out!" (*Vigorous applause.*)

Many Voices. "Open it!—open the sack!"

Mr. Burgess made a slit in the sack, slid his hand in and brought out an envelope. In it were a couple of folded notes. He said:

"One of these is marked, 'Not to be examined until all written communications which have been addressed to the Chair—if any—shall have been read.' The other is marked *'The Test.'* Allow me. It is worded—to wit:

" 'I do not require that the first half of the remark which was made to me by my benefactor shall be quoted with exactness, for it was not striking, and could be forgotten; but its closing fifteen words are quite striking, and I think easily rememberable; unless *these* shall be accurately reproduced, let the applicant be regarded as an impostor. My benefactor began by saying he seldom gave advice to any one, but that it always bore the hall-mark of high value when he did give it. Then he said this—and it has never faded from my memory: *"You are far from being a bad man—"* ' "

Fifty Voices. "That settles it—the money's Wilson's! Wilson! Wilson! Speech! Speech!"

People jumped up and crowded around Wilson, wringing his hand and congratulating fervently—meantime the Chair was hammering with the gavel and shouting:

"Order, gentlemen! Order! Order! Let me finish reading, please." When quiet was restored, the reading was resumed—as follows:

" ' *"Go, and reform—or, mark my words—some day, for your sins, you will die and go to hell or Hadleyburg*—TRY AND MAKE IT THE FORMER." ' "

A ghastly silence followed. First an angry cloud began to settle darkly upon the faces of the citizenship; after a pause the cloud began to rise, and a tickled expression tried to take its place; tried so hard that it was only kept under with great and painful difficulty; the reporters, the Brixtonites, and other strangers bent their heads down and shielded their faces with their hands, and managed to hold in by main strength and heroic courtesy. At this most inopportune time burst upon the stillness the roar of a solitary voice—Jack Halliday's:

"*That's* got the hall-mark on it!"

Then the house let go, strangers and all. Even Mr. Burgess's gravity broke down presently, then the audience considered itself officially absolved from all restraint, and it made the most of its privilege. It was a good long laugh, and a tempestuously whole-hearted one, but it ceased at last—long enough for Mr. Burgess to try to resume, and for the people to get their eyes partially wiped; then it broke out again; and afterward yet again; then at last Burgess was able to get out these serious words:

"It is useless to try to disguise the fact—we find ourselves in the presence of a matter of grave import. It involves the honor of your town, it strikes at the town's good name. The difference of a single word between the test-remarks offered by Mr. Wilson and Mr. Billson was itself a serious thing, since it indicated that one or the other of these gentlemen had committed a theft—"

The two men were sitting limp, nerveless, crushed; but at these words both were electrified into movement, and started to get up—

"Sit down!" said the Chair, sharply, and they obeyed. "That, as I have said, was a serious thing. And it was—but for only one of them. But the matter has become graver; for the honor of *both* is now in formidable peril. Shall I go even further, and say in inextricable peril? *Both* left out the crucial fifteen words." He paused. During several moments he allowed the pervading stillness to gather and deepen its impressive effects, then added: "There would seem to be but one way whereby this could happen. I ask these gentlemen—Was there *collusion?—agreement?*"

A low murmur sifted through the house; its import was, "He's got them both."

Billson was not used to emergencies; he sat in a helpless collapse. But Wilson was a lawyer. He struggled to his feet, pale and worried, and said:

"I ask the indulgence of the house while I explain this most painful matter. I am sorry to say what I am about to say, since it must inflict irreparable injury upon Mr. Billson, whom I have always esteemed and respected until now, and in whose invulnerability to temptation I entirely believed—as did you all. But for the preservation of my own honor I must speak—and with frankness. I confess with shame—and I now beseech your pardon for it—that I said to the ruined stranger all of the words contained in the test-remark, including the disparaging fifteen. [*Sensation.*] When the late publication was made I recalled them, and I resolved to claim the sack of coin, for by every right I was entitled to it. Now I will ask you to consider this point, and weigh it well: that stranger's gratitude to me that night knew no bounds; he said himself that he could find no words for it that were adequate, and that if he should ever be able he would repay me a thousandfold. Now, then, I ask you this: could I expect—could I believe—could I even remotely imagine—that, feeling as he did, he would do so ungrateful a thing as to add those quite unnecessary fifteen words to his test?—set a trap for me?—expose me as a slanderer of my own town before my own people assembled in a public hall? It was preposterous; it was impossible. His test would contain only the kindly opening clause of my remark. Of that I had no shadow of doubt. You would have thought as I did. You would not have expected a base betrayal from one whom you had befriended and against whom you had committed no offence. And so, with perfect confidence, perfect trust, I wrote on a piece of paper the opening words—ending with 'Go, and reform,'—and signed it. When I was about to put it in an envelope I was called into my back office, and without thinking I left the paper lying open on my desk." He stopped, turned his head slowly toward Billson, waited a moment, then added: "I ask you to note this: when I returned, a little later, Mr. Billson was retiring by my street door." (*Sensation.*)

In a moment Billson was on his feet and shouting:

"It's a lie! It's an infamous lie!"

The Chair. "Be seated, sir! Mr. Wilson has the floor."

Billson's friends pulled him into his seat and quieted him, and Wilson went on:

"Those are the simple facts. My note was now lying in a different place on the table from where I had left it. I noticed that, but attached no importance to it, thinking a draught had blown it there. That Mr. Billson would read a private paper was a thing which could not occur to me; he was an honorable man, and he would be above that. If you will allow me to say it, I think his extra word *'very'* stands explained; it is attributable to a defect of memory. I was the only man in the world who could furnish here any detail of the test-mark—by *honorable* means. I have finished."

There is nothing in the world like a persuasive speech to fuddle the mental apparatus and upset the convictions and debauch the emotions of an audience not practised in the tricks and delusions of oratory. Wilson sat down victorious. The house submerged him in tides of approving applause; friends swarmed to him and shook him by the hand and congratulated him, and Billson was shouted down and not allowed to say a word. The Chair hammered and hammered with its gavel, and kept shouting,

"But let us proceed, gentlemen, let us proceed!"

At last there was a measurable degree of quiet, and the hatter said,

"But what is there to proceed with, sir, but to deliver the money?"

Voices. "That's it! That's it! Come forward, Wilson!"

The Hatter. "I move three cheers for Mr. Wilson, Symbol of the special virtue which—"

The cheers burst forth before he could finish; and in the midst of them—and in the midst of the clamor of the gavel also—some enthusiasts mounted Wilson on a big friend's shoulder and were going to fetch him in triumph to the platform. The Chair's voice now rose above the noise—

"Order! To your places! You forget that there is still a document to be read." When quiet had been restored he took up the document, and was going to read it, but laid it down again, saying, "I forgot; this is not to be read until all written communications received by me have first been read." He took an envelope out of his pocket, removed its enclosure, glanced at it—seemed astonished—held it out and gazed at it—stared at it.

Twenty or thirty voices cried out:

"What is it? Read it! read it!"

And he did—slowly, and wondering:

" 'The remark which I made to the stranger—[*Voices.* "Hello! how's this?"]—was this: "You are far from being a bad man. [*Voices.* "Great Scott!"] Go, and reform." ' [*Voice.* "Oh, saw my leg off!"] Signed by Mr. Pinkerton the banker."

The pandemonium of delight which turned itself loose now was of a sort to make the judicious weep. Those whose withers were unwrung laughed till the tears ran down; the reporters, in throes of laughter, set down disordered pot-hooks which would never in the world be decipherable; and a sleeping dog jumped up, scared out of its wits, and barked itself crazy at the turmoil. All manner of cries were scattered through the din: "We're getting rich—*two* Symbols of Incorruptibility!—without counting Billson!" "*Three!*—count Shadbelly in—we can't have too many!" "All right—Billson's elected!" "Alas, poor Wilson—victim of *two* thieves!"

A Powerful Voice. "Silence! The Chair's fished up something more out of its pocket."

Voices. "Hurrah! Is it something fresh? Read it! read! read!"

The Chair (*reading*). " 'The remark which I made,' etc. 'You are far from being a bad man. Go,' etc. Signed, 'Gregory Yates.' "

Tornado of Voices. "Four Symbols!" " 'Rah for Yates!" "Fish again!"

The house was in a roaring humor now, and ready to get all the fun out of the occasion that might be in it. Several Nineteeners, looking pale and distressed, got up and began to work their way toward the aisles, but a score of shouts went up:

"The doors, the doors—close the doors; no Incorruptible shall leave this place! Sit down, everybody!"

The mandate was obeyed.

"Fish again! Read! read!"

The Chair fished again, and once more the familiar words began to fall from its lips—" 'You are far from being a bad man—' "

"Name! name! What's his name?"

" 'L. Ingoldsby Sargent.' "

"Five elected! Pile up the Symbols! Go on, go on!"

" 'You are far from being a bad—' "

"Name! name!"

" 'Nicholas Whitworth.' "

"Hooray! hooray! it's a symbolical day!"

Somebody wailed in, and began to sing this rhyme (leaving out "it's") to the lovely *Mikado* tune of "When a man's afraid of a beautiful maid"; the audience joined in, with joy; then, just in time, somebody contributed another line—

"And don't you this forget—"

The house roared it out. A third line was at once furnished—

"Corruptibles far from Hadleyburg are—"

The house roared that one too. As the last note died, Jack Halliday's voice rose high and clear, freighted with a final line—

"But the Symbols are here, you bet!"

That was sung, with booming enthusiasm. Then the happy house started in at the beginning and sang the four lines through twice, with immense swing and dash, and finished up with a crashing three-times-three and a tiger for "Hadleyburg the Incorruptible and all Symbols of it which we shall find worthy to receive the hall-mark to-night."

Then the shoutings at the Chair began again, all over the place:

"Go on! go on! Read! read some more! Read all you've got!"

"That's it—go on! We are winning eternal celebrity!"

A dozen men got up now and began to protest. They said that this farce was the work of some abandoned joker, and was an insult to the whole community. Without a doubt these signatures were all forgeries—

"Sit down! sit down! Shut up! You are confessing. We'll find *your* names in the lot."

"Mr. Chairman, how many of those envelopes have you got?"

The Chair counted.

"Together with those that have been already examined, there are nineteen."

A storm of derisive applause broke out.

"Perhaps they all contain the secret. I move that you open them all and read every signature that is attached to a note of that sort—and read also the first eight words of the note."

"Second the motion!"

It was put and carried—uproariously. Then poor old Richards got up, and his wife rose and stood at his side. Her head was bent down, so that none might see that she was crying. Her husband gave her his arm, and so supporting her, he began to speak in a quavering voice:

"My friends, you have known us two—Mary and me—all our lives, and I think you have liked us and respected us—"

The Chair interrupted him:

"Allow me. It is quite true—that which you are saying, Mr. Richards; this town *does* know you two; it *does* like you; it *does* respect you; more—it honors you and *loves* you—"

Halliday's voice rang out:

"That's the hall-marked truth, too! If the Chair is right, let the house speak up and say it. Rise! Now, then—hip! hip! hip!—all together!"

The house rose in mass, faced toward the old couple eagerly, filled the air with a snow-storm of waving handkerchiefs, and delivered the cheers with all its affectionate heart.

The Chair then continued:

"What I was going to say is this: We know your good heart, Mr. Richards, but this is not a time for the exercise of charity toward offenders. [Shouts of "Right! right!"] I see your generous purpose in your face, but I cannot allow you to plead for these men—"

"But I was going to—"

"Please take your seat, Mr. Richards. We must examine the rest of these notes—simple fairness to the men who have already been exposed requires this. As soon as that has been done—I give you my word for this—you shall be heard."

Many Voices. "Right!—the Chair is right—no interruption can be permitted at this stage! Go on!—the names! the names!—according to the terms of the motion!"

The old couple sat reluctantly down, and the husband whispered to the wife, "It is pitifully hard to have to wait; the shame will be greater than ever when they find we were only going to plead for *ourselves.*"

Straightway the jollity broke loose again with the reading of the names.

" 'You are far from being a bad man—' Signature, 'Robert J. Titmarsh.'

" 'You are far from being a bad man—' Signature, 'Eliphalet Weeks.'

" 'You are far from being a bad man—' Signature, 'Oscar B. Wilder.' "

At this point the house lit upon the idea of taking the eight words out of the Chairman's hands. He was not unthankful for that. Thenceforward he held up each note in its turn, and waited. The house droned out the eight words in a massed and measured and musical deep volume of sound (with a daringly close resemblance to a well-known church chant)—" 'You are f-a-r from being a b-a-a-a-d man.' " Then the Chair said, "Signature, 'Archibald Wilcox.' " And so on, and so on, name after name, and everybody had an increasingly and gloriously good time except the wretched Nineteen. Now and then, when a particularly shining name was called, the house made the Chair wait while it chanted the whole of the test-remark from the beginning to the closing words, "And go to hell or Hadleyburg—try and make it the for-or-m-e-r!" and in these special cases they added a grand and agonized and imposing "A-a-a-a-*men*!"

The list dwindled, dwindled, dwindled, poor old Richards keeping tally of the count, wincing when a name resembling his own was pronounced, and waiting in miserable suspense for the time to come when it would be his humiliating privilege to rise with Mary and finish his plea, which he was intending to word thus: "... for until now we have never done any wrong thing, but have gone our humble way unreproached. We are very poor, we are old, and have no chick nor child to help us; we were sorely tempted, and we fell. It was my purpose when I got up before to make confession and beg that my name might not be read out in this public place, for it seemed to us that we could not bear it; but I was prevented. It was just; it was our place to suffer with the rest. It has been hard for us. It is the first time we have ever heard our name fall from any one's lips—sullied. Be merciful—for the sake of the better days; make our shame as light to bear as in your charity you can." At this point in his revery Mary nudged him, perceiving that his mind was absent. The house was chanting, "You are f-a-r," etc.

"Be ready," Mary whispered. "Your name comes now; he has read eighteen."

The chant ended.

"Next! next! next!" came volleying from all over the house.

Burgess put his hand into his pocket. The old couple, trembling, began to rise. Burgess fumbled a moment, then said,

"I find I have read them all."

Faint with joy and surprise, the couple sank into their seats, and Mary whispered,

"Oh, bless God, we are saved!—he has lost ours—I wouldn't give this for a hundred of those sacks!"

The house burst out with its *Mikado* travesty, and sang it three times with ever-increasing enthusiasm, rising to its feet when it reached for the third time the closing line—

"But the Symbols are here, you bet!"

and finishing up with cheers and a tiger for "Hadleyburg purity and our eighteen immortal representatives of it."

Then Wingate, the saddler, got up and proposed cheers "for the cleanest man in town, the one solitary important citizen in it who didn't try to steal that money—Edward Richards."

They were given with great and moving heartiness; then somebody proposed that Richards be elected sole Guardian and Symbol of the now Sacred Hadleyburg Tradition, with power and right to stand up and look the whole sarcastic world in the face.

Passed, by acclamation; then they sang the *Mikado* again, and ended it with,

"And there's *one* Symbol left, you bet!"

There was a pause; then—

A Voice. "Now, then, who's to get the sack?"

The Tanner (*with bitter sarcasm*). "That's easy. The money has to be divided among the eighteen Incorruptibles. They gave the suffering stranger twenty dollars apiece—and that remark—each in his turn—it took twenty-two minutes for the procession to move past. Staked the stranger—total contribution, $360. All they want is just the loan back—and interest—forty thousand dollars altogether."

Many Voices (*derisively*). "That's it! Divvy! divvy! Be kind to the poor—don't keep them waiting!"

The Chair. "Order! I now offer the stranger's remaining document. It says: 'If no claimant shall appear [*grand chorus of groans*], I desire that you open the sack and count out the money to the principal citizens of your town, they to take it in trust [*Cries of* "*Oh! Oh! Oh!*"], and use it in such ways as to them shall seem best for the propagation and preservation of your community's noble reputation for incorruptible honesty [*more cries*]—a reputation to which their names and their efforts will add a new and far-reaching lustre.' [*Enthusiastic outburst of sarcastic applause.*] That seems to be all. No—here is a postscript:

" 'P. S.—CITIZENS OF HADLEYBURG: There *is* no test-remark—nobody made one. [*Great sensation.*] There wasn't any pauper stranger, nor any twenty-dollar contribution, nor any accompanying benediction and compliment—these are all inventions. [*General buzz and hum of astonishment and delight.*] Allow me to tell my story—it will take but a word or two. I passed through your town at a certain time, and received a deep offence which I had not earned. Any other man would have been content to kill one or two of you and call it square, but to me that would have been a trivial revenge, and inadequate; for the dead do not *suffer*. Besides, I could not kill you all—and, anyway, made as I am, even that would not have satisfied me. I wanted to damage every man in the place, and every woman—and not in their bodies or in their estate, but in their vanity—the place where feeble and foolish people are most vulnerable. So I disguised myself, and came back and studied you. You were easy game. You had an old and lofty reputation for honesty, and naturally you were proud of it—it was your treasure of treasures, the very apple of your eye. As soon as I found out that you carefully and vigilantly kept yourselves and your children *out of temptation*, I knew how to proceed. Why, you simple creatures, the weakest of all weak things is a virtue which has not been tested in the fire.[5] I laid a plan, and gathered a list of names. My project was to corrupt Hadleyburg the Incorruptible. My idea was to make liars and thieves of nearly half a hundred smirchless men and women who had never in their lives uttered a lie or stolen a penny. I was afraid of Goodson. He was neither born nor reared in Hadleyburg. I was afraid that if I started to operate my scheme by getting my letter laid before you, you would say to yourselves, "Goodson is the only man among us who would give away twenty dollars to a poor devil"—and then you might not bite at my bait. But Heaven took Goodson; then I knew I was safe, and I set my trap and baited it. It may be that I shall not catch all the men to whom I mailed the pretended test secret, but I shall catch the most of them, if I know Hadleyburg nature. [*Voices.* "Right—he got every last one of them."] I believe they will even steal ostensible *gamble*-money, rather than miss, poor, tempted, and mistrained fellows. I am hoping to eternally and everlastingly squelch your vanity and give Hadleyburg a new renown—one that will *stick*—and spread far. If I have succeeded, open the sack and summon the Committee on Propagation and Preservation of the Hadleyburg Reputation.' "

A Cyclone of Voices. "Open it! Open it! The Eighteen to the front! Committee on Propagation of the Tradition! Forward—the Incorruptibles!"

The Chair ripped the sack wide, and gathered up a handful of bright, broad, yellow coins, shook them together, then examined them—

"Friends, they are only gilded disks of lead!"

There was a crashing outbreak of delight over this news, and when the noise had subsided, the tanner called out:

"By right of apparent seniority in this business, Mr. Wilson is Chairman of the Committee on Propagation of the Tradition. I suggest that he step forward on behalf of his pals, and receive in trust the money."

A Hundred Voices. "Wilson! Wilson! Wilson! Speech! Speech!"

Wilson (*in a voice trembling with anger*). "You will allow me to say, and without apologies for my language, *damn* the money!"

A Voice. "Oh, and him a Baptist!"

A Voice. "Seventeen Symbols left! Step up, gentlemen, and assume your trust!"

There was a pause—no response.

The Saddler. "Mr. Chairman, we've got *one* clean man left, anyway, out of the late aristocracy; and he needs money, and deserves it. I move that you appoint Jack Halliday to get up there and auction off that sack of gilt twenty-dollar pieces, and give the result to the right man—the man whom Hadleyburg delights to honor[6]—Edward Richards."

This was received with great enthusiasm, the dog taking a hand again; the saddler started the bids at a dollar, the Brixton folk and Barnum's representative fought hard for it, the people cheered every jump that the bids made, the excitement climbed moment by moment higher and higher, the bidders got on their mettle and grew steadily more and more daring, more and more determined, the jumps went from a dollar up to five, then to ten, then to twenty, then fifty, then to a hundred, then—

At the beginning of the auction Richards whispered in distress to his wife: "Oh, Mary, can we allow it? It—it—you see, it is an honor-reward, a testimonial to purity of character, and—and—can we allow it? Hadn't I better get up and—Oh, Mary, what ought we to do?—what do you think we—" (*Halliday's voice. "Fifteen I'm bid!—fifteen for the sack!—twenty!—ah, thanks!—thirty—thanks again! Thirty, thirty, thirty!—do I hear forty?—forty it is! Keep the ball rolling, gentlemen, keep it rolling!—fifty!—thanks, noble Roman!—going at fifty, fifty, fifty!—seventy!—ninety!—splendid!—a hundred!—pile it up, pile it up!—hundred and twenty—forty!—just in time!—hundred and fifty!—*TWO *hundred!—superb! Do I hear two h—thanks!—two hundred and fifty!—"*)

"It is another temptation, Edward—I'm all in a tremble—but, oh, we've escaped *one* temptation, and that ought to warn us, to— [*"Six did I hear?—thanks!—six fifty, six f*—SEVEN *hundred!"*] And yet, Edward, when you think—nobody susp— [*"Eight hundred dollars!—hurrah!—make it nine!—Mr. Parsons, did I hear you say—thanks!—nine!—this noble sack of virgin lead going at only nine hundred dollars, gilding and all—come! do I hear—a thousand!—gratefully yours!—did some one say eleven?—a sack which is going to be the most celebrated in the whole Uni—"*] Oh, Edward" (beginning to sob), "we are *so* poor!—but—but—do as you think best—do as you think best."

Edward fell—that is, he sat still; sat with a conscience which was not satisfied, but which was overpowered by circumstances.

Meantime a stranger, who looked like an amateur detective gotten up as an impossible English earl, had been watching the evening's proceedings with manifest interest, and with a contented expression in his face; and he had been privately commenting to himself. He was now soliloquizing somewhat like this: "None of the Eighteen are bidding; that is not satisfactory; I must change that—the dramatic unities require it; they must buy the sack they tried to steal; they must pay a heavy price, too—some of them are rich. And another thing, when I make a mistake in Hadleyburg nature the man that puts that error upon me is entitled to a high honorarium, and some one must pay it. This poor old Richards has brought my judgment to shame; he is an honest man:—I don't understand it, but I acknowledge it. Yes, he saw my deuces-*and* with a straight flush, and by rights the pot is his. And it shall be a jack-pot, too, if I can manage it. He disappointed me, but let that pass."

He was watching the bidding. At a thousand, the market broke; the prices tumbled swiftly. He waited—and still watched. One competitor dropped out; then another, and another. He put in a bid or two, now. When the bids had sunk to ten dollars, he added a five; some one raised him a three; he waited a moment, then flung in a fifty-dollar jump, and the sack was his—at $1282. The house broke out in cheers—then stopped; for he was on his feet, and had lifted his hand. He began to speak.

"I desire to say a word, and ask a favor. I am a speculator in rarities, and I have dealings with persons interested in numismatics all over the world. I can make a profit on this purchase, just as it stands; but there is a way, if I can get your approval, whereby I can make every one of these leaden twenty-dollar pieces worth its face in gold, and perhaps more. Grant me that approval, and I will give part of my gains to your Mr.

Richards, whose invulnerable probity you have so justly and so cordially recognized to-night; his share shall be ten thousand dollars, and I will hand him the money tomorrow. [*Great applause from the house.* But the "invulnerable probity" made the Richardses blush prettily; however, it went for modesty, and did no harm.] If you will pass my proposition by a good majority—I would like a two-thirds vote—I will regard that as the town's consent, and that is all I ask. Rarities are always helped by any device which will rouse curiosity and compel remark. Now if I may have your permission to stamp upon the faces of each of these ostensible coins the names of the eighteen gentlemen who—"

Nine-tenths of the audience were on their feet in a moment—dog and all—and the proposition was carried with a whirlwind of approving applause and laughter.

They sat down, and all the Symbols except "Dr." Clay Harkness got up, violently protesting against the proposed outrage, and threatening to—

"I beg you not to threaten me," said the stranger, calmly. "I know my legal rights, and am not accustomed to being frightened at bluster." (*Applause.*) He sat down. "Dr." Harkness saw an opportunity here. He was one of the two very rich men of the place, and Pinkerton was the other. Harkness was proprietor of a mint; that is to say, a popular patent medicine. He was running for the Legislature on one ticket, and Pinkerton on the other. It was a close race and a hot one, and getting hotter every day. Both had strong appetites for money; each had bought a great tract of land, with a purpose: there was going to be a new railway, and each wanted to be in the Legislature and help locate the route to his own advantage; a single vote might make the decision, and with it two or three fortunes. The stake was large, and Harkness was a daring speculator. He was sitting close to the stranger. He leaned over while one or another of the other Symbols was entertaining the house with protests and appeals, and asked, in a whisper,

"What is your price for the sack?"

"Forty thousand dollars."

"I'll give you twenty."

"No."

"Twenty-five."

"No."

"Say thirty."

"The price is forty thousand dollars; not a penny less."

"All right, I'll give it. I will come to the hotel at ten in the morning. I don't want it known; will see you privately."

"Very good." Then the stranger got up and said to the house:

"I find it late. The speeches of these gentlemen are not without merit, not without interest, not without grace; yet if I may be excused I will take my leave. I thank you for the great favor which you have shown me in granting my petition. I ask the Chair to keep the sack for me until tomorrow, and to hand these three five-hundred dollar notes to Mr. Richards." They were passed up to the Chair. "At nine I will call for the sack, and at eleven will deliver the rest of the ten thousand to Mr. Richards in person, at his home. Goodnight."

Then he slipped out, and left the audience making a vast noise, which was composed of a mixture of cheers, the *Mikado* song, dog-disapproval, and the chant, "You are f-a-r from being a b-a-a-d man—a-a-a-a-men!"

IV

At home the Richardses had to endure congratulations and compliments until midnight. Then they were left to themselves. They looked a little sad, and they sat silent and thinking. Finally Mary sighed and said,

"Do you think we are to blame, Edward—*much* to blame?" and her eyes wandered to the accusing triplet of big banknotes lying on the table, where the congratulators had been gloating over them and reverently fingering them. Edward did not answer at once; then he brought out a sigh and said, hesitatingly:

"We—we couldn't help it, Mary. It—well, it was ordered. *All* things are."

Mary glanced up and looked at him steadily, but he didn't return the look. Presently she said:

"I thought congratulations and praises always tasted good. But—it seems to me, now— Edward?"

"Well?"

"Are you going to stay in the bank?"

"N-no."

"Resign?"

"In the morning—by note."

"It does seem best."

Richards bowed his head in his hands and muttered:

"Before, I was not afraid to let oceans of people's money pour through my hands, but— Mary, I am so tired, so tired—"

"We will go to bed."

At nine in the morning the stranger called for the sack and took it to the hotel in a cab. At ten Harkness had a talk with him privately. The stranger asked for and got five checks on a metropolitan bank—drawn to "Bearer,"—four for $1500 each, and one for $34,000. He put one of the former in his pocket-book, and the remainder, representing $38,500, he put in an envelope, and with these he added a note, which he wrote after Harkness was gone. At eleven he called at the Richards house and knocked. Mrs. Richards peeped through the shutters, then went and received the envelope, and the stranger disappeared without a word. She came back flushed and a little unsteady on her legs, and gasped out:

"I am sure I recognized him! Last night it seemed to me that maybe I had seen him somewhere before."

"He is the man that brought the sack here?"

"I am almost sure of it."

"Then he is the ostensible Stephenson too, and sold[7] every important citizen in this town with his bogus secret. Now if he has sent checks instead of money, we are sold too, after we thought we had escaped. I was beginning to feel fairly comfortable once more, after my night's rest, but the look of that envelope makes me sick. It isn't fat enough; $8500 in even the largest bank-notes makes more bulk than that."

"Edward, why do you object to checks?"

"Checks signed by Stephenson! I am resigned to take the $8500 if it could come in bank-notes—for it does seem that it was so ordered, Mary—but I have never had much courage, and I have not the pluck to try to market a check signed with that disastrous name. It would be a trap. That man tried to catch me; we escaped somehow or other; and now he is trying a new way. If it is checks—"

"Oh, Edward, it is *too* bad!" and she held up the checks and began to cry.

"Put them in the fire! quick! we mustn't be tempted. It is a trick to make the world laugh at *us*, along with the rest, and— Give them to *me*, since you can't do it!" He snatched them and tried to hold his grip till he could get to the stove; but he was human, he was a cashier, and he stopped a moment to make sure of the signature. Then he came near to fainting.

"Fan me, Mary, fan me! They are the same as gold!"

"Oh, how lovely, Edward! Why?"

"Signed by Harkness. What can the mystery of that be, Mary?"

"Edward, do you think—"

"Look here—look at this! Fifteen—fifteen—fifteen—thirty-four. Thirty-eight thousand five hundred! Mary, the sack isn't worth twelve dollars, and Harkness—apparently—has paid about par for it."

"And does it all come to us, do you think—instead of the ten thousand?"

"Why, it looks like it. And the checks are made to 'Bearer,' too."

"Is that good, Edward? What is it for?"

"A hint to collect them at some distant bank, I reckon. Perhaps Harkness doesn't want the matter known. What is that—a note?"

"Yes. It was with the checks."

It was in the "Stephenson" handwriting, but there was no signature. It said:

> "I am a disappointed man. Your honesty is beyond the reach of temptation. I had a different idea about it, but I wronged you in that, and I beg pardon, and do it sincerely. I honor you—and that is sincere, too. This town is not worthy to kiss the hem of your garment. Dear sir, I made a square bet with myself that there were nineteen debauchable men in your self-righteous community. I have lost. Take the whole pot, you are entitled to it."

Richards drew a deep sigh, and said:

"It seems written with fire—it burns so. Mary—I am miserable again."

"I, too. Ah, dear, I wish—"

"To think, Mary—he *believes* in me."

"Oh, don't, Edward—I can't bear it."

"If those beautiful words were deserved, Mary—and God knows I believed I deserved them once—I think I could give the forty thousand dollars for them. And I would put that paper away, as representing more than gold and jewels, and keep it always. But now— We could not live in the shadow of its accusing presence, Mary."

He put it in the fire.

A messenger arrived and delivered an envelope. Richards took from it a note and read it; it was from Burgess.

> "You saved me, in a difficult time. I saved you last night. It was at cost of a lie, but I made the sacrifice freely, and out of a grateful heart. None in this village knows so well as I know how brave and good and noble you are. At bottom you cannot respect me, knowing as you do of that matter of which I am accused, and by the general voice condemned; but I beg that you will at least believe that I am a grateful man; it will help me to bear my burden.
>
> [Signed] BURGESS"

"Saved, once more. And on such terms!" He put the note in the fire. "I—I wish I were dead, Mary, I wish I were out of it all."

"Oh, these are bitter, bitter days, Edward. The stabs, through their very generosity, are so deep—and they come so fast!"

Three days before the election each of two thousand voters suddenly found himself in possession of a prized memento—one of the renowned bogus double-eagles. Around one of its faces was stamped these words: "THE REMARK I MADE TO THE POOR STRANGER WAS—" Around the other face was stamped these: "GO, AND REFORM. (SIGNED) PINKERTON." Thus the entire remaining refuse of the renowned joke was emptied upon a single head, and with calamitous effect. It revived the recent vast laugh and concentrated it upon Pinkerton; and Harkness's election was a walk-over.

Within twenty-four hours after the Richardses had received their checks their consciences were quieting down, discouraged; the old couple were learning to reconcile themselves to the sin which they had committed. But they were to learn, now, that a sin takes on new and real terrors when there seems a chance that it is going to be found out. This gives it a fresh and most substantial and important aspect. At church the morning sermon was of the usual pattern; it was the same old things said in the same old way; they had heard them a thousand times and found them innocuous, next to meaningless, and easy to sleep under; but now it was different: the sermon seemed to bristle with accusations; it seemed aimed straight and specially at people who were concealing deadly sins. After church they got away from the mob of congratulators as soon as they could, and hurried homeward, chilled to the bone at they did not know what—vague, shadowy, indefinite fears. And by chance they caught a glimpse of Mr. Burgess as he turned a corner. He paid no attention to their nod of recognition! He hadn't seen it; but they did not know that. What could his conduct mean? It might mean—it might mean—oh, a dozen dreadful things. Was it possible that he knew that Richards could have cleared him of guilt in that bygone time, and had been silently waiting for a chance to even up accounts? At home, in their distress they got to imagining that their servant might have been in the next room listening when Richards revealed the secret to his wife that he knew of Burgess's innocence; next, Richards began to imagine that he had heard the swish of a gown in there at that time; next, he was sure he *had* heard it. They would call Sarah in, on a pretext, and watch her face; if she had been betraying them to Mr. Burgess, it would show in her manner. They asked her some questions—questions which were so random and incoherent and seemingly purposeless that the girl felt sure that the old people's minds had been affected by their sudden good fortune; the sharp and watchful gaze which they bent upon her frightened her, and that completed the business. She blushed, she became nervous and confused, and to the old people these were plain signs of guilt—guilt of some fearful sort or other—without doubt she was a spy and a traitor. When they were alone again they began to piece many unrelated things together and get horrible results out of the combination. When things had got about to the worst, Richards was delivered of a sudden gasp, and his wife asked,

"Oh, what is it?—what is it?"

"The note—Burgess's note! Its language was sarcastic, I see it now." He quoted: " 'At bottom you cannot respect me, *knowing,* as you do, of *that matter* of which I am accused'—oh, it is perfectly plain, now, God help me! He knows that I know! You see the ingenuity of the phrasing. It was a trap—and like a fool, I walked into it. And Mary—?"

"Oh, it is dreadful—I know what you are going to say—he didn't return your transcript of the pretended test-remark."

"No—kept it to destroy us with. Mary, he has exposed us to some already. I know it—I know it well. I saw it in a dozen faces after church. Ah, he wouldn't answer our nod of recognition—*he* knew what he had been doing!"

In the night the doctor was called. The news went around in the morning that the old couple were rather seriously ill—prostrated by the exhausting excitement growing out of their great windfall, the congratulations, and the late hours, the doctor said. The town was sincerely distressed; for these old people were about all it had left to be proud of, now.

Two days later the news was worse. The old couple were delirious, and were doing strange things. By witness of the nurses, Richards had exhibited checks—for $8500? No—for an amazing sum—$38,500! What could be the explanation of this gigantic piece of luck?

The following day the nurses had more news—and wonderful. They had concluded to hide the checks, lest harm come to them; but when they searched they were gone from under the patient's pillow—vanished away. The patient said:

"Let the pillow alone; what do you want?"

"We thought it best that the checks—"

"You will never see them again—they are destroyed. They came from Satan. I saw the hell-brand on them, and I knew they were sent to betray me to sin." Then he fell to gabbling strange and dreadful things which were not clearly understandable, and which the doctor admonished them to keep to themselves.

Richards was right; the checks were never seen again.

A nurse must have talked in her sleep, for within two days the forbidden gabblings were the property of the town; and they were of a surprising sort. They seemed to indicate that Richards had been a claimant for the sack himself, and that Burgess had concealed that fact and then maliciously betrayed it.

Burgess was taxed with this and stoutly denied it. And he said it was not fair to attach weight to the chatter of a sick old man who was out of his mind. Still, suspicion was in the air, and there was much talk.

After a day or two it was reported that Mrs. Richards's delirious deliveries were getting to be duplicates of her husband's. Suspicion flamed up into conviction, now, and the town's pride in the purity of its one undiscredited important citizen began to dim down and flicker toward extinction.

Six days passed, then came more news. The old couple were dying. Richards's mind cleared in his latest hour, and he sent for Burgess. Burgess said:

"Let the room be cleared. I think he wishes to say something in privacy."

"No!" said Richards; "I want witnesses. I want you all to hear my confession, so that I may die a man, and not a dog. I was clean—artificially—like the rest; and like the rest I fell when temptation came. I signed a lie, and claimed the miserable sack. Mr. Burgess remembered that I had done him a service, and in gratitude (and ignorance) he suppressed my claim and saved me. You know the thing that was charged against Burgess years ago. My testimony, and mine alone, could have cleared him, and I was a coward, and left him to suffer disgrace—"

"No—no—Mr. Richards, you—"

"My servant betrayed my secret to him—"

"No one has betrayed anything to me—"

—"and then he did a natural and justifiable thing; he repented of the saving kindness which he had done me, and he *exposed* me—as I deserved—"

"Never!—I make oath—"

"Out of my heart I forgive him."

Burgess's impassioned protestations fell upon deaf ears; the dying man passed away without knowing that once more he had done poor Burgess a wrong. The old wife died that night.

The last of the sacred Nineteen had fallen a prey to the fiendish sack; the town was stripped of the last rag of its ancient glory. Its mourning was not showy, but it was deep.

By act of the Legislature—upon prayer and petition—Hadleyburg was allowed to change its name to (never mind what—I will not give it away), and leave one word out of the motto that for many generations had graced the town's official seal.

It is an honest town once more, and the man will have to rise early that catches it napping again.

[1899]

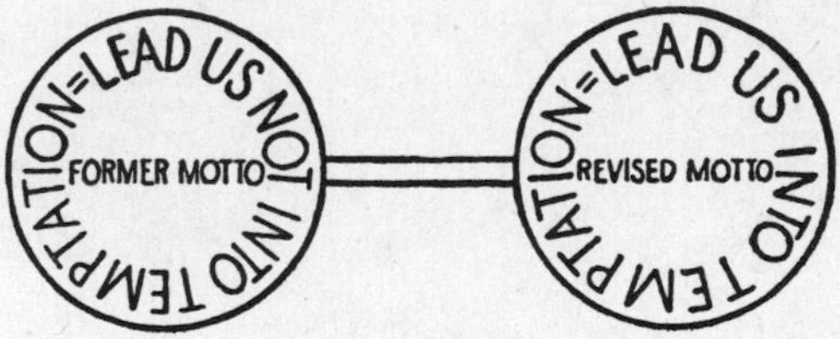

The $30,000 Bequest

I

Lakeside was a pleasant little town of five or six thousand inhabitants, and a rather pretty one, too, as towns go in the Far West. It had church-accommodations for 35,000, which is the way of the Far West and the South, where everybody is religious, and where each of the Protestant sects is represented and has a plant of its own. Rank was unknown in Lakeside—unconfessed, anyway; everybody knew everybody and his dog, and a sociable friendliness was the prevailing atmosphere.

Saladin Foster[1] was bookkeeper in the principal store, and the only high-salaried man of his profession in Lakeside. He was thirty-five years old, now; he had served that store for fourteen years; he had begun in his marriage-week at four hundred dollars a year, and had climbed steadily up, a hundred dollars a year for four years; from that time forth his wage had remained eight hundred—a handsome figure indeed, and everybody conceded that he was worth it.

His wife, Electra,[2] was a capable helpmeet, although—like himself—a dreamer of dreams and a private dabbler in romance. The first thing she did, after her marriage—child as she was, aged only nineteen—was to buy an acre of ground on the edge of the town, and pay down the cash for it—twenty-five dollars, all her fortune. Saladin had less, by fifteen. She instituted a vegetable garden there, got it farmed on shares by the nearest neighbor, and made it pay her a hundred per cent. a year. Out of Saladin's first year's wage she put thirty dollars in the savings-bank, sixty out of his second, a hundred out of his third, a hundred and fifty out of his fourth. His wage went to eight hundred a year, then, and meantime two children had arrived and increased the expenses, but she banked two hundred a year from the salary, nevertheless, thenceforth. When she had been married seven years she built and furnished a pretty and comfortable two-thousand-dollar house in the midst of her garden-acre, paid half of the money down, and moved her family in. Seven years later she was out of debt and had several hundred dollars out earning its living.

Earning it by the rise in landed estate; for she had long ago bought another acre or two and sold the most of it at a profit to pleasant people who were willing to build, and would be good neighbors and furnish a genial comradeship for herself and her growing family. She had an independent income from safe investments of about a hundred dollars a year; her children were growing in years and grace; and she was a pleased and happy woman. Happy in her husband, happy in her children, and the husband and the children were happy in her. It is at this point that this history begins.

The youngest girl, Clytemnestra[3]—called Clytie for short—was eleven; her sister, Gwendolen[4]—called Gwen for short—was thirteen; nice girls, and comely. The names betray the latent romance-tinge in the parental blood,[5] the parents' names indicate that the tinge was an inheritance. It was an affectionate family, hence all four of its members had pet names. Saladin's was a curious and unsexing one[6]—Sally; and so was Electra's—Aleck. All day long Sally was a good and diligent bookkeeper and salesman; all day long Aleck was a good and faithful mother and housewife, and thoughtful and calculating business-woman; but in the cosy living-room at night they put the plodding world away and lived in another and a fairer, reading romances to each other, dreaming dreams,[7] comrading with kings and princes and stately lords and ladies in the flash and stir and splendor of noble palaces and grim and ancient castles.

II

Now came great news! Stunning news, joyous news, in fact. It came from a neighboring State, where the family's only surviving relative lived. It was Sally's relative—a sort of vague and indefinite uncle or second or third cousin by the name of Tilbury Foster, seventy and a bachelor, reputed well-off and correspondingly sour and crusty. Sally had tried to make up to him once, by letter, in a bygone time, and had not made that mistake again. Tilbury now wrote to Sally, saying he should shortly die, and should leave him thirty thousand dollars, cash; not for love, but because money had given him most of his troubles and exasperations, and he wished to place it where there was good hope that it would continue its malignant work. The bequest would be found in his will, and would be paid over. *Provided,* that Sally should be able to prove to the executors that he had *taken no notice of the gift by spoken word or by letter, had made no inquiries concerning the moribund's progress toward the everlasting tropics, and had not attended the funeral.*

As soon as Aleck had partially recovered from the tremendous emotions created by the letter, she sent to the relative's habitat and subscribed for the local paper.

Man and wife entered into a solemn compact, now, to never mention the great news to any one while the relative lived, lest some ignorant person carry the fact to the deathbed and distort it and make it appear that they were disobediently thankful for the bequest, and just the same as confessing it and publishing it, right in the face of the prohibition.

For the rest of the day Sally made havoc and confusion with his books, and Aleck could not keep her mind on her affairs, nor even take up a flower-pot or book or a stick of wood without forgetting what she had intended to do with it. For both were dreaming.

"Thir-ty thousand dollars!"

All day long the music of those inspiring words sang through those people's heads.

From his marriage-day forth, Aleck's grip had been upon the purse, and Sally had seldom known what it was to be privileged to squander a dime on non-necessities.

"Thir-ty thousand dollars!" the song went on and on. A vast sum, an unthinkable sum!

All day long Aleck was absorbed in planning how to invest it, Sally in planning how to spend it.

There was no romance-reading that night. The children took themselves away early, for the parents were silent, distraught, and strangely unentertaining. The good-night kisses might as well have been impressed upon vacancy, for all the response they got; the parents were not aware of the kisses, and the children had been gone an hour before their absence was noticed. Two pencils had been busy during that hour—note-making; in the way of plans. It was Sally who broke the stillness at last. He said, with exultation—

"Ah, it'll be grand, Aleck! Out of the first thousand we'll have a horse and a buggy for summer, and a cutter and a skin lap-robe for winter."

Aleck responded, with decision and composure—

"Out of the *capital*? Nothing of the kind. Not if it was a million!"

Sally was deeply disappointed; the glow went out of his face.

"Oh, Aleck!" he said, reproachfully. "We've always worked so hard and been so scrimped; and now that we are rich, it does seem—"

He did not finish, for he saw her eye soften; his supplication had touched her. She said, with gentle persuasiveness—

"We must not spend the capital, dear, it would not be wise. Out of the income from it—"

"That will answer, that will answer, Aleck! How dear and good you are! There will be a noble income, and if we can spend that—"

"Not *all* of it, dear, not all of it, but you can spend a part of it. That is, a reasonable part. But the whole of the capital—every penny of it—must be put right to work, and kept at it. You see the reasonableness of that, don't you?"

"Why, ye-s. Yes, of course. But we'll have to wait so long. Six months before the first interest falls due."

"Yes—maybe longer."

"Longer, Aleck? Why? Don't they pay half-yearly?"

"*That* kind of an investment—yes; but I sha'n't invest in that way."

"What way then?"

"For big returns."

"Big. That's good. Go on, Aleck. What is it?"

"Coal. The new mines. Cannel. I mean to put in ten thousand. Ground floor. When we organize, we'll get three shares for one."

"By George but it sounds good, Aleck! Then the shares will be worth—how much? And when?"

"About a year. They'll pay ten per cent. half-yearly, and be worth thirty thousand. I know all about it; the advertisement is in the Cincinnati paper here."

"Land, thirty thousand for ten—in a year! Let's jam in the whole capital and pull out ninety! I'll write and subscribe right now—to-morrow it may be too late."

He was flying to the writing-desk, but Aleck stopped him and put him back in his chair. She said—

"Don't lose your head so. We mustn't subscribe till we've got the money; don't you know that?"

Sally's excitement went down a degree or two, but he was not wholly appeased.

"Why, Aleck, we'll *have* it, you know—and so soon, too. He's probably out of his troubles before this, it's a hundred to nothing he's selecting his brimstone-shovel this very minute. Now, I think—"

Aleck shuddered, and said—

"How *can* you, Sally! Don't talk in that way, it is perfectly scandalous."

"Oh, well, make it a halo, if you like, *I* don't care for his outfit, I was only just talking. Can't you let a person talk?"

"But why should you *want* to talk in that dreadful way? How would you like to have people talk so about *you,* and you not cold yet?"

"Nor likely to be, for *one* while, I reckon, if my last act was giving away money for the sake of doing somebody a harm with it. But never mind about Tilbury, Aleck, let's talk about something worldly. It does seem to me that that mine is the place for the whole thirty. What's the objection?"

"All the eggs in one basket—that's the objection."

"All right, if you say so. What about the other twenty? What do you mean to do with that?"

"There is no hurry; I am going to look around before I do anything with it."

"All right, if your mind's made up," sighed Sally. He was deep in thought, a while, then he said—

"There'll be twenty thousand profit coming from the ten a year from now. We can spend that, can't we, Aleck?"

Aleck shook her head.

"No, dear," she said, "it won't sell high till we've had the first semiannual dividend. You can spend part of that."

"Shucks, only *that*—and a whole year to wait! Confound it, I—"

"Oh, do be patient! It might even be declared in three months—it's quite within the possibilities."

"Oh, jolly! oh, thanks!" and Sally jumped up and kissed his wife in gratitude. "It'll be three thousand—three whole thousand! how much of it can we spend, Aleck? Make it liberal—do, dear, that's a good fellow."

Aleck was pleased; so pleased that she yielded to the pressure and conceded a sum which her judgment told her was a foolish extravagance—a thousand dollars. Sally kissed her half a dozen times and even in that way could not express all his joy and thankfulness. This new access of gratitude and affection carried Aleck quite beyond the bounds of prudence, and before she could restrain herself she had made her darling another grant—a couple of thousand out of the fifty or sixty which she meant to clear within a year out of the twenty which still remained of the bequest. The happy tears sprang to Sally's eyes, and he said—

"Oh, I want to hug you!" And he did it. Then he got his notes and sat down and began to check off, for first purchase, the luxuries which he should earliest wish to secure. "Horse—buggy—cutter—lap-robe

—patent-leathers—dog—plug hat—church-pew—stem-winder—new teeth—*say,* Aleck!"

"Well?"

"Ciphering away, aren't you? That's right. Have you got the twenty thousand invested yet?"

"No, there's no hurry about that; I must look around first, and think."

"But you are ciphering; what's it about?"

"Why, I have to find work for the thirty thousand that comes out of the coal, haven't I?"

"Scott, what a head! I never thought of that. How are you getting along? Where have you arrived?"

"Not very far—two years or three. I've turned it over twice; once in oil and once in wheat."

"Why, Aleck, it's splendid! How does it aggregate?"

"I think—well, to be on the safe side, about a hundred and eighty thousand clear, though it will probably be more."

"My! isn't it wonderful? By gracious, luck has come our way at last, after all the hard sledding. Aleck!"

"Well?"

"I'm going to cash-in a whole three hundred on the missionaries—what real right have we to care for expenses!"

"You couldn't do a nobler thing, dear; and it's just like your generous nature, you unselfish boy."

The praise made Sally poignantly happy, but he was fair and just enough to say it was rightfully due to Aleck rather than to himself, since but for her he should never have had the money.

Then they went up to bed, and in their delirium of bliss they forgot and left the candle burning in the parlor. They did not remember until they were undressed; then Sally was for letting it burn; he said they could afford it, if it was a thousand. But Aleck went down and put it out.

A good job, too; for on her way back she hit on a scheme that would turn the hundred and eighty thousand into half a million before it had had time to get cold.

III

The little newspaper which Aleck had subscribed for was a Thursday sheet; it would make the trip of five hundred miles from Tilbury's village and arrive on Saturday. Tilbury's letter had started on Friday, more than a day too late for the benefactor to die and get into that week's issue, but in plenty of time to make connection for the next output. Thus the Fosters had to wait almost a complete week to find out whether anything of a satisfactory nature had happened to him or not. It was a long, long week, and the strain was a heavy one. The pair could hardly have borne it if their minds had not had the relief of wholesome diversion. We have seen that they had that. The woman was piling up fortunes right along, the man was spending them—spending all his wife would give him a chance at, at any rate.

At last the Saturday came, and the *Weekly Sagamore* arrived. Mrs. Eversly Bennett was present. She was the Presbyterian parson's wife, and was working the Fosters for a charity. Talk now died a sudden death—on the Foster side. Mrs. Bennett presently discovered that her hosts were not hearing a word she was saying; so she got up, wondering and indignant, and went away. The moment she was out of the house, Aleck eagerly tore the wrapper from the paper, and her eyes and Sally's swept the columns for the death notices. Disappointment! Tilbury was not anywhere mentioned. Aleck was a Christian from the cradle, and duty and the force of habit required her to go through the motions. She pulled herself together and said, with a pious two-per-cent. trade joyousness:

"Let us be humbly thankful that he has been spared; and—"

"Damn his treacherous hide, I wish—"

"Sally! For shame!"

"I don't care!" retorted the angry man. "It's the way *you* feel, and if you weren't so immorally pious you'd be honest and say so."

Aleck said, with wounded dignity:

"I do not see how you can say such unkind and unjust things. There is no such thing as immoral piety."

Sally felt a pang, but tried to conceal it under a shuffling attempt to save his case by changing the form of it—as if changing the form while retaining the juice could deceive the expert he was trying to placate. He said:

"I didn't mean so bad as that, Aleck; I didn't really mean immoral piety, I only meant—meant—well, conventional piety, you know; er—shop piety; the—the—why, *you* know what I mean, Aleck—the—well, where you put up the plated article and play it for solid, you know, without intending anything improper, but just out of trade habit, ancient policy, petrified custom, loyalty to—to—hang it, I can't find the right words, but *you* know what I mean, Aleck, and that there isn't any harm in it. I'll try again. You see, it's this way. If a person—"

"You have said quite enough," said Aleck, coldly; "let the subject be dropped."

"*I'm* willing," fervently responded Sally, wiping the sweat from his forehead and looking the thankfulness he had no words for. Then, musingly, he apologized to himself. "I certainly held threes—I *know* it—but I drew and didn't fill. That's where I'm so often weak in the game. If I had stood pat—but I didn't. I never do. I don't know enough."

Confessedly defeated, he was properly tame now and subdued. Aleck forgave him with her eyes.

The grand interest, the supreme interest, came instantly to the front again; nothing could keep it in the background many minutes on a stretch. The couple took up the puzzle of the absence of Tilbury's death notice. They discussed it every whichway, more or less hopefully, but they had to finish where they began, and concede that the only really sane explanation of the absence of the notice must be—and without doubt was—that Tilbury was not dead. There was something sad about it, something even a little unfair, maybe, but there it was, and had to be put up with. They were agreed as to that. To Sally it seemed a strangely inscrutable dispensation; more inscrutable than usual, he thought; one of the most unnecessarily inscrutable he could call to mind, in fact—and said so, with some feeling; but if he was hoping to draw Aleck he failed; she reserved her opinion, if she had one; she had not the habit of taking injudicious risks in any market, worldly or other.

The pair must wait for next week's paper—Tilbury had evidently postponed. That was their thought and their decision. So they put the subject away, and went about their affairs again, with as good heart as they could.

Now, if they had but known it, they had been wronging Tilbury all the time. Tilbury had kept faith, kept it to the letter; he was dead, he had died to schedule. He was dead more than four days now and used to it; entirely dead, perfectly dead, as dead as any other new person in the cemetery; dead in abundant time to get into that week's *Sagamore,* too, and only shut out by an accident; an accident which could not happen to a metropolitan journal, but which happens easily to a poor little village rag like the *Sagamore.* On this occasion, just as the editorial page was being locked up, a gratis quart of strawberry water-ice arrived from Hostetter's Ladies' and Gents' Ice-Cream Parlors, and the stickful[8] of rather chilly regret over Tilbury's translation got crowded out to make room for the editor's frantic gratitude.

On its way to the standing-galley Tilbury's notice got pied.[9] Otherwise it would have gone into some future edition, for weekly *Sagamores* do not waste "live" matter, and in their galleys "live" matter is immortal, unless a pi accident intervene. But a thing that gets pied is dead, and for such there is no resurrection; its chance of seeing print is gone, forever and ever. And so, let Tilbury like it or not, let him rave in his grave to his fill, no matter—no mention of his death would ever see the light in the *Weekly Sagamore.*

IV

Five weeks drifted tediously along. The *Sagamore* arrived regularly on the Saturdays, but never once contained a mention of Tilbury Foster. Sally's patience broke down at this point, and he said, resentfully:

"Damn his livers, he's immortal!"

Aleck gave him a very severe rebuke, and added, with icy solemnity:

"How would you feel if you were suddenly cut off just after such an awful remark had escaped out of you?"

Without sufficient reflection Sally responded:

"I'd feel I was lucky I hadn't got caught with it *in* me."

Pride had forced him to say something, and as he could not think of any rational thing to say he flung that out. Then he stole a base—as he called it—that is, slipped from the presence, to keep from getting brayed in his wife's discussion-mortar.

Six months came and went. The *Sagamore* was still silent about Tilbury. Meantime Sally had several times thrown out a feeler—that is, a hint that he would like to know. Aleck had ignored the hints. Sally now resolved to brace up and risk a frontal attack. So he squarely proposed to disguise himself and go to Tilbury's village and surreptitiously find out as to the prospects. Aleck put her foot on the dangerous project with energy and decision. She said:

"What can you be thinking of? You do keep my hands full! You have to be watched all the time, like a little child, to keep you from walking into the fire. You'll stay right where you are!"

"Why, Aleck, I could do it and not be found out—I'm certain of it."

"Sally Foster, don't you know you would have to inquire around?"

"Of course, but what of it? Nobody would suspect who I was."

"Oh, listen to the man! Some day you've got to prove to the executors that you never inquired. What then?"

He had forgotten that detail. He didn't reply; there wasn't anything to say. Aleck added:

"Now then, drop that notion out of your mind, and don't ever meddle with it again. Tilbury set that trap for you. Don't you know it's a trap?

He is on the watch, and fully expecting you to blunder into it. Well, he is going to be disappointed—at least while I am on deck. Sally!"

"Well?"

"As long as you live, if it's a hundred years, don't you ever make an inquiry. Promise!"

"All right," with a sigh and reluctantly.

Then Aleck softened and said:

"Don't be impatient. We are prospering; we can wait; there is no hurry. Our small dead-certain income increases all the time; and as to futures, I have not made a mistake yet—they are piling up by the thousands and the tens of thousands. There is not another family in the State with such prospects as ours. Already we are beginning to roll in eventual wealth. You know that, don't you?"

"Yes, Aleck, it's certainly so."

"Then be grateful for what God is doing for us, and stop worrying. You do not believe we could have achieved these prodigious results without His special help and guidance, do you?"

Hesitatingly, "N-no, I suppose not." Then, with feeling and admiration, "And yet, when it comes to judiciousness in watering a stock or putting up a hand to skin Wall Street I don't give in that *you* need any outside amateur help, if I do I wish I—"

"Oh, *do* shut up! I know you do not mean any harm or any irreverence, poor boy, but you can't seem to open your mouth without letting out things to make a person shudder. You keep me in constant dread. For you and for all of us. Once I had no fear of the thunder, but now when I hear it I—"

Her voice broke and she began to cry, and could not finish. The sight of this smote Sally to the heart, and he took her in his arms and petted her and comforted her and promised better conduct, and upbraided himself and remorsefully pleaded for forgiveness. And he was in earnest, and sorry for what he had done and ready for any sacrifice that could make up for it.

And so, in privacy he thought long and deeply over the matter, resolving to do what should seem best. It was easy to *promise* reform; indeed he had already promised it. But would that do any real good, any permanent good? No, it would be but temporary—he knew his weakness, and confessed it to himself with sorrow—he could not keep the promise. Something surer and better must be devised; and he devised it. At cost of precious money which he had long been saving up, shilling by shilling, he put a lightning-rod on the house.

At a subsequent time he relapsed.

What miracles habit can do! and how quickly and how easily habits are acquired—both trifling habits and habits which profoundly change us. If by accident we wake at two in the morning a couple of nights in succession, we have need to be uneasy, for another repetition can turn the accident into a habit; and a month's dallying with whiskey—but we all know these commonplace facts.

The castle-building habit, the day-dreaming habit—how it grows! what a luxury it becomes; how we fly to its enchantments at every idle moment, how we revel in them, steep our souls in them, intoxicate ourselves with their beguiling fantasies—oh, yes, and how soon and how easily our dream-life and our material life become so intermingled and so fused together that we can't quite tell which is which, any more.

By and by Aleck subscribed for a Chicago daily and for the *Wall Street Pointer.* With an eye single to finance she studied these as diligently all the week as she studied her Bible Sundays. Sally was lost in admiration, to note with what swift and sure strides her genius and judgment developed and expanded, in the forecasting and handling of the securities of both the material and spiritual markets. He was proud of her nerve and daring in exploiting worldly stocks, and just as proud of her conservative caution in working her spiritual deals. He noted that she never lost her head in either case; that with a splendid courage she often went short on worldly futures, but heedfully drew the line there—she was always long on the others. Her policy was quite sane and simple, as she explained it to him: what she put into earthly futures was for speculation, what she put into spiritual futures was for investment; she was willing to go into the one on a margin, and take chances, but in the case of the other, "margin her no margins"—she wanted to cash-in a hundred cents per dollar's-worth, and have the stock transferred on the books.

It took but a very few months to educate Aleck's imagination and Sally's. Each day's training added something to the spread and effectiveness of the two machines. As a consequence, Aleck made imaginary money much faster than at first she had dreamed of making it, and Sally's competency in spending the overflow of it kept pace with the strain put upon it, right along. In the beginning Aleck had given the coal speculation a twelvemonth in which to materialize, and had been loath to grant that this term might possibly be shortened by nine months. But that was the feeble work, the nursery-work, of a financial fancy that had had no teaching, no experience, no practice. These aids soon came, then that nine months vanished, and the imaginary ten-thousand-dollar investment came marching home with three hundred per cent. profit on its back!

It was a great day for the pair of Fosters. They were speechless for joy. Also speechless for another reason: after much watching of the market, Aleck had lately, with fear and trembling, made her first flyer on a "margin," using the remaining twenty thousand of the bequest in this risk. In her mind's eye she had seen it climb, point by point—always with a chance that the market would break—until at last her anxieties were too great for further endurance—she being new to the margin-business and unhardened, as yet—and she gave her imaginary broker an imaginary order by imaginary telegraph to sell. She said forty thousand dollars profit was enough. The sale was made on the very day that the coal-venture had returned with its rich freight. As I have said, the couple were speechless. They sat dazed and blissful, that night, trying to realize the immense fact, the overwhelming fact, that they were actually worth a hundred thousand dollars in clean imaginary cash. Yet so it was.

It was the last time that ever Aleck was afraid of a margin; at least afraid enough to let it break her sleep and pale her cheek to the extent that this first experience in that line had done.

Indeed it was a memorable night. Gradually the realization that they were rich sank securely home into the souls of the pair, then they began to place the money. If we could have looked out through the eyes of these dreamers, we should have seen their tidy little wooden house disappear, and a two-story brick with a cast-iron fence in front of it take its place; we should have seen a three-globed gas-chandelier grow down from the parlor ceiling; we should have seen the homely rag carpet turn to noble Brussels, a dollar and a half a yard; we should have seen the plebeian fireplace vanish away and a recherché big base-burner with isinglass windows take position and spread awe around. And we should have seen other things, too; among them the buggy, the lap-robe, the stove-pipe hat, and so on.

From that time forth, although the daughters and the neighbors saw only the same old wooden house there, it was a two-story brick to Aleck and Sally; and not a night went by that Aleck did not worry about the imaginary gas bills, and get for all comfort Sally's reckless retort, "What of it? we can afford it."

Before the couple went to bed, that first night that they were rich, they had decided that they must celebrate. They must give a party—that was the idea. But how to explain it—to the daughters and the neighbors? They could not expose the fact that they were rich. Sally was willing, even anxious, to do it; but Aleck kept her head and would not allow it. She said that although the money was as good as in, it would be as well to wait until it was actually in. On that policy she took her stand, and would not budge. The great secret must be kept, she said—kept from the daughters and everybody else.

The pair were puzzled. They must celebrate, they were determined to celebrate, but since the secret must be kept, what could they celebrate? No birthdays were due for three months. Tilbury wasn't available, evidently he was going to live forever; what the nation *could* they celebrate? That was Sally's way of putting it; and he was getting impatient, too, and harassed. But at last he hit it—just by sheer inspiration, as it seemed to him—and all their troubles were gone in a moment; they would celebrate the Discovery of America. A splendid idea!

Aleck was almost too proud of Sally for words—she said *she* never would have thought of it. But Sally, although he was bursting with delight in the compliment and with wonder at himself, tried not to let on, and said it wasn't really anything, anybody could have done it. Whereat Aleck, with a prideful toss of her happy head, said—

"Oh, certainly! Anybody could—oh, anybody! Hosannah Dilkins, for instance! Or maybe Adelbert Peanut—oh, *dear*—yes! Well, I'd like to see them try it, that's all. Dear-me-suz, if they could think of the discovery of a forty-acre island it's more than *I* believe they could; and as for a whole continent, why, Sally Foster, you know perfectly well it would strain the livers and lights out of them and *then* they couldn't!"

The dear woman, she knew he had talent; and if affection made her overestimate the size of it a little, surely it was a sweet and gentle crime, and forgiveable for its source's sake.

V

The celebration went off well. The friends were all present, both the young and the old. Among the young were Flossie and Gracie Peanut and their brother Adelbert, who was a rising young journeyman tinner, also Hosannah Dilkins, Jr., journeyman plasterer, just out of his apprenticeship. For many months Adelbert and Hosannah had been showing interest in Gwendolen and Clytemnestra Foster, and the parents of the girls had noticed this with private satisfaction. But they suddenly realized now that that feeling had passed. They recognized that the changed financial conditions had raised up a social bar between their daughters and the young mechanics. The daughters could now look higher—and must. Yes, must. They need marry nothing below the grade of lawyer or merchant; poppa and momma would take care of this; there must be no mésalliances.

However, these thinkings and projects of theirs were private, and did not show on the surface, and therefore threw no shadow upon the celebration. What showed upon the surface was a serene and lofty contentment and a dignity of carriage and gravity of deportment which compelled the admiration and likewise the wonder of the company. All noticed it, all commented upon it, but none was able to divine the secret of it. It was a marvel and a mystery. Three several persons remarked, without suspecting what clever shots they were making:

"It's as if they'd come into property."

That was just it, indeed.

Most mothers would have taken hold of the matrimonial matter in the old regulation way; they would have given the girls a talking to, of a solemn sort and untactful—a lecture calculated to defeat its own purpose, by producing tears and secret rebellion; and the said mothers would have further damaged the business by requesting the young mechanics to discontinue their attentions. But this mother was different. She was practical. She said nothing to any of the young people concerned, nor to any one else except Sally. He listened to her and understood; understood and admired. He said:

"I get the idea. Instead of finding fault with the samples on view, thus hurting feelings and obstructing trade without occasion, you merely offer a higher class of goods for the money, and leave nature to take her course. It's wisdom, Aleck, solid wisdom, and sound as a nut. Who's your fish? Have you nominated him yet?"

No, she hadn't. They must look the market over—which they did. To start with, they considered and discussed Bradish, rising young lawyer, and Fulton, rising young dentist. Sally must invite them to dinner. But not right away; there was no hurry, Aleck said. Keep an eye on the pair, and wait; nothing would be lost by going slowly in so important a matter.

It turned out that this was wisdom, too; for inside of three weeks Aleck made a wonderful strike which swelled her imaginary hundred thousand to four hundred thousand of the same quality. She and Sally were in the clouds that evening. For the first time they introduced champagne at dinner. Not real champagne, but plenty real enough for the amount of imagination expended on it. It was Sally that did it, and Aleck weakly submitted. At bottom both were troubled and ashamed, for he was a high-up Son of Temperance, and at funerals wore an apron which no dog could look upon and retain his reason and his opinion; and she was a W. C. T. U.,[10] with all that that implies of boiler-iron virtue and unendurable holiness. But there it was: the pride of riches was beginning its disintegrating work. They had lived to prove, once more, a sad truth which had been proven many times before in the world: that whereas principle is a great and noble protection against showy and degrading vanities and vices, poverty is worth six of it. More than four hundred thousand dollars to the good! They took up the matrimonial matter again. Neither the dentist nor the lawyer was mentioned; there was no occasion; they were out of the running. Disqualified. They discussed the son of the pork-packer and the son of the village banker. But finally, as in the previous case, they concluded to wait and think, and go cautiously and sure.

Luck came their way again. Aleck, ever watchful, saw a great and risky chance, and took a daring flyer. A time of trembling, of doubt, of awful uneasiness followed, for non-success meant absolute ruin and nothing short of it. Then came the result, and Aleck, faint with joy, could hardly control her voice when she said:

"The suspense is over, Sally—and we are worth a cold million!"

Sally wept for gratitude, and said:

"Oh, Electra, jewel of women, darling of my heart, we are free at last, we roll in wealth, we need never scrimp again. It's a case for Veuve Cliquot!" and he got out a pint of spruce-beer and made sacrifice, he saying "Damn the expense," and she rebuking him gently with reproachful but humid and happy eyes.

They shelved the pork-packer's son and the banker's son, and sat down to consider the Governor's son and the son of the Congressman.

VI

It were a weariness to follow in detail the leaps and bounds the Foster fictitious finances took from this time forth. It was marvellous, it was dizzying, it was dazzling. Everything Aleck touched turned to fairy gold, and heaped itself glittering toward the firmament. Millions upon millions poured in, and still the mighty stream flowed thundering along, still its vast volume increased. Five millions—ten millions—twenty—thirty—was there never to be an end?

Two years swept by in a splendid delirium, the intoxicated Fosters scarcely noticing the flight of time. They were now worth three hundred million dollars; they were in every board of directors of every prodigious combine in the country; and still, as time drifted along, the millions went on piling up, five at a time, ten at a time, as fast as they could tally them off, almost. The three hundred doubled itself—then doubled again—and yet again—and yet once more!

Twenty-four hundred millions!

The business was getting a little confused. It was necessary to take an account of stock, and straighten it out. The Fosters knew it, they felt it, they realized that it was imperative; but they also knew that to do it properly and perfectly the task must be carried to a finish without a break when once it was begun. A ten-hours' job; and where could *they* find ten leisure hours in a bunch? Sally was selling pins and sugar and calico all day and every day; Aleck was cooking and washing dishes and sweeping and making beds all day and every day, with none to help, for the daughters were being saved up for high society. The Fosters knew there was one way to get the ten hours, and only one. Both were ashamed to name it; each waited for the other to do it. Finally Sally said—

"Somebody's got to give in. It's up to me. Consider that I've named it—never mind pronouncing it out loud."

Aleck colored, but was grateful. Without further remark, they fell. Fell, and broke the Sabbath. For that was their only free ten-hour stretch. It was but another step in the downward path. Others would follow. Vast wealth has temptations which fatally and surely undermine the moral structure of persons not habituated to its possession.

They pulled down the shades and broke the Sabbath. With hard and patient labor they overhauled their holdings, and listed them. And a long-drawn procession of formidable names it was! Starting with the Railway Systems, Steamer Lines, Standard Oil, Ocean Cables, Diluted Telegraph, and all the rest, and winding up with Klondike, De Beers, Tammany Graft, and Shady Privileges in the Post-office Department.

Twenty-four hundred millions, and all safely planted in Good Things, gilt-edged and interest-bearing. Income, $120,000,000 a year. Aleck fetched a long purr of soft delight, and said—

"Is it enough?"

"It is, Aleck."

"What shall we do?"

"Stand pat."

"Retire from business?"

"That's it."

"I am agreed. The good work is finished; we will take a long rest and enjoy the money."

"Good! Aleck?"

"Yes, dear?"

"How much of the income can we spend?"

"The whole of it."

It seemed to her husband that a ton of chains fell from his limbs. He did not say a word; he was happy beyond the power of speech.

After that, they broke the Sabbaths right along, as fast as they turned up. It is the first wrong steps that count. Every Sunday they put in the whole day, after morning service, on inventions—inventions of ways to spend the money. They got to continuing this delicious dissipation until past midnight; and at every séance Aleck lavished millions upon great charities and religious enterprises, and Sally lavished like sums upon matters to which (at first) he gave definite names. Only at first. Later the names gradually lost sharpness of outline, and eventually faded into "sundries," thus becoming entirely—but safely—undescriptive. For Sally was crumbling. The placing of these millions added seriously and most uncomfortably to the family expenses—in tallow candles. For a while Aleck was worried. Then, after a little, she ceased to worry, for the occasion of it was gone. She was pained, she was grieved, she was ashamed; but she said nothing, and so became an accessory. Sally was taking candles; he was robbing the store. It is ever thus. Vast wealth, to the person unaccustomed to it, is a bane; it eats into the flesh and bone of his morals. When the Fosters were poor, they could have been trusted with untold candles. But now they—but let us not dwell upon it. From candles to apples is but a step: Sally got to taking apples; then soap; then maple-sugar; then canned goods; then crockery. How easy it is to go from bad to worse, when once we have started upon a downward course!

Meantime, other effects had been milestoning the course of the Fosters' splendid financial march. The fictitious brick dwelling had given place to an imaginary granite one with a checker-board mansard roof; in time this one disappeared and gave place to a still grander home—and so on and so on. Mansion after mansion, made of air, rose, higher, broader, finer, and each in its turn vanished away; until now, in these latter great days, our dreamers were in fancy housed, in a distant region, in a sumptuous vast palace which looked out from a leafy summit upon a noble prospect of vale and river and receding hills steeped in tinted mists—and all private, all the property of the dreamers; a palace swarming with liveried servants, and populous with guests of fame and power, hailing from all the world's capitals, foreign and domestic.

This palace was far, far away toward the rising sun, immeasurably remote, astronomically remote, in Newport, Rhode Island, Holy Land of High Society, ineffable Domain of the American Aristocracy. As a rule, they spent a part of every Sabbath—after morning service—in this sumptuous home, the rest of it they spent in Europe, or in dawdling around in their private yacht. Six days of sordid and plodding fact-life at home on the ragged edge of Lakeside and straitened means, the seventh in Fairyland—such had become their programme and their habit.

In their sternly restricted fact-life they remained as of old—plodding, diligent, careful, practical, economical. They stuck loyally to the little Presbyterian Church, and labored faithfully in its interests and stood by its high and tough doctrines with all their mental and spiritual energies. But in their dream-life they obeyed the invitations of their fancies, whatever they might be, and howsoever the fancies might change. Aleck's fancies were not very capricious, and not frequent, but Sally's scattered a good deal. Aleck, in her dream-life, went over to the Episcopal camp, on account of its large official titles; next she became High-church on account of the candles and shows; and next she naturally changed to Rome, where there were cardinals and more candles. But these excursions were as nothing to Sally's. His dream-life was a glowing and continuous and persistent excitement, and he kept every part of it fresh and sparkling by frequent changes, the religious part along with the rest. He worked his religions hard, and changed them with his shirt.

The liberal spendings of the Fosters upon their fancies began early in their prosperities, and grew in prodigality step by step with their advancing fortunes. In time they became truly enormous. Aleck built a university or two per Sunday; also a hospital or two; also a Rowton hotel[11] or so; also a batch of churches; now and then a cathedral; and once, with untimely and ill-chosen playfulness, Sally said, "It was a cold day when she didn't ship a cargo of missionaries to persuade unreflecting Chinamen to trade off twenty-four carat Confucianism for counterfeit Christianity."

This rude and unfeeling language hurt Aleck to the heart, and she went from the presence crying. That spectacle went to his own heart, and in his pain and shame he would have given worlds to have those unkind words back. She had uttered no syllable of reproach—and that cut him. Not one suggestion that he look at his own record—and she could have made, oh, so many, and such blistering ones! Her generous silence brought a swift revenge, for it turned his thoughts upon himself, it summoned before him a spectral procession, a moving vision of his life as he had been leading it these past few years of limitless prosperity, and as he sat there reviewing it his cheeks burned and his soul was steeped in humiliation. Look at her life—how fair it was, and tending ever upward; and look at his own—how frivolous, how charged with mean vanities, how selfish, how empty, how ignoble! And its trend—never upward, but downward, ever downward!

He instituted comparisons between her record and his own. He had found fault with her—so he mused—*he!* And what could he say for himself? When she built her first church what was he doing? Gathering other blasé multimillionaires into a Poker Club; defiling his own palace with it; losing hundreds of thousands to it at every sitting, and sillily vain of the admiring notoriety it made for him. When she was building her first university, what was he doing? Polluting himself with a gay and dissipated secret life in the company of other fast bloods, multimillionaires in money and paupers in character. When she was building her first foundling asylum, what was he doing? Alas! When she was projecting her noble Society for the Purifying of the Sex, what was he doing? Ah, what, indeed! When she and the W. C. T. U. and the Woman with the Hatchet,[12] moving with resistless march, were sweeping the fatal bottle from the land, what was he doing? Getting drunk three times a day. When she, builder of a hundred cathedrals, was being gratefully welcomed and blest in papal Rome and decorated with the Golden Rose which she had so honorably earned, what was he doing? Breaking the bank at Monte Carlo.

He stopped. He could go no farther; he could not bear the rest. He rose up, with a great resolution upon his lips: this secret life should be revealed, and confessed; no longer would he live it clandestinely; he would go and tell her All.

And that is what he did. He told her All; and wept upon her bosom; wept, and moaned, and begged for her forgiveness. It was a profound shock, and she staggered under the blow, but he was her own, the core of her heart, the blessing of her eyes, her all in all, she could deny him nothing, and she forgave him. She felt that he could never again be quite to her what he had been before; she knew that he could only repent, and not reform; yet all morally defaced and decayed as he was, was he not her own, her very own, the idol of her deathless worship? She said she was his serf, his slave, and she opened her yearning heart and took him in.

VII

One Sunday afternoon some time after this they were sailing the summer seas in their dream-yacht, and reclining in lazy luxury under the awning of the after-deck. There was silence, for each was busy with his own thoughts. These seasons of silence had insensibly been growing more and more frequent of late; the old nearness and cordiality were waning. Sally's terrible revelation had done its work; Aleck had tried hard to drive the memory of it out of her mind, but it would not go, and the shame and bitterness of it were poisoning her gracious dream-life. She could see now (on Sundays) that her husband was becoming a bloated and repulsive Thing. She could not close her eyes to this, and in these days she no longer looked at him, Sundays, when she could help it.

But she—was she herself without blemish? Alas, she knew she was not. She was keeping a secret from him, she was acting dishonorably toward him, and many a pang it was costing her. *She was breaking the compact, and concealing it from him.* Under strong temptation she had gone into business again; she had risked their whole fortune in a purchase of all the railway systems and coal and steel companies in the country on a margin, and she was now trembling, every Sabbath hour, lest through some chance word of hers he find it out. In her misery and remorse for this treachery she could not keep her heart from going out to him in pity; she was filled with compunctions to see him lying there, drunk and content, and never suspecting. Never suspecting—trusting her with a perfect and pathetic trust, and she holding over him by a thread a possible calamity of so devastating a—

"*Say*—Aleck?"

The interrupting words brought her suddenly to herself. She was grateful to have that persecuting subject from her thoughts, and she answered, with much of the old-time tenderness in her tone:

"Yes, dear."

"Do you know, Aleck, I think we are making a mistake—that is, you are. I mean about the marriage business." He sat up, fat and froggy and benevolent, like a bronze Buddha, and grew earnest. "Consider—it's more than five years. You've continued the same policy from the start: with every rise, always holding on for five points higher. Always when I think we are going to have some weddings, you see a bigger thing ahead, and I undergo another disappointment. *I* think you are too hard to please. Some day we'll get left. First, we turned down the dentist and the lawyer. That was all right—it was sound. Next, we turned down the banker's son and the pork-butcher's heir—right again, and sound. Next, we turned down the Congressman's son and the Governor's—right as a trivet, I confess it. Next, the Senator's son and the son of the Vice-President of the United States—perfectly right, there's no permanency about those little distinctions. Then you went for the aristocracy; and I thought we had struck oil at last—yes. We would make a plunge at the Four Hundred, and pull in some ancient lineage, venerable, holy, ineffable, mellow with the antiquity of a hundred and fifty years, disinfected of the ancestral odors of salt cod and pelts all of a century ago, and unsmirched by a day's work since; and then! why, then the marriages, of course. But no, along comes a pair of real aristocrats from Europe, and straightway you throw over the half-breeds. It was awfully discouraging, Aleck! Since then, what a procession! You turned down the baronets for a pair of barons; you turned down the barons for a pair of viscounts; the viscounts for a pair of earls; the earls for a pair of marquises; the marquises for a brace of dukes. *Now,* Aleck, cash in!—you've played the limit. You've got a job lot of four dukes under the hammer; of four nationalities; all sound in wind and limb and pedigree, all bankrupt and in debt up to the ears. They come high, but we can afford it. Come, Aleck, don't delay any longer, don't keep up the suspense: take the whole lay-out, and leave the girls to choose!"

Aleck had been smiling blandly and contentedly all through this arraignment of her marriage-policy; a pleasant light, as of triumph with perhaps a nice surprise peeping out through it, rose in her eyes, and she said, as calmly as she could—

"Sally, what would you say to—*royalty*?"

Prodigious! Poor man, it knocked him silly, and he fell over the garboard-strake and barked his shin on the cat-heads. He was dizzy for a moment, then he gathered himself up and limped over and sat down by his wife and beamed his old-time admiration and affection upon her in floods, out of his bleary eyes.

"By George!" he said, fervently, "Aleck, you *are* great—the greatest woman in the whole earth! I can't ever learn the whole size of you. I can't ever learn the immeasurable deeps of you. Here I've been considering myself qualified to criticise your game. *I!* Why, if I had stopped to think, I'd have known you had a lone hand up your sleeve. Now, dear heart, I'm all red-hot impatience—tell me about it!"

The flattered and happy woman put her lips to his ear and whispered a princely name. It made him catch his breath, it lit his face with exultation.

"Land!" he said, "it's a stunning catch! He's got a gambling-hell, and a graveyard, and a bishop, and a cathedral—all his very own. And all gilt-edged five-hundred-per-cent. stock, every detail of it; the tidiest little property in Europe. And that graveyard—it's the selectest in the world:

none but suicides admitted; *yes,* sir, and the free-list suspended, too, *all* the time. There isn't much land in the principality, but there's enough: eight hundred acres in the graveyard and forty-two outside. It's a *sovereignty*—that's the main thing; *land's* nothing. There's plenty land, Sahara's drugged with it."

Aleck glowed; she was profoundly happy. She said—

"Think of it, Sally—it is a family that has never married outside the Royal and Imperial Houses of Europe: our grandchildren will sit upon thrones!"

"True as you live, Aleck—and bear sceptres, too; and handle them as naturally and nonchalantly as I handle a yardstick. It's a grand catch, Aleck. He's corralled, is he? Can't get away? You didn't take him on a margin?"

"No. Trust me for that. He's not a liability, he's an asset. So is the other one."

"Who is it, Aleck?"

"His Royal Highness Sigismund-Siegfried-Lauenfeld-Dinkelspiel-Schwartzenberg Blutwurst, Hereditary Grand Duke of Katzenyammer."

"No! You can't mean it!"

"It's as true as I'm sitting here, I give you my word," she answered.

His cup was full, and he hugged her to his heart with rapture, saying—

"How wonderful it all seems, and how beautiful! It's one of the oldest and noblest of the three hundred and sixty-four ancient German principalities, and one of the few that was allowed to retain its royal estate when Bismarck got done trimming them. I know that farm, I've been there. It's got a ropewalk and a candle-factory and an army. Standing army. Infantry and cavalry. Three soldiers and a horse. Aleck, it's been a long wait, and full of heartbreak and hope deferred, but God knows I am happy now. Happy, and grateful to you, my own, who have done it all. When is it to be?"

"Next Sunday."

"Good. And we'll want to do these weddings up in the very regalest style that's going. It's properly due to the royal quality of the parties of the first part. Now as I understand it, there is only one kind of marriage that is sacred to royalty, exclusive to royalty: it's the morganatic."

"What do they call it that for, Sally?"

"I don't know; but anyway it's royal, and royal only."

"Then we will insist upon it. More—I will compel it. It is morganatic marriage or none."

"That settles it!" said Sally, rubbing his hands with delight. "And it will be the very first in America. Aleck, it will make Newport sick."

Then they fell silent, and drifted away upon their dream-wings to the far regions of the earth to invite all the crowned heads and their families and provide gratis transportation for them.

VIII

During three days the couple walked upon air, with their heads in the clouds. They were but vaguely conscious of their surroundings, they saw all things dimly, as through a veil, they were steeped in dreams, often they did not hear when they were spoken to, they often did not understand when they heard; they answered confusedly or at random; Sally sold molasses by weight, sugar by the yard, and furnished soap when asked for candles, and Aleck put the cat in the wash and fed milk to the soiled linen. Everybody was stunned and amazed, and went about muttering, "What *can* be the matter with the Fosters?"

Three days. Then came events! Things had taken a happy turn, and for forty-eight hours Aleck's imaginary corner had been booming. Up—up—still up! Cost-point was passed. Still up—and up—and up! Five points above cost—then ten—fifteen—twenty! Twenty points cold profit on the vast venture, now, and Aleck's imaginary brokers were shouting frantically by imaginary long-distance, "Sell! sell! for Heaven's sake *sell*!"

She broke the splendid news to Sally, and he, too, said "Sell! sell—oh, don't make a blunder, now, you own the earth!—sell, sell!" But she set her iron will and lashed it amidships, and said she would hold on for five points more if she died for it.

It was a fatal resolve. The very next day came the historic crash, the record crash, the devastating crash, when the bottom fell out of Wall Street, and the whole body of gilt-edged stocks dropped ninety-five points in five hours, and the multimillionaire was seen begging his bread in the Bowery. Aleck sternly held her grip and "put up" as long as she could, but at last there came a call which she was powerless to meet, and her imaginary brokers sold her out. Then, and not till then, the man in her was vanquished, and the woman in her resumed sway. She put her arms about her husband's neck and wept, saying—

"I am to blame, do not forgive me, I cannot bear it. We are paupers! Paupers, and I am so miserable. The weddings will never come off; all that is past; we could not even buy the dentist, now."

A bitter reproach was on Sally's tongue: "I *begged* you to sell, but you—" He did not say it; he had not the heart to add a hurt to that broken and repentant spirit. A nobler thought came to him and he said—

"Bear up, my Aleck, all is not lost! You really never invested a penny of my uncle's bequest, but only its unmaterialized future; what we have lost was only the increment harvested from that future by your incomparable financial judgment and sagacity. Cheer up, banish these griefs; we still have the thirty thousand untouched; and with the experience which you have acquired, think what you will be able to do with it in a couple of years! The marriages are not off, they are only postponed."

These were blessed words. Aleck saw how true they were, and their influence was electric; her tears ceased to flow, and her great spirit rose to its full stature again. With flashing eye and grateful heart, and with hand uplifted in pledge and prophecy, she said—

"Now and here I proclaim—"

But she was interrupted by a visitor. It was the editor and proprietor of the *Sagamore*. He had happened into Lakeside to pay a duty-call upon an obscure grandmother of his who was nearing the end of her pilgrimage, and with the idea of combining business with grief[13] he had looked up the Fosters, who had been so absorbed in other things for the past four years that they had neglected to pay up their subscription. Six dollars due. No visitor could have been more welcome. He would know all about Uncle Tilbury and what his chances might be getting to be, cemeterywards. They could of course ask no questions, for that would squelch the bequest, but they could nibble around on the edge of the subject and hope for results. The scheme did not work. The obtuse editor did not know he was being nibbled at; but at last, chance accomplished what art had failed in. In illustration of something under discussion which required the help of metaphor, the editor said—

"Land, it's as tough as Tilbury Foster!—as *we* say."

It was sudden, and it made the Fosters jump. The editor noticed it, and said, apologetically—

"No harm intended, I assure you. It's just a saying; just a joke, you know—nothing in it. Relation of yours?"

Sally crowded his burning eagerness down, and answered with all the indifference he could assume—

"I—well, not that I know of, but we've heard of him." The editor was thankful, and resumed his composure. Sally added, "Is he—is he—well?"

"Is he *well*? Why, bless you he's in Sheol these five years!"

The Fosters were trembling with grief, though it felt like joy. Sally said, non-committally—and tentatively:

"Ah, well, such is life, and none can escape—not even the rich are spared."

The editor laughed.

"If you are including Tilbury," said he, "it don't apply. *He* hadn't a cent; the town had to bury him."

The Fosters sat petrified for two minutes; petrified and cold. Then, white-faced and weak-voiced, Sally asked:

"Is it true? Do you *know* it to be true?"

"Well, I should say! I was one of the executors. He hadn't anything to leave but a wheelbarrow, and he left that to me. It hadn't any wheel, and wasn't any good. Still, it was something, and so, to square up, I scribbled off a sort of a little obituarial send-off for him, but it got crowded out."

The Fosters were not listening—their cup was full, it could contain no more. They sat with bowed heads, dead to all things but the ache at their hearts.

An hour later. Still they sat there, bowed, motionless, silent, the visitor long ago gone, they unaware.

Then they stirred, and lifted their heads wearily, and gazed at each other wistfully, dreamily, dazed; then presently began to twaddle to each other in a wandering and childish way. At intervals they lapsed into silences, leaving a sentence unfinished, seemingly either unaware of it or losing their way. Sometimes, when they woke out of these silences, they had a dim and transient consciousness that something had happened to their minds; then with a dumb and yearning solicitude they would softly caress each other's hands in mutual compassion and support, as if they would say: "I am near you, I will not forsake you, we will bear it together; somewhere there is release and forgetfulness, somewhere there is a grave and peace; be patient, it will not be long."

They lived yet two years, in mental night, always brooding, steeped in vague regrets and melancholy dreams, never speaking; then release came to both on the same day.

Toward the end the darkness lifted from Sally's ruined mind for a moment, and he said:

"Vast wealth, acquired by sudden and unwholesome means, is a snare. It did us no good, transient were its feverish pleasures; yet for its sake we threw away our sweet and simple and happy life—let others take warning by us."

He lay silent a while, with closed eyes; then as the chill of death crept upward toward his heart, and consciousness was fading from his brain, he muttered:

"Money had brought him misery, and he took his revenge upon us, who had done him no harm. He had his desire: with base and cunning calculation he left us but thirty thousand, knowing we would try to increase it, and ruin our life and break our hearts. Without added expense he could have left us far above desire of increase,[14] far above the temptation to speculate, and a kinder soul would have done it; but in him was no generous spirit, no pity, no—"

[1904]

Eve's Diary

TRANSLATED FROM THE ORIGINAL

SATURDAY—I am almost a whole day old now. I arrived yesterday. That is as it seems to me. And it must be so, for if there was a day-before-yesterday I was not there when it happened, or I should remember it. It could be, of course, that it did happen, and that I was not noticing. Very well; I will be very watchful, now, and if any day-before-yesterdays happen I will make a note of it. It will be best to start right and not let the record get confused, for some instinct tells me that these details are going to be important to the historian some day. For I feel like an experiment, I feel exactly like an experiment, it would be impossible for a person to feel more like an experiment than I do, and so I am coming to feel convinced that that is what I *am*—an experiment; just an experiment, and nothing more.

Then if I am an experiment, am I the whole of it? No, I think not; I think the rest of it is part of it. I am the main part of it, but I think the rest of it has its share in the matter. Is my position assured, or do I have to watch it and take care of it? The latter, perhaps. Some instinct tells me that eternal vigilance is the price of supremacy.[1] [That is a good phrase, I think, for one so young.]

Everything looks better to-day than it did yesterday. In the rush of finishing up yesterday, the mountains were left in a ragged condition, and some of the plains were so cluttered with rubbish and remnants that the aspects were quite distressing. Noble and beautiful works of art should not be subjected to haste; and this majestic new world is indeed a most noble and beautiful work. And certainly marvellously near to being perfect, notwithstanding the shortness of the time. There are too many stars in some places and not enough in others, but that can be remedied presently, no doubt. The moon got loose last night, and slid down and fell out of the scheme—a very great loss; it breaks my heart to think of it. There isn't another thing among the ornaments and decorations that is comparable to it for beauty and finish. It should have been fastened better. If we can only get it back again—

But of course there is no telling where it went to. And besides, whoever gets it will hide it; I know it because I would do it myself. I believe I can be honest in all other matters, but I already begin to realize that the core and centre of my nature is love of the beautiful, a passion for the beautiful, and that it would not be safe to trust me with a moon that belonged to another person and that person didn't know I had it. I could give up a moon that I found in the daytime, because I should be afraid some one was looking; but if I found it in the dark, I am sure I should find some kind of an excuse for not saying anything about it. For I do love moons, they are so pretty and so romantic. I wish we had five or six; I would never go to bed; I should never get tired lying on the moss-bank and looking up at them.

Stars are good, too. I wish I could get some to put in my hair. But I suppose I never can. You would be surprised to find how far off they are, for they do not look it. When they first showed, last night, I tried to knock some down with a pole, but it didn't reach, which astonished me; then I tried clods till I was all tired out, but I never got one. It was because I am left-handed and cannot throw good. Even when I aimed at the one I wasn't after I couldn't hit the other one, though I did make some close shots, for I saw the black blot of the clod sail right into the midst of the golden clusters forty or fifty times, just barely missing them, and if I could have held out a little longer maybe I could have got one.

So I cried a little, which was natural, I suppose, for one of my age, and after I was rested I got a basket and started for a place on the extreme rim of the circle, where the stars were close to the ground and I could get them with my hands, which would be better, anyway, because I could gather them tenderly then, and not break them. But it was farther than I thought, and at last I had to give it up; I was so tired I couldn't drag my feet another step; and besides, they were sore and hurt me very much.

I couldn't get back home; it was too far and turning cold; but I found some tigers and nestled in among them and was most adorably comfortable, and their breath was sweet and pleasant, because they live on strawberries. I had never seen a tiger before, but I knew them in a minute by the stripes. If I could have one of those skins, it would make a lovely gown.

To-day I am getting better ideas about distances. I was so eager to get hold of every pretty thing that I giddily grabbed for it, sometimes when it was too far off, and sometimes when it was but six inches away but seemed a foot—alas, with thorns between! I learned a lesson; also I made an axiom, all out of my own head—my very first one: *The scratched Experiment shuns the thorn.* I think it is a very good one for one so young.

I followed the other Experiment around, yesterday afternoon, at a distance, to see what it might be for, if I could. But I was not able to make out. I think it is a man. I had never seen a man, but it looked like one, and I feel sure that that is what it is. I realize that I feel more curiosity about it than about any of the other reptiles. If it is a reptile, and I suppose it is; for it has frowsy hair and blue eyes, and looks like a reptile. It has no hips; it tapers like a carrot; when it stands, it spreads itself apart like a derrick; so I think it is a reptile, though it may be architecture.

I was afraid of it at first, and started to run every time it turned around, for I thought it was going to chase me; but by-and-by I found it was only trying to get away, so after that I was not timid any more, but tracked it along, several hours, about twenty yards behind, which made it nervous and unhappy. At last it was a good deal worried, and climbed a tree. I waited a good while, then gave it up and went home.

To-day the same thing over. I've got it up the tree again.

SUNDAY—It is up there yet. Resting, apparently. But that is a subterfuge: Sunday isn't the day of rest; Saturday is appointed for that. It looks to me like a creature that is more interested in resting than anything else. It would tire me to rest so much. It tires me just to sit around and watch the tree. I do wonder what it is for; I never see it do anything.

They returned the moon last night, and I was *so* happy! I think it is very honest of them. It slid down and fell off again, but I was not distressed; there is no need to worry when one has that kind of neighbors; they will fetch it back. I wish I could do something to show my appreciation. I would like to send them some stars, for we have more than we can use. I mean I, not we, for I can see that the reptile cares nothing for such things.

It has low tastes, and is not kind. When I went there yesterday evening in the gloaming it had crept down and was trying to catch the little speckled fishes that play in the pool, and I had to clod it to make it go up the tree again and let them alone. I wonder if *that* is what it is for? Hasn't it any heart? Hasn't it any compassion for those little creatures? Can it be that it was designed and manufactured for such ungentle work? It has the look of it. One of the clods took it back of the ear, and it used language. It gave me a thrill, for it was the first time I had ever heard speech, except my own. I did not understand the words, but they seemed expressive.

When I found it could talk I felt a new interest in it, for I love to talk; I talk all day, and in my sleep, too, and I am very interesting, but if I had another to talk to I could be twice as interesting, and would never stop, if desired.

If this reptile is a man, it isn't an *it,* is it? That wouldn't be grammatical, would it? I think it would be *he.* I think so. In that case one would parse it thus: nominative, *he;* dative, *him;* possessive, *his'n.* Well, I will consider it a man and call it he until it turns out to be something else. This will be handier than having so many uncertainties.

NEXT WEEK SUNDAY—All the week I tagged around after him and tried to get acquainted. I had to do the talking, because he was so shy, but I didn't mind it. He seemed pleased to have me around, and I used the sociable "we" a good deal, because it seemed to flatter him to be included.

WEDNESDAY—We are getting along very well indeed, now, and getting better and better acquainted. He does not try to avoid me any more, which is a good sign, and shows that he likes to have me with him. That pleases me, and I study to be useful to him in every way I can, so as to increase his regard. During the last day or two I have taken all the work of naming things off his hands, and this has been a great relief to him, for he has no gift in that line, and is evidently very grateful. He can't think of a rational name to save him, but I do not let him see that I am aware of his defect. Whenever a new creature comes along I name it before he has time to expose himself by an awkward silence. In this way I have saved him many embarrassments. I have no defect like his. The minute I set eyes on an animal I know what it is. I don't have to reflect a moment; the right name comes out instantly, just as if it were an inspiration, as no doubt it is, for I am sure it wasn't in me half a minute before. I seem to know just by the shape of the creature and the way it acts what animal it is.

When the dodo came along he thought it was a wildcat—I saw it in his eye. But I saved him. And I was careful not to do it in a way that could hurt his pride. I just spoke up in a quite natural way of pleased surprise, and not as if I was dreaming of conveying information, and said, "Well, I do declare if there isn't the dodo!" I explained—without seeming to be explaining—how I knew it for a dodo, and although I thought maybe he was a little piqued that I knew the creature when he didn't, it was quite evident that he admired me. That was very agreeable, and I thought of it more than once with gratification before I slept. How little a thing can make us happy when we feel that we have earned it.

THURSDAY—My first sorrow. Yesterday he avoided me and seemed to wish I would not talk to him. I could not believe it, and thought there was some mistake, for I loved to be with him, and loved to hear him talk, and so how could it be that he could feel unkind towards me when I had not done anything? But at last it seemed true, so I went away and sat lonely in the place where I first saw him the morning that we were made and I did not know what he was and was indifferent about him; but now it was a mournful place, and every little thing spoke of him, and my heart was very sore. I did not know why very clearly, for it was a new feeling; I had not experienced it before, and it was all a mystery, and I could not make it out.

But when night came I could not bear the lonesomeness, and went to the new shelter which he has built, to ask him what I had done that was wrong and how I could mend it and get back his kindness again; but he put me out in the rain, and it was my first sorrow.

SUNDAY—It is pleasant again, now, and I am happy; but those were heavy days; I do not think of them when I can help it.

I tried to get him some of those apples, but I cannot learn to throw straight. I failed, but I think the good intention pleased him. They are forbidden, and he says I shall come to harm; but so I come to harm through pleasing him, why shall I care for that harm?

MONDAY—This morning I told him my name, hoping it would interest him. But he did not care for it. It is strange. If he should tell me his name, I would care. I think it would be pleasanter in my ears than any other sound.

He talks very little. Perhaps it is because he is not bright, and is sensitive about it and wishes to conceal it. It is such a pity that he should feel so, for brightness is nothing; it is in the heart that the values lie. I wish I could make him understand that a loving good heart is riches, and riches enough, and that without it intellect is poverty.

Although he talks so little he has quite a considerable vocabulary. This morning he used a surprisingly good word. He evidently recognized, himself, that it was a good one, for he worked it in twice afterward, casually. It was not good casual art, still it showed that he possesses a certain quality of perception. Without a doubt that seed can be made to grow, if cultivated.

Where did he get that word? I do not think I have ever used it.

No, he took no interest in my name. I tried to hide my disappointment, but I suppose I did not succeed. I went away and sat on the moss-bank with my feet in the water. It is where I go when I hunger for companionship, some one to look at, some one to talk to. It is not enough—that lovely white body painted there in the pool—but it is something, and something is better than utter loneliness. It talks when I talk; it is sad when I am sad;

it comforts me with its sympathy; it says, "Do not be downhearted, you poor friendless girl; I will be your friend." It *is* a good friend to me, and my only one; it is my sister.

That first time that she forsook me! ah, I shall never forget that—never, never. My heart was lead in my body! I said, "She was all I had, and now she is gone!" In my despair I said, "Break, my heart; I cannot bear my life any more!" and hid my face in my hands, and there was no solace for me. And when I took them away, after a little, there she was again, white and shining and beautiful, and I sprang into her arms!

That was perfect happiness; I had known happiness before, but it was not like this, which was ecstasy. I never doubted her afterwards. Sometimes she stayed away—maybe an hour, maybe almost the whole day, but I waited and did not doubt; I said, "She is busy, or she is gone a journey, but she will come." And it was so: she always did. At night she would not come if it was dark, for she was a timid little thing; but if there was a moon she would come. I am not afraid of the dark, but she is younger than I am; she was born after I was. Many and many are the visits I have paid her; she is my comfort and my refuge when my life is hard—and it is mainly that.

TUESDAY—All the morning I was at work improving the estate; I purposely kept away from him in the hope that he would get lonely and come. But he did not.

At noon I stopped for the day and took my recreation by flitting all about with the bees and the butterflies and revelling in the flowers, those beautiful creatures that catch the smile of God out of the sky and preserve it! I gathered them, and made them into wreaths and garlands and clothed myself in them whilst I ate my luncheon—apples, of course; then I sat in the shade and wished and waited. But he did not come.

But no matter. Nothing would have come of it, for he does not care for flowers. He calls them rubbish, and cannot tell one from another, and thinks it is superior to feel like that. He does not care for me, he does not care for flowers, he does not care for the painted sky at eventide—is there anything he does care for, except building shacks to coop himself up in from the good clean rain, and thumping the melons, and sampling the grapes, and fingering the fruit on the trees, to see how those properties are coming along?

I laid a dry stick on the ground and tried to bore a hole in it with another one, in order to carry out a scheme that I had, and soon I got an awful fright. A thin, transparent bluish film rose out of the hole, and I dropped everything and ran! I thought it was a spirit, and I *was* so frightened! But I looked back, and it was not coming; so I leaned against a rock and rested and panted, and let my limbs go on trembling until they got steady again; then I crept warily back, alert, watching, and ready to fly if there was occasion; and when I was come near, I parted the branches of a rose-bush and peeped through—wishing the man was about, I was looking so cunning and pretty—but the sprite was gone. I went there, and there was a pinch of delicate pink dust in the hole. I put my finger in, to feel it, and said *ouch!* and took it out again. It was a cruel pain. I put my finger in my mouth; and by standing first on one foot and then the other, and grunting, I presently eased my misery; then I was full of interest, and began to examine.

I was curious to know what the pink dust was. Suddenly the name of it occurred to me, though I had never heard of it before. It was *fire*! I was as certain of it as a person could be of anything in the world. So without hesitation I named it that—fire.

I had created something that didn't exist before; I had added a new thing to the world's uncountable properties; I realized this, and was proud of my achievement, and was going to run and find him and tell him about it, thinking to raise myself in his esteem—but I reflected, and did not do it. No—he would not care for it. He would ask what it was good for, and what could I answer? for if it was not *good* for something, but only beautiful, merely beautiful—

So I sighed, and did not go. For it wasn't good for anything; it could not build a shack, it could not improve melons, it could not hurry a fruit crop; it was useless, it was a foolishness and a vanity; he would despise it and say cutting words. But to me it was not despicable; I said, "Oh, you fire, I love you, you dainty pink creature, for you are *beautiful*—and that is enough!" and was going to gather it to my breast. But refrained. Then I made another maxim out of my own head, though it was so nearly like the first one that I was afraid it was only a plagiarism: *"The burnt Experiment shuns the fire."*

I wrought again; and when I had made a good deal of fire-dust I emptied it into a handful of dry brown grass, intending to carry it home and keep it always and play with it; but the wind struck it and it sprayed up and spat out at me fiercely, and I dropped it and ran. When I looked back the blue spirit was towering up and stretching and rolling away like a cloud, and instantly I thought of the name of it—*smoke!*—though, upon my word, I had never heard of smoke before.

Soon, brilliant yellow-and-red flares shot up through the smoke, and

I named them in an instant—*flames!*—and I was right, too, though these were the very first flames that had ever been in the world. They climbed the trees, they flashed splendidly in and out of the vast and increasing volume of tumbling smoke, and I had to clap my hands and laugh and dance in my rapture, it was so new and strange and so wonderful and so beautiful!

He came running, and stopped and gazed, and said not a word for many minutes. Then he asked what it was. Ah, it was too bad that he should ask such a direct question. I had to answer it, of course, and I did. I said it was fire. If it annoyed him that I should know and he must ask, that was not my fault; I had no desire to annoy him. After a pause he asked,

"How did it come?"

Another direct question, and it also had to have a direct answer.

"I made it."

The fire was travelling farther and farther off. He went to the edge of the burned place and stood looking down, and said,

"What are these?"

"Fire-coals."

He picked up one to examine it, but changed his mind and put it down again. Then he went away. *Nothing* interests him.

But I was interested. There were ashes, gray and soft and delicate and pretty—I knew what they were at once. And the embers; I knew the embers, too. I found my apples, and raked them out, and was glad; for I am very young and my appetite is active. But I was disappointed; they were all burst open and spoiled. Spoiled apparently; but it was not so; they were better than raw ones. Fire is beautiful; some day it will be useful, I think.

FRIDAY—I saw him again, for a moment, last Monday at nightfall, but only for a moment. I was hoping he would praise me for trying to improve the estate, for I had meant well and had worked hard. But he was not pleased, and turned away and left me. He was also displeased on another account: I tried once more to persuade him to stop going over the Falls. That was because the fire had revealed to me a new passion—quite new, and distinctly different from love, grief, and those others which I had already discovered—*fear.* And it is horrible!—I wish I had never discovered it; it gives me dark moments, it spoils my happiness, it makes me shiver and tremble and shudder. But I could not persuade him, for he has not discovered fear yet, and so he could not understand me.

EXTRACT FROM ADAM'S DIARY

Perhaps I ought to remember that she is very young, a mere girl, and make allowances. She is all interest, eagerness, vivacity, the world is to her a charm, a wonder, a mystery, a joy; she can't speak for delight when she finds a new flower, she must pet it and caress it and smell it and talk to it, and pour out endearing names upon it. And she is color-mad: brown rocks, yellow sand, gray moss, green foliage, blue-sky; the pearl of the dawn, the purple shadows on the mountains, the golden islands floating in crimson seas at sunset, the pallid moon sailing through the shredded cloud-rack, the star-jewels glittering in the wastes of space—none of them is of any practical value, so far as I can see, but because they have color and majesty, that is enough for her, and she loses her mind over them. If she could quiet down and keep still a couple of minutes at a time, it would be a reposeful spectacle. In that case I think I could enjoy looking at her; indeed I am sure I could, for I am coming to realize that she is a quite remarkably comely creature—lithe, slender, trim, rounded, shapely, nimble, graceful; and once when she was standing marble-white and sun-drenched on a boulder, with her young head tilted back and her hand shading her eyes, watching the flight of a bird in the sky, I recognized that she was beautiful.

MONDAY NOON—If there is anything on the planet that she is not interested in it is not in my list. There are animals that I am indifferent to, but it is not so with her. She has no discrimination, she takes to all of them, she thinks they are all treasures, every new one is welcome.

When the mighty brontosaurus came striding into camp, she regarded it as an acquisition, I considered it a calamity; that is a good sample of the lack of harmony that prevails in our views of things. She wanted to domesticate it, I wanted to make it a present of the homestead and move out. She believed it could be tamed by kind treatment and would be a good pet; I said a pet twenty-one feet high and eighty-four feet long would be no proper thing to have about the place, because, even with the best intentions and without meaning any harm, it could sit down on the house and mash it, for any one could see by the look of its eye that it was absent-minded.

Still, her heart was set upon having that monster, and she couldn't give it up. She thought we could start a dairy with it, and wanted me to help her milk it; but I wouldn't; it was too risky. The sex wasn't right, and we hadn't any ladder anyway. Then she wanted to ride it, and look at the scenery. Thirty or forty feet of its tail was lying on the ground, like a fallen tree, and she thought she could climb it, but she was mistaken; when she got to the steep place it was too slick and down she came, and would have hurt herself but for me.

Was she satisfied now? No. Nothing ever satisfies her but demonstration; untested theories are not in her line, and she won't have them. She was born scientific. It is the right spirit, I concede it; it attracts me; I feel the influence of it; if I were with her more I think I should take it up myself. Well, she had one theory remaining about this colossus: she thought that if we could tame him and make him friendly we could stand him in the river and use him for a bridge. It turned out that he was already plenty tame enough—at least as far as she was concerned—so she tried her theory, but it failed: every time she got him properly placed in the river and went ashore to cross over on him, he came out and followed her around like a pet mountain. Like the other animals. They all do that.

TUESDAY—WEDNESDAY—THURSDAY—AND TO-DAY—: all without seeing him. It is a long time to be alone; still, it is better to be alone than unwelcome.

I *had* to have company—I was made for it, I think—so I made friends with the animals. They are just charming, and they have the kindest disposition and the politest ways; they never look sour, they never let you feel that you are intruding, they smile at you and wag their tail, if they've got one, and they are always ready for a romp or an excursion or anything you want to propose. I think they are perfect gentlemen. All these days we have had such good times, and it hasn't been lonesome for me, ever. Lonesome! No, I should say not. Why, there's always a swarm of them around—sometimes as much as four or five acres—you can't count them; and when you stand on a rock in the midst and look out over the furry expanse it is so mottled and splashed and gay with color and frisking sheen and sunflash, and so rippled with stripes, that you might think it was a lake, only you know it isn't; and there's storms of sociable birds, and hurricanes of whirring wings; and when the

sun strikes all that feathery commotion, you have a blazing up of all the colors you can think of, enough to put your eyes out.

We have made long excursions, and I have seen a great deal of the world; almost all of it, I think; and so I am the first traveller, and the only one. When we are on the march, it is an imposing sight—there's nothing like it anywhere. For comfort I ride a tiger or a leopard, because it is soft and has a round back that fits me, and because they are such pretty animals; but for long distance or for scenery I ride the elephant. He hoists me up with his trunk, but I can get off myself; when we are ready to camp, he sits and I slide down the back way.

The birds and animals are all friendly to each other, and there are no disputes about anything. They all talk, and they all talk to me, but it must be a foreign language, for I cannot make out a word they say; yet they often understand me when I talk back, particularly the dog and the elephant. It makes me ashamed. It shows that they are brighter than I am, and are therefore my superiors. It annoys me, for I want to be the principal Experiment myself—and I intend to be, too.

I have learned a number of things and am educated, now, but I wasn't at first. I was ignorant at first. At first it used to vex me because, with all my watching, I was never smart enough to be around when the water was running up-hill; but now I do not mind it. I have experimented and experimented until now I know it never does run up-hill, except in the dark. I know it does in the dark, because the pool never goes dry; which it would, of course, if the water didn't come back in the night. It is best to prove things by actual experiment; then you *know;* whereas if you depend on guessing and supposing and conjecturing, you will never get educated.

Some things you *can't* find out; but you will never know you can't by guessing and supposing: no, you have to be patient and go on experimenting until you find out that you can't find out. And it is delightful to have it that way, it makes the world so interesting. If there wasn't anything to find out, it would be dull. Even trying to find out and not finding out is just as interesting as trying to find out and finding out, and I don't know but more so. The secret of the water was a treasure until I *got* it; then the excitement all went away, and I recognized a sense of loss.

By experiment I know that wood swims, and dry leaves, and feathers, and plenty of other things; therefore by all that cumulative evidence you know that a rock will swim; but you have to put up with simply knowing it, for there isn't any way to prove it—up to now. But I shall find a way—then *that* excitement will go. Such things make me sad; be-

cause by-and-by when I have found out everything there won't be any more excitements, and I do love excitements so! The other night I couldn't sleep for thinking about it.

At first I couldn't make out what I was made for, but now I think it was to search out the secrets of this wonderful world and be happy and thank the Giver of it all for devising it. I think there are many things to learn yet—I hope so; and by economizing and not hurrying too fast I think they will last weeks and weeks. I hope so. When you cast up a feather it sails away on the air and goes out of sight; then you throw up a clod and it doesn't. It comes down, every time. I have tried it and tried it, and it is always so. I wonder why it is? Of course it *doesn't* come down, but why should it *seem* to? I suppose it is an optical illusion. I mean, one of them is. I don't know which one. It may be the feather, it may be the clod; I can't prove which it is, I can only demonstrate that one or the other is a fake, and let a person take his choice.

By watching, I know that the stars are not going to last. I have seen some of the best ones melt and run down the sky. Since one can melt, they can all melt; since they can all melt, they can all melt the same night. That sorrow will come—I know it. I mean to sit up every night and look at them as long as I can keep awake; and I will impress those sparkling fields on my memory, so that by-and-by when they are taken away I can by my fancy restore those lovely myriads to the black sky and make them sparkle again, and double them by the blur of my tears.

AFTER THE FALL

When I look back, the Garden is a dream to me. It was beautiful, surpassingly beautiful, enchantingly beautiful; and now it is lost, and I shall not see it any more.

The Garden is lost, but I have found *him,* and am content. He loves me as well as he can; I love him with all the strength of my passionate nature, and this, I think, is proper to my youth and sex. If I ask myself why I love him, I find I do not know, and do not really much care to know; so I suppose that this kind of love is not a product of reasoning and statistics, like one's love for other reptiles and animals. I think that this must be so. I love certain birds because of their song; but I do not love Adam on account of his singing—no, it is not that; the more he sings the more I do not get reconciled to it. Yet I ask him to sing, because I wish to learn to like everything he is interested in. I am sure I can learn, because at first I could not stand it, but now I can. It sours the milk, but it doesn't matter; I can get used to that kind of milk.

It is not on account of his brightness that I love him—no, it is not that. He is not to blame for his brightness, such as it is, for he did not make it himself; he is as God made him, and that is sufficient. There was a wise purpose in it, *that* I know. In time it will develop, though I think it will not be sudden; and besides, there is no hurry; he is well enough just as he is.

It is not on account of his gracious and considerate ways and his delicacy that I love him. No, he has lacks in these regards, but he is well enough just so, and is improving.

It is not on account of his industry that I love him—no, it is not that. I think he has it in him, and I do not know why he conceals it from me. It is my only pain. Otherwise he is frank and open with me, now. I am sure he keeps nothing from me but this. It grieves me that he should have a secret from me, and sometimes it spoils my sleep, thinking of it, but I will put it out of my mind; it shall not trouble my happiness, which is otherwise full to overflowing.

It is not on account of his education that I love him—no, it is not that. He is self-educated, and does really know a multitude of things, but they are not so.

It is not on account of his chivalry that I love him—no, it is not that. He told on me, but I do not blame him; it is a peculiarity of sex, I think, and he did not make his sex. Of course I would not have told on him, I would have perished first; but that is a peculiarity of sex, too, and I do not take credit for it, for I did not make my sex.

Then why is it that I love him? *Merely because he is masculine,* I think.

At bottom he is good, and I love him for that, but I could love him without it. If he should beat me and abuse me, I should go on loving him. I know it. It is a matter of sex, I think.

He is strong and handsome, and I love him for that, and I admire him and am proud of him, but I could love him without those qualities. If he were plain, I should love him; if he were a wreck, I should love him; and I would work for him, and slave over him, and pray for him, and watch by his bedside until I died.

Yes, I think I love him merely because he is *mine* and is *masculine.* There is no other reason, I suppose. And so I think it is as I first said: that this kind of love is not a product of reasonings and statistics. It just *comes*—none knows whence—and cannot explain itself. And doesn't need to.

It is what I think. But I am only a girl, and the first that has examined this matter, and it may turn out that in my ignorance and inexperience I have not got it right.

FORTY YEARS LATER

It is my prayer, it is my longing, that we may pass from this life together—a longing which shall never perish from the earth, but shall have place in the heart of every wife that loves, until the end of time; and it shall be called by my name.

But if one of us must go first, it is my prayer that it shall be I; for he is strong, I am weak, I am not so necessary to him as he is to me—life without him would not be life; how could I endure it? This prayer is also immortal, and will not cease from being offered up while my race continues. I am the first wife; and in the last wife I shall be repeated.

AT EVE'S GRAVE

ADAM: Wheresoever she was, *there* was Eden.

[1905]

Captain Stormfield's Visit to Heaven

Note. I knew Captain Stormfield well. I made three long sea-voyages with him in his ship. He was a rugged, weather-tanned sailor, with a picked-up education, a sterling good heart, an iron will, abundant pluck, unshakable beliefs and convictions, and a confidence in himself which had no discoverable limits. He was open, frank, communicative, affectionate, and as honest, simple and genuine as a dog. He was deeply religious, by nature and by the training of his mother, and a fluent and desolating swearer by the training of his father and by the necessities of his occupation. He was born in his father's ship, he had spent his entire life at sea, had seen the edges of all lands and the interiors of none, and when I first knew him he was sixty-five years old and his glossy black hair and whiskers were beginning to show threads of gray; but there was no trace of age in his body, yet, nor in his determined spirit, and the fires that burned in his eyes were the fires of youth. He was a lovable man when people pleased him, but a tough person to deal with when the case was otherwise.

He had a good deal of imagination, and it probably colored his statements of fact; but if this was so, he was not aware of it. He made no statement which he did not believe to be true. When he told me about his strange and uncanny adventures in the Devil's Race-Track[1]—a vast area in the solitudes of the South Pacific where the needle of the compass is powerless to exercise its office and whizzes madly and continuously around—I spared him the hurt of suggesting that he had dreamed the tale, for I saw that he was in earnest; but in secret I believed it was only a vision, a dream. Privately I think his visit to the Other World was a

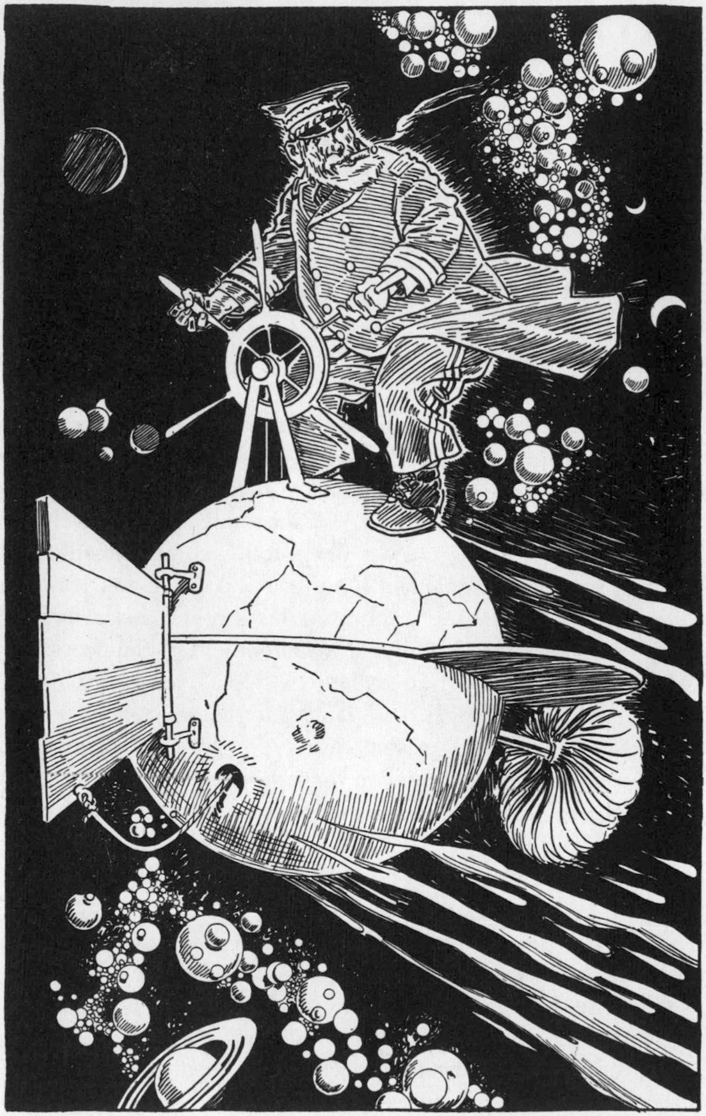

dream, also, but I did not wound him with the expression of the thought. He believed that the visit was an actual experience; I accepted it on those terms, listened to it attentively, took down the details of each day's revelations in short-hand, by his permission, then afterward reduced the result to long-hand. I have polished some of the ruggednesses out of his grammar and construction, and in places I have cooled off his language a little; otherwise his tale stands here as he told it.

Mark Twain

CHAPTER 1

I was dying, and I knew it. I was making gasps, with long spaces between, and they were standing around the bed, quiet and still, waiting for me to go. Now and then they spoke; and what they said got dimmer and dimmer, and further and further away. I heard it all, though. The mate said—

"He's going out with the tide."

Chips the carpenter said—

"How do you know? No tide out here in the middle of the ocean."

"Yes there is. And anyway, they always do."

It was still again, a while—only the heaving and creaking, and the dull lanterns swinging this way and that, and the wind wheezing and piping, far off. Then I heard a voice, away off—

"Eight bells, sir."

"Make it so," said the mate.

"Aye-aye, sir."

Another voice—

"Freshening up, sir—coming on to blow."

"Sheet home," says the mate. "Reef tops'ls and sky-scrapers, and stand by."

"Aye-aye, sir."

By the by the mate says—

"How's it now?"

"He's cold, up to his ribs," says the doctor. "Give him ten minutes."

"Everything ready, Chips?"

"Canvas, cannon balls and all, sir."

"Bible and burial service?"

"All handy, sir."

Quiet again, for a while—wind so vague it sounded like dream-wind. Then the doctor's voice—

"Is he prepared for the change, do you think?"

"To hell? Oh, I guess so."

"I reckon there ain't any doubt."

It was Chips said it; kind of mournful, too.

"Doubt?" said the mate. "Hadn't any himself, if that's any sign."

"No," says Chips, "he always said he judged he was booked for there."

Long, long stillness. Then the doctor's voice, so far off and dim it sounded like it was down a deep well—

"There—it's over! Just at 12:14!"

Dark? Oh, pitch dark—all in a second! I was dead, and I knew it.

I felt myself make a plunge, and recognised that I was flashing through the air like a bird. I had a quick, dim glimpse of the sea and the ship, then everything was black darkness, and nothing visible, and I went whizzing through it. I said to myself, "I'm all here, clothes and all, nothing missing; they'll sink a counterfeit in the sea; it's not me, I'm all here."

Next, it began to get light, and straight off I plunged into a whole universe of blinding fire, and straight through it. It was 12:22 by my watch.

Do you know where I was? In the sun. That was my guess, and it turned out afterwards that I was right. Eight minutes out from port. It gave me my gait—exactly the speed of light, 186,000 miles a second. Ninety-three million miles in eight minutes by the watch. There wasn't ever a prouder ghost. I was as pleased as a child, and wished I had something to race with.

Before I was done thinking these things I was out on the other side and the sun shriveling up to a luminous wad behind me. It was less than a million miles in diameter, and I was through before I had time to get warm. I was in the dark again, now. In the dark; but I myself wasn't dark. My body gave out a soft and ghostly glow and I felt like a lightning bug. I couldn't make out the why of this, but I could read my watch by it, and that was more to the point.

Presently I noticed a glow like my own a little way off, and was glad, and made a trumpet of my hands and hailed it—

"Shipmate ahoy!"

"Same to you!"

"Where from?"

"Chatham street."

"Whither bound?"

"I vish I knew—aind it?"

"I reckon you're going my way. Name?"

"Solomon Goldstein. Yours?"

"Captain Ben Stormfield, late of Fairhaven and 'Frisco. Come alongside, friend."

He did it. It was a great improvement, having company. I was born sociable, and never could stand solitude. I was trained to a prejudice against Jews[2]—Christians always are, you know—but such of it as I had was in my head, there wasn't any in my heart. But if I had been full of it it would have disappeared then, I was so lonesome and so anxious for company. Dear me, when you are going to—to—where I was going—you are humble-mindeder than you used to be, and thankful for whatever you can get, never mind the quality of it.

We spun along together, and talked, and got acquainted and had a good time. I thought it would be a kindness to Solomon to dissipate his doubts, so that he would have a quiet mind. I could never be comfortable in a state of doubt myself. So I reasoned the thing out, and showed him that his being pointed the same as me was proof of where he was bound for. It cost him a good deal of distress, but in the end he was reconciled and said it was probably best the way it was, he wouldn't be suitable company for angels and they would turn him down if he tried to work in; he had been treated like that in New York, and he judged that the ways of high society were about the same everywhere. He wanted me not to desert him when we got to where we were going, but stay by him, for he would be a stranger and friendless. Poor fellow, I was touched; and promised—"to all eternity."

Then we were quiet a long time, and I let him alone, and let him think. It would do him good. Now and then he sighed, and by and by I found he was crying. You know, I was mad with him in a minute; and says to myself, "Just like a Jew! he has promised some hayseed or other a coat for four dollars, and now he has made up his mind that if he was back he could work off a worse one on him for five. They haven't any heart—that race—nor any principles."

He sobbed along to himself, and I got colder and colder and harder and harder towards him. At last I broke out and said—

"Cheese it! Damn the coat! Drop it out of your mind."

"Goat?"

"Yes. Find something else to cry about."

"Why, I vasn't crying apoud a goat."

"What then?"

"Oh, captain, I loss my little taughter, and now I never, never see her again any more. It break my heart!"

By God, it went through me like a knife! I wouldn't feel so mean again, and so grieved, not for a fleet of ships. And I spoke out and said what I felt; and went on damning myself for a hound till he was so distressed I had to stop; but I wasn't half through. He begged me not to talk so, and said I oughtn't to make so much of what I had done; he said it was only a mistake, and a mistake wasn't a crime.

There now—wasn't it magnanimous? I ask you—wasn't it? I think so. To my mind there was the stuff in him for a Christian; and I came out flat-footed and told him so. And if it hadn't been too late I would have reformed him and made him one, or died in the act.

We were good friends again, and he didn't need to keep his sorrows to himself any more, he could pour them right into my heart, which was wide open and ready; and he did; till it seemed to me I couldn't bear it. Lord, the misery of it! She was his pet, his playfellow, the apple of his eye; she was ten years old, and dead six months, and he was glad to die, himself, so he could have her in his arms again and be with her always—and now that dream was over. Why she was gone—*forever.* The word had a new meaning. It took my breath, it made me gasp. All our lives we believe we are going to see our lost friends again—we are not disturbed with doubts, we think we *know* it. It is what keeps us alive. And here, in this father's heart that hope was dead, I had never seen that before. This was the first time. And I—why it was I that had killed it. If I had only thought! If I had only kept still, and left him to find it out for himself. He let his tears run, and now and then his trouble wrung a groan out of him, and his lips quivered and he said—

"Poor little Minnie—and poor me."

And to myself I said the same—

"Poor little Minnie—and poor me."

That feeling stayed by me, and never left me. And many's the time, when I was thinking of that poor Jew's disaster, I have said in my thoughts, "I wish I was bound for heaven, and could trade places with him, so he could see his child, damned if I wouldn't do it." If ever you are situated like that, you will understand the feeling.

CHAPTER 2

We talked late, and fell asleep pretty tired, about two in the morning; had a sound sleep, and woke refreshed and fine towards noon. Pitch dark, still. We were not hungry, but I could have smoked with a relish, if I had had the things. Also, I could have enjoyed a drink.

We had to stop and think a minute, when we woke, before we came fully to ourselves and realized our situation, for we thought we had been dreaming. In fact it was hard to get rid of the idea that it was all a dream. But we had to get rid of it, and we did. Then a ghastly cold shock went through us—we remembered where we were pointed for. Next, we were astonished. Astonished because we hadn't arrived. Astonished and glad. Glad we hadn't arrived. Hopeful that we might not arrive for some little time yet.

"How far is it that ve haf come, Captain Sthormfilt?"

"Eleven or twelve hundred million miles."

"Ach Gott, it is a speed!"

"Right you are. There isn't anything that can pass us but thought. It would take the lightning express twenty-four or twenty-five days to fly around the globe; we could do it four times in a second—yes, sir, and do it easy. Solomon, I wish we had something to race with."

Along in the afternoon we saw a soft blur of light a little way off, north-east-by-east-half-east, about two points off the weather bow, and hailed it. It closed up on us, and turned out to be a corpse by the name of Bailey, from Oshkosh, that had died at 7:10 the night before. A good creature, but mooney and reflective. Republican in politics, and had the idea that nothing could save civilization but that party. He was melancholy, and we got him to talk, so as to cheer him up; and along by spells, as he got to feeling better, his private matters got to leaking out—among others, the fact that he had committed suicide. You know, we had suspected it; he had a hole through his forehead that you couldn't have plugged with a marlin-spike.

By and by his spirits sagged again. Then the cause came out. He was delicate and sensitive in his morals, and he had been doing something in politics, the last thing, which he was wondering if it was exactly straight. There was an election to fill a vacancy in his town government, and it was such a close fit that his one vote would decide it. He wasn't going to be there to vote—he was going to be up here, with us. But if he could keep a democrat from voting that would answer just as well, and the republican candidate would pull through. So, when he was ready for suicide he went to a rigidly honorable friend who was a democrat, and got him to pair off with him. The republican ticket was safe, then, and he killed himself. So he was a little troubled about it, and uncertain; afraid that maybe he hadn't played quite fair, for a Presbyterian.

But Solomon admired him, and thought it was an amazingly smart idea, and just gloated over him with envy, and grinned that Jew grin of intense satisfaction, you know, and slapped his thigh and said—

"Py Chorge, Pailey, almost thou persuadest me to pe a Ghristian."[3]

It was about his girl that he killed himself—Candace Miller. He couldn't ever quite get her to say she loved him, though she seemed to, and he had good hopes. But the thing that decided him was a note from her, in which she told him she loved him as a friend, and hoped they would always be friends, but she found her heart belonged to another. Poor Bailey, he broke down, there and cried.

Curious! Just then we sighted a blue light a little astern, and hailed it, and when it ranged up alongside Bailey shouted—

"Why Tom Wilson! what a happy surprise; what ever brought you here, comrade?"

Wilson gave him an appealing look that was sort of heartbreaking to see, and said—

"Don't welcome me like that, George, I'm not worthy. I'm a low-down dog, and not fit for any clean man's company."

"Don't," said Bailey. "Don't talk like that. What is it?"

"George, I did a treacherous thing. To think I could do it to an old playfellow like you, that I was born and raised with! But it was only a silly practical joke, and I never dreamed that any harm could come of it. *I* wrote that letter. She loved you, George."

"My God!"

"Yes, she did. She was the first one to the house; and when she saw you lying dead in your blood and the letter by you, signed with her name, she read it and knew! She flung herself on your corpse, and kissed your face and your eyes, and poured out her love and her grief and despair, and I saw it. I had murdered you, I had broken her heart, I couldn't bear it—and I am here."

Another suicide, you see. Bailey—well, he couldn't go back, you know, and it was pitiful to see him, he was so frantic over what he had lost by killing himself before ever stopping to find out whether she wrote the letter or not. He kept on regretting and lamenting and wishing he had waited and been more rational, and arranging over and over again in different ways, how he ought to have acted, and how he would act now, if he could only have the chance over again. All no good, of course, and made us miserable to hear it, for he couldn't ever have his chance again forever—we realized that, and the whole ghastliness of the situation. Some people think you are at rest when you die. Let them wait, they'll see.

Solomon took Bailey aside to comfort him—a good idea; people that carry griefs in their hearts know how to comfort others' griefs.

We whizzed along about a week before we picked up another straggler. This time it was a nigger. He was about thirty-eight or forty, and had been a slave nearly half of his life. Named Sam. A cheerful, good-natured cuss, and likable. As I learned later, a pick-up is a depressing influence upon the company for some time, because he is full of thinkings about his people at home and their grief over losing him; and so his talk is all about that, and he wants sympathy, and cries a good deal, and tells you how dear and good his wife was, or his poor old mother, or his sisters and brothers; and of course in common kindness you have to listen, and it keeps the company feeling desolate and wretched for days and days together, and starts up their own sorrows over their own loss of family and friends; but when the pick-up is a young person that has lost a sweetheart, that is the worst. There isn't any end to their talk, and their sorrow and their tears. And dear, dear, that one tiresome everlasting question that they keep on asking till you are worn to the bone with it: *don't* we think he (or she) will die soon and come? What can you say? There's only one thing: *yes,* we hope he will. And when you have said it a couple of thousand times, you lose patience and wish you hadn't died. But dead people are people, just the same, and they bring their habits with them, which is natural. On the earth, when you arrive in a city—any city on the globe—the people peck at you with the same old regular questions—

"First time you have visited our city?"

"How does it impress you?"

"When did you arrive?"

"How long are you going to stay?"

Sometimes you have to leave next day, to get a rest. We arranged differently with the lovers, by and by: we bunched them together to themselves and made them burn their own smoke. And it was no harm: they liked it best that way. There was plenty of sympathy and sentiment, and that was what they wanted.

Sam had pipe, tobacco and matches; I cannot tell you how glad I was. But only for a little moment; then there was a sharp disappointment: the matches wouldn't light. Bailey explained it: there was no atmosphere there in space, and the match couldn't burn without oxygen. I said we would keep the things—we might strike through the atmosphere of a planet or a sun, some time or other, and if it was a big one we might have time for one whiff, anyway. But he said no, it wasn't in the cards.

"Ours are spiritualized bodies and spiritualized clothes and things," he said, "otherwise they would have been consumed in a flash when we first darted through the earth's atmosphere. This is spiritualized tobacco, and fire-proof."

It was very annoying. But I said we would keep it, just the same—

"It will burn in hell, anyway."

When the nigger found that that was where I was going, it filled him with distress, and he hoped I was mistaken, and did his best to persuade me I was; but I hadn't any doubts, and so he had to give in. He was as grieved about it as my best friend could be, and tried his best to believe it wouldn't be as hot there as people said, and hoped and believed I would get used to it after a while, and not mind it. His kindly talk won me completely; and when he gave me the pipe and tobacco, and begged me to think of him sometimes when I was smoking, I was a good deal moved. He was a good chap, and like his race: I have seen but few niggers that hadn't their hearts in the right place.

As week after week slipped along by, we picked up a straggler at intervals, and at the end of the first year our herd numbered 36. It looked like a flock of glow-worms, and was a quite pretty sight. We could have had a regiment if we had kept all we came across, but the speeds were various and that was an interference. The slowest ship makes the pace for the fleet, of course. I raised our gait a little, as an accommodation, and established it at 200,000 miles a second. Some wanted to get on faster, on account of wanting to join lost friends, so we let them go. I was not in a particular hurry, myself—my business would keep. Some that had been consumptives and such like, were rickety and slow, and they dropped behind and disappeared. Some that were troublesome and disagreeable, and always raising Cain over any little thing that didn't suit them, I ordered off the course, with a competent cursing and a warning to stand clear. We had all sorts left, young and old, and on the whole they were satisfactory enough, though a few of them were not up to standard, I will admit.

CHAPTER 3

Well, when I had been dead about thirty years, I begun to get a little anxious. Mind you, I had been whizzing through space all that time, like a comet.—*Like* a comet! Why, Peters, I laid over the lot of them! Of course there warn't any of them going my way, as a steady thing, you know, because they travel in a long circle like the loop of a lasso, whereas I was pointed as straight as a dart for the Hereafter; but I happened on one every now and then that was going my way for an hour or so, and then we had a bit of a brush together. But it was generally pretty one-sided, because I sailed by them the same as if they were standing still. An ordinary comet don't make more than about 200,000 miles a minute. Of course when I came across one of that sort—like Encke's and Halley's comets,[4] for instance—it warn't anything but a flash of light and a vanish, you see, you couldn't rightly call it a race. It was as if the comet was a gravel-train and I was a telegraph dispatch. But after I got outside of our astronomical system, I used to flush a comet occasionally that was something *like*! *We* haven't got any such comets—ours don't begin. One night I was swinging along at a good round gait, everything taut and trim, and the wind in my favor—I judged I was going about a million miles a minute—it might have been more, it couldn't have been less—when I flushed a most uncommon big one about three points off my starboard bow. By his stern-lights I judged he was bearing about northeast-and-by-north-half-east. Well, it was so near my course that I wouldn't throw away the chance; so I fell off a point, steadied my helm, and went for him. You should have heard me whiz, and seen the electric fur fly! In about a minute and a half I was fringed-out with an electrical nimbus that flamed around for miles and miles and lit up all space like broad day. The comet was burning blue in the distance, like a sickly torch, when I first sighted him, but he begun to grow bigger and bigger as I crept up on him. I slipped up on him so fast that when I had gone about 150,000,000 miles I was close enough to be swallowed up in the phosphorescent glory of his wake, and I couldn't see anything for the glare. Thinks I, it won't do to run into him, so I shunted to one side and tore along. By and by I closed up abreast of his tail. Do you know what it was like? It was like a gnat closing up on the continent of America. I forged along. By and by I had sailed along his coast for a little upwards of a hundred and fifty million miles, and then I could see by the shape of him that I hadn't even got up to his waistband yet. Why, Peters, *we* don't know anything about comets, down here. If you want to see comets that *are* comets, you've got to go outside of our system—where there's room for them, you understand! My friend, I've seen comets out there that couldn't even lay down inside the *orbits* of our nobbiest comets without their tails hanging over.

Well, I boomed along another hundred and fifty million miles, and got up abreast his shoulder, as you may say. I was feeling pretty fine, I tell you; but just then I noticed the officer of the deck come to the side and hoist his glass in my direction. Straight off I heard him sing out—

"Below there, ahoy! Shake her up, shake her up! Heave on a hundred million billion tons of brimstone!"

"Aye-aye, sir!"

"Pipe the stabboard watch! All hands on deck!"

"Aye-aye, sir!"

"Send two hundred thousand million men aloft to shake out royals and sky-scrapers!"

"Aye-aye, sir!"

"Hand the stuns'ls! Hang out every rag you've got! Clothe her from stem to rudder-post!"

"Aye-aye, sir!"

In about a second I begun to see I'd woke up a pretty ugly customer, Peters. In less than ten seconds that comet was just a blazing cloud of red-hot canvas. It was piled up into the heavens clean out of sight—the old thing seemed to swell out and occupy all space; the sulphur-smoke from the furnaces—oh, well, nobody can describe the way it rolled and tumbled up into the skies, and nobody can half describe the way it smelt. Neither can anybody begin to describe the way that monstrous craft begun to crash along. And such another pow-wow—thousands of bo's'n's whistles screaming at once, and a crew like the population of a hundred thousand worlds like ours all swearing at once. Well, *I* never heard the like of it before.

We roared and thundered along side by side, both doing our level best, because I'd never struck a comet before that could lay over me, and so I was bound to beat this one or break something. I judged I had some reputation in space, and I calculated to keep it. I noticed I wasn't gaining as fast, now, as I was before, but still I was gaining. There was a power of excitement on board the comet. Upwards of a hundred billion passengers swarmed up from below and rushed to the side and begun to bet on the race. Of course this careened her and damaged her speed. My, but wasn't the mate mad! He jumped at that crowd, with his trumpet in his hand, and sung out—

"Amidships, amidships, ——* you, or I'll brain the last idiot of you!"

Well, sir, I gained and gained, little by little, till at last I went skimming sweetly by the magnificent old conflagration's nose. By this time the captain of the comet had been rousted out, and he stood there in the red glare for'ard, by the mate, in his shirt-sleeves and slippers, his hair all rat's-nests and one suspender hanging; and how sick those two men did look!

I just simply couldn't help putting my thumb to my nose, as I glided away, and singing out—

"Ta-ta! ta-ta! Any word to send to your family?"

*The captain could not remember what this word was. He said it was in a foreign tongue.

Peters, that was a mistake. Yes, sir, I've often regretted that—it was a mistake. You see, the captain had given up the race, but that remark was too tedious for him—he couldn't stand it. He turned to the mate, and says he—

"Have we got brimstone enough of our own to make the trip?"

"Yes, sir."

"Sure?"

"Yes, sir—more than enough."

"How much have we got in cargo for Satan?"

"Eighteen hundred thousand billion quintillions of kazarks."

"Very well, then, let his boarders freeze till the next comet comes. Lighten ship! Lively, now, lively, men! Heave the whole cargo overboard!"

"Peters, look me in the eye and be calm. I found out, over there, that a kazark is exactly the bulk of *a hundred and sixty-nine worlds like ours*! They hove all that load overboard. When it fell it wiped out a considerable raft of stars just as clean as if they'd been candles and somebody blow'd them out. As for the race, *that* was at an end. The minute she was lightened, the comet swung along by me the same as if I was anchored. The captain stood on the stern, by the after-davits, and put his thumb to his nose and sung out—

"Ta-ta! ta-ta! Maybe *you've* got some message to send to your friends in the Everlasting Tropics!"

Then he hove up his other suspender and started for'ard, and inside of three quarters of an hour his craft was only a pale torch again in the distance. Yes, it was a mistake, Peters—that remark of mine. I don't reckon I'll ever get over being sorry about it. I'd 'a' beat the bully of the firmament if I'd kept my mouth shut.

But I've wandered a little off the track of my tale; I'll get back on my course again. Now you can see what kind of speed I was making. So, as I said, when I had been tearing along this way about thirty years, I begun to get uneasy. Oh, it was pleasant enough, with a good deal to be seen and a good deal to find out, but then it was kind of lonesome, you know. Besides, I wanted to get somewhere. I hadn't shipped with the idea of cruising forever. First off, I liked the delay, because I judged I was going to fetch up in pretty warm quarters when I got through; but towards the last I begun to feel that I'd rather go to—to—well, most any place, so as to finish up the uncertainty.

Well, one night—it was always night, except when I was rushing by some star that was occupying the whole universe with its fire and its glare—light enough then, of course, but I necessarily left it behind in a minute or two and plunged into a solid week of darkness again. The stars ain't so close together as they look to be. Where was I? Oh, yes; one night I was sailing along, when I discovered a tremendous long row of blinking lights away in the horizon ahead. As I approached, they begun to tower and swell, and look like mighty furnaces. Says I to myself—"By George, I've arrived at last—and at the wrong place, just as I expected!"

Then I fainted. I don't know how long I was insensible, but it must have been a good while, for when I came to, the darkness was all gone and there was the loveliest sunshine and the balmiest, fragrantest air in its place. And there was such a marvelous world spread out before me—such a glowing, beautiful, bewitching country! The things I took for furnaces were gates, miles high, made all of flashing jewels, and they pierced a wall of solid gold that you couldn't see the top of, nor yet the end of, in either direction. I was pointed straight for one of these gates and a-coming like a house afire. Now I noticed that the skies were black with millions of people pointed for those gates. What a roar they made, rushing through the air! The ground was as thick as ants with people, too—billions of them, I judge.

I lit. I drifted up to a gate with a swarm of people, and when it was my turn the head clerk says, in a business-like way—

"Well, quick! Where are you from?"

"San Francisco," says I.

"San fran- *what*?" says he.

"San Francisco."

He scratched his head and looked puzzled, then he says—

"Is it a planet?"

By George, Peters, think of it! *"Planet,"* says I, "it's a city. And moreover, it's one of the biggest, and finest and—"

"There, there!" says he, "no time here for conversation. We don't deal in cities here. Where are you from in a *general* way?"

"Oh," I says, "I beg pardon. Put me down for California."

I had him *again,* Peters. He puzzled a second, then he says, sharp and irritable—

"I don't know any such planet—is it a constellation?"

"Oh, my goodness!" says I. "Constellation, says you? No—it's a State."

"Man, we don't deal in States here. *Will* you tell me where you are from *in general*—AT LARGE, don't you understand?"

"O, now I get your idea," I says. "I'm from America—the United States of America."

Peters, do you know I had him *again*? If I didn't I'm a clam. His face was as blank as a target after a militia shooting-match. He turned to an under-clerk and says—

"Where is America? *What* is America?"

The under-clerk answered up prompt and says—

"There ain't any such orb."

"Orb," says I. "Why, what are you talking about, young man? It ain't an orb; it's a country; it's a continent. Columbus discovered it; I reckon likely you've heard of *him,* anyway. America—why, sir, America—"

"Silence!" says the head clerk. "Once for all, where—are—you—*from*?"

"Well," says I, "I don't know anything more to say—unless I lump things, and just say I'm from the world."

"Ah," says he brightening up, "now that's something like. *What* world?"

Peters, he had *me,* that time. I looked at him, puzzled, he looked at me worried. Then he burst out—

"Come, come, what world?"

Says I, "Why, *the* world, of course."

"*The* world!" he says. "Hm! There's billions of them! . . . . Next!"

That meant for me to stand aside. I did so, and a sky-blue man with seven heads and only one leg hopped into my place. I took a walk. It just occurred to me, then, that all the myriads I had seen swarming to that gate, up to this time, were just like that creature. I tried to run across somebody I was acquainted with, but they were out of acquaintances of mine just then. So I thought the thing all over and finally sidled back there pretty meek and feeling rather stumped, as you may say.

"Well?" says the head clerk.

"Well, sir," I says, pretty humble, "I don't seem to make out which world it is I'm from. But you may know it from this—it's the one the Savior saved."

He bent his head at the Name. Then he says, gently—

"The worlds He has saved are like to the gates of heaven in number—none can count them. What astronomical system is your world in?—perhaps that may assist."

"It's the one that has the sun in it—and the moon—and Mars"—he shook his head at each name—hadn't ever heard of them, you see—"and Neptune—and Uranus—and Jupiter—"

"Hold on!" says he, "hold on a minute. Jupiter . . . . Jupiter . . . . seems to me we had a man from there eight or nine hundred years ago—but people from that system very seldom enter by this gate." All of a sudden he begun to look me so straight in the eye that I thought he was going to bore through me. Then he says, very deliberate, "Did you come *straight here* from your system?"

"Yes, sir," I says—but I blushed the least little bit in the world when I said it.

He looked at me very stern, and says—

"That is not true; and this is not the place for prevarication. You wandered from your course. How did that happen?"

Says I, blushing again—

"I'm sorry, and I take back what I said, and confess. I raced with a comet one day—only just the least little bit—only the tiniest lit—"

"So-so," says he—and without any sugar in his voice, to speak of.

I went on, and says—

"But I only fell off just a bare point, and I went right back on my course again the minute the race was over."

"No matter—that divergence has made all this trouble. It has brought you to a gate that is billions of leagues from the right one. If you had gone to your own gate they would have known all about your world at once and there would have been no delay. But we will try to accommodate you." He turned to an under-clerk and says—

"What system is Jupiter in?"

"I don't remember sir, but I think there is such a planet in one of the little new systems away out in one of the thinly-worlded corners of the universe. I will see."

He got a balloon and sailed up and up and up, in front of a map that was as big as Rhode Island. He went on up till he was out of sight, and by and by he came down and got something to eat; and went up again. To cut a long story short, he kept on doing this for a day or two, and finally he came down and said he thought he had found that solar system, but it might be fly-specks. So he got a microscope and went back. It turned out better than he feared. He had rousted out our system, sure enough. He got me to describe our planet and its distance from our sun, and then he says to his chief—

"Oh, I know the one he means, now, sir. It is on the map. It is called the Wart."

Says I to myself, "Young man, it wouldn't be wholesome for you to go down *there* and call it the Wart."

Well, they let me in, then, and told me I was safe forever and wouldn't have any more troubles.

Then they turned from me and went on with their work the same as if they considered my case all complete and shipshape. I was a good deal surprised at this, but I was diffident about speaking up and reminding them. I did so hate to do it, you know; it seemed a pity to bother them, they had so much on their hands. Twice I thought I would give up and let the thing go; so twice I started to leave, but immediately I thought what a figure I should cut stepping out amongst the redeemed in such a rig, and that made me hang back and come to anchor again. People got to eyeing me—clerks, you know—wondering why I didn't get under weigh.[5] I couldn't stand this long—it was too uncomfortable. So at last I plucked up courage and tipped the head clerk a signal. He says—

"What, you here yet? What's wanting?"

Says I, in a low voice and very confidential, making a trumpet with my hands at his ear—

"I beg pardon, and you mustn't mind my reminding you, and seeming to meddle, but hain't you forgot something?"

He studied a second, and says—

"Forgot something? . . . . No, not that I know of."

"Think," says I.

He thought. Then he says—

"No, I can't seem to have forgot anything. What is it?"

"Look at me," say I; "look me all over."

He done it.

"Well?" says he.

"Well," says I, "you don't notice anything? If I branched out amongst the elect looking like this, wouldn't I attract considerable attention?—wouldn't I be a little conspicuous?"

"Well," he says, "I don't see anything the matter. What do you lack?"

"Lack! Why I lack my harp, and my wreath, and my halo, and my hymn-book, and my palm branch—I lack everything that a body naturally requires up here, my friend."

Puzzled? Peters, he was the worst puzzled man you ever saw. Finally he says—

"Well, you seem to be a curiosity every way a body takes you. I never heard of these things before."

I looked at that man a while in solid astonishment; then I says—

"Now I hope you won't take it as an offense, for I don't mean any, but really, for a man that has been in the Kingdom as long as I reckon you have, you do seem to know powerful little about its customs."

"Its customs!" says he. "Heaven is a large place, good friend. Large empires have many and diverse customs. Even small dominions have, as you doubtless know by what you have seen of the matter on a small scale in the Wart. How can you imagine if I could ever learn the varied customs of the countless kingdoms of heaven? It makes my head ache to think of it. I know the customs that prevail in those portions inhabited by peoples that are appointed to enter by my own gate—and harkye, that is quite enough knowledge for one individual to try to pack into his head in the thirty-seven millions of years I have devoted night and day to that study. But the idea of learning the customs of the whole appalling expanse of heaven—O man, how insanely you talk! Now I don't doubt that this odd costume you talk about is the fashion in that district of heaven you belong to, but you won't be conspicuous in this section without it."

I felt all right, if that was the case, so I bade him good day and left. All day I walked toward the far end of a prodigious hall of the office, hoping to come out into heaven any moment, but it was a mistake. That hall was built on the general heavenly plan—it naturally couldn't be small. At last I got so tired I couldn't go any farther; so I sat down to rest, and begun to tackle the queerest sort of strangers and ask for information; but I didn't get any; they couldn't understand my language, and I could not understand theirs. I got dreadfully lonesome. I was so down-hearted and homesick I wished a hundred times I never had died. I turned back, of course. About noon next day I got back at last and I was on hand at the booking office once more. Says I to the head-clerk—

"I begin to see that a man's got to be in his own heaven to be happy."

"Perfectly correct," says he. "Did you imagine the same heaven would suit all sorts of men?"

"Well I had that idea—but I see the foolishness of it. Which way am I to go to get to my district?"

He called the under-clerk that had examined the map, and he gave me the general directions. I thanked him and started; but he says—

"Wait a minute; it is millions of leagues from here. Go outside and stand on that red wishing-carpet; shut your eyes, hold your breath, and wish yourself there."

"I'm much obliged," says I, "why didn't you dart me through when I first arrived?"

"We have a good deal to think of here; it was your place to think of it and ask for it. Good-bye, we probably shan't see you in this region again for a thousand centuries or so."

"In that case, *o revoor*," says I.

I hopped onto the carpet and held my breath and shut my eyes and wished I was in the booking-office of my own section. The very next instant a voice I knew sung out in a business kind of a way—

"A harp and a hymn-book, pair of wings and a halo, size No. 13, for Cap'n Eli Stormfield of San Francisco!—make him out a clean bill of health, and let him in."

I opened my eyes. Sure enough, it was a Pi Ute Injun I used to know in Tulare county; mighty good fellow—I remembered being at his funeral, which consisted of him being burnt and the other Injuns gauming their faces with his ashes and howling like wild-cats. He was powerful glad to see me, and you can make up your mind I was just as glad to see him, and feel that I was in the right kind of a heaven at last.

Just as far as your eye could reach, there was swarms of clerks, running and bustling around, tricking out thousands of Yanks, and Mexicans, and English, and A-rabs, and all sorts of people, in their new outfits; and when they gave me my kit and I put on my halo and took a look in the glass, I could have jumped over a house for joy I was so happy. "Now *this* is something like!" says I. "Now," says I, "I'm all right—show me a cloud."

Inside of fifteen minutes I was a mile on my way toward the cloud-banks, and about a million people along with me. Most of us tried to fly, but some got crippled and nobody made a success of it. So we concluded to walk, for the present, till we had had some wing-practice.

We begun to meet swarms of folks who were coming back. Some had harps and nothing else; some had hymn-books and nothing else; some had nothing at all; all of them looked meek and uncomfortable; one young fellow hadn't anything left but his halo, and he was carrying that in his hand; all of a sudden he offered it to me and says—

"Will you hold it for me a minute?"

Then he disappeared in the crowd. I went on. A woman asked me to hold her palm branch, and then *she* disappeared. A girl got me to hold her harp for her, and by George, *she* disappeared; and so on and so on, till I was about loaded down to the guards. Then comes a smiling old gentleman and asked me to hold *his* things. I swabbed off the perspiration, and says I, pretty tart—

"I'll have to get you to excuse me, my friend—*I* ain't no hat-rack."

About this time I begun to run across piles of those traps, laying in the road. I just quietly dumped my extra cargo along with them. I looked around, and Peters, that whole nation that was following me were loaded down, same as I'd been. The return crowd had got them to hold their things a minute, you see. They all dumped their loads, too, and we went on.

When I found myself perched on a cloud with a million other people, I never felt so good in my life. Says I, "Now this is according to the promises; I've been having my doubts, but now I *am* in heaven, sure enough." I gave my palm branch a wave or two, for luck, and then I tautened up my harp-strings and struck in. Well, Peters, you can't imagine anything like the row we made. It was grand to listen to, and made a body thrill all over, but there was considerable many tunes going at once, and that was a drawback to the harmony, you understand; and then there was a lot of Injun tribes and they kept up such another war-whooping that they kind of took the tuck out of the music. By and by I quit performing, and judged I'd take a rest. There was quite a nice mild old gentleman sitting next me, and I noticed he didn't take a hand; I encouraged him, but he said he was naturally bashful, and was afraid to try before so many people. By and by the old gentleman said he never could seem to enjoy music, somehow. The fact was, I was beginning to feel the same way; but I didn't say anything. Him and I had a considerable long silence, then, but of course it warn't noticeable in that place. After about sixteen or seventeen hours, during which I played and sung a little, now and then—always the same tune, because I didn't know any other—I laid down my harp and begun to fan myself with my palm branch. Then we both got to sighing, pretty regular. Finally, says he—

"Don't you know any tune but the one you've been pegging at all day?"

"Not another blessed one," says I.

"Don't you reckon you could learn another one?" says he.

"Never," says I; "I've tried to, but I couldn't manage it."

"It's a long time to hang to the one—eternity, you know."

"Don't break my heart," says I; "I'm getting low-spirited enough already."

After another long silence, says he—

"Are you glad to be here?"

Says I, "Old man, I'll be frank with you. This *ain't* just as near my idea of bliss as I thought it was going to be, when I used to go to church."

Says he, "What do you say to knocking off and calling it half a day?"

"That's me," says I; "I never wanted to get off watch so bad in my life."

So we started. Millions were coming to the cloud-bank all the time, happy and hosannahing, millions were leaving it all the time, looking mighty quiet I tell you. We laid for the newcomers, and pretty soon I'd got them to hold all my things a minute, and then I was a free man again and most outrageously happy. Just then I ran across old Sam Bartlett, who had been dead a long time, and stopped to have a talk with him. Says I—

"Now tell me—is this to go on forever? Ain't there anything else for a change?"

Says he—

"I'll set you right on that point very quick. People take the figurative language of the Bible and the allegorists for literal, and the first thing they ask for when they get here is a halo and a harp, and so on. Nothing that's harmless and reasonable is refused a body here, if he asks it in the right spirit. So they are outfitted with these things without a word. They go and sing and play just about one day, and that's the last you'll ever see them in the choir. They don't need anybody to tell them that that sort of thing wouldn't make a heaven—at least not a heaven that a sane man could stand a week and remain sane. That cloud-bank is placed where the noise can't disturb the old inhabitants, and so there ain't any harm in letting everybody get up there and cure himself as soon as he comes.

"Now you just remember this—heaven is as blissful and lovely as it can be; but it's just the busiest place you ever heard of. There ain't any idle people here—after the first day. Singing hymns and waving palm branches through all eternity is mighty pretty when you hear about it in the pulpit, but it's as poor a way to put in valuable time as a body could contrive. It would just make a heaven of warbling ignoramuses, don't you see? Eternal Rest sounds mighty comforting in the pulpit, too. Well, you try it once, and see how heavy time will hang on your hands. Why Stormfield, a man like you, that had been active and stirring all his life, would go mad in six months in a heaven where he hadn't anything to do. Heaven is the very last place to come to to *rest* in!—and don't you be afraid to bet on that!"

Says I—

"Sam, I'm as glad to hear it as I thought I'd be sorry. I'm glad I come, now."

Says he—

"Cap'n, ain't you pretty physically tired?"

Says I—

"Sam, it ain't any name for it. Fiddling and singing all day on a damp cloud ain't rest, as I look at it. I'm dog-tired."

"Just so—just so. You've earned a good sleep, and you'll get it. You've earned a good appetite and you'll enjoy your dinner. It's the same here it is on earth—you've got to earn a thing, square and honest, before you enjoy it. You can't enjoy first and earn afterwards. But there's this difference, here: you can choose your own occupation, and all the powers of heaven will be put forth to help you make a success of it, if you do your level best. The shoemaker on earth that had the soul of a poet in him, won't have to make shoes here."

"Now that's all reasonable and right," says I. "Plenty of work, and the kind you hanker after; no more pain, no more suffering—"

"O, hold on; there's plenty of pain here—but it don't kill. There's plenty of suffering, here, but it don't last. You see, happiness ain't a *thing in itself*—it's only a *contrast* with something that ain't pleasant. That's all it is. There ain't a thing you can mention that is happiness in its own self—it's only so by contrast with the other thing. And mind you, as soon as the novelty is over and the force of the contrast dulled, it ain't happiness any longer, and you've got to get up something fresh. Well, there's plenty of pain and suffering in heaven—consequently there's plenty of contrasts, and just no end of happiness."

Says I, "It's the sensiblest heaven I ever heard of, Sam, though it's about as different from the one I was brought up on as a live princess is from her own wax-figger."

Along in the first months I knocked around about the Kingdom, making friends and looking at the country, and finally settled down in a pretty likely region, to have a rest before taking another start. I went on making acquaintances and gathering up information.

I had a good deal of talk with an old bald-headed angel by the name of Sandy McWilliams. He was from somewheres in New Jersey. I went about with him, considerable. We used to lay around, warm afternoons, in the shade of a rock, on some meadow-ground that was pretty high and out of the marshy slush of his cranberry farm, and there we used to talk about all kinds of things, and smoke pipes. One day, says I—

"About how old might you be, Sandy?"

"Seventy-two."

"I judged so. How long you been in heaven?"

"Twenty-seven years, come Christmas."

"How old was you when you come up?"

"Why seventy-two, of course."

"You can't mean it."

"Why can't I mean it?"

"Because, if you was seventy-two then, you are naturally ninety-nine, now."

"No, but I ain't. I stay the same age I was when I come."

"Well," says I, "come to think, there's something just there that I want to ask about. Down below, I always had an idea that in heaven we would all be young, and bright, and spry."

"Well, you *can* be young, if you want to. You've only got to wish."

"Well, then, why didn't you wish?"

"I did. They all do. You'll try it, some day, like enough; but you'll get tired of the change, pretty soon."

"Why?"

"Well, I'll tell you. Now you've always been a sailor; did you ever try some other business?"

"Yes, I tried keeping grocery, once, up in the mines; but I couldn't stand it; it was too dull—no stir, no storm, no life about it; it was like being part dead and part alive, both at the same time. I wanted to be one thing or t'other. I shut up shop pretty quick and went to sea."

"That's it. Grocery people like it, but you couldn't. You see, you wasn't used to it. Well, I wasn't used to being young, and I couldn't seem to take any interest in it. I was strong, and handsome, and had curly hair,—yes, and wings too!—gay wings like a butterfly. I went to picnics and dances and parties with the fellows, and tried to carry on and talk nonsense with the girls, but it wasn't any use, I couldn't take to it—fact is, it was an awful bore. What I wanted was early to bed and early to rise, and something to *do;* and when my work was done, I wanted to sit quiet, and smoke and think—not tear around with a parcel of giddy young kids. You can't think what I suffered whilst I was young."

"How long was you young?"

"Only two weeks. That was plenty for me. Laws, I was so lonesome! You see, I was full of the knowledge and experience of seventy-two years; the deepest subject those young folks could strike was only *a-b-c* to me. And to hear them argue—Oh, my! It would have been funny, if it hadn't been so pitiful. Well, I was so hungry for the ways and the sober talk I was used to, that I tried to ring in with the old people, but they wouldn't have it. They considered me a conceited young upstart, and gave me the cold shoulder. Two weeks was a plenty for me. I was glad to get back my bald head again, and my pipe, and my old drowsy reflections in the shade of a rock or a tree."

"Well," says I, "do you mean to say you're going to stand still at seventy-two, forever?"

"I don't know, and I ain't particular. But I ain't going to drop back to twenty-five any more—I know that, mighty well. I know a sight more than I did twenty-seven years ago, and I enjoy learning all the time, but

I don't seem to get any older. That is, bodily—my mind gets older, and stronger, and better seasoned, and more satisfactory."

Says I, "If a man comes here at ninety, don't he ever set himself back?"

"Of course he does. He sets himself back to fourteen; tries it a couple of hours, and feels like a fool; sets himself forward to twenty; it ain't much improvement; tries thirty, fifty, eighty, and finally ninety—finds he is more at home and comfortable at the same old figure he is used to than any other way. Or, if his mind begun to fail him on earth at eighty, that's where he finally sticks, up here. He sticks at the place where his mind was last at its best, for there's where his enjoyment is best, and his ways most set and established."

"Does a chap of twenty-five stay always twenty-five, and look it?"

"If he is a fool, yes. But if he is bright, and ambitious and industrious, the knowledge he gains and the experiences he has, change his ways and thoughts and likings, and make him find his best pleasure in the company of people above that age; so he allows his body to take on the look of as many added years as he needs to make him comfortable and proper in that sort of society; he lets his body go on taking the look of age, according as he progresses, and by and by he will be bald and wrinkled outside, and wise and deep within."

"Babies the same?"

"Babies the same. Laws, what asses we used to be, on earth, about these things! We said we'd be always young, in heaven. We didn't say *how* young—we didn't think of that, perhaps—that is, we didn't all think alike, anyway. When I was a boy of seven, I suppose I thought we'd all be twelve, in heaven; when I was twelve, I suppose I thought we'd all be eighteen or twenty in heaven; when I was forty, I begun to go back; I remember I hoped we'd all be about *thirty* years old, in heaven. Neither a man nor a boy ever thinks the age he *has* is exactly the best one—he puts the *right* age a few years older or a few years younger than he is. Then he makes that ideal age the general age of the heavenly people. And he expects everybody *to stick* at that age—stand stock still—and expects them to enjoy it! Now just think of the idea of standing still in heaven! Think of a heaven made up entirely of hoop-rolling, marble-playing cubs of seven years!—or of awkward, diffident, sentimental immaturities of nineteen!—or of vigorous people of thirty, healthy-minded, brimming with ambition, but chained hand and foot to that one age and its limitations like so many helpless galley-slaves! Think of the dull sameness of a society made up of people all of one age and one set of looks, habits, tastes and feelings. Think how superior to it earth would be, with its variety of types and faces and ages, and the enlivening attrition of the myriad interests that come into pleasant collision in such a variegated society."

"Look here," says I, "do you know what you're doing?"

"Well, what am I doing?"

"You are making heaven pretty comfortable in one way, but you are playing the mischief with it in another."

"How do you mean?"

"Well," I says, "take a young mother that's lost her child, and—"

"Sh!" he says, "Look!"

It was a woman. Middle-aged, and had grizzled hair. She was walking slow, and her head was bent down, and her wings hanging limp and droopy; and she looked ever so tired, and was crying, poor thing. She passed along by, with her head down, that way, and the tears running down her face, and didn't see us. Then Sandy said, low and gentle and full of pity—

"*She's* hunting for her child! No, *found* it, I reckon. Lord, how she's changed. But I reconnized her in a minute, though it's twenty-seven years since I saw her. A young mother she was, about twenty-two or four, or along there; and blooming and lovely and sweet? oh, just a flower! And all her heart and all her soul was wrapped up in her child, her little girl, two years old. And it died, and she went wild with grief, just wild! Well, the only comfort she had, was that she'd see her child again, in heaven—'never more to part,' she said, and kept saying it over and over, 'never more to part.' And the words made her happy; yes they did, they made her joyful; and when I was dying, twenty-seven years ago, she told me to find her child the first thing, and say she was coming—'soon, soon, *very* soon, she hoped and believed!' "

"Why, it's pitiful, Sandy."

He didn't say anything for a while, but sat looking at the ground, thinking. Then he says, kind of mournful—

"And now she's come!"

"Well? Go on."

"Stormfield, maybe she hasn't found the child, but *I* think she has. Looks so to me. I've seen cases before. You see, she's kept that child in her head just the same as it was when she jounced it in her arms a little chubby thing. But here it didn't elect to *stay* a child. No, it elected to grow up, which it did. And in these twenty-seven years it has learned all the deep scientific learning there *is* to learn, and is studying and studying and learning and learning more and more, all the time, and don't give a damn for anything *but* learning; just learning, and discussing gigantic problems with people like herself."

"Well?"

"Stormfield, don't you see? Her mother knows *cranberries,* and how to tend them, and pick them, and put them up, and market them; and not another blamed thing! Her and her daughter can't be any more company for each other *now* than mud-turtle and bird o' paradise. Poor thing, she was looking for a baby to jounce; *I* think she's struck a disapp'intment."

"Sandy, what will they do—stay unhappy forever in heaven?"

"No, they'll come together and get adjusted by and by. But not this year and not next. By and by."

CHAPTER 4

I had been having considerable trouble with my wings. The day after I helped the choir, I made a dash or two with them, but I was not lucky. First-off, I flew thirty yards, and then fouled an Irishman and brought him down—brought us both down, in fact. Next, I had a collision with a Bishop—and bowled him down, of course. We had some sharp words, and I felt pretty cheap, to come banging into a grave old person like that, with a million strangers looking on and smiling to themselves.

I saw I hadn't got the hang of the steering, and so couldn't rightly tell where I was going to bring up when I started. I went afoot the rest of the day, and let my wings hang. Early next morning I went to a private place to have some practice. I got up on a pretty high rock, and got a good start, and went swooping down, aiming for a bush a little over three hundred yards off; but I couldn't seem to calculate for the wind, which was about two points abaft my beam. I could see I was going considerable to looard of the bush, so I worked my starboard wing slow and went ahead strong on the port one, but it wouldn't answer; I could see I was going to broach to, so I slowed down on both, and lit. I went back to the rock and took another chance at it. I aimed two or three points to starboard of the bush—yes, more than that—enough so as to make it nearly a head-wind. I done well enough, but made pretty poor time. I could see plain enough, that on a head-wind, wings was a mistake. I could see that a body could sail pretty close to the wind, but he couldn't go in the wind's eye. I could see that if I wanted to go a visiting any distance from home, and the wind was ahead, I might have to wait days, maybe, for a change; and I could see, too, that these things could not be any use at all in a gale; if you tried to run before the wind, you would make a mess of it, for there isn't any way to shorten sail—like reefing, you know—you have to take it *all* in—shut your feathers down flat to your sides. That would *land* you, of course. You could lay to, with your head to the wind—That is the best you could do, and right hard work you'd find it, too. If you tried any other game, you would founder, sure.

I judge it was about a couple of weeks or so after this, that I dropped old Sandy McWilliams a note one day—it was a Tuesday—and asked him to come over and take his manna and quails[6] with me next day; and the first thing he did when he stepped in, was to twinkle his eye in a sly way, and say—

"Well, Cap., what you done with your wings?"

I saw in a minute that there was some sarcasm done up in that rag somewheres, but I never let on. I only says—

"Gone to the wash."

"Yes," he says, in a dry sort of way, "they mostly go to the wash—about this time—I've often noticed it. Fresh angels are powerful neat. When do you look for 'em back?"

"Day after to-morrow," says I.

He winked at me, and smiled.

Says I—

"Sandy, out with it. Come—no secrets among friends. I notice you don't ever wear wings—and plenty others don't. I've been making an ass of myself—is that it?"

"That is about the size of it. But it is no harm. We all do it—at first. It's perfectly natural. You see, on earth we jump to such foolish conclusions as to things up here. In the pictures we always saw the angels with wings on—and that was all right; but we jumped to the conclusion that that was their way of getting around—and that was all wrong. The wings ain't anything but a uniform, that's all. When they are in the field—so to speak—they always wear them; you never see an angel going with a message anywhere without his wings, any more than you would see a military officer presiding at a court martial without his uniform, or a postman delivering letters, or a policeman walking his beat, in plain clothes. But laws, they ain't to *fly* with! The wings are for show, not for use. Old experienced angels are like officers of the regular army—they dress plain, when they are off duty. New angels are like the militia—never shed the uniform—always fluttering and floundering around in their wings, butting people down, flapping here, and there, and everywhere, always showing off and always imagining they are attracting the admiring eye—well, they just think they are the very most important people in heaven. And when you see one of them come swooping sailing around with one wing tipped up and t'other down, you can make up your mind he is saying to himself, 'I wish Mary Ann in Arkansaw could see me now! I reckon she wishes she hadn't shook me.' No, they're just for show, that's all—only just for show."

"I judge you've got it put up about right, Sandy," says I.

"Why, look at it yourself," says he. "*You* ain't built for wings—no man is. You know what a grist of years it took you to come here from the earth—and yet you were booming along faster than any cannon ball could go. Suppose you had had to fly that distance with your wings—wouldn't eternity have been over before you got here? Certainly. Well, angels have to go to the earth every day—millions of them—to appear in visions to dying children and good people, you know—it's the heft of their business. They appear with their wings, of course, because they are on official service, and because the dying persons wouldn't know they were angels if they hadn't wings—but do you reckon they fly with them? It stands to reason they don't. The wings would wear out before they got half way; even the pin-feathers would be gone; the wing-frames would be as bare as kite-sticks before the paper is pasted on. The distances in heaven are billions of times greater; angels have to go all over heaven every day; could they do it with their wings alone? No indeed; they wear the wings for style, but they travel any distance in an instant by *wishing*. The wishing-carpet of the Arabian Nights was a sensible idea—but our earthly idea of angels flying these awful distances with their clumsy wings was foolish.

"Our young saints, of both sexes, wear wings all the time—blazing red ones, and blue and green, and gold, and variegated, and rainbowed, and ring-streaked-and-striped ones—and nobody finds fault. It is suitable to their time of life. The things are beautiful, and they set the young people off. They are the most striking and lovely part of their outfit—a halo don't *begin*."

"Well," says I, "I've tucked mine away in the cupboard, and I allow to let them lay there till there's mud."

"Yes—or a reception."

"What's that?"

"Well, you can see one to-night if you want to. There's a barkeeper from Jersey City going to be received."

"Go on—tell me about it."

"This barkeeper got converted at a Moody and Sankey[7] meeting, in

New York, and started home on the ferry boat, and there was a collision and he got drowned. He is of a class that think all heaven goes wild with joy when a particularly hard lot like him is saved; they think all heaven turns out hosannahing to welcome them; they think there isn't anything talked about in the realms of the blest, but their case, for that day. This barkeeper thinks there hasn't been such another stir here in years, as his coming is going to raise. And I've always noticed this peculiarity about a dead barkeeper—he not only expects all hands to turn out when he arrives, but he expects to be received with a torchlight procession."

"I reckon he is disappointed, rhen."

"No he isn't. No man is allowed to be disappointed here. Whatever he wants when he comes—that is, any reasonable and unsacrilegious thing—he can have. There's always a few millions or billions of young folks around who don't want any better entertainment than to fill up their lungs and swarm out with their torches and have a high time over a barkeeper. It tickles the barkeeper till he can't rest, it makes a charming lark for the young folks, it don't do anybody any harm, it don't cost a rap, and it keeps up the place's reputation for making all comers happy and content."

"Very good. I'll be on hand and see them land the barkeeper."

"It is manners to go in full dress. You want to wear your wings, you know, and your other things."

"Which oncs?"

"Halo, and harp, and palm branch, and all that."

"Well," says I, "I reckon I ought to be ashamed of myself, but the fact is I left them laying around that day I resigned from the choir. I haven't got a rag to wear but this robe and the wings."

"That's all right. You'll find they've been raked up and saved for you. Send for them."

"I'll do it, Sandy. But what was it you was saying about the unsacrilegious things, which people expect to get, and will be disappointed about?"

"O, there are a lot of such things that people expect and don't get. For instance, there's a Brooklyn preacher by the name of Talmage,[8] who is laying up a considerable disappointment for himself. He says every now and then in his sermons, that the first thing he does when he gets to heaven, will be to fling his arms around Abraham, Isaac and Jacob, and kiss them and weep on them. There's millions of people down there on earth that are promising themselves the same thing. As many as sixty thousand people arrive here every single day, that want to run straight to

Abraham, Isaac and Jacob, and hug them and weep on them. Now mind you, sixty thousand a day is a pretty heavy contract for those old people. If they were a mind to allow it, they wouldn't ever have anything to do, year in and year out, but stand up and be hugged and wept on thirty-two hours in the twenty-four. They would be tired out and as wet as muskrats all the time. What would heaven be, to *them*? It would be a mighty good place to get out of—you know that, yourself. Those are kind and gentle old Jews, but they ain't any fonder of kissing the emotional highlights of Brooklyn than you be. You mark my words, Mr. T.'s endearments are going to be declined, with thanks. There are limits to the privileges of the elect, even in heaven. Why, if Adam was to show himself to every new-comer that wants to call and gaze at him and strike him for his autograph, he would never have time to do anything else but just that. Talmage has said he is going to give Adam some of his attentions, as well as A., I., and J. But he will have to change his mind about that."

"Do you think Talmage will really come here?"

"Why certainly he will; but don't you be alarmed; he will run with his own kind, and there's plenty of them. That is the main charm of heaven—there's all kinds here—which wouldn't be the case if you let the preachers tell it. Anybody can find the sort he prefers here, and he just lets the others alone, and they let *him* alone. When the Deity builds a heaven, it is built right, and on a liberal plan."

Sandy sent home for his things, and I sent for mine, and about nine in the evening we begun to dress. Sandy says—

"This is going to be a grand time for you, Stormy. Like as not some of the patriarchs will turn out."

"No, but will they?"

"Like as not. Of course they are pretty exclusive. They hardly ever show themselves to the common public. I believe they never turn out except for an eleventh-hour convert. They wouldn't do it then, only earthly tradition makes a grand show pretty necessary on that kind of an occasion."

"Do they all turn out, Sandy?"

"Who?—all the patriarchs? Oh, no—hardly ever more than a couple. You will be here fifty thousand years—maybe more—before you get a glimpse of all the patriarchs and prophets. Since I have been here, Job has been to the front once, and once Ham and Jeremiah[9] both at the same time. But the finest thing that has happened in my day was a year or so ago, that was Charles Peace's reception—him they called 'the Bannercross Murderer'[10]—an Englishman. There were four patriarchs and two prophets on the Grand Stand that time—there hasn't been anything like it since Captain Kidd[11] came; Abel was there—the first time in twelve hundred years. A report got around that Adam was coming; well, of course Abel was enough to bring a crowd, all by himself, but there is nobody that can draw like Adam. It was a false report, but it got around, anyway, as I say, and it will be a long day before I see the like of it again. The reception was in the English department, of course, which is eight hundred and eleven million miles from the New Jersey line. I went, along with a good many of my neighbors, and it was a sight to see, I can tell you. Flocks came from all the departments. I saw Esquimaux there, and Tartars, negroes, Chinamen—people from everywhere. You see a mixture like that in the Grand Choir, the first day you land here, but you hardly ever see it again. There were billions of people; when they were singing or hosannahing, the noise was wonderful; and even when their tongues were still, the drumming of the wings was nearly enough to burst your head, for all the sky was as thick as if it was snowing angels. Although Adam was not there, it was a great time anyway, because we had three Archangels on the Grand Stand—it is a seldom thing that even one comes out."

"What did they look like, Sandy?"

"Well, they had shining faces, and shining robes, and wonderful rainbow wings, and they stood eighteen feet high, and wore swords, and held their heads up in a noble way, and looked like soldiers."

"Did they have halos?"

"No—anyway, not the hoop kind. The archangels and the upper-class patriarchs wear a finer thing than that. It is a round, solid, splendid glory of gold, that is blinding to look at. You have often seen a patriarch in a picture, on earth, with that thing on—you remember it?—he looks as if he had his head in a brass platter. That don't give you the right idea of it at all—it is much more shining and beautiful."

"Did you talk with those archangels and patriarchs, Sandy?"

"Who—*I*? Why what can you be thinking about, Stormy? I ain't worthy to speak to such as they."

"Is Talmage?"

"Of course not. You have got the same mixed-up idea about these things that everybody has, down there. I had it once but I got over it. Down there they talk of the heavenly King—and that is right—but they go right on speaking as if this was a Republic and everybody was on a dead level with everybody else, and privileged to fling his arms around anybody he comes across, and be hail-fellow-well-met with all the elect, from the highest down. How tangled up and absurd that is! How are you going to have a republic under a king? How are you going to have a republic at all, where the head of the government is absolute, holds his place forever, and has no parliament, no council to meddle or make in his affairs, nobody voted for, nobody elected, nobody in the whole universe with a voice in the government, nobody asked to take a hand in its matters, and nobody *allowed* to do it? Fine republic, ain't it?"

"Well, yes—it *is* a little different from the idea I had—but I thought I might go around and get acquainted with the grandees, anyway—not exactly splice the main-brace with them, you know, but shake hands and pass the time of day."

"Could Tom, Dick, and Harry call on the Cabinet of Russia and do that?—on Prince Gortschakoff,[12] for instance?"

"I reckon not, Sandy."

"Well, this is Russia—only more so. There's not the shadow of a republic about it anywhere. There are ranks, here. There are viceroys, princes, governors, sub-governors, sub-sub-governors, and a hundred orders of nobility, grading along down from grand-ducal archangels, stage by stage, till the general level is struck, where there ain't any titles. Do you know what a prince of the blood is, on earth?"

"No."

"Well, a prince of the blood don't belong to the royal family exactly, and he don't belong to the mere nobility of the kingdom; he is lower than the one, and higher than t'other. That's about the position of the patriarchs and prophets, here. There's some mighty high nobility here—people that you and I ain't worthy to polish sandals for—and *they* ain't worthy to polish sandals for the patriarchs and prophets. That gives you a kind of an idea of their rank, don't it? You begin to see how high up they are, don't you? Just to get a two-minute glimpse of one of them is a thing for a body to remember and tell about for a thousand years. Why Captain, just think of this: if Abraham was to set his foot down here by this door, there would be a railing set up around that foot-track right away, and a shelter put over it, and people would flock here from all over heaven, for hundreds and hundreds of years, to look at it. Abraham is one of the parties that Mr. Talmage, of Brooklyn, is going to embrace, and kiss, and weep on, when he comes. He wants to lay in a good stock of tears, you know, or five to one he will go dry before he gets a chance to do it."

"Sandy," says I, "I had an idea that *I* was going to be equals with everybody here, too, but I will let that drop. It don't matter, and I am plenty happy enough anyway."

"Captain, you are happier than you would be, the other way. These old patriarchs and prophets have got ages the start of you; they know more in two minutes than you know in a year. Did you ever try to have a sociable improving-time discussing winds, and currents, and variations of compass with an undertaker?"

"I get your idea, Sandy. He couldn't interest me. He would be an ignoramus in such things—he would bore me, and I would bore him."

"You have got it. You would bore the patriarchs when you talked, and when they talked they would shoot over your head. By and by you would say, 'Good morning, your Eminence, I will call again'—but you wouldn't. Did you ever ask the slush-boy[13] to come up in the cabin and take dinner with you?"

"I get your drift again, Sandy. I wouldn't be used to such grand people as the patriarchs and prophets, and I would be sheepish and tongue-tied in their company, and mighty glad to get out of it. Sandy, which is the highest rank, patriarch, or prophet?"

"Oh, the prophets hold over the patriarchs. The newest prophet, even, is of a sight more consequence than the oldest patriarch. Yes, sir, Adam himself has to walk behind Shakspere."

"Was Shakspere a prophet?"

"Of course he was; and so was Homer, and heaps more. But Shakspere and the rest have to walk behind a common tailor from Tennessee, by the name of Billings; and behind a horse-doctor named Sakka, from Afghanistan. Jeremiah and Billings and Buddha walk together, side by side, right behind a crowd from planets not in our astrononomy; next come a dozen or two from Jupiter and other worlds; next come Daniel, and Sakka and Confucius; next a lot from systems outside of ours; next come Ezekiel, Mahomet, Zoroaster,[14] and a knife-grinder from ancient Egypt; then there is a long string, and after them, away down toward the bottom, come Shakspere and Homer and a shoemaker named Marais, from the back settlements of France."

"Have they really rung in Mahomet and all those other heathens?"

"Yes—they all had their message; and they all get their reward. The man who don't get his reward on earth, needn't bother—he will get it here, sure."

"But why did they throw off on Shakspere, that way, and put him away down there below those shoemakers and horse-doctors, and knife-grinders—a lot of people nobody ever heard of?"

"That is the heavenly justice of it—they warn't rewarded according to their deserts on earth, but here they get their rightful rank. That tailor Billings, from Tennessee, wrote poetry that Homer and Shakspere couldn't begin to come up to; but nobody would print it, nobody read it but his neighbors, an ignorant lot, and they laughed at it. Whenever the village had a drunken frolic and a dance, they would drag him in and crown him with cabbage leaves, and pretend to bow down to him; and one night when he was sick and nearly starved to death, they had him out and crowned him, and then they rode him on a rail about the village, and everybody followed along beating tin pans and yelling. Well, he died before morning. He wasn't ever expecting to go to heaven, much less that there was going to be any fuss made over him, so I reckon he was a good deal surprised when the reception broke on him."

"Was you there, Sandy?"

"Bless you, no!"

"Why? Didn't you know it was going to come off?"

"Well, I judge I did. It was the talk of these realms—not for a day, like this barkeeper business, but for twenty years before the man died."

"Why the mischief didn't you go, then?"

"Now, how you talk! The like of me go meddling around at the reception of a prophet? A mudsill[15] like me trying to push in and help receive an awful grandee like Edward J. Billings? Why I should have been laughed at for a billion miles around. I shouldn't ever heard the last of it."

"Well, who did go, then?"

"Mighty few people that you and I will ever get a chance to see, Captain. Not a solitary commoner ever has the luck to see a reception of a prophet, I can tell you. All the nobility, and all the patriarchs and prophets—every last one of them—and all the archangels, and all the princes and governors and viceroys, were there,—and no small fry—not a single one. And mind you, I'm not talking about only the grandees from *our* world, but the princes and patriarchs and so-on from *all* the worlds that shine in our sky, and from billions more that belong in systems upon systems away outside of the one our sun is in. There were some prophets and patriarchs there that ours ain't a circumstance to, for rank and illustriousness and all that. Some were from Jupiter and other worlds in our own system, but the most celebrated were three poets, Saa, Bo, and Soof, from great planets in three different and very remote systems. These three names are common and familiar in every nook and corner of heaven, clear from one end of it to the other—fully as well known as the eighty Supreme Archangels, in fact—whereas our Moses, and Adam, and the rest, have not been heard of outside of our world's little corner of heaven, except by a few very learned men scattered here and there—and they always spell their names wrong, and get the performances of one mixed up with the doings of another, and they almost always locate them simply *in our solar system,* and think that is enough without going into little details such as naming the particular world they are from. It is like a learned Hindoo showing off how much he knows by saying Longfellow lives in the United States—as if he lived all over the United States, and as if the country was so small you couldn't throw a brick there without hitting him. Between you and me, it does gravel me, the cool way people from those monster worlds outside our system snub our little world, and even our system. Of course we think a good deal of Jupiter, because our world is only a potato to it, for size; but then there are worlds in other systems that Jupiter isn't even a mustard seed to—like the planet Goobra, for instance, which you couldn't squeeze inside the orbit of Halley's comet without straining the rivets. Tourists from Goobra (I mean parties that lived and died there—natives,) come here, now and then, and inquire about our world, and when they find out it is so little that a streak of lightning can flash clear around it in the eighth of a second, they have to lean up against something to laugh. Then they screw a glass into their eye[16] and go to examining *us* as if we were a curious kind of foreign bug, or something of that sort. One of them asked me how long our day was; and when I told him it was twelve hours long, as a general thing, he asked me if people where I was from considered it worth while to get up and wash for such a day as that. That is the way with those Goobra people—they can't seem to let a chance go by to throw it in your face that their day is three hundred and twenty-two of our years long. This young snob was just of age—he was six or seven thousand of his days old—say two million of our years—and he had all the puppy airs that belong to that time of life—that turning point when a person has got over being a boy and yet ain't quite a man exactly. If it had been anywhere else but in heaven, I would have given him a piece of my mind. Well, anyway, Billings had the grandest reception that has been seen in thousands of centuries, and I think it will have a good effect. His name will be carried pretty far, and it will make our system talked about, and maybe our world, too, and raise us in the respect of the general public of heaven. Why look here—Shakspere walked backward before that tailor from Tennessee, and scattered flowers for him to walk on, and Homer stood behind his chair and waited on him at the banquet.

Of course that didn't go for much *there,* amongst all those big foreigners from other systems, as they hadn't heard of Shakspere or Homer either, but it would amount to considerable down there on our little earth if they could know about it. I wish there was something *in* that miserable spiritualism, so we could send them word. That Tennessee village would set up a monument to Billings, then, and his autograph would outsell Satan's. Well, they had grand times at that reception—a small-fry noble from Hoboken told me all about it—Sir Richard Duffer, Baronet."

"What, Sandy, a nobleman from Hoboken? How is that?"

"Easy enough. Duffer kept a sausage shop, and never saved a cent in his life because he used to give all his spare meat to the poor, in a quiet way. Not tramps,—no, the other sort—the sort that will starve before they will beg—honest square people out of work. Dick used to watch hungry-looking men and women and children, and track them home, and find out all about them from the neighbors, and then feed them and find them work. As nobody ever *saw* him give anything to anybody, he had the reputation of being mean; he died with it, too, and everybody said it was a good riddance; but the minute he landed here, they made him a baronet, and the very first words Dick the sausage-maker of Hoboken heard when he stepped upon the heavenly shore, were, 'Welcome, Sir Richard Duffer!' It surprised him some, because he thought he had reasons to believe he was pointed for a warmer climate than this one."

All of a sudden the whole region fairly rocked under the crash of eleven hundred and one thunder-blasts, all let off at once, and Sandy says—

"There, that's for the barkeep."

I jumped up and says—

"Then let's be moving along, Sandy, we don't want to miss any of this thing, you know."

"Keep your seat," he says, "he is only just telegraphed, that is all."

"How?"

"That blast only means that he has been sighted from the signal station. He is off Sandy Hook. The committee will go down to meet him, now, and escort him in. There will be ceremonies and delays, they won't be coming up the Bay for a considerable time, yet. It is several billion miles away, anyway."

"*I* could have been a barkeeper and a hard lot just as well as not," says I, remembering the lonesome way I arrived, and how there wasn't any committee nor anything.

"I notice some regret in your voice," says Sandy, "and it is natural enough; but let bygones be bygones; you went according to your lights, and it is too late now to mend the thing."

"No, let it slide, Sandy, I don't mind. But you've got a Sandy Hook *here,* too, have you?"

"We've got everything here, just as it is below. All the States and Territories of the Union, and all the kingdoms of the earth and the islands of the sea are laid out here just as they are on the globe—all the same shape they are down there, and all graded to the relative sizes, only each State and realm and island is a good many billion times bigger here than it is below. There goes another blast."

"What is that one for?"

"That is only another fort answering the first one. They each fire eleven hundred and one thunder-claps at a single dash—it is the usual salute for an eleventh-hour guest; a hundred for each hour and an extra one for the guest's sex; if it was a woman we would know it by their leaving off the extra gun."

"How do we know there's eleven hundred and one, Sandy, when they all go off at once?—and yet we certainly do know."

"Our intellects are a good deal sharpened up, here, in some ways, and that is one of them. Numbers and sizes and distances are so great, here, that we have to be made so we can *feel* them—our old ways of counting and measuring and ciphering wouldn't ever give us an idea of them, but would only confuse us and oppress us and make our heads ache."

After some more talk about this, I says—

"Sandy, I notice that I hardly ever see a white angel; where I run across one white angel, I strike as many as a hundred million copper colored ones—people that can't speak English. How is that?"

"Well, you will find it the same in any State or Territory of the American corner of heaven you choose to go to. I have shot along a whole week on a stretch, and gone millions and millions of miles, through perfect swarms of angels, without ever seeing a single white one, or hearing a word I could understand. You see, America was occupied a billion years and more, by Injuns and Aztecs, and that sort of folks, before a white man ever set his foot in it. During the first three hundred years after Columbus's discovery, there wasn't ever more than one good lecture audience of white people, all put together, in America,—I mean the whole thing, British Possessions and all; in the beginning of our century there were only 6,000,000 or 7,000,000—say seven; 12,000,000 or 14,000,000 in 1825; say 23,000,000 in 1850; 40,000,000 in 1875. Our death rate has always been 20 in 1,000 per annum. Well, 140,000 died the first year of the century; 280,000 the twenty-fifth year; 500,000 the fiftieth year; about a million the seventy-fifth year. Now I am going to be liberal about this thing, and consider that fifty million whites have died in America, from the beginning up to to-day—make it sixty, if you want to; make it a hundred million—it's no difference about a few millions one way or t'other. Well, now, you can see, yourself, that when you come to spread a little dab of people like that over these hundreds of billions of miles of American territory here in heaven, it is like scattering a ten-cent box of homœopathic pills over the great Sahara and expecting to find them again. You can't expect us to amount to anything in heaven, and we *don't*—now that is the simple fact, and we have got to do the best we can with it. The learned men from other planets and other systems come here and hang around a while, when they are touring around the Kingdom and then go back to their own section of heaven and write a book of travels, and they give America about five lines in it. And what do they say about us? They say this wilderness is populated with a scattering few hundred thousand billions of red angels, with now and then a curiously complected *diseased* one. You see, they think we whites, and the occasional nigger, are Injuns that have been bleached out or blackened by some leprous disease or other—for some peculiarly rascally *sin*, mind you. It is a mighty sour pill for us all, my friend—even the modestest of us, let alone the other kind, that think they are going to be received like a long-lost government bond, and hug Abraham into the bargain. I haven't asked you any of the particulars, Captain, but I judge it goes without saying—if my experience is worth anything—that there wasn't much of a hooraw made over you when you arrived—now was there?"

"Don't mention it, Sandy," says I, coloring up a little, "I wouldn't have had the family see it for any amount you are a mind to name. Change the subject, Sandy, change the subject."

"Well, do you think of settling in the Californian department of bliss?"

"I don't know. I wasn't calculating on doing anything really definite in that direction till the family come. I thought I would just look around, meantime, in a quiet way, and make up my mind. Besides, I know a good many dead people, and I was calculating to hunt them up and swap a little gossip with them about friends, and old times, and one thing or another, and ask them how they like it here as far as they have got. I reckon my wife will want to camp in the Californian range, though, because most all her departed will be there, and she likes to be with folks she knows."

"Don't you let her. You see what the Jersey district of heaven is for whites; well, the Californian district is a thousand times worse. It swarms with a mean kind of leather-headed mud-colored angels—Digger Injuns, mainly—and your nearest white neighbor is likely to be a million miles away. *What a man mostly misses, in heaven, is company*—company of his own sort and color and language. I have come near settling in the European part of heaven once or twice on that account."

"Well, why didn't you, Sandy?"

"Oh, various reasons. For one thing, although you *see* plenty of whites there, you can't understand any of them, hardly, and so you go about as hungry for talk as you do here. I like to look at a Russian or a German or an Italian—I even like to look at a Frenchman if I ever have the luck to catch him engaged in anything that ain't indelicate—but *looking* don't cure the hunger—what you want is talk."

"Well, there's England, Sandy—the English district of heaven."

"Yes, but it is not so very much better than this end of the heavenly domain. As long as you run across Englishmen born this side of three hundred years ago, you are all right; but the minute you get back of Elizabeth's time the language begins to fog up, and the further back you go the foggier it gets. I had some talk with one Langland and a man by the name of Chaucer—old-time poets—but it was no use, I couldn't quite understand them, and they couldn't quite understand me. I have had letters from them since, but it is such broken English I can't make it out. Back of those men's time the English are just simply foreigners, nothing more, nothing less; they talk Danish, German, Norman French, and sometimes a mixture of all of these; back of *them,* they talk Latin, and ancient British, Irish, and Gaelic; and then back of these comes billions and billions of pure savages that talk a gibberish that Satan himself couldn't understand. The fact is, where you strike one man in the English settlements that you can understand, you wade through awful swarms that talk something you can't make head nor tail of. You see, every country on earth has been overlaid so often, in the course of a billion years, with different kinds of people and different sorts of languages that this sort of mongrel business was bound to be the result in heaven."

"Sandy," says I, "did you see a good many of the great people history tells about?"

"Yes—plenty. I saw kings and all sorts of distinguished people."

"Do the kings rank just as they did below?"

"No; a body can't bring his rank up here with him. Divine right is a good enough earthly romance, but it don't go, here. Kings drop down to the general level as soon as they reach the realms of grace. I knew Charles the Second very well—one of the most popular comedians in the English section—draws first rate. There are better, of course—people that were never heard of on earth—but Charles is making a very good reputation indeed, and is considered a rising man. Richard the Lion-hearted is in the prize ring, and coming into considerable favor. Henry the Eighth is a tragedian, and the scenes where he kills people are done to the very life. Henry the Sixth keeps a religious-book stand."

"Did you ever see Napoleon, Sandy?"

"Often—sometimes in the Corsican range, sometimes in the French. He always hunts up a conspicuous place, and goes frowning around with his arms folded and his field glass under his arm, looking as grand, gloomy, and peculiar as his reputation calls for, and very much bothered because he don't stand as high here, for a soldier, as he expected to."

"Why, who stands higher?"

"Oh, a *lot* of people *we* never heard of before—the shoemaker and horse-doctor and knife-grinder kind, you know—clod-hoppers from goodness knows where, that never handled a sword or fired a shot in their lives—but the soldiership was in them, though they never had a chance to show it.[17] But here they take their right place, and Caesar and Napoleon and Alexander have to take a back seat. The greatest military genius our world ever produced was a bricklayer from somewhere back of Boston—died during the Revolution—by the name of Absalom Jones. Wherever he goes, crowds flock to see him. You see, everybody knows that if he had had a chance he would have shown the world some generalship that would have made all generalship before look like child's-play and 'prentice-work. But he never got a chance; he tried heaps of times to enlist as a private, but he had lost both thumbs and a couple of front teeth, and the recruiting surgeon wouldn't pass him. However, as I say, everybody knows, now, what he *would* have been, and so they flock by the million to get a glimpse of him whenever they hear he is going to be anywhere. Caesar, and Hannibal, and Alexander, and Napoleon are all on his staff, and ever so many more great generals, but the public hardly care to look at *them* when *he* is around. Boom! There goes another salute. The barkeeper's off quarantine, now."

Sandy and I put on our things. Then we made a wish, and in a second we were at the reception-place. We stood on the edge of the ocean of space, and looked out over the dimness, but couldn't make out anything. Close by us was the Grand Stand. Tier on tier of dim thrones rising up toward the zenith. From each side of it spread away the tiers of seats for the general public. They spread away for leagues and leagues—you couldn't see the ends. They were empty and still, and hadn't a cheerful look, but looked dreary, like a theatre before anybody comes—gas turned down. Sandy says—

"We'll sit down here and wait. We'll see the head of the procession come in sight away off yonder pretty soon, now."

Says I—

"It's pretty lonesome, Sandy; I reckon there's a hitch somewheres. Nobody but just you and me—it ain't much of a display for the barkeeper."

"Don't you fret, it's all right. There'll be one more gun-fire—then you'll see."

In a little while we noticed a sort of a lightish flush away off on the horizon.

"Head of the torchlight procession," says Sandy.

It spread, and got lighter and brighter; soon it had a strong glare like a locomotive headlight; it kept on getting brighter and brighter till it was like the sun peeping above the horizon-line at sea—the big red rays shot high up into the sky.

"Keep your eyes on the Grand Stand and the miles of seats—sharp!" says Sandy, "and listen for the gun-fire."

Just then it burst out "Boom-boom-boom!" like a million thunderstorms in one, and made the whole heavens rock. Then there was a sudden and awful glare of light all about us, and in that very instant every one of the millions of seats was occupied, and as far as you could see, in both directions, was just a solid pack of people, and the place was all splendidly lit up! It was enough to take a body's breath away. Sandy says—

"That is the way we do it here. No time fooled away; nobody straggling in after the curtain's up. Wishing is quicker work than traveling. A matter of a second ago these folks were millions of miles from here. When they heard the last signal, all they had to do was to wish, and here they are."

The prodigious choir struck up—

"We long to hear thy voice,
To see thee face to face."

It was noble music but the uneducated chipped in and spoilt it, just as the congregations used to do on earth.

The head of the procession began to pass, now, and it was a wonderful sight. It swept along, thick and solid, five hundred thousand angels abreast, and every angel carrying a torch and singing—the whirring thunder of the wings made a body's head ache. You could follow the line of the procession back, and slanting upward into the sky, far away in a glittering snaky rope, till it was only a faint streak in the distance. The rush went on and on, for a long time, and at last, sure enough, along comes the barkeeper, and then everybody rose and a cheer went up that made the heavens shake, I tell you! He was all smiles, and had his halo tilted over one ear in a cocky way and was the most satisfied-looking saint I ever saw. While he marched up the steps of the Grand Stand, the choir struck up—

"The whole wide heaven groans,
And waits to hear that voice."

There were four gorgeous tents standing side by side in the place of honor, on a broad railed platform in the centre of the Grand Stand, with a shining guard of honor round about them. The tents had been shut up, all this time. As the barkeeper climbed along up, bowing and smirking to everybody, and at last got to the platform, these tents were jerked up aloft, all of a sudden, and we saw four noble thrones of gold, all caked with jewels, and in the two middle ones sat old white-whiskered men, and in the two others a couple of the most glorious and gaudy giants, with platter-halos and beautiful armor. All the millions went down on their knees, and stared, and looked glad, and burst out into a joyful kind of murmurs. They said—

"Two archangels!—that is splendid. Who can the others be?"

The archangels gave the barkeeper a stiff little military bow; the two old men rose; one of them said, "Moses and Esau welcome thee!" and then all the four vanished and the thrones were empty.

The barkeeper looked a little disappointed, for he was calculating to hug those old people, I judge; but it was the gladdest and proudest multitude you ever saw—because they had seen Moses and Esau. Everybody was saying, "Did you see them?—*I* did—Esau's side face was to me, but I saw Moses full in the face, just as plain as I see you this minute!"

The procession took up the barkeeper and moved on with him again, and the crowd broke up and scattered. As we went along home, Sandy said it was a great success, and the barkeeper would have a right to be proud of it forever. And he said *we* were in luck, too; said we might attend receptions for forty thousand years to come, and not have a chance to see a brace of such grand moguls as Moses and Esau. We found afterwards that we had come near seeing another patriarch, and likewise a genuine prophet besides, but at the last moment they sent regrets. Sandy said there would be a monument put up there, where Moses and Esau had stood, with the date and the circumstances, and all about the whole business, and travelers would come for thousands of years, and gawk at it, and climb over it, and scribble their names on it.

CHAPTER 5

Captain Stormfield Resumes

I

When I had been in heaven some time I begun to feel restless, the same as I used to on earth when I had been ashore a month, so I sejested to Sandy that we do some excursions. He said all right, and with that we started with a whiz—not that you could *hear* us go, but it was as if you ought to. On account of our going so fast, for you go by *thought*. If you went only as fast as light or electricity you would be forever getting to any place, heaven is so big. Even when you are traveling by thought it takes you days and days and days to cover the territory of any Christian State, and days and days and days to cover the uninhabited stretch between that State and the next one.

"You can't put it into miles," Sandy says.

"Why can't you?" says I.

"Becuz there ain't enough of them. If you had all the miles God ever made they wouldn't reach from the Catholic camp to the High Church Piscopalian—nor half way, for that matter; and yet they are the nearest together of any. Professor Higgins tries to work the miles on the measurements, on account of old earthly habit, and p'raps he gets a sort of grip on the distances out of the result, but you couldn't, and I can't."

"How do *you* know I couldn't, Sandy? Speak for yourself, hadn't you better? You just tell me his game, and wait till I look at my hand."

"Well, it's this. He used to be astronomical professor of astronomy at Harvard—"

"This was before he was dead?"

"Cert'nly. How could he be *after* he was dead?"

"Oh, well, it ain't important. But a *soldier* can be a soldier after he's dead. And he can breed, too. There's eleven million dead soldiers drawing pension at home, now—some that's been dead 125 years—and we've never had those millions on the pay-roll since the first Fourth of July. Go on, Sandy. Maybe it was before he was dead, maybe it wasn't; but it ain't important."

"Well, he was astronomical professor, and can't get rid of his habits. So he tries to figure out these heavenly distances by astronomical measurements. That is to say, he computes them in light-years."

"What is a light-year, Sandy?"

"He says light travels 186,000 miles a second, and—"

"How many?"

"186,000."

"In a *second,* Sandy—not a week?"

"No, in a second. He says the sun is 93,000,000 miles from the earth, and it takes light 8 minutes to cover the distance. Then he ciphers out how far the light would travel in a year of 365 days, at that gait, and he calls that distance a light-year."

"It's considerable, ain't it, Sandy?"

"Don't you doubt it!"

"How far is it, Sandy?"

"It's 63,280 times the distance from the earth to the sun."

"Land! Say it again, Sandy, and say it slow."

"63,280 times 93,000,000 miles."

"Sandy it beats the band. Do you think there's room for a straight stretch like that? Don't you reckon it would come to the edge and stick out over? What does a light-year foot up, Sandy, in a lump?"

"Six thousand million miles."

"Sandy, it is certainly a corker! Is there any known place as far off as a light-year?"

"Shucks, Stormy, *one* light-year is nothing. He says it's *four* light-years from our earth to the nearest star—and nothing between."

"*Nothing* between? Nothing but just emptiness?"

"That's it; nothing but emptiness. And he says there's not a star in the Milky Way nor anywhere else in the sky that's not *further* away from its nearest neighbor than that."

"Why, Sandy, if that is true, the sky is emptier than heaven."

"Oh, indeed, no! Far from it. In the Milky Way, the professor says, no star is more than six or seven light-years distant from its nearest neighbor, but there ain't any Christian sect in heaven that is nearer than 5,000 light-years from the camp of the next sect. Oh, no, he says the sky *is* a howling wilderness, but it can't howl with heaven. No, sir, he says of all the lonesome places that ever was, give him heaven. Every now and then he gets so lonesome here that he makes an excursion amongst the stars, so's to have a sense of company."

"Why, Sandy, what have they made heaven so large, for?"

"So's to have room in the future. The redeemed will still be coming for billions and billions and billions and billions of years, but there'll always be room, you see. *This* heaven ain't built on any 'Gates Ajar' proportions."[18]

. . . . Time drifted along. We went on excursioning amongst the colonies and over the monstrous spaces between, till at last I was so weighed down by the awful bigness of heaven that I said I'd got to see something small to get back my natural focus and lift off some of the load, I couldn't stand it any longer. Sandy says,

"Well, then, suppose we try an asterisk, or asteroid, or whatever the professor calls them. *They're* little enough to fit the case, I reckon."

II

Journey to the Asterisk

So we went, and it was quite interesting. It was a very nice little world, twenty-five or thirty miles in circumference; almost exactly a thousand times smaller than the earth, and just a miniature of it, in every way: little wee Atlantic oceans and Pacific oceans and Indian oceans, all in the right places; the same with the rivers, the same with the lakes; the same old familiar mountain ranges, the same continents and islands, the same Sahara—all in the right proportions and as exact as a photograph. We walked around it one afternoon, and waded the oceans, and had a most uncommon good time. We spent weeks and weeks walking around over it and getting acquainted with the nations and their ways.

Nice little dollies, they were, and not bigger than Gulliver's Lilliput people. Their ways were like ours. In their America they had a republic on our own plan, and in their Europe, their Asia and their Africa they had monarchies and established churches, and a pope and a czar, and all the rest of it. They were not afraid of us; in fact they held us in rather frank contempt, because we were giants. Giants have never been respected, in any world. These people had a quite good opinion of themselves, although they were no bigger than a banana, and many of them no bigger than a clothespin. In church it was a common thing for the preacher to look out over his congregation and speak of them as the noblest work of God—and never a clothespin smiled! These little animals were having wars all the time, and raising armies and building navies, and striving after the approval of God every way they could. And wherever there was a savage country that needed civilizing, they went there and took it, and divided it up among the several enlightened monarchs, and civilized it—each monarch in his own way, but generally with Bibles and bullets and taxes. And the way they did whoop-up Morals, and Patriotism, and Religion, and the Brotherhood of Man was noble to see.

I couldn't see that they differed from us, except in size. It was like looking at ourselves through the wrong end of the spyglass. But Sandy said there was one difference, and a big one. It was this: each person could look right into every other person's mind and read what was in it, but he thought his own mind was concealed from everybody but himself!

CHAPTER 6

From Captain Stormfield's Reminiscences

One day, whilst I was there in Heaven, I says to Sandy—

"Sandy," I says, "You was telling me, a while back, that you knowed how the human race came to be created; and now, if you don't mind," I says, "I'd like you to pull off the narrative, for I reckon it's intresting."

So he done it. This is it.

Sandy's Narrative

Well, it was like this. I got it from Slattery. Slattery was there at the time, being an eye witness, you see; and so Slattery, he—

"Who's Slattery, Sandy?"

One of the originals.

"Original *which*?"

Original inventions. He used to be an angel, in the early times, two hunderd thousand years ago; and so, as it happened—

"Two hun—do you mean to say—"

Yes, I *do.* It was two hunderd thousand years ago. Slattery was born here in Heaven, and so time don't count. As I was a-telling you, he was an angel, first-off, but when Satan fell, he fell, too, becuz he was a connexion of Satan's, by marriage or blood or somehow or other, and it put him under suspicion, though they warn't able to prove anything on him. Still, they judged a little term down below in the fires would be a lesson to him and do him good, so they give him a thousand years down in them tropics, and—

"A *thousand,* Sandy?"

Cert'nly. It ain't anything to these people, Cap'n Stormfield. When you've been here as long as I have—but never mind about that. When he got back, he was different. The vacation done him good. You see, he had had experience, and it sharpened him up. And besides, he had traveled, and it made him important, which he warn't, before. Satan come near getting a thousand years himself, that time—

"But I thought he *did,* Sandy. I thought he went down for good and all."

No, sir, not that time.

"What saved him?"

Influence.

"M-m. So they have it here, too, do they?"

Oh, well, I sh'd *think*! Satan has fell a lot of times, but he hasn't ever been sent down permanent, yet—but only the small fry.

"Just the same it used to was, down on the earth, Sandy. Ain't it intresting? Go on. Slattery he got reinstated, as I understand it?"

Yes, so he did. And he was a considerable person by now, as I was a-saying, partly on accounts of his relative, and partly on accounts of him having been abroad, and all that, and affecting to talk with a foreign accent, which he picked up down below. So he was around when the first attempts was made. They had a mould for a man, and a mould for a woman, and they mixed up the materials and poured it in. They come out very handsome to look at, and everybody said it was a success. So they made some more, and kept on making them and setting them one side to dry, till they had about ten thousand. Then they blew in the breath, and put the dispositions in, and turned them loose in a pleasant piece of territory, and told them to go it.

"Put in the *dispositions*?"

Yes, The *Moral Qualities.* That's what makes disposition. They distributed 'em around perfectly fair and honorable. There was 28 of them, according to the plans and specifications, and the whole 28 went to each man and woman in equal measure, nobody getting more of a quality than anybody else, nor less. I'll give you the list, just as Slattery give it to me:

1. Magnanimity.	2. Meanness.
3. Moral courage—	4. Moral cowardice.
5. Physical courage.	6. Physical cowardice.
7. Honesty....	8. Dishonesty.
9. Truthfulness...	10. Untruthfulness.

11. Love......	12. Hate.
13. Chastity......	14. Unchastity.
15. Firmness....	16. Unfirmness.
17. Diligence...	18. Indolence.
19. Selfishness...	20. Unselfishness.
21. Prodigality....	22. Stinginess.
23. Reverence....	24. Irreverence.
25. Intellectuality...	26. Unintellectuality.
27. Self-Conceit.	28. Humility.

"And a mighty good layout, Sandy. And all fair and square, too; and no favors to anybody. I like it. Looks to me elegant, and the way it had ought to be. Blamed if it ain't intresting. Go on."

Well, the new creatures settled in the territory that was app'inted for them, and begun to hatch, and multiply and replenish, and all that, and everything went along to the queen's taste, as the saying is. But by and by Slattery noticed something, and got Satan to go out there and take a look, which he done, and says,

"Well, something the matter, you think? What is it?"

"I'll show you," Slattery says. "Warn't they to be something fresh, something new and surprising?"

"Cert'nly," Satan says, "Ain't they?"

"Oh, well," says Slattery, "if you come right down to the fine shades, I ain't able to deny that they *are* new—but *how* new? That's the idea? Moreover, what I want to know is, what's now an *improvement*?"

"Go on," says Satan, a little impatient, "what's your point? Get at it!"

"Well, it's this. These new people don't differ from the angels. Except that they hain't got wings, and they don't get sick, and they don't die. Otherwise they're just angels—just the old usual thing. They're all the same size, they're all exactly alike—hair, eyes, noses, gait, everything—just the same as angels. Now, then, here's the point: The only solitary new thing about 'em is a new arrangement of their morals. It's the only fresh thing."

"Very well," says Satan, "ain't that enough? What are you complaining about?"

"No, it *ain't* enough, unless it's an improvement over the old regular arrangement."

"Come, get down to particulars!" says Satan, in that snappish way some people has.

"All right. Look at the old arrangement, and what do you find? Just this: the entire and complete and rounded-out sum of an angel's morals is *goodness*—plain, simple *goodness.* What's his equipment—a great long string of Moral Qualities with 28 specifications in it? No, there's only one—*Love.* It's the whole outfit. They can't hate, they don't know how, becuz they can't help loving everything and everybody. Just the same, they don't know anything about envy, or jealousy, or avarice, or meanness, or lying, or selfishness, or *any* of those things. And so they're never unhappy, there not being any way for them to *get* unhappy. It makes *character,* don't it? And A-1."

"Correct. Go on."

"Now then, look at these new creatures. They've got an immense lay-out in the way of Moral Qualities, and you'd think they'd have a stunning future in front of them—but it ain't so. For why? Because they've got Love *and* Hate, in the same proportions. The one neutralizes the other. They don't really love, and they don't really hate! They *can't,* you see. It's the same with the whole invoice: Honesty and Dishonesty, exactly the same quantity of each; selfishness and unselfishness; reverence and irreverence; courage and cowardice—and so on and so on. They are all exactly alike, inside and out, these new people—and *characterless.* They're ciphers, nothings, just wax-works. What do you say?"

"I see the point," says Satan. "The old arrangement was better."

Well, they got to talking around, and by and by others begun to see the point—and criticize. But not loud—only continuous. In about two hundred thousand years it got all around and come to be common talk everywheres. So at last it got to the Authorities.

"Would it take all that time, Sandy?"

"Here? Yes. It ain't long here, where a thousand years is as a day. It ain't six months, heavenly time. You've often noticed, in history, where the awful oppression of a nation has been going on eight or nine hundred years before Providence interferes, and everybody surprised at the delay. Providence *does* interfere, and mighty prompt, too, as you reconnize when you come to allow for the difference betwixt heavenly time and real time."

"By gracious I never thought of that before! I've been unfair to Providence a many and a many a time, but it was becuz I didn't think. Russia's a case in point; it looks like procasturation,[19] but I see now, it ain't."

"Yes, you see, a thousand years earthly time, being exactly a day of heavenly time, then of course a year of earthly time is only just a shade over a minute of heavenly time; and if you don't keep these facts in mind you are naturally bound to think Providence is procrasturing when it's just the other way. It's on accounts of this ignorance that many and many a person has got the idea that prayer ain't ever answered, and stuck to it to his dying day; whereas, prayer is *always* answered. Take praying for rain, f'rinstance. The prayer comes up; Providence reflects a minute, judges it's all right, and says to the Secatry of State, 'Turn it on.' Down she comes, in a flood. But don't do any good of course, becuz it's a year late. Providence reflecting a minute has made all the trouble, you see. If people would only take the Bible at its word, and reconnize the difference betwixt heavenly time and earthly time, they'd pray for rain a year before they want it, and then they'd be all right. Prayer is always answered, but not inside of a year, becuz Providence has *got* to have a minute to reflect. Otherwise there'd be mistakes, on accounts of too much hurry."

"Why, Sandy, blamed if it don't make everything perfectly plain and understandable, which it never was before. Well, go on about what we was talking about."

"All right. The Authorities got wind of the talk, so They reckoned They would take a private view of them wax figures and see what was to be done. The end was, They concluded to start another Race, and do it better this time. Well, this was the Human Race."

"Wasn't the other the human race too, Sandy?"

"No. That one is neither one thing nor t'other. It ain't human because it's immortal; and it ain't any account, becuz everybody is just alike and hasn't any character. The Holy Doughnuts—that is what they're called, in private."

"Can we go and see them, some time, Sandy?" I says.

"Certn'ly. There's excursions every week-day. Well, the Authorities started out on the hypotheneuse[20] that the thing to go for in the new race was *variety*. You see, that's where the Doughnuts failed. Now then, was the Human Race an easy job? Yes, sir, it was. They made rafts of moulds, this time, no two of them alike—so there's your *physical* differentiations, till you can't rest! Then all They had to do was to take the same old 28 Moral Qualities, and mix them up, helter-skelter, in all sorts of different proportions, and ladle them into the moulds—and there's your *dispositional* differentiations, b'George! *Variety?* Oh don't mention it! Slattery says to me, 'Sandy,' he says, 'this dreamy old quiet heaven of ourn has been asleep for ages, but if that Human Race didn't wake it up don't you believe *me* no more!'

"Wake it up? Oh, yes, that's what it done. Slattery says the Authorities was awful surprised when They come to examine that Human Race and see how careless They'd been in the distribution of them Qualities, and the results that was a-flowing from it.

" 'Sandy,' he says, 'there wasn't any foreman to the job, nor any plan about the distributing. Anybody could help that wanted to; no instructions, only look out and provide *variety*. So these 'commodating volunteers would heave a dipperful of Hate into a mould and season it with a teaspoon of Love, and there's your *Murderer*, all ready for business. And into another mould they'd heave a teaspoonful of Chastity, and flavor it up with a dipperful of Unchastity—and so on and so on. A dipperful of Honesty and a spoonful of Dishonesty; a dipperful of Moral Courage and a spoonful of Moral Cowardice—and there's your splendid man, ready to stand up for an unpopular cause and stake his life on it; in another mould they'd dump considerable Magnanimity, and then dilute it down with Meanness till there wasn't any strength left in it—and so on and so—the worst mixed-up mess of good and bad dispositions and half-good and half-bad ones a body could imagine—just a tagrag-and-bobtail Mob of nondescripts, and not worth propagating, of course; but what could the Authorities *do*? Not a thing. It was too late.' "

[1909/1995]

Letter from the Recording Angel

Office of the Recording Angel,
Dept. of Petitions, Jan. 20.

Andrew Langdon,[1]
Coal Dealer, Buffalo, N.Y.

I have the honor, as per command, to inform you that your recent act of benevolence and self-sacrifice has been recorded upon a page by itself of the Book called Golden Deeds of Men; a distinction, I am permitted to remark, which is not merely extraordinary, it is unique.

As regards your prayers, for the week ending the 19th, I have the honor to report as follows:

1. For weather to advance hard coal 15 cents per ton. Granted.

2. For influx of laborers to reduce wages 10 per cent. Granted.

3. For a break in rival soft-coal prices. Granted.

4. For a visitation upon the man, or upon the family of the man, who has set up a competing retail coal-yard in Rochester. Granted, as follows: diphtheria, 2, 1 fatal; scarlet fever, 1, to result in deafness and imbecility. Note. This prayer should have been directed against this subordinate's principals, the N.Y. Central RR Co.

5. For deportation to Sheol, of annoying swarms of persons who apply daily for work, or for favors of one sort or another. Taken under advisement for later decision and compromise, this petition appearing to conflict with another one of same date, which will be cited further along.

6. For application of some form of violent death to neighbor who

threw brick at family cat, whilst the which was serenading. Reserved for consideration and compromise, because of conflict with a prayer of even date to be cited further along.

7. To "damn the missionary cause." Reserved also—as above.

8. To increase December profits of $22,230 to $45,000 for January, and perpetuate a proportionate monthly increase thereafter—"which will satisfy you." The prayer granted; the added remark accepted with reservations.

9. For cyclone, to destroy the works and fill up the mine of the North Pennsylvania Co. NOTE: Cyclones are not kept in stock in the winter season. A reliable article of fire-damp can be furnished upon application.

Especial note is made of the above list, they being of particular moment. The 298 remaining supplications classifiable under the head of Special Providences, Schedule A, for week ending 19th, are granted in a body, except that 3 of the 32 cases requiring immediate death have been modified to incurable disease.

This completes the week's invoice of petitions known to this office under the technical designation of Secret Supplications of the Heart, and which for a reason which may suggest itself, always receive our first and especial attention.

The remainder of the week's invoice falls under the head of what we term Public Prayers, in which classification we place prayers uttered in Prayer Meeting, Sunday School, Class Meeting, Family Worship, etc. These kinds of prayers have value according to classification of Christian uttering them. By rule of this office, Christians are divided into two grand classes, to-wit: 1, Professing Christians; 2, Professional Christians. These, in turn, are minutely subdivided and classified by Size, Species, and Family; and finally, Standing is determined by carats, the minimum being 1, the maximum 1,000.

As per balance-sheet for quarter ending Dec. 31st, 1847, you stood classified as follows:

Grand Classification, Professing Christian.

Size, one-fourth of maximum.

Species, Human-Spiritual.

Family, A of the Elect, Division 16.

Standing, 322 carats fine.

As per balance-sheet for quarter just ended,—that is to say, forty years later,—you stand classified as follows:

Grand Classification, Professional Christian.

Size, six one-hundredths of maximum.

Species, Human-Animal.

Family, W of the Elect, Division 1547.

Standing, 3 carats fine.

I have the honor to call your attention to the fact that you seem to have deteriorated.

To resume report upon your Public Prayers—with the side remark that in order to encourage Christians of your grade and of approximate grades, it is the custom of this office to grant many things to them which would not be granted to Christians of a higher grade—partly because they would not be asked for:

Prayer for weather mercifully tempered to the needs of the poor and the naked. Denied. This was a Prayer-Meeting prayer. It conflicts with Item 1 of this Report, which was a Secret Supplication of the Heart. By a rigid rule of this office, certain sorts of Public Prayers of Professional Christians are forbidden to take precedence of Secret Supplications of the Heart.

Prayer for better times and plentier food "for the hard handed son of toil whose patient and exhausting labors make comfortable the homes, and pleasant the ways, of the more fortunate, and entitle him to our vigilant and effective protection from the wrongs and injustices which grasping avarice would do him, and to the tenderest offices of our grateful hearts." Prayer-Meeting Prayer. Refused. Conflicts with Secret Supplication of the Heart No. 2.

Prayer "that such as in any way obstruct our preferences may be generously blessed, both themselves and their families, we here calling our hearts to witness that in their worldly prosperity we are spiritually blessed, and our joys made perfect." Prayer-Meeting Prayer. Refused. Conflicts with Secret Supplications of the Heart Nos. 3 and 4.

"Oh, let none fall heir to the pains of perdition through words or acts of ours." Family Worship. Received fifteen minutes in advance of Secret Supplication of the Heart No. 5, with which it distinctly conflicts. It is suggested that one or the other of these prayers be withdrawn, or both of them modified.

"Be mercifully inclined toward all who would do us offence in our persons or our property." Includes man who threw brick at cat. Family Prayer. Received some minutes in advance of No. 6, Secret Supplications of the Heart. Modification suggested, to reconcile discrepancy.

"Grant that the noble missionary cause, the most precious labor entrusted to the hands of men, may spread and prosper without let or limit in all heathen lands that do as yet reproach us with their spiritual darkness." Uninvited prayer shoved in at meeting of American Board. Received nearly half a day in advance of No. 7, Secret Supplications of the Heart. This office takes no stock in missionaries, and is not connected in any way with the American Board. We should like to grant one of these prayers, but cannot grant both. It is suggested that the American Board one be withdrawn.

This office desires for the twentieth time to call urgent attention to your remark appended to No. 8. It is a chestnut.

Of the 464 specifications contained in your Public Prayers for the week, and not previously noted in this report, we grant 2, and deny the rest. To-wit: Granted, (1), "that the clouds may continue to perform their office; (2), and the sun his." It was the divine purpose anyhow; it will gratify you to know that you have not disturbed it. Of the 462 details refused, 61 were uttered in Sunday School. In this connection I must once more remind you that we grant no Sunday School Prayers of Professional Christians of the classification technically known in this office as the John Wanamaker grade.[2] We merely enter them as "words," and they count to his credit according to number uttered within certain limits of time, 3,000 per quarter-minute required, or no score; 4,200 in a possible 5,000 is a quite common Sunday School score, among experts, and counts the same as two hymns and a bouquet furnished by young ladies in the assassin's cell, execution-morning. Your remaining 401 details count for wind only. We bunch them and use them for head-winds in retarding the ships of improper people, but it takes so many of them to make an impression that we cannot allow anything for their use.

I desire to add a word of my own to this report. When certain sorts of people do a sizeable good deed, we credit them up a thousand-fold more for it than we would in the case of a better man—on account of the strain. You stand far away above your classification-record here, because of certain self-sacrifices of yours which greatly exceed what could have been expected of you. Years ago, when you were worth only $100,000, and sent $2 to your impoverished cousin the widow, when she appealed to you for help, there were many in heaven who were not able to believe it, and many more who believed that the money was counterfeit. Your character went up many degrees when it was shown that these suspicions were unfounded. A year or two later, when you sent the poor girl $4 in answer to another appeal, everybody believed it, and you were all the talk here for days together. Two years later you sent $6, upon supplication, when the widow's youngest child died, and that act made perfect your good fame. Everybody in heaven said, "Have you heard about Andrew?"—for you are now affectionately called Andrew here. Your increasing donation, every two or three years, has kept your name on all lips, and warm in all hearts. All heaven watches you Sundays, as you drive to church in your handsome carriage; and when your hand retires from the contribution plate, the glad shout is heard even to the ruddy walls of remote Sheol, "Another nickel from Andrew!" But the climax came a few days ago, when the widow wrote and said she could get a school in a far village to teach if she had $50 to get herself and her two surviving children over the long journey; and you counted up last month's clear profit from your three coal mines—$22,230—and added to it the certain profit for the current month—$45,000 and a possible fifty—and then got down your pen and your check-book and mailed her *fifteen whole dollars*! Ah, Heaven bless and keep you forever and ever, generous heart! There was not a dry eye in the realms of bliss; and amidst the hand-shakings, and embracings, and praisings, the decree was thundered forth from the shining mount, that this deed should out-honor all the historic self-sacrifices of men and angels, and be recorded by itself upon a page of its own, for that the strain of it upon you had been heavier and bitterer than the strain it costs ten thousand martyrs to yield up their lives at the fiery stake; and all said, "What is the giving up of life, to a noble soul, or to ten thousand noble souls, compared with the giving up of fifteen dollars out of the greedy grip of the meanest white man that ever lived on the face of the earth?"

And it was a true word. And Abraham, weeping, shook out the contents of his bosom and pasted the eloquent label there, "RESERVED"; and Peter, weeping, said, "He shall be received with a torchlight procession when he comes"; and then all heaven boomed, and was glad you were going there. And so was hell.

[Signed]
THE RECORDING ANGEL [seal]

By command.

[1887/1946]

The Great Dark

BEFORE IT HAPPENED

STATEMENT BY MRS. EDWARDS

We were in no way prepared for this dreadful thing. We were a happy family, we had been happy from the beginning; we did not know what trouble was, we were not thinking of it nor expecting it.

My husband was thirty-five years old, and seemed ten years younger, for he was one of those fortunate people who by nature are overcharged with breezy spirits and vigorous health, and from whom cares and troubles slide off without making any impression. He was my ideal, and indeed my idol. In my eyes he was everything that a man ought to be, and in spirit and body beautiful. We were married when I was a girl of 16, and we now had two children, comely and dear little creatures: Jessie, 8 years old, and Bessie, 6.

The house had been in a pleasant turmoil all day, this 19th of March, for it was Jessie's birthday.[1] Henry (my husband) had romped with the children till I was afraid he would tire them out and unfit them for their party in the evening, which was to be a children's fancy dress dance; and so I was glad when at last in the edge of the evening he took them to our bedroom to show them the grandest of all the presents, the microscope. I allowed them fifteen minutes for this show. I would put the children into their costumes, then, and have them ready to receive their great flock of little friends and the accompanying parents. Henry would then be free to jot down in short-hand (he was a past-master in that art) an essay which he was to read at the social club the next night. I would show the children to him in their smart costumes when the party should be over and the good-night kisses due.

I left the three in a state of great excitement over the microscope, and at the end of the fifteen minutes I returned for the children. They and their papa were examining the wonders of a drop of water through a powerful lens. I delivered the children to a maid and they went away. Henry said—

"I will take forty winks and then go to work. But I will make a new experiment with the drop of water first. Won't you please strengthen the drop with the merest touch of Scotch whisky and stir up the animals?"

Then he threw himself on the sofa and before I could speak he uttered a snore. That came of romping the whole day. In reaching for the whisky decanter I knocked off the one that contained brandy and it broke. The noise stopped the snore. I stooped and gathered up the broken glass hurriedly in a towel, and when I rose to put it out of the way he was gone. I dipped a broomstraw in the Scotch whisky and let a wee drop fall upon the glass slide where the water-drop was, then I crossed to the glass door to tell him it was ready. But he had lit the gas and was at his table writing. It was the rule of the house not to disturb him when he was at work; so I went about my affairs in the picture gallery, which was our house's ballroom.

STATEMENT BY MR. EDWARDS

We were experimenting with the microscope. And pretty ignorantly. Among the little glass slides in the box we found one labeled "section of a fly's eye." In its centre was faintly visible a dot. We put it under a low-power lens and it showed up like a fragment of honey-comb. We put it under a stronger lens and it became a window-sash. We put it under the most powerful lens of all, then there was room in the field for only one pane of the several hundred. We were childishly delighted and astonished at the magnifying capacities of that lens, and said, "Now we can find out if there really are living animals in a drop of water, as the books say."

We brought some stale water from a puddle in the carriage-house where some rotten hay lay soaking, sucked up a dropperful and allowed a tear of it to fall on a glass slide. Then we worked the screws and brought the lens down until it almost touched the water; then shut an eye and peered eagerly down through the barrel. A disappointment—nothing showed. Then we worked the screws again and made the lens *touch* the water. Another disappointment—nothing visible. Once more we worked the screws and projected the lens hard *against* the glass slide itself. *Then* we saw the animals! Not frequently, but now and then. For a time there would be a great empty blank; then a monster would enter one horizon of this great white sea made so splendidly luminous by the reflector and go plowing across and disappear beyond the opposite horizon. Others would come and go at intervals and disappear. The lens was pressing *against* the glass slide; therefore how could those bulky creatures crowd through between and not get stuck? Yet they swam with perfect freedom; it was plain that they had all the room and all the water that they needed. Then how unimaginably little they must be! Moreover, that wide circular sea which they were traversing was only a small part of our drop of stale water; it was not as big as the head of a pin; whereas the entire drop, flattened out on the glass, was as big around as a child's finger-ring. If we could have gotten the whole drop under the lens we could have seen those gruesome fishes swim leagues and leagues before they dwindled out of sight at the further shore!

I threw myself on the sofa profoundly impressed by what I had seen, and oppressed with thinkings. An ocean in a drop of water—and unknown, uncharted, unexplored by man! By man, who gives all his time to the Africas and the poles, with this unsearched marvelous world right at his elbow. Then the Superintendent of Dreams appeared at my side, and we talked it over. He was willing to provide a ship and crew, but said—

"It will be like any other voyage of the sort—not altogether a holiday excursion."

"That is all right; it is not an objection."

"You and your crew will be much diminished, as to size, but you need not trouble about that, as you will not be aware of it. Your ship itself, stuck upon the point of a needle, would not be discoverable except through a microscope of very high power."

"I do not mind these things. Get a crew of whalers. It will be well to have men who will know what to do in case we have trouble with those creatures."

"Better still if you avoid them."

"I shall avoid them if I can, for they have done me no harm, and I would not wantonly hurt any creature, but I shan't run from them. They have an ugly look, but I thank God I am not afraid of the ugliest that ever plowed a drop of water."

"You think so *now*, with your five feet eight, but it will be a different matter when the mote that floats in a sunbeam is Mont Blanc compared to you."

"It is no matter; you have seen me face dangers before—"

"Finish with your orders—the night is slipping away."

"Very well, then. Provide me a naturalist to tell me the names of the creatures we see; and let the ship be a comfortable one and perfectly appointed and provisioned, for I take my family with me."

Half a minute later (as it seemed to me), a hoarse voice broke on my ear—

"Topsails all—let go the lee brace—sheet home the stuns'l boom—hearty, now, and all together!"

I turned out, washed the sleep out of my eyes with a dash of cold water, and stepped out of my cabin, leaving Alice quietly sleeping in her berth. It was a blustering night and dark, and the air was thick with a driving mist out of which the tall masts and bellying clouds of sail towered spectrally, faintly flecked here and there aloft by the smothered signal lanterns. The ship was heaving and wallowing in the heavy seas, and it was hard to keep one's footing on the moist deck. Everything was dimmed to obliteration, almost; the only thing sharply defined was the foamy mane of white water, sprinkled with phosphorescent sparks, which broke away from the lee bow. Men were within twenty steps of me, but I could not make out their figures; I only knew they were there by their voices. I heard the quartermaster report to the second mate—

"Eight bells, sir."

"Very well—make it so."

Then I heard the muffled sound of the distant bell, followed by a faroff cry—

"Eight bells and a cloudy morning—anchor watch turn out!"

I saw the glow of a match photograph a pipe and part of a face against a solid bank of darkness, and groped my way thither and found the second mate.

"What of the weather, mate?"

"I don't see that it's any better, sir, than it was the first day out, ten days ago; if anything it's worse—thicker and blacker, I mean. You remember the spitting snow-flurries we had that night?"

"Yes."

"Well, we've had them again to-night. And hail and sleet besides, b'George! And here it comes again."

We stepped into the sheltering lee of the galley, and stood there listening to the lashing of the hail along the deck and the singing of the wind in the cordage. The mate said—

"I've been at sea thirty years, man and boy, but for a level ten-day stretch of unholy weather this bangs anything I ever struck, north of the

Horn—if we *are* north of it. For I'm blest if I know *where* we are—do you?"

It was an embarrassing question. I had been asked it very confidentially by my captain, long ago, and had been able to state that I didn't know; and had been discreet enough not to go into any particulars; but this was the first time that any officer of the ship had approached me with the matter. I said—

"Well, no, I'm not a sailor, but I am surprised to hear *you* say you don't know where we are."

He was caught. It was his turn to be embarrassed. First he began to hedge, and vaguely let on that perhaps he did know, after all; but he made a lame fist of it, and presently gave it up and concluded to be frank and take me into his confidence.

"I'm going to be honest with you, sir—and don't give me away." He put his mouth close to my ear and sheltered it against the howling wind with his hand to keep from having to shout, and said impressively, "Not only I don't know where we are, sir, but by God the captain himself don't know!"

I had met the captain's confession by pretending to be frightened and distressed at having engaged a man who was ignorant of his business; and then he had changed his note and told me he had only meant that he had lost his bearings in the thick weather—a thing which would rectify itself as soon as he could get a glimpse of the sun. But I was willing to let the mate tell me all he would, so long as I was not to "give it away."

"No, sir, he don't know where he is; lets on to, but he don't. I mean, he lets on to the crew, and his daughters, and young Phillips the purser, and of course to you and your family, but here lately he don't let on any more to the chief mate and me. And worried? I tell you he's worried plumb to his vitals."

"I must say I don't much like the look of this, Mr. Turner."

"Well, don't let on, sir; keep it to yourself—maybe it'll come out all right; hope it will. But you look at the facts—just look at the facts. We sail north—see? North-and-by-east-half-east, to be exact. Noon the fourth day out, heading for Sable island[2]—ought to see it, weather rather thin for *this* voyage. *Don't* see it. Think the dead reckoning ain't right, maybe. We bang straight along, all the afternoon. No Sable island. *Damned if we didn't run straight over it!* It warn't there. What do you think of that?"

"Dear me, it is awful—awful—if true."

"*If* true. Well, it *is* true. True as anything that ever was, I take my oath on it. And then Greenland. We three banked our hopes on Greenland.

Night before last we couldn't sleep for uneasiness; just anxiety, you know, to see if Greenland was going to be there. By the dead reckoning she was due to be in sight along anywhere from five to seven in the morning, if clear enough. But we staid on deck all night. Of course two of us had no business there, and had to scuttle out of the way whenever a man came along, or they would have been suspicious. But five o'clock came, seven o'clock, eight o'clock, ten o'clock, and at last twelve—and then the captain groaned and gave in! He knew well enough that if there had been any Greenland left we'd have knocked a corner off of it long before that."

"This is appalling!"

"You may hunt out a bigger word than that and it won't cover it, sir. And Lord, to see the captain, gray as ashes, sweating and worrying over his chart all day yesterday and all day to-day, and spreading his compasses here and spreading them there, and getting suspicious of his chronometer, and damning the dead-reckoning—just suffering death and taxes, you know, and me and the chief mate helping and suffering, and that purser and the captain's oldest girl spooning and cackling around, just in heaven! I'm a poor man, sir, but if I could buy out half of each of 'em's ignorance and put it together and make it a whole, blamed if I wouldn't put up my last nickel to do it, you hear *me*. Now—"

A wild gust of wind drowned the rest of his remark and smothered us in a fierce flurry of snow and sleet. He darted away and disappeared in the gloom, but first I heard his voice hoarsely shouting—

"Turn out, all hands, shorten sail!"

There was a rush of feet along the deck, and then the gale brought the dimmed sound of far-off commands—

"Mizzen foretop halyards there—all clue-garnets heave and away—now then, with a will—sheet home!"

And then the plaintive notes that told that the men were handling the kites—

"If you get there, before I do—
Hi-ho-o-o, roll a man down;
If you get there before I do,
O, give a man time to roll a man down!"

By and by all was still again. Meantime I had shifted to the other side of the galley to get out of the storm, and there Mr. Turner presently found me.

"That's a specimen," said he. "I've never struck any such weather anywheres. You are bowling along on a wind that's as steady as a sermon, and just as likely to last, and before you can say Jack Robinson the wind whips around from weather to lee, and if you don't jump for it you'll have your canvas blown out of the cat-heads and sailing for heaven in rags and tatters. I've never seen anything to begin with it. But then I've never been in the middle of Greenland before—in a *ship*—middle of where it *used* to be, I mean. Would it worry you if I was to tell you something, sir?"

"Why, no, I think not. What is it?"

"Let me take a turn up and down, first, to see if anybody's in earshot." When he came back he said, "What should you think if you was to see a whale with hairy spider-legs to it as long as the foretogallant backstay and as big around as the mainmast?"

I recognized the creature; I had seen it in the microscope. But I didn't say so. I said—

"I should think I had a little touch of the jimjams."[3]

"The very thing *I* thought, so help me! It was the third day out, at a quarter to five in the morning. I was out astraddle of the bowsprit in the drizzle, bending on a scuttle-butt, for I don't trust that kind of a job to a common sailor, when all of a sudden that creature plunged up out of the sea the way a porpoise does, not a hundred yards away—I saw two hundred and fifty feet of him and his fringes—and then he turned in the air like a triumphal arch, shedding Niagaras of water, and plunged head first under the sea with an awful swash of sound, and by that time we were close aboard him and in another ten yards we'd have hit him. It was my belief that he tried to hit *us*, but by the mercy of God he was out of practice. The lookout on the foc'sle was the only man around, and thankful I was, or there could have been a mutiny. He was asleep on the binnacle—they always sleep on the binnacle, it's the best place to see from—and it woke him up and he said, "Good land, what's that, sir?" and I said, "It's nothing, but it *might* have been, for any good a stump like you is for a lookout." I was pretty far gone, and said I was sick, and made him help me onto the foc'sle; and then I went straight off and took the pledge; for I had been going it pretty high for a week before we sailed, and I made up my mind that I'd rather go dry the rest of my life than see the like of that thing again."

"Well, I'm glad it was only the jimjams."

"Wait a minute, I ain't done. Of course I didn't enter it on the log—"

"Of course not—"

"For a man in his right mind don't put nightmares in the log. He only puts the word 'pledge' in, and takes credit for it if anybody inquires; and knows it will please the captain, and hopes it'll get to the owners. Well, two days later the chief mate took the pledge!"

"You don't mean it!"

"Sure as I'm standing here. I saw the word on the book. I didn't say anything, but I felt encouraged. Now then, listen to this: day before yesterday I'm dumm'd if the *captain* didn't take the pledge!"

"Oh, come!"

"It's a true bill—I take my oath. There was the word. Then we begun to put this and that together, and next we began to look at each other kind of significant and willing, you know; and of course giving the captain the pre*cee*dence, for it wouldn't become *us* to begin, and we nothing but mates. And so yesterday, sure enough, out comes the captain—and we called his hand. Said he was out astern in a snow-flurry about dawn, and saw a creature shaped like a wood-louse and as big as a turreted monitor, go racing by and tearing up the foam, in chase of a fat animal the size of an elephant and creased like a caterpillar—and saw it dive after it and disappear; and so he begun to prepare *his* soul for the pledge and break it to his entrails."

"It's terrible!"

"The pledge?—you bet your bottom dollar. If I—"

"No, I don't mean the pledge; I mean it is terrible to be lost at sea among such strange, uncanny brutes."

"Yes, there's something in that, too, I don't deny it. Well, the thing that the mate saw was like one of these big long lubberly canal boats, and it was ripping along like the Empire Express;[4] and the look of it gave him the cold shivers, and so he begun to arrange *his* earthly affairs and go for the pledge."

"Turner, it is dreadful—dreadful. Still, good has been done; for these pledges—"

"Oh, they're off!"

"Off?"

"Cert'nly. Can't be jimjams; couldn't all three of us have them at once, it ain't likely. What do you want with a pledge when there ain't any occasion for it? *There* he goes!"

He was gone like a shot, and the night swallowed him up. Now all of a sudden, with the wind still blowing hard, the seas went down and the deck became as level as a billiard table! Were *all* the laws of Nature suspended? It made my flesh creep; it was like being in a haunted ship.

Pretty soon the mate came back panting, and sank down on a cable-tier, and said—

"Oh, this is an awful life; I don't think we can stand it long. There's too many horribles in it. Let me pant a little, I'm in a kind of a collapse."

"What's the trouble?"

"Drop down by me, sir—I mustn't shout. There—now you're all right." Then he said sorrowfully, "I reckon we've got to take it again."

"Take what?"

"The pledge."

"Why?"

"Did you see that thing go by?"

"What thing?"

"A *man.*"

"No. What of it?"

"This is four times that *I*'ve seen it; and the mate has seen it, and so has the captain. Haven't you ever seen it?"

"I suppose not. Is there anything extraordinary about it?"

"Extra-*or*dinary? Well, I should *say*!"

"How is it extraordinary?"

He said in an awed voice that was almost like a groan—

"Like this, for instance: you put your hand on him and *he ain't there.*"

"What do you mean, Turner?"

"It's as true as I'm sitting here, I wish I may never stir. The captain's getting morbid and religious over it, and says he wouldn't give a damn for ship and crew if that thing stays aboard."

"You curdle my blood. What is the man like? Isn't it just one of the crew, that you glimpse and lose in the dark?"

"You take note of *this:* it wears a broad slouch hat and a long cloak. Is that a whaler outfit, I'll ask you? A minute ago I was as close to him as I am to you; and I made a grab for him, and what did I get? A handful of air, that's all. There warn't a sign of him left."

"I do hope the pledge will dispose of it. It must be a work of the imagination, or the crew would have seen it."

"We're afraid they have. There was a deal of whispering going on last night in the middle watch. The captain dealt out grog, and got their minds on something else; but he is mighty uneasy, because of course he don't want you or your family to hear about that man, and would take my scalp if he knew what I'm doing now; and besides, if such a thing got a start with the crew, there'd be a mutiny, sure."

"I'll keep quiet, of course; still, I think it must be an output of imaginations overstrung by the strange fishes you think you saw; and I am hoping that the pledge—"

"I want to take it now. And I will."

"I'm witness to it. Now come to my parlor and I'll give you a cup of hot coffee and—"

"Oh, my goodness, there it is again! . . . It's gone. . . . Lord, it takes a body's breath. . . . It's the jimjams I've got—I know it for sure. I want the coffee; it'll do me good. If you could help me a little, sir—I feel as weak as Sabbath grog."

We groped along the sleety deck to my door and entered, and there in the bright glare of the lamps sat (as I was half expecting) the man of the long cloak and the slouch hat, on the sofa,—my friend the Superintendent of Dreams. I was annoyed, for a moment, for of course I expected Turner to make a jump at him, get nothing, and be at once in a more miserable state than he already was. I reached for my cabin door and closed it, so that Alice might not hear the scuffle and get a fright. But there wasn't any. Turner went on talking, and took no notice of the Superintendent. I gave the Superintendent a grateful look; and it was an honest one, for this thing of making himself visible and scaring people could do harm.

"Lord, it's good to be in the light, sir," said Turner, rustling comfortably in his yellow oilskins, "it lifts a person's spirits right up. I've noticed that these cussed jimjam blatherskites ain't as apt to show up in the light as they are in the dark, except when you've got the trouble in your attic pretty bad." Meantime we were dusting the snow off each other with towels. "You're mighty well fixed here, sir—chairs and carpets and rugs and tables and lamps and books and everything lovely, and so warm and comfortable and homy; and the roomiest parlor I ever struck in a ship, too. Land, hear the wind, don't she sing! And not a sign of motion!—rip goes the sleet again!—ugly, you bet!—and here? why here it's only just the more cosier on account of it. Dern that jimjam, if I had him in here once I bet you I'd sweat him. Because I don't mind saying that I don't grab at him as earnest as I want to, outside there, and ain't as disappointed as I ought to be when I don't get him; but here in the light I ain't afraid of *no* jimjam."

It made the Superintendent of Dreams smile a smile that was full of pious satisfaction to hear him. I poured a steaming cup of coffee and handed it to Turner and told him to sit where he pleased and make himself comfortable and at home; and before I could interfere he had sat down in the Superintendent of Dreams' lap!—no, sat down *through* him. It cost me a gasp, but only that, nothing more. [The] Superintendent of

Dreams' head was larger than Turner's, and *surrounded* it, and was a transparent spirit-head fronted with a transparent spirit-face; and this latter smiled at me as much as to say give myself no uneasiness, it is all right. Turner was smiling comfort and contentment at me at the same time, and the double result was very curious, but I could tell the smiles apart without trouble. The Superintendent of Dreams' body enclosed Turner's, but I could see Turner through it, just as one sees objects through thin smoke. It was interesting and pretty. Turner tasted his coffee and set the cup down in front of him with a hearty—

"Now I call that prime! 'George, it makes me feel the way old Cap'n Jimmy Starkweather did, I reckon, the first time he tasted grog after he'd been off his allowance three years. The way of it was this. It was there in Fairhaven by New Bedford, away back in the old early whaling days before I was born; but I heard about it the first day I *was* born, and it was a ripe old tale then, because they keep only the one fleet of yarns in commission down New Bedfordway, and don't ever re-stock and don't ever repair. And I came near hearing it in old Cap'n Jimmy's own presence once, when I was ten years old and he was ninety-two; but I didn't, because the man that asked Cap'n Jimmy to tell about it got crippled and the thing didn't materialize. It was Cap'n Jimmy that crippled him. Land, I thought I sh'd die! The very recollection of it—"

The very recollection of it so powerfully affected him that it shut off his speech and he put his head back and spread his jaws and laughed himself purple in the face. And while he was doing it the Superintendent of Dreams emptied the coffee into the slop bowl and set the cup back where it was before. When the explosion had spent itself Turner swabbed his face with his handkerchief and said—

"There—that laugh has scoured me out and done me good; I hain't had such another one—well, not since I struck *this* ship, now that's sure. I'll whet up and start over."

He took up his cup, glanced into it, and it was curious to observe the two faces that were framed in the front of his head. Turner's was long and distressed; the Superintendent of Dreams' was wide, and broken out of all shape with a convulsion of silent laughter. After a little, Turner said in a troubled way—

"I'm dumm'd if *I* recollect drinking that."

I didn't say anything, though I knew he must be expecting me to say something. He continued to gaze into the cup a while, then looked up wistfully and said—

"Of course I must have drunk it, but I'm blest if I can recollect whether I did or not. Lemme see. First you poured it out, then I set down and put it before me here; next I took a sup and said it was good, and set it down and begun about old Cap'n Jimmy—and then—and then—" He was silent a moment, then said, "It's as far as I can get. It beats me. I reckon that after that I was so kind of full of my story that I didn't notice whether I—." He stopped again, and there was something almost pathetic about the appealing way in which he added, "But I *did* drink it, *didn't* I? You *see* me do it—*didn't* you?"

I hadn't the heart to say no.

"Why, yes, I think I did. I wasn't noticing particularly, but it seems to me that I saw you drink it—in fact, I am about certain of it."

I was glad I told the lie, it did him so much good, and so lightened his spirits, poor old fellow.

"Of course I done it! I'm such a fool. As a general thing I wouldn't care, and I wouldn't bother anything about it; but when there's jimjams around the least little thing makes a person suspicious, you know. If you don't mind, sir—thanks, ever so much." He took a large sup of the new supply, praised it, set the cup down—leaning forward and fencing it around with his arms, with a labored pretense of not noticing that he was doing that—then said—

"Lemme see—where was I? Yes. Well, it happened like this. The Washingtonian Movement started up in those old times, you know, and it was Father Matthew[5] here and Father Matthew there and Father Matthew yonder—nothing but Father Matthew and temperance all over everywheres. And temperance societies? There was millions of them, and everybody joined and took the pledge. We had one in New Bedford. Every last whaler joined—captain, crew and all. All, down to old Cap'n Jimmy. He was an old bach, his grog was his darling, he owned his ship and sailed her himself, he was independent, and he wouldn't give in. So at last they gave it up and quit pestering him. Time rolled along, and he got awful lonesome. There wasn't anybody to drink with, you see, and it got unbearable. So finally the day he sailed for Bering Strait he caved, and sent in his name to the society. Just as he was starting, his mate broke his leg and stopped ashore and he shipped a stranger in his place from down New York way. This fellow didn't belong to any society, and he went aboard fixed for the voyage. Cap'n Jimmy was out three solid years; and all the whole time he had the spectacle of that mate whetting up every day and leading a life that was worth the trouble; and it nearly killed him for envy to see it. Made his mouth water, you know, in a way that was pitiful. Well, he used to get out on the peak of the bowsprit where it was private, and set there and cuss. It was his only relief from his sufferings. Mainly he cussed himself; but when he had used up all his words and couldn't think of any new rotten things to call himself, he would turn his vocabulary over and start fresh and lay into Father Matthew and give *him* down the banks;[6] and then the society; and so put in his watch as satisfactory as he could. Then he would count the days he was out, and try to reckon up about when he could hope to get home and resign from the society and start in on an all-compensating drunk that would make up for lost time. Well, when he was out three thousand years—which was *his* estimate, you know, though really it was only three years—he came rolling down the home-stretch with every rag stretched on his poles. Middle of winter, it was, and terrible cold and stormy. He made the landfall just at sundown and had to stand watch on deck all night of course, and the rigging was caked with ice three inches thick, and the yards was bearded with icicles five foot long, and the snow laid nine inches deep on the deck and hurricanes more of it being shoveled down onto him out of the skies. And so he plowed up and down all night, cussing himself and Father Matthew and the society, and doing it better than he ever done before; and his mouth was watering so, on account of the mate whetting up right in his sight all the time, that every cuss-word come out damp, and froze solid as it fell, and in his insufferable indignation he would hit it a whack with his cane and knock it a hundred yards, and one of them took the mate in the mouth and fetched away a rank of teeth and lowered *his* spirits considerable. He made the dock just at early breakfast time and never waited to tie up, but jumped ashore with his jug in his hand and rushed for the society's quarters like a deer. He met the seckatary coming out and yelled at him—

" 'I've resigned my membership!—I give you just two minutes to scrape my name off your log, d'ye hear?'

"And then the seckatary told him he'd been black-balled three years before—*hadn't ever been a member!*[7] Land, I can't hold in, it's coming again!"

He flung up his arms, threw his head back, spread his jaws, and made the ship quake with the thunder of his laughter, while the Superintendent of Dreams emptied the cup again and set it back in its place. When Turner came out of his fit at last he was limp and exhausted, and sat mopping his tears away and breaking at times into little feebler and feebler barks and catches of expiring laughter. Finally he fetched a deep sigh of comfort and satisfaction, and said—

"Well, it *does* do a person good, no mistake—on a voyage like *this*. I reckon—"

His eye fell on the cup. His face turned a ghastly white—

"By God she's empty again!"

He jumped up and made a sprawling break for the door. I was frightened; I didn't know what he might do—jump overboard, maybe. I sprang in front of him and barred the way, saying, "Come, Turner, be a man, be a man! don't let your imagination run away with you like this"; and over his shoulder I threw a pleading look at the Superintendent of Dreams, who answered my prayer and refilled the cup from the coffee urn.

"Imagination you call it, sir! Can't I *see*?—with my own eyes? Let me go—don't stop me—I can't stand it, I can't stand it!"

"Turner, be reasonable—you know perfectly well your cup isn't empty, and *hasn't* been."

That hit him. A dim light of hope and gratitude shone in his eye, and he said in a quivery voice—

"Say it again—and say it's true. *Is* it true? Honor bright—you wouldn't deceive a poor devil that's—"

"Honor bright, man, I'm not deceiving you—look for yourself."

Gradually he turned a timid and wary glance toward the table; then the terror went out of his face, and he said humbly—

"Well, you see I reckon I hadn't quite got over thinking it happened the first time, and so maybe without me knowing it, that made me kind of suspicious that it would happen again, because the jimjams make you untrustful that way; and so, sure enough, I didn't half look at the cup, and just jumped to the conclusion it *had* happened." And talking so, he moved toward the sofa, hesitated a moment, and then sat down in that figure's body again. "But I'm all right, now, and I'll just shake these feelings off and be a man, as you say."

The Superintendent of Dreams separated himself and moved along the sofa a foot or two away from Turner. I was glad of that; it looked like a truce. Turner swallowed his cup of coffee; I poured another; he began to sip it, the pleasant influence worked a change, and soon he was a rational man again, and comfortable. Now a sea came aboard, hit our deck-house a stunning thump, and went hissing and seething aft.

"Oh, that's the ticket," said Turner, "the dummdest weather that ever I went pleasure-excursioning in. And how did it get aboard?—You answer me that: there ain't any motion to the ship. These mysteriousnesses—well, they just give me the cold shudders. And that reminds me. Do you mind my calling your attention to another peculiar thing or two?—on conditions as before—solid secrecy, you know."

"I'll keep it to myself. Go on."

"The Gulf Stream's gone to the devil!"[8]

"What do you mean?"

"It's the fact, I wish I may never die. From the day we sailed till now, the water's been the same temperature right along, I'll take my oath. The Gulf Stream don't exist any more; she's gone to the devil."

"It's incredible, Turner! You make me gasp."

"Gasp away, if you want to; if things go on so, you ain't going to forget how for want of practice. It's the wooliest voyage, take it by and large—why, look here! You are a landsman, and there's no telling what a landsman can't overlook if he tries. For instance, have you noticed that the nights and days are exactly alike, and you can't tell one from tother except by keeping tally?"

"Why, yes, I have noticed it in a sort of indifferent general way, but—"

"Have you kept a tally, sir?"

"No, it didn't occur to me to do it."

"I thought so. Now you know, you couldn't keep it in your head, because you and your family are free to sleep as much as you like, and as it's always dark, you sleep a good deal, and you are pretty irregular, naturally. You've all been a little seasick from the start—tea and toast in your own parlor here—no regular time—order it as each of you pleases. You see? You don't go down to meals—*they* would keep tally for you. So you've lost your reckoning. I noticed it an hour ago."

"How?"

"Well, you spoke of *to-night.* It ain't to-night at all; it's just noon, now."

"The fact is, I don't believe I have often thought of its being day, since we left. I've got into the habit of considering it night all the time; it's the same with my wife and the children."

"There it is, you see. Mr. Edwards, it's perfectly awful; now ain't it, when you come to look at it? Always night—and such dismal nights, too. It's like being up at the pole in the winter time. And I'll ask you to notice another thing: this sky is as empty as my sou-wester there."

"Empty?"

"Yes, sir. I know it. You can't get up a day, in a Christian country, that's so solid black the sun can't make a blurry glow of *some* kind in the sky at high noon—now can you?"

"No, you can't."

"Have you ever seen a suspicion of any such a glow in this sky?"

"Now that you mention it, I haven't."

He dropped his voice and said impressively—

"Because there ain't any *sun.* She's gone where the Gulf Stream twineth."[9]

"Turner! Don't talk like that."

"It's confidential, or I wouldn't. And the moon. She's at the full—by the almanac she is. Why don't *she* make a blur? Because there *ain't* any moon. And moreover—you might rake this on-completed sky a hundred year with a drag-net and you'd never scoop a star! Why? Because there *ain't* any. Now then, what is your opinion about all this?"

"Turner, it's so gruesome and creepy that I don't like to think about it—and I haven't any. What is yours?"

He said, dismally—

"That the world has come to an end. Look at it yourself. Just look at the facts. Put them together and add them up, and what have you got? No Sable island; no Greenland; no Gulf Stream; no day, no proper night; weather that don't jibe with any sample known to the Bureau; animals that would start a panic in any menagerie, chart no more use than a horse-blanket, and the heavenly bodies gone to hell! And on top of it all, that jimjam that I've put my hand on more than once and he warn't there—I'll swear it. The ship's bewitched. You don't believe in the jim, and I've sort of lost faith myself, here in the bright light; but if this cup of coffee was to—"

The cup began to glide slowly away, along the table. The hand that moved it was not visible to him. He rose slowly to his feet and stood trembling as if with an ague, his teeth knocking together and his glassy eyes staring at the cup. It slid on and on, noiseless; then it rose in the air, gradually reversed itself, poured its contents down the Superintendent's throat—I saw the dark stream trickling its way down through his hazy breast—then it returned to the table, and without sound of contact, rested there. The mate continued to stare at it for as much as a minute; then he drew a deep breath, took up his sou-wester, and without looking to the right or the left, walked slowly out of the room like one in a trance, muttering—

"I've *got* them—I've had the proof."

I said, reproachfully—

"Superintendent, why do you do that?"

"Do what?"

"Play these tricks."

"What harm is it?"

"Harm? It could make that poor devil jump overboard."

"No, he's not as far gone as that."

"For a while he was. He is a good fellow, and it was a pity to scare him so. However there are other matters that I am more concerned about just now."

"Can I help?"

"Why yes, you can; and I don't know any one else that can."

"Very well, go on."

"By the dead-reckoning we have come twenty-three hundred miles."

"The actual distance is twenty-three-fifty."

"Straight as a dart in the one direction—mainly."

"Apparently."

"Why do you say apparently? Haven't we come straight?"

"Go on with the rest. What were you going to say?"

"This. Doesn't it strike you that this is a pretty large drop of water?"

"No. It is about the usual size—six thousand miles across."

"Six thousand miles!"

"Yes."

"Twice as far as from New York to Liverpool?"

"Yes."

"I must say it is more of a voyage than I counted on. And we are not a great deal more than halfway across, yet. When shall we get in?"

"It will be some time yet."

"That is not very definite. Two weeks?"

"More than that."

I was getting a little uneasy.

"But how *much* more? A week?"

"All of that. More, perhaps."

"Why don't you tell me? A month more, do you think?"

"I am afraid so. Possibly two—possibly longer, even."

I was getting seriously disturbed by now.

"Why, we are sure to run out of provisions and water."

"No you'll not. I've looked out for that. It is what you are loaded with."

"Is that so? How does that come?"

"Because the ship is chartered for a voyage of discovery. Ostensibly she goes to England, takes aboard some scientists, then sails for the South pole."

"I see. You are deep."

"I understand my business."

I turned the matter over in my mind a moment, then said—

"It is more of a voyage than I was expecting, but I am not of a worrying disposition, so I do not care, so long as we are not going to suffer hunger and thirst."

"Make yourself easy, as to that. Let the trip last as long as it may, you will not run short of food and water, I go bail for that."

"All right, then. Now explain this riddle to me. Why is it always night?"

"That is easy. All of the drop of water is outside the luminous circle of the microscope except one thin and delicate rim of it. We are in the shadow; consequently in the dark."

"In the shadow of what?"

"Of the brazen end of the lens-holder."

"How can it cover such a spread with its shadow?"

"Because it is several thousand miles in diameter. For dimensions, that is nothing. The glass slide which it is pressing against, and which forms the bottom of the ocean we are sailing upon, is thirty thousand miles long, and the length of the microscope barrel is a hundred and twenty thousand. Now then, if—"

"You make me dizzy. I—"

"If you should thrust that glass slide through what you call the 'great' globe, eleven thousand miles of it would stand out on each side—it would be like impaling an orange on a table-knife. And so—"

"It gives me the head-ache. Are these the fictitious proportions which we and our surroundings and belongings have acquired by being reduced to microscopic objects?"

"They are the proportions, yes—but they are not fictitious. You do not notice that you yourself are in any way diminished in size, do you?"

"No, I am my usual size, so far as I can see."

"The same with the men, the ship and everything?"

"Yes—all natural."

"Very good; nothing but the laws and conditions have undergone a change. You came from a small and very insignificant world. The one you are in now is proportioned according to microscopic standards—that is to say, it is inconceivably stupendous and imposing."[10]

It was food for thought. There was something overpowering in the situation, something sublime. It took me a while to shake off the spell and drag myself back to speech. Presently I said—

"I am content; I do not regret the voyage—far from it. I would not change places with any man in that cramped little world. But tell me—is it always going to be dark?"

"Not if you ever come into the luminous circle under the lens. Indeed you will not find *that* dark!"

"If we ever. What do you mean by that? We are making steady good time; we are cutting across this sea on a straight course."

"Apparently."

"There is no apparently about it."

"You might be going around in a small and not rapidly widening circle."

"Nothing of the kind. Look at the tell-tale compass over your head."

"I see it."

"We changed to this easterly course to satisfy—well, to satisfy everybody but me. It is a pretense of aiming for England—in a drop of water! Have you noticed that needle before?"

"Yes, a number of times."

"To-day, for instance?"

"Yes—often."

"Has it varied a jot?"

"Not a jot."

"Hasn't it always kept the place appointed for it—from the start?"

"Yes, always."

"Very well. First we sailed a northerly course; then tilted easterly; and now it is more so. How is *that* going around in a circle?"

He was silent. I put it at him again. He answered with lazy indifference—

"I merely threw out the suggestion."

"All right, then; cornered; let it stand at that. Whenever you happen to think of an argument in support of it, I shall be glad to hear about it."

He did not like that very well, and muttered something about my being a trifle airy. I retorted a little sharply, and followed it up by finding fault with him again for playing tricks on Turner. He said Turner called him a blatherskite. I said—

"No matter; you let him alone, from this out. And moreover, stop appearing to people—stop it entirely."

His face darkened. He said—

"I would advise you to moderate your manner. I am not used to it, and I am not pleased with it."

The rest of my temper went, then. I said, angrily—

"You may like it or not, just as you choose. And moreover, if my style doesn't suit you, you can end the dream as soon as you please—right now, if you like."

He looked me steadily in the eye for a moment, then said, with deliberation—

"The dream? *Are you quite sure it is a dream?*"

It took my breath away.

"What do you mean? *Isn't* it a dream?"

He looked at me in that same way again; and it made my blood chilly, this time. Then he said—

"You have spent your whole life in this ship. And this is *real* life. Your other life was the dream!"

It was as if he had hit me, it stunned me so. Still looking at me, his lip curled itself into a mocking smile, and he wasted away like a mist and disappeared.

I sat a long time thinking uncomfortable thoughts.

We are strangely made.[11] We think we are wonderful creatures. Part of the time we think that, at any rate. And during that interval we consider with pride our mental equipment, with its penetration, its power of analysis, its ability to reason out clear conclusions from confused facts, and all the lordly rest of it; and then comes a rational interval and disenchants us. Disenchants us and lays us bare to ourselves, and we see that intellectually we are really no great things; that we seldom really know the thing we think we know; that our best-built certainties are but sand-houses and subject to damage from any wind of doubt that blows.

So little a time before, I *knew* that this voyage was a dream, and nothing more; a wee little puff or two of doubt had blown against that certainty, unhelped by fact or argument, and already it was dissolving away. It seemed an incredible thing, and it hurt my pride of intellect, but it had to be confessed.

When I came to consider it, these ten days had been such intense realities!—so intense that by comparison the life I had lived before them seemed distant, indistinct, slipping away and fading out in a far perspective—exactly as a dream does when you sit at breakfast trying to call back its details. I grew steadily more and more nervous and uncomfortable—and a little frightened, though I would not quite acknowledge this to myself.

Then came this disturbing thought: if this transformation goes on, how am I going to conceal it from my wife? Suppose she should say to me, "Henry, there is something the matter with you, you are acting strangely; something is on your mind that you are concealing from me; tell me about it, let me help you"—what answer could I make?

I was *bound* to act strangely if this went on—bound to bury myself in deeps of troubled thought; I should not be able to help it. She had a swift eye to notice, where her heart was concerned, and a sharp intuition, and I was an impotent poor thing in her hands when I had things to hide and she had struck the trail.

I have no large amount of fortitude, staying power. When there is a fate before me I cannot rest easy until I know what it is. I am not able to wait. I want to know, right away. So, I would call Alice, now, and take the consequences. If she drove me into a corner and I found I could not escape, I would act according to my custom—come out and tell her the truth. She had a better head than mine, and a surer instinct in grouping facts and getting their meaning out of them. If I was drifting into dangerous waters, now, she would be sure to detect it and as sure to set me right and save me. I would call her, and keep out of the corner if I could; if I couldn't, why—I couldn't, that is all.

She came, refreshed with sleep, and looking her best self: that is to say, looking like a girl of nineteen, not a matron of twenty-five; she wore a becoming wrapper, or tea gown, or whatever it is called, and it was trimmed with ribbons and limp stuff—lace, I suppose; and she had her hair balled up and nailed to its place with a four-pronged tortoise-shell comb. She brought a basket of pink and gray crewels with her, for she was crocheting a jacket—for the cat, probably, judging by the size of it. She sat down on the sofa and set the basket on the table, expecting to have a chance to get to work by and by; not right away, because a kitten was curled up in it asleep, fitting its circle snugly, and the repose of the children's kittens was a sacred thing and not to be disturbed. She said—

"I noticed that there was no motion—it was what waked me, I think—and I got up to enjoy it, it is such a rare thing."

"Yes, rare enough, dear: we do have the most unaccountably strange weather."

"Do you think so, Henry? Does it seem strange weather to you?"

She looked so earnest and innocent that I was rather startled, and a little in doubt as to what to say. Any sane person could see that it was perfectly devilish[12] weather and crazy beyond imagination, and so how could she feel uncertain about it?

"Well, Alice, I may be putting it too strong, but I don't think so; I think a person may call our weather by any hard name he pleases and be justified."

"Perhaps you are right, Henry. I have heard the sailors talk the same way about it, but I did not think that that meant much, they speak so extravagantly about everything. You are not always extravagant in your speech—often you are, but not always—and so it surprised me a little to hear you." Then she added tranquilly and musingly, "I don't remember any different weather."

It was not quite definite.

"You mean on *this* voyage, Alice."

"Yes, of course. Naturally. I haven't made any other."

She was softly stroking the kitten—and apparently in her right mind. I said cautiously, and with seeming indifference—

"You mean you haven't made any other this year. But the time we went to Europe—well, that was very different weather."

"The time we went to Europe, Henry?"

"Certainly, certainly—when Jessie was a year old."

She stopped stroking the kitty, and looked at me inquiringly.

"I don't understand you, Henry."

She was not a joker, and she was always truthful. Her remark blew another wind of doubt upon my wasting sand-edifice of certainty. Had I only *dreamed* that we went to Europe? It seemed a good idea to put this thought into words.

"Come, Alice, the first thing you know you will be imagining that we went to Europe in a dream."

She smiled, and said—

"Don't let me spoil it, Henry, if it is pleasant to you to think we went. I will consider that we did go, and that I have forgotten it."

"But Alice dear we *did* go!"

"But Henry dear we *didn't* go!"

She had a good head and a good memory, and she was always truthful. My head had been injured by a fall when I was a boy, and the physicians had said at the time that there could be ill effects from it some day. A cold wave struck me, now; perhaps the effects had come. I was losing confidence in the European trip. However, I thought I would make another try.

"Alice, I will give you a detail or two; then maybe you will remember."

"A detail or two from the dream?"

"I am not at all sure that it was a dream; and five minutes ago I was sure that it wasn't. It was seven years ago. We went over in the *Batavia*. Do you remember the *Batavia*?"

"I don't, Henry."

"Captain Moreland.[13] Don't you remember him?"

"To me he is a myth, Henry."

"Well, it beats anything. We lived two or three months in London, then six weeks in a private hotel in George Street, Edinburgh—Veitch's. Come!"

"It sounds pleasant, but I have never heard of these things before, Henry."

"And Doctor John Brown,[14] of *Rab and His Friends*—you were ill, and he came every day; and when you were well again he still came every day and took us all around while he paid his visits, and we waited in his carriage while he prescribed for his patients. And he was so dear and lovely. You *must* remember all that, Alice."

"None of it, dear; it is only a dream."

"Why, Alice, have you ever had a dream that remained as distinct as that, and which you could remember so long?"

"So long? It is more than likely that you dreamed it last night."

"No indeed! It has been in my memory seven years."

"Seven years in a dream, yes—it is the way of dreams. They put seven years into two minutes, without any trouble—isn't it so?"

I had to acknowledge that it was.

"It seems almost as if it couldn't have been a dream, Alice; it seems as if you ought to remember it."

"Wait! It begins to come back to me." She sat thinking a while, nodding her head with satisfaction from time to time. At last she said, joyfully, "I remember almost the whole of it, now."

"Good!"

"I am glad I got it back. Ordinarily I remember my dreams very well; but for some reason this one—"

"*This* one, Alice? Do you really consider it a dream, yet?"

"I don't consider anything about it, Henry, I know it; I know it positively."

The conviction stole through me that she must be right, since she felt so sure. Indeed I almost knew she was. I was privately becoming ashamed of myself now, for mistaking a clever illusion for a fact. So I gave it up, then, and said I would let it stand as a dream. Then I added—

"It puzzles me; even now it seems almost as distinct as the microscope."

"Which microscope?"

"Well, Alice, there's only the one."

"Very well, which one is *that*?"

"Bother it all, the one we examined this ocean in, the other day."

"Where?"

"Why, at home—of course."

"What home?"

"Alice, it's provoking—why, *our* home. In Springport."

"Dreaming again. I've never heard of it."

That was stupefying. There was no need of further beating about the bush; I threw caution aside, and came out frankly.

"Alice, what do you call the life we are leading in this ship? Isn't it a dream?"

She looked at me in a puzzled way and said—

"A dream, Henry? Why should I think that?"

"Oh, dear me, *I* don't know! I thought I did, but I don't. Alice, haven't we ever had a home? Don't you remember one?"

"Why, yes—three. That is, dream-homes, not real ones. I have never regarded them as realities."

"Describe them."

She did it, and in detail; also our life in them. Pleasant enough homes, and easily recognizable by me. I could also recognize an average of 2 out of 7 of the episodes and incidents which she threw in. Then I described the home and the life which (as it appeared to me) we had so recently left. She recognized it—but only as a dream-home. She remembered nothing about the microscope and the children's party. I was in a corner; but it was not the one which I had arranged for.

"Alice, if those were dream-homes, how long have you been in this ship?—you say this is the only voyage you have ever made."

"I don't know. I don't remember. It *is* the only voyage we have made—unless breaking it to pick up this crew of strangers in place of the friendly dear men and officers we had sailed with so many years makes two voyages of it. How I do miss them—Captain Hall, and Williams the sail-maker, and Storrs the chief mate, and—"

She choked up, and the tears began to trickle down her cheeks. Soon she had her handkerchief out and was sobbing.

I realized that I remembered those people perfectly well. Damnation![15] I said to myself, are we real creatures in a real world, all of a sudden, and have we been feeding on dreams in an imaginary one since nobody knows when—or how *is* it? My head was swimming.

"Alice! Answer me this. Do you know the Superintendent of Dreams?"

"Certainly."

"Have you seen him often?"

"Not often, but several times."

"When did you see him first?"

"The time that Robert the captain's boy was eaten."

"Eaten?"

"Yes. Surely you haven't forgotten that?"

"But I have, though. I never heard of it before." (I spoke the truth. For the moment I could not recal the incident.)

Her face was full of reproach.

"I am sorry, if that is so. He was always good to you. If you are jesting, I do not think it is in good taste."

"Now don't treat me like that, Alice, I don't deserve it. I am not jesting, I am in earnest. I mean the boy's memory no offence, but although I remember him I do not remember the circumstance—I swear it. Who ate him?"

"Do not be irreverent, Henry, it is out of place. It was not a *who,* at all."

"What then—a *which?*"

"Yes."

"What kind of a which?"

"A spider-squid. *Now* you remember it I hope."

"Indeed and deed and double-deed I don't, Alice, and it is the real truth. Tell me about it, please."

"I suppose you see, now, Henry, what your memory is worth. You can remember dream-trips to Europe well enough, but things in real life—even the most memorable and horrible things—pass out of your memory in twelve years. There is something the matter with your mind."

It was very curious. How *could* I have forgotten that tragedy? It must have happened; she was never mistaken in her facts, and she never spoke with positiveness of a thing which she was in any degree uncertain about. And this tragedy—*twelve years* ago—

"Alice, how long *have* we been in this ship?"

"Now how can I know, Henry? It goes too far back. Always, for all I know. The earliest thing I can call to mind was papa's death by the sun-heat and mamma's suicide the same day. I was four years old, then. Surely you must remember that, Henry."

"Yes.... Yes. But it is so dim. Tell me about it—refresh my memory."

"Why, you must remember that we were in the edge of a great white glare once for a little while—a day, or maybe two days,—only a little while, I think, but I remember it, because it was the only time I was ever out of the dark, and there was a great deal of talk of it for long afterwards—why, Henry, you *must* remember a wonderful thing like that."

"Wait. Let me think." Gradually, detail by detail the whole thing came back to me; and with it the boy's adventure with the spider-squid; and then I recalled a dozen other incidents, which Alice verified as incidents of our ship-life, and said I had set them forth correctly.

It was a puzzling thing—my freaks of memory; Alice's, too. By testing, it was presently manifest that the vacancies in my ship-life memories were only apparent, not real; a few words by way of reminder enabled me to fill them up, in almost all cases, and give them clarity and vividness. What had caused these temporary lapses? Didn't these very lapses indicate that the ship-life was a dream, and not real?

It made Alice laugh.

I did not see anything foolish in it, or anything to laugh at, and I told her so. And I reminded her that her own memory was as bad as mine, since many and many a conspicuous episode of our land-life was gone from her, even so striking an incident as the water-drop exploration with the microscope—

It made her shout.

I was wounded; and said that if I could not be treated with respect I would spare her the burden of my presence and conversation. She stopped laughing, at once, and threw her arms about my neck. She said she would not have hurt me for the world, but she supposed I was joking; it was quite natural to think I was not in earnest in talking gravely about this and that and the other dream-phantom as if it were a reality.

"But Alice I *was* in earnest, and I *am* in earnest. Look at it—examine it. If the land-life was a dream-life, how is it that you remember so much of it exactly as *I* remember it?"

She was amused again, inside—I could feel the quiver; but there was no exterior expression of it, for she did not want to hurt me again.

"Dear heart, throw the whole matter aside! Stop puzzling over it; it isn't worth it. It is perfectly simple. It is true that I remember a little of that dream-life just as you remember it—but that is an accident; the rest of it—and by far the largest part—does not correspond with your recollections. And how *could* it? People can't be expected to remember each other's dreams, but only their own. You have put me into your land-dreams a thousand times, but I didn't always know I was there; so how could I remember it? Also I have put you into my land-dreams a thousand times when you didn't know it—and the natural result is that when I name the circumstances you don't always recall them. But how different it is with this real life, this genuine life in the ship! Our recollections of it are just alike. You have been forgetting episodes of it to-day—I don't know why; it has surprised me and puzzled me—but the lapse was only temporary; your memory soon rallied again. Now it hasn't rallied in the case of land-dreams of mine—in most cases it hasn't. And it's not going to, Henry. You can be sure of that."

She stopped, and tilted her head up in a thinking attitude and began to unconsciously tap her teeth with the ivory knob of a crochet needle. Presently she said, "I think I know what is the matter. I have been neglecting you for ten days while I have been grieving for our old shipmates and pretending to be seasick so that I might indulge myself with solitude; and here is the result—you haven't been taking exercise enough."

I was glad to have a reason—any reason that would excuse my memory—and I accepted this one, and made confession. There was no truth in the confession, but I was already getting handy with these evasions. I was a little sorry for this, for she had always trusted my word, and I had honored this trust by telling her the truth many a time when it was a sharp sacrifice to me to do it. She looked me over with gentle reproach in her eye, and said—

"Henry, how can you be so naughty? I watch you so faithfully and make you take such good care of your health that you owe me the grace to do my office for me when for any fair reason I am for a while not on guard. When have you boxed with George last?"

What an idea it was! It was a good place to make a mistake, and I came near to doing it. It was on my tongue's end to say that I had never boxed with anyone; and as for boxing with a colored man-servant—and so on; but I kept back my remark, and in place of it tried to look like a person who didn't know what to say. It was easy to do, and I probably did it very well.

"You do not say anything, Henry. I think it is because you have a good reason. When have you fenced with him? Henry, you are avoiding my eye. Look up. Tell me the truth: have you fenced with him a single time in the last ten days?"

So far as I was aware I knew nothing about foils, and had never handled them; so I was able to answer—

"I will be frank with you, Alice—I haven't."

"I suspected it. Now, Henry, what can you say?"

I was getting some of my wits back, now, and was not altogether unprepared, this time.

"Well, Alice, there hasn't been much fencing weather, and when there was any, I—well, I was lazy, and that is the shameful truth."

"There's a chance now, anyway, and you mustn't waste it. Take off your coat and things."

She rang for George, then she got up and raised the sofa-seat and began to fish out boxing-gloves, and foils and masks from the locker under it, softly scolding me all the while. George put his head in, noted the preparations, then entered and put himself in boxing trim. It was his turn to take the witness stand, now.

"George, didn't I tell you to keep up Mr. Henry's exercises just the same as if I were about?"

"Yes, madam, you did."

"Why haven't you done it?"

George chuckled, and showed his white teeth and said—

"Bless yo' soul, honey, I dasn't."

"Why?"

"Because the first time I went to him—it was that Tuesday, you know, when it was ca'm—he wouldn't hear to it, and said he didn't want no exercise and warn't going to take any, and tole me to go 'long. Well, I didn't stop there, of course, but went to him agin, every now and then, trying to persuade him, tell at last he let into me" (he stopped and comforted himself with an unhurried laugh over the recollection of it,) "and give me a most solid good cussing, and tole me if I come agin he'd take and thow me overboard—there, ain't that so, Mr. Henry?"

My wife was looking at me pretty severely.

"Henry, what have you to say to that?"

It was my belief that it hadn't happened, but I was steadily losing confidence in my memory; and moreover my new policy of recollecting whatever anybody required me to recollect seemed the safest course to pursue in my strange and trying circumstances; so I said—

"Nothing, Alice—I did refuse."

"Oh, I'm not talking about that; of course you refused—George had already said so."

"Oh, I see."

"Well, why do you stop?"

"Why do I stop?"

"Yes. Why don't you answer my question?"

"Why, Alice, I've answered it. You asked me—you asked me—What *is* it I haven't answered?"

"Henry, you know very well. You broke a promise; and you are trying to talk around it and get me away from it; but I am not going to let you. You know quite well you promised me you wouldn't swear any more in calm weather. And it is such a little thing to do. It is hardly ever calm, and—"

"Alice, dear, I beg ever so many pardons! I had clear forgotten it; but I won't offend again, I give you my word. Be good to me, and forgive."

She was always ready to forgive, and glad to do it, whatever my crime might be; so things were pleasant again, now, and smooth and happy. George was gloved and skipping about in an imaginary fight, by this time, and Alice told me to get to work with him. She took pencil and paper and got ready to keep game. I stepped forward to position—then a curious thing happened: I seemed to remember a thousand boxing-bouts with George, the whole boxing art came flooding in upon me, and I knew just what to do! I was a prey to no indecisions, I had no trouble. We fought six rounds, I held my own all through, and I finally knocked George out. I was not astonished; it seemed a familiar experience. Alice showed no surprise, George showed none; apparently it was an old story to them.

The same thing happened with the fencing. I suddenly knew that I was an experienced old fencer; I expected to get the victory, and when I got it, it seemed but a repetition of something which had happened numberless times before.

We decided to go down to the main saloon and take a regular meal in the regular way—the evening meal. Alice went away to dress. Just as I had finished dressing, the children came romping in, warmly and prettily clad, and nestled up to me, one on each side, on the sofa, and began to chatter. Not about a former home; no, not a word of that, but only about this ship-home and its concerns and its people. After a little I threw out some questions—feelers. They did not understand. Finally I asked them if they had known no home but this one. Jessie said, with some little enthusiasm—

"Oh, yes, dream-homes. They are pretty—some of them." Then, with a shrug of her shoulders, "But they *are* so queer!"

"How, Jessie?"

"Well, you know, they have such curious things in them; and they fade, and don't stay. Bessie doesn't like them at all."

"Why don't you, Bessie?"

"Because they scare me so."

"What is it that scares you?"

"Oh, everything, papa. Sometimes it is so light. That hurts my eyes. And it's too many lamps—little sparkles all over, up high, and large ones that are dreadful. They could fall on me, you know."

"But I am not much afraid," said Jessie, "because mamma says they are not real, and if they did fall they wouldn't hurt."

"What else do you see there besides the lights, Bessie?"

"Ugly things that go on four legs like our cat, but bigger."

"Horses?"

"I forget names."

"Describe them, dear."

"I can't, papa. They are not alike; they are different kinds; and when I wake up I can't just remember the shape of them, they are so dim."

"And I wouldn't wish to remember them," said Jessie, "they make me feel creepy. Don't let's talk about them, papa, let's talk about something else."

"That's what I say, too," said Bessie.

So then we talked about our ship. That interested them. They cared for no other home, real or unreal, and wanted no better one. They were innocent witnesses and free from prejudice.

When we went below we found the roomy saloon well lighted and brightly and prettily furnished, and a very comfortable and inviting place altogether. Everything seemed substantial and genuine, there was nothing to suggest that it might be a work of the imagination.

At table the captain (Davis) sat at the head, my wife at his right with the children, I at his left, a stranger at my left. The rest of the company consisted of Rush Phillips, purser, aged 27; his sweetheart the Captain's daughter Lucy, aged 22; her sister Connie (short for Connecticut), aged 10; Arnold Blake, surgeon, 25; Harvey Pratt, naturalist, 36; at the foot sat Sturgis the chief mate, aged 35, and completed the snug assemblage. Stewards waited upon the general company, and George and our nurse Germania had charge of our family. Germania was not the nurse's name, but that was our name for her because it was shorter than her own. She was 28 years old, and had always been with us; and so had George. George was 30, and had once been a slave, according to my record, but I was losing my grip upon that, now, and was indeed getting shadowy and uncertain about all my traditions.

The talk and the feeding went along in a natural way, I could find nothing unusual about it anywhere. The captain was pale, and had a jaded and harassed look, and was subject to little fits of absence of mind; and these things could be said of the mate, also, but this was all natural enough considering the grisly time they had been having, and certainly there was nothing about it to suggest that they were dream-creatures or that their troubles were unreal.

The stranger at my side was about 45 years old, and he had the half-subdued, half-resigned look of a man who had been under a burden of trouble a long time. He was tall and thin; he had a bushy black head, and black eyes which burned when he was interested, but were dull and expressionless when his thoughts were far away—and that happened every time he dropped out of the conversation. He forgot to eat, then, his hands became idle, his dull eye fixed itself upon his plate or upon vacancy, and now and then he would draw a heavy sigh out of the depths of his breast.

These three were exceptions; the others were chatty and cheerful, and they were like a pleasant little family party together. Phillips and Lucy were full of life, and quite happy, as became engaged people; and their furtive love-passages had everybody's sympathy and approval. Lucy was a pretty creature, and simple in her ways and kindly, and Phillips was a blithesome and attractive young fellow. I seemed to be familiarly acquainted with everybody, I didn't quite know why. That is, with everybody except the stranger at my side; and as he seemed to know me well, I had to let on to know him, lest I cause remark by exposing the fact that I didn't know him. I was already tired of being caught up for ignorance at every turn.

The captain and the mate managed to seem comfortable enough until Phillips raised the subject of the day's run, the position of the ship, distance out, and so on; then they became irritable, and sharp of speech, and were unkinder to the young fellow than the case seemed to call for. His sweetheart was distressed to see him so treated before all the company, and she spoke up bravely in his defence and reproached her father for making an offence out of so harmless a thing. This only brought her into trouble, and procured for her so rude a retort that she was consumed with shame, and left the table crying.

The pleasure was all gone, now; everybody felt personally affronted and wantonly abused. Conversation ceased and an uncomfortable silence fell upon the company; through it one could hear the wailing of the wind and the dull tramp of the sailors and the muffled words of command overhead, and this made the silence all the more dismal. The dinner was a failure. While it was still unfinished the company began to break up and slip out, one after another; and presently none was left but me.[16]

I sat long, sipping black coffee and smoking. And thinking; groping about in my dimming land-past. An incident of my American life would rise upon me, vague at first, then grow more distinct and articulate, then sharp and clear; then in a moment it was gone, and in its place was a dull and distant image of some long-past episode whose theatre was this ship—and then *it* would develop, and clarify, and become strong and real. It was fascinating, enchanting, this spying among the elusive mysteries of my bewitched memory, and I went up to my parlor and continued it, with the help of punch and pipe, hour after hour, as long as I could keep awake. With this curious result: that the main incidents of both my lives were now recovered, but only those of one of them persistently gathered strength and vividness—our life in the ship! Those of our land-life were good enough, plain enough, but in minuteness of detail they fell perceptibly short of those others; and in matters of feeling—joy, grief, physical pain, physical pleasure—immeasurably short!

Some mellow notes floated to my ear, muffled by the moaning wind—six bells in the morning watch. So late! I went to bed. When I woke in the middle of the so-called day the first thing I thought of was my night's experience. Already my land-life had faded a little—but not the other.

BOOK II
CHAPTER I

I have long ago lost Book I, but it is no matter. It served its purpose—writing it was an entertainment to me. We found out that our little boy set it adrift on the wind, sheet by sheet, to see if it would fly. It did. And so two of us got entertainment out of it. I have often been minded to begin Book II, but natural indolence and the pleasant life of the ship interfered.

There have been little happenings, from time to time. The principal one, for us of the family, was the birth of our Harry, which stands recorded in the log under the date of June 8, and happened about three months after we shipped the present crew, poor devils! They still think we are bound for the South Pole, and that we are a long time on the way. It is pathetic, after a fashion. They regard their former life in the World as their real life and this present one as—well, they hardly know what; but sometimes they get pretty tired of it, even at this late day. We hear of it now and then through the officers—mainly Turner, who is a puzzled man.

During the first four years we had several mutinies, but things have been reasonably quiet during the past two. One of them had really a serious look. It occurred when Harry was a month old, and at an anxious time, for both he and his mother were weak and ill. The master spirit of it was Stephen Bradshaw the carpenter, of course—a hard lot I know, and a born mutineer I think.

In those days I was greatly troubled, for a time, because my wife's memories still refused to correspond with mine. It had been an ideal life, and naturally it was a distress not to be able to live it over again in its entirety with her in our talks. At first she did not feel about it as I did, and said she could not understand my interest in those dreams, but when she found how much I took the matter to heart, and that to me the dreams had come to have a seeming of reality and were freighted with tender and affectionate impressions besides, she began to change her mind and wish she could go back in spirit with me to that mysterious land. And so she tried to get back that forgotten life. By my help, and by patient probing and searching of her memory she succeeded. Gradually it all came back, and her reward was sufficient. We now had the recollections of two lives to draw upon, and the result was a double measure of happiness for us. We even got the children's former lives back for them—with a good deal of difficulty—next the servants'. It made a new world for us all, and an entertaining one to explore. In the beginning George the colored man was an unwilling subject, because by heredity he was superstitious, and believed that no good could come of meddling with dreams; but when he presently found that no harm came of it his disfavor dissolved away.

Talking over our double-past—particularly our dream-past—became our most pleasant and satisfying amusement, and the search for missing details of it our most profitable labor. One day when the baby was about a month old, we were at this pastime in our parlor. Alice was lying on the sofa, propped with pillows—she was by no means well. It was a still and solemn black day, and cold; but the lamps made the place cheerful, and as for comfort, Turner had taken care of that; for he had found a kerosene stove with an ising-glass front among the freight, and had brought it up and lashed it fast and fired it up, and the warmth it gave and the red glow it made took away all chill and cheerlessness from the parlor and made it homelike. The little girls were out somewhere with George and Delia (the maid).

Alice and I were talking about the time, twelve years before, when Captain Hall's boy had his tragic adventure with the spider-squid, and I was reminding her that she had misstated the case when she mentioned it to me, once. She had said the squid *ate* the boy. Out of my memory I could call back all the details, now, and I remembered that the boy was only badly hurt, not eaten.

For a month or two the ship's company had been glimpsing vast animals at intervals of a few days, and at first the general terror was so great that the men openly threatened, on two occasions, to seize the ship unless the captain turned back; but by a resolute bearing he tided over the difficulty; and by pointing out to the men that the animals had shown no disposition to attack the ship and might therefore be considered harmless, he quieted them down and restored order. It was good grit in the captain, for privately he was very much afraid of the animals himself and had but a shady opinion of their innocence. He kept his gatlings in order, and had gun-watches, which he changed with the other watches.

I had just finished correcting Alice's history of the boy's adventure with the squid when the ship, plowing through a perfectly smooth sea, went heeling away down to starboard and stayed there! The floor slanted like a roof, and every loose thing in the room slid to the floor and glided down against the bulkhead. We were greatly alarmed, of course. Next we heard a rush of feet along the deck and an uproar of cries and shoutings, then the rush of feet coming back, with a wilder riot of cries. Alice exclaimed—

"Go find the children—quick!"

I sprang out and started to run aft through the gloom, and then I saw the fearful sight which I had seen twelve years before when that boy had had his shocking misadventure. For the moment I turned the corner of the deck-house and had an unobstructed view astern, there it was—apparently two full moons rising close over the stern of the ship and lighting the decks and rigging with a sickly yellow glow—the eyes of the colossal squid. His vast beak and head were plain to be seen, swelling up like a hill above our stern; he had flung one tentacle forward and gripped it around the peak of the main-mast and was pulling the ship over; he had gripped the mizzen-mast with another, and a couple more were writhing about dimly away above our heads searching for something to take hold of. The stench of his breath was suffocating everybody.

I was like the most of the crew, helpless with fright; but the captain and the officers kept their wits and courage. The gatlings on the starboard side could not be used, but the four on the port side were brought to bear, and inside of a minute they had poured more than two thousand bullets into those moons. That blinded the creature, and he let go; and by squirting a violent Niagara of water out of his mouth which tore the sea into a tempest of foam he shot himself backward three hundred yards and the ship forward as far, drowning the deck with a racing flood which swept many of the men off their feet and crippled some, and washed all loose deck-plunder overboard. For five minutes we could hear him thrashing about, there in the dark, and lashing the sea with his giant tentacles in his pain; and now and then his moons showed, then vanished again; and all the while we were rocking and plunging in the booming seas he made. Then he quieted down. We took a thankful full breath, believing him dead.

Now I thought of the children, and ran all about inquiring for them, but no one had seen them. I thought they must have been washed overboard, and for a moment my heart stopped beating. Then the hope came that they had taken refuge with their mother; so I ran there; and almost swooned when I entered the place, for it was vacant. I ran out shouting the alarm, and after a dozen steps almost ran over her. She was lying against the bulwarks drenched and insensible. The surgeon and young Phillips helped me carry her in; then the surgeon and I began to work over her and Phillips rushed away to start the hunt for the children. It was all of half an hour before she showed any sign of life; then her eyes opened with a dazed and wondering look in them, then they recognized me and into them shot a ghastly terror.

"The children! the children!" she gasped; and I, with the heart all gone out of me, answered with such air of truth as I could assume—

"They are safe."

I could never deceive her. I was transparent to her.

"It is not true! The truth speaks out all over you—they are lost, oh they are lost, they are lost!"

We were strong, but we could not hold her. She tore loose from us and was gone in a moment, flying along the dark decks and shrieking the children's names with a despairing pathos that broke one's heart to hear it. We fled after her, and urged that the flitting lanterns meant that all were searching, and begged her for the children's sake and mine if not for her own to go to bed and save her life. But it went for nothing, she would not listen. For she was a mother, and her children were lost. That says it all. She would hunt for them as long as she had strength to move. And that is what she did, hour after hour, wailing and mourning, and touching the hardest hearts with her grief, until she was exhausted and fell in a swoon. Then the stewardess and I put her to bed, and as soon as she came to and was going to creep out of her bed and take up her search again the doctor encouraged her in it and gave her a draught to restore her strength; and it put her into a deep sleep, which was what he expected.

We left the stewardess on watch and went away to join the searchers. Not a lantern was twinkling anywhere, and every figure that emerged from the gloom moved upon tip-toe. I collared one of them and said angrily—

"What does this mean? Is the search stopped?"

Turner's voice answered—very low: "—'sh! Captain's orders. The beast ain't dead—it's hunting for us."

It made me sick with fear.

"Do you mean it, Turner? How do you know?"

"Listen."

There was a muffled swashing sound out there somewhere, and then the two moons appeared for a moment, then turned slowly away and were invisible again.

"He's been within a hundred yards of us, feeling around for us with his arms. He could reach us, but he couldn't locate us because he's blind. Once he mighty near had us; one of his arms that was squirming around up there in the dark just missed the foremast, and he hauled in the slack of it without suspecting anything. It made my lungs come up into my throat. He has edged away, you see, but he ain't done laying for us." Pause. Then in a whisper, "He's wallowing around closer to us again, by gracious. Look—look at that. See it? Away up in the air—writhing around like a crooked mainmast. Dim, but—there, *now* don't you see it?"

We stood dead still, hardly breathing. Here and there at little distances the men were gathering silently together and watching and pointing. The deep hush lay like a weight upon one's spirit. Even the faintest quiver of air that went idling by gave out a ghost of sound. A couple of mellow notes floated lingering and fading down from forward:

Booooom——booooom. (Two bells in the middle watch.)

A hoarse low voice—the captain's:

"Silence that damned bell!"

Instantly there was a thrashing commotion out there, with a thundering rush of discharged water, and the monster came charging for us. I caught my breath, and had to seize Turner or I should have fallen, so suddenly my strength collapsed. Then vaguely we saw the creature, waving its arms aloft, tear past the ship stern first, pushing a vast swell ahead and trailing a tumultuous wake behind, and the next moment it was far away and we were plunging and tossing in the sea it made.

"Thank God, *he's* out of practice!" said Turner, with emotion.

The majestic blind devil stopped out there with its moons toward us, and we were miserable again. We had so hoped it would go home.

I resumed my search. Below I found Phillips and Lucy Davis and a number of others searching, but with no hope. They said they had been everywhere, and were merely going over the ground again and again because they could not bear to have it reported to the mother that the search had ceased. She must be told that they were her friends and that she could depend upon them.

Four hours later I gave it up, wearied to exhaustion, and went and sat down by Alice's bed, to be at hand and support her when she should wake and have to hear my desolate story. After a while she stirred, then opened her eyes and smiled brightly and said—

"Oh, what bliss it is! I dreamed that the children—" She flung her arms about me in a transport of grief. "I remember—oh, my God it is true!"

And so, with sobs and lamentations and frantic self-reproaches she poured out her bitter sorrow, and I clasped her close to me, and could not find one comforting word to say.

"Oh, Henry, Henry, your silence means—oh, we cannot live, we cannot bear it!"

There was a flurry of feet along the deck, the door was burst in, and Turner's voice shouted—

"They're found, by God they're found!"

A joy like that brings the shock of a thunderbolt, and for a little while we thought Alice was gone; but then she rallied, and by that time the children were come, and were clasped to her breast, and she was steeped in a happiness for which there were no words. And she said she never dreamed that profanity could sound so dear and sweet, and she asked the mate to say it again; and he did, but left out the profanity and spoiled it.

The children and George and Delia had seen the squid come and lift its moons above our stern and reach its vast tentacles aloft; and they had not waited, but had fled below, and had not stopped till they were deep down in the hold and hidden in a tunnel among the freight. When found, they had had several hours' sleep and were much refreshed.

Between seeing the squid, and getting washed off her feet, and losing the children, the day was a costly one for Alice. It marks the date of her first gray hairs. They were few, but they were to have company.

We lay in a dead calm, and helpless. We could not get away from the squid's neighborhood. But I was obliged to have some sleep, and I took it. I took all I could get, which was six hours. Then young Phillips came and turned me out and said there were signs that the spirit of mutiny was abroad again and that the captain was going to call the men aft and talk to them. Phillips thought I would not want to miss it.

He was right. We had private theatricals, we had concerts, and the other usual time-passers customary on long voyages; but a speech from the captain was the best entertainment the ship's talent could furnish. There was character back of his oratory. He was all sailor. He was sixty years old, and had known no life but sea life. He had no gray hairs, his beard was full and black and shiny; he wore no mustache, therefore his lips were exposed to view; they fitted together like box and lid, and expressed the pluck and resolution that were in him. He had bright black eyes in his old bronze face and they eloquently interpreted all his moods, and his moods were many: for at times he was the youngest man in the ship, and the most cheerful and vivacious and skittish; at times he was the best-natured man in the ship, and he was always the most lovable; sometimes he was sarcastic, sometimes he was serious even to solemnity, sometimes he was stern, sometimes he was as sentimental as a school-girl; sometimes he was silent, quiet, withdrawn within himself, sometimes he was talkative and argumentative; he was remarkably and sincerely and persistently pious, and marvelously and scientifically profane; he was much the strongest man in the ship, and he was also the largest, excepting that plotting, malicious and fearless devil, Stephen Bradshaw the carpenter; he could smile as sweetly as a girl, and it was a pleasure to see him do it. He was entirely self-educated, and had made a vast and picturesque job of it. He was an affectionate creature, and in his family relations he was beautiful; in the eyes of his daughters he was omniscient, omnipotent, a mixed sun-god and storm-god, and they feared him and adored him accordingly. He was fond of oratory, and thought he had the gift of it; and so he practiced it now and then, upon occasion, and did it with easy confidence. He was a charming man and a manly man, with a right heart and a fine and daring spirit.

Phillips and I slipped out and moved aft. Things had an unusual and startling aspect. There were flushes of light here and there and yonder; the captain stood in one of them, the officers stood a little way back of him.

"How do matters stand, Phillips?"

"You notice that the battle-lanterns are lit, all the way forward?"

"Yes. The gun-watches are at their posts; I see that. The captain means business, I reckon."

"The gun-watches are mutineers!"

I steadied my voice as well as I could, but there was still a quaver in it when I said—

"Then they've sprung a trap on us, and we are at their mercy, of course."

"It has the look of it. They've caught the old man napping, and we are in a close place this time."

We joined the officers, and just then we heard the measured tramp of the men in the distance. They were coming down from forward. Soon they came into view and moved toward us until they were within three or four paces of the captain.

"Halt!"

They had a leader this time, and it was he that gave the command—Stephen Bradshaw, the carpenter. He had a revolver in his hand. There was a pause, then the captain drew himself up, put on his dignity, and prepared to transact business in a properly impressive and theatrical way. He cleared his voice and said, in a fatherly tone—

"Men, this is your spokesman, duly appointed by you?"

Several responded timidly—

"Yes, sir."

"You have a grievance, and you desire to have it redressed?"

"Yes, sir."

"He is not here to represent himself, lads, but only you?"

"Yes, sir."

"Very well. Your complaint shall be heard, and treated with justice." (Murmur of approbation from the men.) Then the captain's soft manner hardened a little, and he said to the carpenter, "Go on."

Bradshaw was eager to begin, and he flung out his words with aggressive confidence—

"Captain Davis, in the first place this crew wants to know where they *are.* Next, they want this ship put about and pointed for home—straight off, and no fooling. They are tired of this blind voyage, and they ain't going to have any more of it—and that's the word with the bark on it." He paused a moment, for his temper was rising and obstructing his breath; then he continued in a raised and insolent voice and with a showy flourish of his revolver. "Before, they've had no leader, and you talked them down and cowed them; but that ain't going to happen this time. And they hadn't any plans, and warn't fixed for business; but it's different, now." He grew exultant. "Do you see this?"—his revolver. "And do you see that?" He pointed to the gatlings. "We've got the guns; we are boss of the ship. Put her about! That's the order, and it's going to be obeyed."

There was an admiring murmur from the men. After a pause the captain said, with dignity—

"Apparently you are through. Stand aside."

"Stand aside, is it? Not till I have heard what answer you—"

The captain's face darkened and an evil light began to flicker in his eyes, and his hands to twitch. The carpenter glanced at him, then stepped a pace aside, shaking his head and grumbling. "Say your say, then, and cut it short, for I've got something more to say when you're done, if it ain't satisfactory."

The captain's manner at once grew sweet, and even tender, and he turned toward the men with his most genial and winning smile on his face, and proceeded to take them into his confidence.

"You want to know where you are, boys. It is reasonable; it is natural. If we don't know where we are—if we are lost—who is worst off, you or me? You have no children in this ship—I have. If we are in danger have I put us there intentionally? Would I have done it purposely—with my children aboard? Come, what do you think?"

There was a stir among the men, and an approving nodding of heads which conceded that the point was well taken.

"Don't I know my trade, or am I only an apprentice to it? Have I sailed the seas for sixty years and commanded ships for thirty to be taught what to do in a difficulty by—by a damned carpenter?"

He was talking in such a pleading way, such an earnest, and moving and appealing way that the men were not prepared for the close of his remark, and it caught them out and made some of them laugh. He had scored one—and he knew it. The carpenter's back was turned—he was playing indifference. He whirled around and covered the captain with his revolver. Everybody shrank together and caught his breath, except the captain, who said gently—

"Don't be afraid—pull the trigger; it isn't loaded."

The carpenter pulled—twice, thrice, and threw the pistol away. Then he shouted—

"Fall back, men—out of the way!" They surged apart, and he fell back himself. The captain and the officers stood alone in the circle of light. "Gun 4, fire!" The officers threw themselves on their faces on the deck, but the captain remained in his place. The gunner spun the windlass around—there was no result. "Gun 3, fire!" The same thing happened again. The captain said—

"Come back to your places, men." They obeyed, looking puzzled, surprised, and a good deal demoralized. The officers got up, looking astonished and rather ashamed. "Carpenter, come back to your place." He did it, but reluctantly, and swearing to himself. It was easy to see that the captain was contented with his dramatic effects. He resumed his speech, in his pleasantest manner—

"You have mutinied two or three times, boys. It is all right—up to now. I would have done it myself in my common-seaman days, I reckon, if my ship was bewitched and I didn't know where I was. Now then, can you be trusted with the facts? Are we rational men, manly men, men who can stand up and face hard luck and a big difficulty that has been brought about by nobody's fault, and say live or die, survive or perish, we are in for it, for good or bad, and we'll stand by the ship if she goes to hell!"[17] (The men let go a tol[erably] hearty cheer.) "Are we men—grown men—salt-sea men—men nursed upon dangers and cradled in storms—men made in the image of God and ready to do when He commands and die when He calls—or are we just sneaks and curs and carpenters!" (This brought both cheers and laughter, and the captain was happy.) "There—that's the kind. And so I'll tell you how the thing stands. *I* don't know where this ship is, but she's in the hands of God, and that's enough for me, it's enough for you, and it's enough for anybody but a carpenter. If it is God's will that we pull through, we pull through—otherwise not. We haven't had an observation for four months, but we are going ahead, and do our best to fetch up somewhere."

[1898/1962]

The Second Advent

Black Jack[1] is a very small village lying far away back in the western wilds and solitudes of Arkansas. It is made up of a few log cabins; its lanes are deep with mud in wet weather; its fences and gates are rickety and decayed; its cornfields and gardens are weedy, slovenly, and poorly cared for; there are no newspapers, no railways, no factories, no library; ignorance, sloth and drowsiness prevail. There is a small log church, but no school. The hogs are many, and they wallow by the doors, they sun themselves in the public places.

It is a frontier village; the border of the Indian Territory is not a day's walk away, and the loafing savage is a common sight in the town. There are some other sleepy villages thereabouts: Tumblinsonville, three or four miles off; Brunner, four or five; Sugarloaf, ten or twelve. In effect, the region is a solitude, and far removed from the busy world and the interests which animate it.

A gentle and comely young girl, Nancy Hopkins, lived in Black Jack, with her parents. The Hopkinses were old residents; in fact neither they nor their forerunners for two generations had ever known any other place than Black Jack. When Nancy was just budding into womanhood, she was courted by several of the young men of the village, but she finally gave the preference to Jackson Barnes the blacksmith, and was promised to him in marriage by her parents. This was soon known to everybody, and of course discussed freely, in village fashion. The young couple were chaffed, joked, and congratulated in the frank, rude, frontier way, and the discarded suitors were subjected to abundance of fat-witted raillery.

Then came a season of quiet, the subject being exhausted; a season wherein tongues were still, there being nothing whatever in that small world to talk about. But by and by a change came; suddenly all tongues were busy again. Busier, too, than they had ever been at any time before, within any one's memory; for never before had they been furnished with anything like so prodigious a topic as now offered itself: Nancy Hopkins, the sweet young bride elect, was—

The news flew from lip to lip with almost telegraphic swiftness; wives told it to their husbands; husbands to bachelors; servants got hold of it and told it to the young misses; it was gossiped over in every corner; rude gross pioneers coarsely joked about it over their whisky in the village grocery, accompanying their witticisms with profane and obscene words and mighty explosions of horse laughter. The unsuspecting blacksmith was called into this grocery and the crushing news sprung upon him with a brutal frankness and directness. At first he was bowed with grief and misery; but very soon anger took the place of these feelings, and he went forth saying he would go and break the engagement. After he was gone, the grocery crowd organized itself into a public meeting to consider what ought to be done with the girl. After brief debate it was resolved—

1. That she must name her betrayer.
2. And immediately marry him.
3. Or be tarred and feathered and banished to the Indian Territory.

The proceedings were hardly ended when Jackson Barnes was seen returning; and, to the general astonishment, his face was seen to be calm, placid, content—even joyful. Everybody crowded around to hear what he might say in explanation of this strange result. There was a deep and waiting silence for some moments; then Barnes said solemnly, and with awe in his voice and manner:

"She has explained it. She has made everything clear. I am satisfied, and have taken her back to my love and protection. She has told me all, and with perfect frankness, concealing nothing. She is pure and undefiled. She will give birth to a son, but no man has had to do with her. God has honored her, God has overshadowed her, and to Him she will bear this child. A joy inexpressible is ours, for we are blessed beyond all mankind."

His face was radiant with a holy happiness while he spoke. Yet when he had finished a brutal jeer went up from the crowd, and everybody mocked at him, and he was assailed on all sides with insulting remarks and questions. One said—

"How does she know it was God?"

Barnes answered: "An angel told her."

"When did the angel tell her?"

"Several months ago."

"Before, or after the act?"

"Before."

"Told her it was going to happen?"

"Yes."

"Did she believe the angel at the time?"

"Yes."

"But didn't mention the matter to you at the time?"

"No."

"Why didn't she?"

"I do not know."

"Did she mention it to the old people?"

"No."

"Why didn't she?"

"I do not know."

"Had she any other evidence as to the facts than the angel?"

"No."

"What did the angel look like?"

"Like a man."

"Naked?"

"No—clothed."

"How?"

"In ancient times the angels came clothed in a robe, the dress of the people of the day. Naturally this one was clothed according to the fashion of our day. He wore a straw hat, a blue jeans roundabout and pants, and cowhide boots."

"How did she know he was an angel?"

"Because he said he was; and angels cannot lie."

"Did he speak English?"

"Of course; else she would not have understood him."

"Did he speak like an American, or with an accent?"

"He had no accent."

"Were there any witnesses?"

"No—she was alone."

"It might have been well to have some witnesses. Have you any evidence to convince you except her word?"

"Yes. While I talked with her, sleep came upon me for a moment, and I dreamed. In my dream I was assured by God that all she had said was true, and He also commanded me to stand by her and marry her."

"How do you know that the dream came from God and not from your dinner? How could you tell?"

"I knew because the voice of the dream distinctly said so."

"You believe, then, that Nancy Hopkins is still pure and undefiled?"

"I know it. She is still a virgin."

"Of course you may know that, and know it beyond doubt or question, if you have applied the right test. Have you done this?"

"I have not applied any test. I do not need to. I know perfectly that she is a virgin, by better evidence than a test."

"By what evidence? How can you know—how do you know—that she is still a virgin?"

"I know it because she told me so herself, with her own lips."

"Yes, and you dreamed it besides."

"I did."

"Absolutely overwhelming proof—isn't it?"

"It seems so to me."

"Isn't it possible that a girl might lie, in such circumstances, to save her good name?"

"To save her good name, yes; but to lie in this case would be to rob herself of the unspeakable honor of being made fruitful by Almighty God. It would be more than human heroism for Nancy Hopkins to lie, in this case, and deny the illustrious fatherhood of her child, and throw away the opportunity to make her name revered and renowned forever in the world. She did right to confess her relations with the Deity. Where is there a girl in Black Jack who would not be glad to enjoy a like experience, and proud to proclaim it?"

"You suspect none but God?"

"How should I?"

"You do not suspect the angel in the straw hat?"

"He merely brought the message, that is all."

"And delivered it and left immediately?"

"I suppose so. I do not know."

"Suppose he had staid away and sent it by mail—or per dream, which is cheaper and saves paper and postage—would the result to Nancy have been the same, do you think?"

"Of course; for the angel had nothing to do but convey the prophecy; his functions ceased there."

"Possibly they did. Still, it would be helpful to hear from the angel. What shall you do with this child when it comes?"

"I shall rear it carefully, and provide for it to the best of my means."

"And call it your own?"

"I would not dare to. It is the child of the most high God. It is holy."

"What shall you call it, if it be a girl?"

"It will not be a girl."

"Then if it be a boy?"

"It shall be called Jesus Christ."

"What—is there to be another Jesus Christ?"

"No, it is the same that was born of Mary, ages ago, not another. This is merely the Second Advent; I was so informed by the Most High in my dream."

"You are in error, manifestly. He is to come the second time not humbly, but in clouds and great glory."

"Yes, but that has all been changed. It was a question if the world would believe it was Jesus if he came in that way, so the former method was reinstituted. He is to be again born of an obscure Virgin, because the world cannot help but believe and be convinced by that circumstance, since it has been convinced by it before."

"To be frank with you, we do not believe a word of this flimsy nonsense you are talking. Nancy Hopkins has gone astray; she is a disgraced girl, and she knows it and you know it and we all know it. She must not venture to show her face among our virtuous daughters; we will not allow it. If you wish to marry her and make an honest woman of her, well and good; but take her away from here, at least till the wind of this great scandal has somewhat blown over."

So the Hopkinses and the blacksmith shut themselves up in their house, and were shunned and despised by the whole village.

But the day of their sorrow was to have an end, in time. They felt it, they knew it, in truth, for their dreams said it. So they waited, and were patient. Meantime the marvelous tale spread abroad; village after village heard of the new Virgin and the new Christ, and presently the matter traveled to the regions of newspapers and telegraphs; then instantly it swept the world as upon myriad wings, and was talked of in all lands.

So at last came certain wise men from the far east, to inquire concerning the matter, and to learn for themselves whether the tale was true or false. These were editors from New York and other great cities, and presidents of Yale and Princeton and Andover and other great colleges. They saw a star shining in the east—it was Venus—and this they resolved to follow. Several astronomers said that a star could not be followed—that a person might as well try to follow a spot on the sun's disk, or any other object that was so far away it could not be seen to move. Other astronomers said that if a star should come down low enough to be valuable as a guide, it would roof the whole earth in, and make total darkness and give forth no relieving light itself—and that then it would be just as useful, as a guide, as is the eternal roof of the Mammoth Cave to the explorer of its maze of halls and chambers. And they also said that a star could not descend thus low without disorganizing the universe and hurling all the worlds together in confusion.

But the wise men were not disturbed. They answered that what had happened once could happen again. And they were right. For this talk had hardly ended when Venus did actually leave her place in the sky and come down and hang over the very building in which the sages were assembled. She gave out a good light, too, and appeared to be no larger than a full moon.

The wise men were greatly rejoiced; and they gathered together their baggage, and their editorial passes, and clerical half-rate tickets, and took the night train westward praising God. In the morning they stopped at Pittsburg and laid over till Venus was visible again in the evening. And so they journeyed on, night after night. At Louisville they got news of the child's birth. That night they resumed their journey; and so continued, by rail and horse conveyance, following the star until it came and stood over the house in Black Jack where the young child lay. Then the star retired into the sky, and they saw it go back and resume its glimmering function in the remote east.

It was about dawn, now; and immediately the whole heavens were filled with flocks of descending angels, and these were joined by a choir of drovers who were ranching in the vicinity, and all broke forth into song—the angels using a tune of their own, and the others an Arkansas tune, but all employing the same words. The wise men assisted, as well as they could, until breakfast time; then the angels returned home, the drovers resumed business, and the wise men retired to the village tavern.

After breakfast, the wise men being assembled privately, the President of Princeton made a brief speech and offered this suggestion:

1. That they all go, in a body, to see the child and hear the evidence;

2. That they all question the witnesses and assist in sifting the testimony;

3. But that the verdict be voted and rendered, not by the full body, but by a jury selected out of it by ballot.

Mr. Greeley, Mr. Bennett and Mr. Beach[2] saw no good reason for this. They said the whole body was as good a jury as a part of it could be.

The President of Princeton replied that the proposed method would simplify matters.

A vote was then taken and the measure carried, in spite of the editorial opposition.

The President of Andover then proposed that the jury consist of six persons, and that only members of some orthodox church be eligible.

Against this the editors loudly protested, and remarked that this would make a packed jury and rule out every editor, since none of their faction would be eligible. Mr. Greeley implored the President of Andover to relinquish his proposition; and reminded him that the church had always been accused of packing juries and using other underhand methods wherever its interests seemed to be concerned; and reminded him, further, as an instance, that church trials of accused clergymen nearly always resulted in a barefaced whitewashing of the accused. He begged that the present opportunity to improve the church's reputation would not be thrown away, but that a fair jury, selected without regard to religious opinion or complexion might be chosen.

The plea failed, however, and a jury composed solely of church members was chosen, the church faction being largely in the majority and voting as a unit. The editors were grieved over the advantage which had been taken of their numerical weakness, but they could not help themselves.

Then the wise men arose and went in a body to see the Hopkinses. There they listened to the evidence offered by Nancy and Barnes; and when the testimony was all in, it was examined and discussed. The religious faction maintained that it was clear, coherent, cogent, and without flaw, discrepancy, or doubtful feature; but the editorial faction stoutly maintained the directly opposite view, and implored the jury to consider well, and not allow their judgment to be influenced by prejudice and what might seem to be ecclesiastical interest.

The jury then retired; and after a brief absence brought in a verdict, as follows:

"We can doubt no whit. We find these to be the facts: An angel informed Nancy Hopkins of what was to happen; this is shown by her unqualified declaration. She is still a virgin; we know this is so, because we have her word for it. The child is the actual child of Almighty God—a fact established by overwhelming testimony, to-wit, the testimony of the angel, of Nancy, and of God Himself, as delivered to Jackson Barnes in a dream. Our verdict, then, is that this child is truly the Christ the Son of God, that his birth is miraculous, and that his mother is still a virgin."

Then the jury and their faction fell upon their knees and worshiped the child, and laid at its feet costly presents: namely, a History of the Church's Dominion During the First Fourteen Centuries; a History of the Presbyterian Dominion in Scotland; a History of Catholic Dominion in England; a History of the Salem Witchcraft; a History of the Holy

Inquisition; in addition, certain toys for the child to play with—these being tiny models of the Inquisition's instruments of torture; and a little Holy Bible with the decent passages printed in red ink.

But the other wise men, the editors, murmured and were not satisfied. Mr. Horace Greeley delivered their opinion. He said:

"Where an individual's life is at stake, hearsay evidence is not received in courts; how, then, shall we venture to receive hearsay evidence in this case, where the eternal life of whole nations is at stake? We have hearsay evidence that an angel appeared; none has seen that angel but one individual, and she an interested person. We have hearsay evidence that the angel delivered a certain message; whether it has come to us untampered with or not, we can never know, there being none to convey it to us but a party interested in having it take a certain form. We have the evidence of dreams and other hearsay evidence—and still, as before, from interested parties—that God is the father of this child, and that its mother remains a virgin: the first a statement which never has been and never will be possible of verification, and the last a statement which could only have been verified before the child's birth, but not having been done then can never hereafter be done. Silly dreams, and the unverifiable twaddle of a family of nobodies who are interested in covering up a young girl's accident and shielding her from disgrace—such is the 'evidence!' 'Evidence' like this could not affect even a dog's case, in any court in Christendom. It is rubbish, it is foolishness. No court would listen to it; it would be an insult to judge and jury to offer it."

Then a young man of the other party, named Talmage,[3] rose in a fury of generous enthusiasm, and denounced the last speaker as a reprobate and infidel, and said he had earned and would receive his right reward in the fulness of time in that everlasting hell created and appointed for his kind by this holy child, the God of the heavens and the earth and all that in them is. Then he sprang high in the air three times, cracking his heels together and praising God. And when he had finally alighted and become in a measure stationary, he shouted in a loud voice, saying:

"Here is divine evidence, evidence from the lips of very God Himself, and it is scoffed at! here is evidence from an angel of God, coming fresh from the fields of heaven, from the shadow of the Throne, with the odors of Eternal Land upon his raiment, and it is derided! here is evidence from God's own chosen handmaid, holy and pure, whom He has fructified without sin, and it is mocked at! here is evidence of one who has spoken face to face with the Most High in a dream, and even his evidence is called lies and foolishness! and on top of all, here is *cumulative* evidence: for the fact that all these things have happened before, in exactly the same way, establishes the genuineness of this second happening beyond shadow or possibility of doubt to all minds not senile, idiotic or given hopelessly over to the possession of hell and the devil! If men cannot believe *these* evidences, taken together, and piled, Pelion on Ossa, mountains high, what *can* they believe!"

Then the speaker flung himself down, with many contortions, and wallowed in the dirt before the child, singing praises and glorifying God.

The Holy Family remained at Black Jack, and in time the world ceased to talk about them, and they were forgotten.

But at the end of thirty years they came again into notice; for news went abroad that Jesus had begun to teach in the churches, and to do miracles. He appointed twelve disciples, and they went about proclaiming Christ's kingdom and doing good. Many of the people believed, and confessed their belief; and in time these became a multitude. Indeed there was a likelihood that by and by all the nation would come into the fold, for the miracles wrought were marvelous, and men found themselves unable to resist such evidences. But after a while there came a day when murmurings began to be heard, and dissatisfaction to show its head. And the cause of this was the very same cause which had worked the opposite effect, previously,—namely, the miracles. The first notable instance was on this wise:

One of the twelve disciples—the same being that Talmage heretofore referred to—was tarrying for a time in Tumblinsonville, healing the sick and teaching in the public places of the village. It was summer, and all the land was parched with a drouth which had lasted during three months. The usual petitions had been offered up, daily at the hearth-stone and on Sundays from the pulpit, but without result—the rain did not come. The governor finally issued his proclamation for a season of fasting and united prayer for rain, naming a certain Sunday for the beginning. St. Talmage sat with the congregation in the Tumblinsonville church that Sunday morning. There was not a cloud in the sky; it was blistering hot; everybody was sad; the preacher said, mournfully, that it was now plain that the rain was withheld for a punishment, and it would be wisest to ask for it no more for the present. At that moment the saint rose up and rebuked the minister before the whole wondering assemblage, for his weak and faltering faith; then he put his two hands together, lifted up his face, and began to pray for rain. With his third sentence an instant darkness came, and with it a pouring deluge! Perhaps one may imagine the faces of the people—it is a thing which cannot be described. The blessed rain continued to come down in torrents all day long, and the happy people talked of nothing but the miracle. Indeed, they were so absorbed in it that it was midnight before they woke up to a sense of the fact that this rain, which began as a blessing, had gradually turned into a calamity—the country was flooded, the whole region was well nigh afloat. Everybody turned out and tried to save cattle, hogs, and bridges; and at this work they wrought despairingly and uselessly two or three hours before it occurred to anybody that *if* that disciple's prayer had brought the deluge, possibly another prayer from him might stop it. Some hurried away and called up the disciple out of his bed, and begged him to stay the flood if he could. He told them to cease from their terrors and bear witness to what was about to happen. He then knelt and offered up his petition. The answer was instantaneous; the rain stopped immediately and utterly.

There was rejoicing in all religious hearts, because the unbelieving had always scoffed at prayer and said the pulpit had claimed that it could accomplish everything, whereas none could prove that it was able to accomplish anything at all. Unbelievers had scoffed when prayers were offered up for better weather, and for the healing of the sick, and the staying of epidemics, and the averting of war—prayers which no living man had ever seen answered, they said. But the holy disciple had shown, now, that special providences were at the bidding of the prayers of the perfect. The evidence was beyond dispute.

But on the other hand there was a widespread discontent among such of the community as had had their all swept away by the flood. It was a feeling which was destined to find a place, later, in other bosoms.

When but a few days had gone by, certain believers came and touched the hem of the disciple's garment and begged that once more he would exert his miraculous powers in the name of Him whom he and they served and worshiped. They desired him to pray for cold weather, for the benefit of a poor widow who was perishing of a wasting fever. He consented; and although it was midsummer, ice formed, and there was a heavy fall of snow. The woman immediately recovered. The destruction of crops by the cold and snow was complete; in addition, a great many persons who were abroad and out of the way of help had their ears and fingers frostbitten, and six children and two old men fell by the wayside, being benumbed by the cold and confused and blinded by the snow, and were frozen to death. Wherefore, although numbers praised God for the miracle, and marveled at it, the relatives and immediate friends of the injured and the killed were secretly discontented, and some of them even gave voice to murmurs.

Now came divers of the elect, praising God, and asked for further changes of the weather, for one reason or another, and the holy disciple, glad to magnify his Lord, willingly gratified them. The calls became incessant. As a consequence, he changed the weather many times, every day. These changes were very trying to the general public, and caused much sickness and death, since alternate drenchings and freezings and scorchings were common, and none could escape colds, in consequence, neither could any ever know, upon going out, whether to wear muslin or furs. A man who dealt in matters of science and had long had a reputation as a singularly accurate weather prophet, found himself utterly baffled by this extraordinary confusion of weather; and his business being ruined, he presently lost his reason and endeavored to take the life of the holy disciple. Eventually so much complaint was made that the saint was induced, by a general petition, to desist, and leave the weather alone. Yet there were many that protested, and were not able to see why they should not be allowed to have prayers offered up for weather to suit their private interests—a thing, they said, which had been done in all ages, and been encouraged by the pulpit, too, until now, when such prayers were found to be worth something. There was a degree of reasonableness in the argument, but it plainly would not answer to listen to it.

An exceedingly sickly season followed the confused and untimely weather, and every house became a hospital. The holy Talmage was urged to interfere with prayer. He did so. The sickness immediately disappeared, and no one was unwell in the slightest degree, during three months. Then the physicians, undertakers and professional nurses of all the region round about rose in a body and made such an outcry that the saint was forced to modify the state of things. He agreed to pray in behalf of special cases, only. Now a young man presently fell sick, and when he was dying his mother begged hard for his life, and the saint yielded, and by his prayers restored him to immediate health. The next day he killed a comrade in a quarrel, and shortly was hanged for it. His mother never forgave herself for procuring the plans of God to be altered. By request of another mother, another dying son was prayed back to health, but it was not a fortunate thing; for he strangely forsook his blameless ways, and in a few months was in a felon's cell for robbing his employer, and his family were broken hearted and longing for death.

By this time the miracles of the Savior himself were beginning to fall under criticism. He had raised many poor people from the dead; and as long as he had confined himself to the poor these miracles brought large harvests of glory and converts, and nobody found fault, or even thought of finding fault. But a change came at last. A rich bachelor died in a neighboring town, leaving a will giving all his property to the Society for the Encouragement of Missions. Several days after the burial, an absent friend arrived home, and learning of the death, came to Black Jack, and prevailed with the Savior to pray him back to life and health. So the man was alive again, but found himself a beggar; the Society had possession of all his wealth and legal counsel warned the officers of the Society that if they gave it up they would be transcending their powers and the Society could come on them for damages in the full amount, and they would unquestionably be obliged to pay. The officers started to say something about Lazarus, but the lawyer said that if Lazarus left any property behind him he most certainly found himself penniless when he was raised from the dead; that if there was any dispute between him and his heirs, the law upheld the latter. Naturally, the Society decided to hold on to the man's property. There was an aggravating lawsuit; the Society proved that the man had been dead and been buried; the court dismissed the case, saying it could not consider the complaints of a corpse. The matter was appealed; the higher court sustained the lower one. It went further, and said that for a dead man to bring a suit was a thing without precedent, a violation of privilege, and hence was plainly contempt of court—whereupon it laid a heavy fine upon the transgressor. Maddened by these misfortunes, the plaintiff killed the presiding officer of the Society and then blew his own brains out, previously giving warning that if he was disturbed again he would make it a serious matter for the disturber.

The Twelve Disciples were the constant though innocent cause of trouble. Every blessing they brought down upon an individual was sure to fetch curses in its train for other people. Gradually the several communities among whom they labored grew anxious and uneasy; these prayers had unsettled everything; they had so disturbed the order of nature, that nobody could any longer guess, one day, what was likely to happen the next. So the popularity of the Twelve wasted gradually away. The people murmured against them, and said they were a pestilent incumbrance and a dangerous power to have in the State. During the time that they meddled with the weather, they made just one friend every time they changed it, and not less than a hundred enemies—a thing which was natural, and to be expected.—When they agreed to let the weather and the public health alone, their popularity seemed regained, for a while, but they soon lost it once more, through indiscretions. To accommodate a procession, they prayed that the river might be divided; this prayer was answered, and the procession passed over dry-shod. The march consumed twenty minutes, only, but twenty minutes was ample time to enable the backed-up waters to overflow all the country for more than a hundred and fifty miles up the river, on both sides; in consequence of which a vast number of farms and villages were ruined, many lives were lost, immense aggregations of live stock destroyed, and thousands of people reduced to beggary. The disciples had to be spirited away and kept concealed for two or three months, after that, so bitter was the feeling against them, and so widespread the desire to poison or hang them.

In the course of time so many restrictions came to be placed upon the disciples' prayers, by public demand, that they were at last confined to two things, raising the dead and restoring the dying to health. Yet at times even these services produced trouble, and sometimes as great in degree as in the case of the rich bachelor who was raised by the Savior. A very rich old man, with a host of needy kin, was snatched from the very jaws of death by the disciples, and given a long lease of life. The needy kin were not slow to deliver their opinions about what they termed "this outrage"; neither were they mild or measured in their abuse of the holy Twelve. Almost every time a particularly disagreeable person died, his relatives had the annoyance of seeing him walk into their midst again within a week. Often, when such a person was about to die, half the village would be in an anxious and uncomfortable state, dreading the interference of the disciples, each individual hoping they would let nature take its course but none being willing to assume the exceedingly delicate office of suggesting it.

However, a time came at last when people were forced to speak. The region had been cursed, for many years, by the presence of a brute named Marvin, who was a thief, liar, drunkard, blackguard, incendiary, a loathsome and hateful creature in every way. One day the news went about that he was dying. The public joy was hardly concealed. Everybody thought of the disciples in a moment, (for they would be sure to raise him up in the hope of reforming him,) but it was too late. A dozen men started in the direction of Marvin's house, meaning to stand guard there and keep the disciples away; but they were too late; the prayer had been offered, and they met Marvin himself, striding down the street, hale and hearty, and good for thirty years more.

An indignation meeting was called, and there was a packed attendance. It was difficult to maintain order, so excited were the people. Intemperate speeches were made, and resolutions offered in which the disciples were bitterly denounced. Among the resolutions finally adopted were these:

Resolved, That the promise "Ask and ye shall receive" shall henceforth be accepted as sound in theory, and true; but it shall stop there; whosoever ventures to actually follow the admonition shall suffer death.

Resolved, That to pray for the restoration of the sick; for the averting of war; for the blessing of rain; and for other special providences, were things righteous and admissible whilst they were mere forms and yielded no effect; but henceforth, whosoever shall so pray shall be deemed guilty of crime and shall suffer death.

Resolved, That if the ordinary prayers of a nation were answered during a single day, the universal misery, misfortune, destruction and desolation which would ensue, would constitute a cataclysm which would take its place side by side with the deluge and so remain in history to the end of time.

Resolved, That whosoever shall utter his belief in special providences in answer to prayer, shall be adjudged insane and shall be confined.

Resolved, That the Supreme Being is able to conduct the affairs of this world without the assistance of any person in Arkansas; and whosoever shall venture to offer such assistance shall suffer death.

Resolved, That since no one can improve the Creator's plans by procuring their alteration, there shall be but one form of prayer allowed in Arkansas henceforth, and that form shall begin and end with the words, *"Lord, Thy will, not mine, be done;"*[4] and whosoever shall add to or take from this prayer, shall perish at the stake.

During several weeks the holy disciples observed these laws, and things moved along, in nature, in a smooth and orderly way which filled the hearts of the harassed people with the deepest gratitude; but at last the Twelve made the sun and moon stand still ten or twelve hours once, to accommodate a sheriff's posse who were trying to exterminate a troublesome band of tramps. The result was frightful. The tides of the ocean being released from the moon's control, burst in one mighty assault upon the shores of all the continents and islands of the globe and swept millions of human beings to instant death. The Savior and the disciples, being warned by friends, fled to the woods, but they were hunted down, one after the other, by the maddened populace, and crucified. With the exception of St. Talmage. For services rendered the detectives, he was paid thirty pieces of silver[5] and his life spared. Thus ended the Second Advent, A.D. 1881.

[1881/1972]

Appendix

Mark Twain not only told stories, he wrote about how to tell them and left information that bears on his techniques of composition. Although Twain's genius is inimitable and the essence of his artistry a unique complex of mental processes, an elusive and untransmittable mystery that lies buried with him, we can at least approach that mystery if not solve it. So although the three items in this appendix do not explain his genius, they at least cast light on it. One thing they all have in common is that they show that he was a conscious artist. He paid attention to his craft and to his audience; he had a marvelous and uncanny sense of the way his words would be received, and because he was a master of the language he chose those words with great care. At the height of his powers he wrote: "The difference between the *almost*-right word & the *right* word is really a large matter—it's the difference between the lightning-bug & the lightning."

The first of the appendix selections is the October 5, 1877, *Detroit Free Press* version of a reporter-stenographer's transcript of a talk Twain gave in Massachusetts that was printed in the *Boston Post* and subsequently reprinted all over the country for the next few months as newspaper exchanges (the *San Jose Pioneer* copied it in its issue of December 29, 1877, and Paul Fatout has a similar version in his book *Mark Twain Speaking*). It is a case in point of how difficult it is to depend on Twain's recollections for an accurate account of his life. It seems to be his first public mention of his Civil War experience. In keeping with the jovial mood of the occasion for which it was prepared, it narrates only humorous incidents and is composed for oral delivery. Comparing it, therefore, with "The Private History of a Campaign That Failed," which was written eight years later and was meant to be read, we see that there are a number of differences between the two accounts, particularly the major one of the inclusion of the fatal ambush in the later piece. Both cannot be complete and true accounts of the incident. If the talk omits essential details, the essay restores them; if those details in the essay are fictitious, then the talk is more accurate. The two pieces were prepared for different although partly overlapping purposes. In both pieces the hand of an artist is apparent, but in the absence of specific biographical facts not only is it impossible to determine which one is the story, it is possible that both were made up.

The second piece, dating from 1894, is the "Private History of the 'Jumping Frog' Story." It is interesting on the face of it, but the "deliciously exact" resemblances of Twain's story and the Greek version Professor Van Dyke of Princeton sent him were not accidental. According to Professor Louis J. Budd, the Greek story was really his own, translated and adapted by Arthur Sidgwick for inclusion in his book *Introduction to Greek Composition, with Exercises.* Van Dyke apparently mistakenly assumed that a story in a book on ancient Greek would have been authentic and so precipitated Twain into analyzing the translation and noting the exact features that he himself had established in the original. It is an instructive case of Twain's recognizing his own hand.

The piece also has a literal retranslation into English of a French translation of the "Jumping Frog." Twain pretends that the French version is defective as a story, but he knows full well the limits of translation, especially of literal translation, and has fun with the translation exercise. In 1880 he appended to *A Tramp Abroad* what became a famous set piece, his essay on "The Awful German Language." In that essay he made the same sort of fun with untranslatable idioms and gender differences between the two languages. After that, in 1883, he provided an introduction to *The New Guide of the Conversation in Portuguese and English* by Pedro Carolino. He finds that book full of "miraculous stupidities" by the author, who honestly and in good faith but erroneously "believed he knew something of the English language." To Twain the book is *perfect* as an example of "unconscious ridiculousness." Apart from the fun of critiquing the French translation, therefore, this second item shows Twain fully aware of the nuances of language and narration, both deliberate and accidental, that make one version of a story immortal and forever fresh and another dead at birth.

"How to Tell a Story" (1895), the third item, includes his famous distinction between the humorous, the comic, and the witty story. Again, this essay concentrates not on the substance of a story but on its manner of delivery, the techniques the narrator uses to make his story successful, even down to the use of the pause, of which Twain was a master. Two anecdotes and one favorite story of his, "The Golden Arm" (which Pascal Covici, Jr., dates in print to 1888), are included in the essay as illustrations of his points.

A good lesson should be entertaining as well as instructive. Twain's comments on the process of writing succeed on both counts.

War Times

Mark Twain's Speech at a Hartford Banquet—The Terrible Tramping His Company Had to Do for Liberty

On Tuesday the Ancient and Honorable Artillery Company held their second day's parade at Hartford, Connecticut, and in the evening a banquet refreshed the warriors who "shouldered their crutches and showed how fields were won." Mark Twain gave an account of how he won a great number of fields by hurriedly tramping over them. His speech is thus reported by the Boston Post:

I wouldn't have missed being here for a good deal. The last time I had the privilege of breaking bread with soldiers was some years ago with the oldest military organization in England, the Ancient and Honorable Artillery Company of London, somewhere about its six hundredth anniversary: and now I have enjoyed this privilege with its eldest child, the oldest military organization in America, the Ancient and Honorable Artillery Company of Massachusetts, on this their two hundred and fortieth anniversary. Fine old stock, both of you; and if you fight as well as you feed, God protect the enemy. I did not assemble at the hotel parlors to day to be received by a committee as a mere civilian guest. No; I assembled at the headquarters of the Putnam Phalanx and insisted upon my right to be escorted to this place as one of the military guests. For I, too, am a soldier. I am inured to war. I have a military history. I have been through a stirring campaign, and there is not even a mention of it in any history of the United States or of the Southern Confederacy. To such lengths can the envy and malignity of the historian go. I will unbosom myself here, where I cannot but find sympathy. I will tell you about it and appeal through you to justice. In the earliest summer days of the war, I slipped out of Hannibal, Missouri, by night, with a friend, and joined a detachment of the rebel General Tom Harris' army, up a gorge behind an old barn in Ralls County. Col. Ralls, of Mexican war celebrity, swore us in. He made us swear to uphold the flag and Constitution of the United States, and to destroy every other military organization that we caught doing the same thing, which being interpreted means that we were to repel invasion. Well, you see this mixed us. We couldn't really tell which side we were on. But we went into camp and left it to the God of battles. For that was the term then. I was made Second Lieutenant and Chief Mogul of a company of eleven men who knew nothing about war—nor anything, for we had no captain. My friend, who was nineteen years old, six feet high, three feet wide and some distance through and just out of the infant school, was made orderly sergeant. His name was Ben Tupper. He had a hard time. When he was mounted, and on the march, he used to go to sleep, and his horse would reach around to bite him on the leg, and then he would wake up and cry and curse and want to go home. The other men pestered him a good deal, too. When they were dismounted they said they couldn't march in double file with him because his feet took up so much room. One night, when we were around the camp-fire, some fellow on the outside in the cold said: "Ben Tupper, put down that newspaper; it throws the whole place into twilight and casts a shadow like a blank." Ben said: "I ain't got any newspaper." Then the other fellow said: "Oh I see; 'twas your ear." We all slept in a corn crib; on the corn, and the rats were very thick. Ben Tupper had been carefully and rightly reared, and when he was ready for bed he would start to pray and a rat would bite him in the heel. And then he would sit up and swear all night and keep everybody awake. He was town-bred and did not seem to have any correct idea of military discipline. If I commanded him to shut up he would say: "Who was your nigger last year?" One evening I ordered him to ride out about three miles on picket duty to the beginning of a prairie. Said he: "What, in the night, and them blamed Union soldiers likely to be prowling around there any time?" So he wouldn't go, and the next morning I ordered him again. Said he: "In the rain? I think I see myself!" He didn't go. Next day I ordered him on picket duty once more. This time he looked hurt. Said he: "What, on Sunday; you must be a d——d fool." Well, picketing might have been a very good thing, but I saw it was impracticable, so I dropped it from my military system. We had a good enough time there at the barn, barring the rats and the musquitoes and the rain. We levied on both parties impartially, and both parties hated us impartially. But one day we heard that the invader was approaching. So we had to pack up and move, of course, and within twenty-four hours he was coming again. So we moved again. Next day he was after us once more. Well, we didn't like it much—but we moved—rather than make trouble. And this went on for a week or ten days, and we saw considerable scenery. Then Ben Tupper's patience was lost. Said he: "War is not what it's cracked up to be. I'm going home if I can't ever git a chance to sit down a minute. Why do these people keep us humpin' around so? Blame their skins, do they think this is an excursion?"

Some of the other town boys got to grumbling. They complained that there was an insufficiency of umbrellas. So I sent around to the farmers and borrowed what I could. Then they complained that the Worcestershire sauce was out. There was mutiny and dissatisfaction all around, and of course, at such a time as this the invader must come around pestering us again; as much as two hours before breakfast, too, when no one wanted to turn out, of course. This was carrying the thing too far. The whole command felt insulted. I detached one of my aides and sent him to the brigadier and asked him to assign us a district where there wasn't so much bother going on. The history of our campaign was laid before him; but instead of being touched by it, what did he do? He sent back an indignant message and said: "You have had a dozen chances inside of two weeks to capture the enemy and he is still at large. (Well, we knew that!) Stay where you are this time or I will court-martial and hang the whole of you." Well, I submitted this brutal message to my battalion and asked their advice. Said the Orderly Sergeant: "If Tom Harris wants the enemy, let him come here and get him. I ain't got any use for my share, and who's Tom Harris anyway, I'd like to know, that's putting on so many frills. Why, I knew him when he wasn't anything but a darned telegraph operator. Gentlemen you can do as you choose. As for me, I've got enough of this sashaying around so's't you can't get a chance to pray, because the time is all required for cussing, so off goes my war-paint. You hear me!" The whole regiment said with one voice, "That's the talk for me." So there and then, on the spot, my brigade disbanded itself and tramped off home, with me in the tail of it. I hung up my own sword and returned to the arts of peace, and there were people who said I hadn't been absent from them yet. We were the first men that went into the service in Missouri; we were the first that went out of it anywhere. This, gentlemen, is the history of the part which my division took in the great rebellion, and such is the military record of its Commander-in-Chief, and this is the first time that the deeds of those warriors have been brought officially to the notice of humanity. Treasure these things in your hearts. And so shall the detectives and truculent historians of this land be brought to shame and confusion. I ask you to fill your glasses and drink with me to the reverent memory of the orderly sergeant and those other neglected and forgotten heroes, my footsore and travel-stained paladins who were first in war, first in peace and were not idle during the interval that lay between.

[1877]

Private History of the "Jumping Frog" Story

Five or six years ago a lady from Finland asked me to tell her a story in our negro dialect, so that she could get an idea of what that variety of speech was like. I told her one of Hopkinson Smith's negro stories, and gave her a copy of *Harper's Monthly* containing it. She translated it for a Swedish newspaper, but by an oversight named me as the author of it instead of Smith. I was very sorry for that, because I got a good lashing in the Swedish press, which would have fallen to his share but for that mistake; for it was shown that Boccaccio had told that very story, in his curt and meagre fashion, five hundred years before Smith took hold of it and made a good and tellable thing out of it.

I have always been sorry for Smith. But my own turn has come now. A few weeks ago Professor Van Dyke, of Princeton, asked this question:

"Do you know how old your Jumping Frog story is?"

And I answered:

"Yes—forty-five years. The thing happened in Calaveras County in the spring of 1849."

"No; it happened earlier—a couple of thousand years earlier; it is a Greek story."

I was astonished—and hurt. I said:

"I am willing to be a literary thief if it has been so ordained; I am even willing to be caught robbing the ancient dead alongside of Hopkinson Smith, for he is my friend and a good fellow, and I think would be as honest as any one if he could do it without occasioning remark; but I am not willing to antedate his crimes by fifteen hundred years. I must ask you to knock off part of that."

But the professor was not chaffing; he was in earnest, and could not abate a century. He named the Greek author, and offered to get the book and send it to me and the college text-book containing the English translation also. I thought I would like the translation best, because Greek makes me tired. January 30th he sent me the English version, and I will presently insert it in this article. It is my Jumping Frog tale in every essential. It is not strung out as I have strung it out, but it is all there.

To me this is very curious and interesting. Curious for several reasons. For instance:

I heard the story told by a man who was not telling it to his hearers as a thing new to them, but as a thing which *they had witnessed and would remember.* He was a dull person, and ignorant; he had no gift as a story-teller, and no invention; in his mouth this episode was merely history—history and statistics; and the gravest sort of history, too; he was entirely serious, for he was dealing with what to him were austere facts, and they interested him solely because they *were* facts; he was drawing on his memory, not his mind; he saw no humor in his tale, neither did his listeners; neither he nor they ever smiled or laughed; in my time I have not attended a more solemn conference. To him and to his fellow gold-miners there were just two things in the story that were worth considering. One was the smartness of its hero, Jim Smiley, in taking the stranger in with a loaded frog; and the other was Smiley's deep knowledge of a frog's nature—for he knew (as the narrator asserted and the listeners conceded) that a frog *likes shot* and is always ready to eat it. Those men discussed those two points, and those only. They were hearty in their admiration of them, and none of the party was aware that a first-rate story had been told in a first-rate way, and that it was brimful of a quality whose presence they never suspected—humor.

Now, then, the interesting question is, *did* the frog episode happen in Angel's Camp in the spring of '49, as told in my hearing that day in the fall of 1865? I am perfectly sure that it did. I am also sure that its duplicate happened in Bœotia a couple of thousand years ago. I think it must be a case of history actually repeating itself, and not a case of a good story floating down the ages and surviving because too good to be allowed to perish.

I would now like to have the reader examine the Greek story and the story told by the dull and solemn Californian, and observe how exactly alike they are in essentials.

[Translation]

The Athenian and the Frog*

An Athenian once fell in with a Bœotian who was sitting by the roadside looking at a frog. Seeing the other approach, the Bœotian said his was a remarkable frog, and asked if he would agree to start a contest of frogs, on condition that he whose frog jumped farthest should receive a large sum of money. The Athenian replied that he would if the other would fetch him a frog, for the lake was near. To this he agreed, and when he was gone the Athenian took the frog, and, opening its mouth, poured some stones into its stomach, so that it did not indeed seem larger than before, but could not jump. The Bœotian soon returned with the other frog, and the contest began. The second frog first was pinched, and jumped moderately; then they pinched the Bœotian frog. And he gathered himself for a leap, and used the utmost effort, but he could not move his body the least. So the Athenian departed with the money. When he was gone the Bœotian, wondering what was the matter with the frog, lifted him up and examined him. And being turned upside down, he opened his mouth and vomited out the stones.

And here is the way it happened in California:

From "The Celebrated Jumping Frog of Calaveras County"

Well, thish-yer Smiley had rat-tarriers, and chicken cocks, and tomcats, and all them kind of things, till you couldn't rest, and you couldn't fetch nothing for him to bet on but he'd match you. He ketched a frog one day, and took him home, and said he cal'lated to educate him; and so he never done nothing for three months but set in his back yard and learn that frog to jump. And you bet you he *did* learn him, too. He'd give him a little punch behind, and the next minute you'd see that frog whirling in the air like a doughnut—see him turn one summerset, or maybe a couple if he got a good start, and come down flat-footed and all right, like a cat. He got him up so in the matter of ketching flies, and kep' him in practice so constant, that he'd nail a fly every time as fur as he could see him. Smiley said all a frog wanted was education, and he could do 'most anything—and I believe him. Why, I've seen him set Dan'l Webster down here on this floor—Dan'l Webster was the name of the frog—and sing out "Flies, Dan'l, flies!" and quicker'n you could wink he'd spring straight up and snake a fly off'n the counter there, and flop down on the floor ag'in as solid as a gob of mud, and fall to scratching the side of his head with his hind foot as indifferent as if he hadn't no idea he'd been doin' any more'n any frog might do. You never see a frog so modest and straightfor'ard as he was, for all he was so gifted.

*Sidgwick, *Greek Prose Composition*, page 116.

And when it come to fair and square jumping on a dead level, he could get over more ground at one straddle than any animal of his breed you ever see. Jumping on a dead level was his strong suit, you understand; and when it came to that, Smiley would ante up money on him as long as he had a red. Smiley was monstrous proud of his frog, and well he might be, for fellers that had travelled and been everywheres all said he laid over any frog that ever *they* see.

Well, Smiley kep' the beast in a little lattice box, and he used to fetch him down-town sometimes and lay for a bet. One day a feller—a stranger in the camp, he was—come acrost him with his box, and says:

"What might it be that you've got in the box?"

And Smiley says, sorter indifferent-like, "It might be a parrot, or it might be a canary, maybe, but it ain't—it's only just a frog."

And the feller took it, and looked at it careful, and turned it round this way and that, and says, "H'm—so 'tis. Well, what's *he* good for?"

"Well," Smiley says, easy and careless, "he's good enough for *one* thing, I should judge—he can outjump any frog in Calaveras County."

The feller took the box again and took another long, particular look, and give it back to Smiley and says, very deliberate, "Well," he says, "I don't see no p'ints about that frog that's any better'n any other frog."

"Maybe you don't," Smiley says. "Maybe you understand frogs and maybe you don't understand 'em; maybe you've had experience, and maybe you ain't only a amature, as it were. Anyways, I've got *my* opinion, and I'll resk forty dollars that he can outjump any frog in Calaveras County."

And the feller studies a minute, and then says, kinder sad like, "Well, I'm only a stranger here, and I ain't got no frog, but if I had a frog I'd bet you."

And then Smiley says: "That's all right—that's all right—if you'll hold my box a minute, I'll go and get you a frog." And so the feller took the box and put up his forty dollars along with Smiley's and set down to wait.

So he set there a good while thinking and thinking to hisself, and then he got the frog out and prized his mouth open and took a teaspoon and filled him full of quail shot—filled him pretty near up to his chin—and set him on the floor. Smiley he went to the swamp and slopped around in the mud for a long time, and finally he ketched a frog and fetched him in and give him to this feller, and says:

"Now, if you're ready, set him alongside of Dan'l, with his fore-paws just even with Dan'l's, and I'll give the word." Then he says, "One—two—three—*git!*" and him and the feller touched up the frogs from behind, and the new frog hopped off lively; but Dan'l give a heave, and hysted up his shoulders—so—like a Frenchman, but it warn't no use—he couldn't budge; he was planted as solid as a church, and he couldn't no more stir than if he was anchored out. Smiley was a good deal surprised, and he was disgusted, too, but he didn't have no idea what the matter was, of course.

The feller took the money and started away; and when he was going out at the door he sorter jerked his thumb over his shoulder—so—at Dan'l, and says again, very deliberate: "Well," he says, "*I* don't see no p'ints about that frog that's any better'n any other frog."

Smiley he stood scratching his head and looking down at Dan'l a long time, and at last he says, "I do wonder what in the nation that frog throw'd off for—I wonder if there ain't something the matter with him—he 'pears to look mighty baggy, somehow." And he ketched Dan'l by the nap of the neck, and hefted him, and says, "Why, blame my cats if he don't weigh five pound!" and turned him upside down, and he belched out a double handful of shot. And then he see how it was, and he was the maddest man—he set the frog down and took out after that feller, but he never ketched him.

The resemblances are deliciously exact. There you have the wily Bœotian and the wily Jim Smiley waiting—two thousand years apart—and waiting, each equipped with his frog and "laying" for the stranger. A contest is proposed—for money. The Athenian would take a chance "if the other would fetch him a frog"; the Yankee says: "I'm only a stranger here, and I ain't got no frog, but if I had a frog I'd bet you." The wily Bœotian and the wily Californian, with that vast gulf of two thousand years between, retire eagerly and go frogging in the marsh; the Athenian and the Yankee remain behind and work a base advantage, the one with pebbles, the other with shot. Presently the contest began. In the one case "they pinched the Bœotian frog"; in the other, "him and the feller touched up the frogs from behind." The Bœotian frog "gathered himself for a leap" (you can just *see* him!), but "could not move his body the least"; the Californian frog "give a heave, but it warn't no use—he couldn't budge." In both the ancient and the modern cases the strangers departed with the money. The Bœotian and the Californian wonder what is the matter with their frogs; they lift them and examine; they turn them upside down and out spills the informing ballast.

Yes, the resemblances are curiously exact. I used to tell the story of the Jumping Frog in San Francisco, and presently Artemus Ward came along and wanted it to help fill out a little book which he was about to publish; so I wrote it out and sent it to his publisher, Carleton; but Carleton thought the book had enough matter in it, so he gave the story to Henry Clapp as a present, and Clapp put it in his *Saturday Press,* and it killed that paper with a suddenness that was beyond praise. At least the paper died with that issue, and none but envious people have ever tried to rob me of the honor and credit of killing it. The "Jumping Frog" was the first piece of writing of mine that spread itself through the newspapers and brought me into public notice. Consequently, the *Saturday Press* was a cocoon and I the worm in it; also, I was the gay-colored literary moth which its death set free. This simile has been used before.

Early in '66 the "Jumping Frog" was issued in book form, with other sketches of mine. A year or two later Madame Blanc translated it into French and published it in the *Revue des Deux Mondes*, but the result was not what should have been expected, for the *Revue* struggled along and pulled through, and is alive yet. I think the fault must have been in the translation. I ought to have translated it myself. I think so because I examined into the matter and finally retranslated the sketch from the French back into English, to see what the trouble was; that is, to see just what sort of a focus the French people got upon it. Then the mystery was explained. In French the story is too confused, and chaotic, and unreposeful, and ungrammatical, and insane; consequently it could only cause grief and sickness—it could not kill. A glance at my re-translation will show the reader that this must be true.

[My Retranslation]

The Frog Jumping of the County of Calaveras

Eh bien! this Smiley nourished some terriers à rats, and some cocks of combat, and some cats, and all sort of things; and with his rage of betting one no had more of repose. He trapped one day a frog and him imported with him (et l'emporta chez lui) saying that he pretended to make his education. You me believe if you will, but during three months he not has nothing done but to him apprehend to jump (apprendre a sauter) in a court retired of her mansion (de sa maison). And I you respond that he have succeeded. He him gives a small blow by behind, and the instant after you shall see the frog turn in the air like a grease-biscuit, make one summersault, sometimes two, when she was well started, and re-fall upon his feet like a cat. He him had accomplished in the art of to gobble the flies (gober des mouches), and him there exercised continually—so well that a fly at the most far that she appeared was a fly lost. Smiley had custom to say that all which lacked to a frog it was the education, but with the education she could do nearly all—and I him believe. Tenez, I him have seen pose Daniel Webster there upon this plank—Daniel Webster was the name of the frog—and to him sing, "Some flies, Daniel, some flies!"—in a flash of the eye Daniel had bounded and seized a fly here upon the counter, then jumped anew at the earth, where he rested truly to himself scratch the head with his behind-foot, as if he no had not the least idea of his superiority. Never you not have seen frog as modest, as natural, sweet as she was. And when he himself agitated to jump purely and simply upon plain earth, she does more ground in one jump than any beast of his species than you can know.

To jump plain—this was his strong. When he himself agitated for that Smiley multiplied the bets upon her as long as there to him remained a red. It must to know, Smiley was monstrously proud of his frog, and he of it was right, for some men who were travelled, who had all seen, said that they to him would be injurious to him compare to another frog. Smiley guarded Daniel in a little box latticed which he carried bytimes to the village for some bet.

One day an individual stranger at the camp him arrested with his box and him said:

"What is this that you have then shut up there within?"

Smiley said, with an air indifferent:

"That could be a paroquet, or a syringe (*ou un serin*), but this no is nothing of such, it not is but a frog."

The individual it took, it regarded with care, it turned from one side and from the other, then he said:

"*Tiens!* in effect!—At what is she good?"

"My God!" respond Smiley, always with an air disengaged, "she is good for one thing, to my notice (*à mon avis*), she can batter in jumping (*elle peut batter en sautant*) all frogs of the county of Calaveras."

The individual re-took the box, it examined of new longly, and it rendered to Smiley in saying with an air deliberate:

"*Eh bien!* I no saw not that that frog had nothing of better than each frog." *(Je ne vois pas que cette grenouille ait rien de mieux qu'aucune grenouille)*. [If that isn't grammar gone to seed, then I count myself no judge.—M. T.]

"Possible that you not it saw not," said Smiley, "possible that you—you comprehend frogs; possible that you not you there comprehend nothing; possible that you had of the experience, and possible that you not be but an amateur. Of all manner (*De toute manière*) I bet forty dollars that she batter in jumping no matter which frog of the county of Calaveras."

The individual reflected a second, and said like sad:

"I not am but a stranger here, I no have not a frog; but if I of it had one, I would embrace the bet."

"Strong, well!" respond Smiley; "nothing of more facility. If you will hold my box a minute, I go you to search a frog (*j'irai vous chercher*)."

Behold, then, the individual, who guards the box, who puts his forty dollars upon those of Smiley, and who attends (*et qui attend*). He attended enough longtimes, reflecting all solely. And figure you that he takes Daniel, him opens the mouth by force and with a teaspoon him fills with shot of the hunt, even him fills just to the chin, then he him puts by the earth. Smiley during these times was at slopping in a swamp. Finally he trapped (*attrape*) a frog, him carried to that individual, and said:

"Now if you be ready, put him all against Daniel, with their before-feet upon the same line, and I give the signal"—then he added: "One, two, three—advance!"

Him and the individual touched their frogs by behind, and the frog new put to jump smartly, but Daniel himself lifted ponderously, exalted the shoulders thus, like a Frenchman—to what good? he could not budge, he is planted solid like a church, he not advance no more than if one him had put at the anchor.

Smiley was surprised and disgusted, but he not himself doubted not of the turn being intended (*mais il ne se doutait pas du tour bien entendu*). The individual empocketed the silver, himself with it went, and of it himself in going is that he no gives not a jerk of thumb over the shoulder—like that—at the poor Daniel, in saying with his air deliberate—(*L'individu empoche l'argent s'en va et en s'en allant est ce qu'il ne donne pas un coup de pouce par-dessus l'épaule, comme ça, au pauvre Daniel, en disant de son air délibéré.*)

"Eh bien! *I no see not that that frog has nothing of better than another.*"

Smiley himself scratched longtimes the head, the eyes fixed upon Daniel, until that which at last he said:

"I me demand how the devil it makes itself that this beast has refused. Is it that she had something? One would believe that she is stuffed."

He grasped Daniel by the skin of the neck, him lifted and said:

"The wolf me bite if he no weigh not five pounds."

He him reversed and the unhappy belched two handfuls of shot (*et le malheureux,* etc.).—When Smiley recognized how it was, he was like mad. He deposited his frog by the earth and ran after that individual, but he not him caught never.

It may be that there are people who can translate better than I can, but I am not acquainted with them.

So ends the private and public history of the Jumping Frog of Calaveras County, an incident which has this unique feature about it—that it is both old and new, a "chestnut" and not a "chestnut"; for it was original when it happened two thousand years ago, and was again original when it happened in California in our own time.

[1894]

How to Tell a Story

The Humorous Story an American Development—Its Difference from Comic and Witty Stories

I do not claim that I can tell a story as it ought to be told. I only claim to know how a story ought to be told, for I have been almost daily in the company of the most expert story-tellers for many years.

There are several kinds of stories, but only one difficult kind—the humorous. I will talk mainly about that one. The humorous story is American, the comic story is English, the witty story is French. The humorous story depends for its effect upon the *manner* of the telling; the comic story and the witty story upon the *matter*.

The humorous story may be spun out to great length, and may wander around as much as it pleases, and arrive nowhere in particular; but the comic and witty stories must be brief and end with a point. The humorous story bubbles gently along, the others burst.

The humorous story is strictly a work of art—high and delicate art—and only an artist can tell it; but no art is necessary in telling the comic and the witty story; anybody can do it. The art of telling a humorous story—understand, I mean by word of mouth, not print—was created in America, and has remained at home.

The humorous story is told gravely; the teller does his best to conceal the fact that he even dimly suspects that there is anything funny about it; but the teller of the comic story tells you beforehand that it is one of the funniest things he has ever heard, then tells it with eager delight, and is the first person to laugh when he gets through. And sometimes, if he has had good success, he is so glad and happy that he will repeat the "nub" of it and glance around from face to face, collecting applause, and then repeat it again. It is a pathetic thing to see.

Very often, of course, the rambling and disjointed humorous story finishes with a nub, point, snapper, or whatever you like to call it. Then the listener must be alert, for in many cases the teller will divert attention from that nub by dropping it in a carefully casual and indifferent way, with the pretence that he does not know it is a nub.

Artemus Ward used that trick a good deal; then when the belated audience presently caught the joke he would look up with innocent surprise, as if wondering what they had found to laugh at. Dan Setchell used it before him, Nye and Riley and others use it to-day.

But the teller of the comic story does not slur the nub; he shouts it at you—every time. And when he prints it, in England, France, Germany, and Italy, he italicizes it, puts some whooping exclamation-points after it, and sometimes explains it in a parenthesis. All of which is very depressing, and makes one want to renounce joking and lead a better life.

Let me set down an instance of the comic method, using an anecdote which has been popular all over the world for twelve or fifteen hundred years. The teller tells it in this way:

THE WOUNDED SOLDIER

In the course of a certain battle a soldier whose leg had been shot off appealed to another soldier who was hurrying by to carry him to the rear, informing him at the same time of the loss which he had sustained; whereupon the generous son of Mars, shouldering the unfortunate, proceeded to carry out his desire. The bullets and cannon-balls were flying in all directions, and presently one of the latter took the wounded man's head off—without, however, his deliverer being aware of it. In no long time he was hailed by an officer, who said:

"Where are you going with that carcass?"

"To the rear, sir—he's lost his leg!"

"His leg, forsooth?" responded the astonished officer; "you mean his head, you booby."

Whereupon the soldier dispossessed himself of his burden, and stood looking down upon it in great perplexity. At length he said:

"It is true, sir, just as you have said." Then after a pause he added, "*But he* TOLD *me* IT WAS HIS LEG!!!!!"

—

Here the narrator bursts into explosion after explosion of thunderous horse-laughter, repeating that nub from time to time through his gaspings and shriekings and suffocatings.

It takes only a minute and a half to tell that in its comic-story form; and isn't worth the telling, after all. Put into the humorous-story form it takes ten minutes, and is about the funniest thing I have ever listened to—as James Whitcomb Riley tells it.

He tells it in the character of a dull-witted old farmer who has just heard it for the first time, thinks it is unspeakably funny, and is trying to repeat it to a neighbor. But he can't remember it; so he gets all mixed up and wanders helplessly round and round, putting in tedious details that don't belong in the tale and only retard it; taking them out conscientiously and putting in others that are just as useless; making minor mistakes now and then and stopping to correct them and explain how he came to make them; remembering things which he forgot to put in in their proper place and going back to put them in there; stopping his narrative a good while in order to try to recall the name of the soldier that was hurt, and finally remembering that the soldier's name was not mentioned, and remarking placidly that the name is of no real importance, anyway—better, of course, if one knew it, but not essential, after all—and so on, and so on, and so on.

The teller is innocent and happy and pleased with himself, and has to stop every little while to hold himself in and keep from laughing outright; and does hold in, but his body quakes in a jelly-like way with interior chuckles; and at the end of the ten minutes the audience have laughed until they are exhausted, and the tears are running down their faces.

The simplicity and innocence and sincerity and unconsciousness of the old farmer are perfectly simulated, and the result is a performance which is thoroughly charming and delicious. This is art—and fine and beautiful, and only a master can compass it; but a machine could tell the other story.

To string incongruities and absurdities together in a wandering and sometimes purposeless way, and seem innocently unaware that they are absurdities, is the basis of the American art, if my position is correct. Another feature is the slurring of the point. A third is the dropping of a studied remark apparently without knowing it, as if one were thinking aloud. The fourth and last is the pause.

Artemus Ward dealt in numbers three and four a good deal. He would begin to tell with great animation something which he seemed to think was wonderful; then lose confidence, and after an apparently absentminded pause add an incongruous remark in a soliloquizing way; and that was the remark intended to explode the mine—and it did.

For instance, he would say eagerly, excitedly, "I once knew a man in

New Zealand who hadn't a tooth in his head"—here his animation would die out; a silent, reflective pause would follow, then he would say dreamily, and as if to himself, "and yet that man could beat a drum better than any man I ever saw."

The pause is an exceedingly important feature in any kind of story, and a frequently recurring feature, too. It is a dainty thing, and delicate, and also uncertain and treacherous; for it must be exactly the right length—no more and no less—or it fails of its purpose and makes trouble. If the pause is too short the impressive point is passed, and the audience have had time to divine that a surprise is intended—and then you can't surprise them, of course.

On the platform I used to tell a negro ghost story that had a pause in front of the snapper on the end, and that pause was the most important thing in the whole story. If I got it the right length precisely, I could spring the finishing ejaculation with effect enough to make some impressible girl deliver a startled little yelp and jump out of her seat—and that was what I was after. This story was called "The Golden Arm," and was told in this fashion. You can practise with it yourself—and mind you look out for the pause and get it right.

THE GOLDEN ARM

Once 'pon a time dey wuz a monsus mean man, en he live 'way out in de prairie all 'lone by hisself, 'cep'n he had a wife. En bimeby she died, en he tuck en toted her way out dah in de prairie en buried her. Well, she had a golden arm—all solid gold, fum de shoulder down. He wuz pow'ful mean—pow'ful; en dat night he couldn't sleep, caze he want dat golden arm so bad.

When it come midnight he couldn't stan' it no mo'; so he git up, he did, en tuck his lantern en shoved out thoo de storm en dug her up en got de golden arm; en he bent his head down 'gin de win', en plowed en plowed en plowed thoo de snow. Den all on a sudden he stop (make a considerable pause here, and look startled, and take a listening attitude) en say: "My *lan'*, what's dat!"

En he listen—en listen—en de win' say (set your teeth together and imitate the wailing and wheezing singsong of the wind), "Bzzz-z-zzz"—en den, way back yonder whah de grave is, he hear a *voice*!—he hear a voice all mix' up in de win'—can't hardly tell 'em 'part—"Bzzz-zzz—W-h-o—g-o-t—m-y—g-o-l-d-e-n *arm*?—zzz—zzz—W-h-o g-o-t m-y g-o-l-d-e-n *arm*? (You must begin to shiver violently now.)

En he begin to shiver en shake, en say, "Oh, my! *Oh,* my lan'!" en de win' blow de lantern out, en de snow en sleet blow in his face en mos' choke him, en he start a-plowin' knee-deep towards home mos' dead, he so sk'yerd—en pooty soon he hear de voice agin, en (pause) it 'us comin' *after* him! "Bzzz—zzz—zzz—W-h-o—g-o-t—m-y—g-o-l-d-e-n—*arm?*"

When he git to de pasture he hear it agin—closter now, en a-*comin'*!—a-comin' back dah in de dark en de storm—(repeat the wind and the voice). When he git to de house he rush up-stairs en jump in de bed en kiver up, head and years, en lay dah shiverin' en shakin'—en den way out dah he hear it *agin*!—en a-*comin'*! En bimeby he hear (pause—awed, listening attitude)—pat—pat—pat—*hit's a-comin' up-stairs*! Den he hear de latch, en he *know* it's in de room!

Den pooty soon he know it's a-*stannin' by de bed*! (Pause.) Den—he know it's a-*bendin' down over him*—en he cain't skasely git his breath! Den—den—he seem to feel someth'n *c-o-l-d,* right down 'most agin his head! (Pause.)

Den de voice say, *right at his year*—"W-h-o—g-o-t—m-y—g-o-l-d-e-n *arm?*" (You must wail it out very plaintively and accusingly; then you stare steadily and impressively into the face of the farthest-gone auditor—a girl, preferably—and let that awe-inspiring pause begin to build itself in the deep hush. When it has reached exactly the right length, jump suddenly at that girl and yell, "*You've* got it!"

If you've got the *pause* right, she'll fetch a dear little yelp and spring right out of her shoes. But you *must* get the pause right; and you will find it the most troublesome and aggravating and uncertain thing you ever undertook.)

[1895]

Notes

Jim Smiley and His Jumping Frog

The brilliance of this story may be appreciated when it is considered as an intricate nest of hoaxes, one inside the other. The outer and most obvious one is on Jim Smiley, but other hoaxes are played on his "fifteen-minute nag," his bull-pup, Andrew Jackson, his frog, Dan'l Webster, and ultimately on the letter-writer narrator, who seems not to understand what has happened and is in doubt whether or not he was outwitted by the seemingly simple Simon Wheeler. Twain picked up the germ of the story from Ben Coon, an inhabitant of the gold-mining community of Angel's Camp, California, which Twain visited from December 1864 to February 1865. Coon told the original version apparently without an idea of its humorous potential. Twain supplied that. This story is also notable for being possibly the first appearance of the "mysterious stranger" motif, which recurs throughout Twain's canon and is always ominous.

1. *Mr. A. Ward:* a reference to Artemus Ward, who visited Virginia City, Nevada Territory, in December 1863. Ward, already a nationally known humorist, and Twain immediately hit it off. Ward had perfected a style of surreptitiously pursuing a thematic line in a droll and seemingly rambling assemblage of comments. Twain recognized what Ward was doing, was captivated by it, and soon assimilated it. The "Jumping Frog" was Twain's response to a letter from Ward soliciting a contribution to a book he was preparing. The story arrived too late for Ward's book, but he passed it on to New York's *Saturday Press* magazine, which published it. It was an immediate success and was widely copied, launching Twain into his writing career.
2. *tuned:* I wish to gratefully acknowledge the advice of Dr. Robert Hirst, editor of the Mark Twain Papers, who informed me of this corrected

replacement for the word *turned* in the otherwise standard text of the story in *Early Tales & Sketches,* vol. 2.

THE STORY OF THE BAD LITTLE BOY WHO DIDN'T COME TO GRIEF

Also known by its alternate titles, "The Story of the Bad Little Boy That Bore a Charmed Life" and "Story of the Bad Little Boy," this story is obviously a parody of the moralistic tales promoted by Sunday schools. Beneath the humor is the clear implication that the Sunday-school tracts were, however well intentioned, hoaxes in that they induced children to believe in unrealistic and therefore false notions of morality.

CANNIBALISM IN THE CARS

Like "Jumping Frog," this tale had its genesis in somebody else's story, in this case a journalistic account Twain read in his brother's newspaper of a passenger train marooned for a week in an Illinois snowbank. Lighter than "A Modest Proposal," Swift's celebrated satire on the same subject, this story sidesteps explicitly naming cannibalism by a series of witty double-entendre circumlocutions and the briskly cheerful tone and urbanity of the stranger's narrative. A level of sharp satire in the story stems from its tongue-in-cheek description of what was really a savage struggle for survival and the way Robert's Rules of Order were ingeniously adapted by the survivors to their macabre political jockeying to formally and "democratically" select victims for eating. Twain drew upon his experience as a journalist covering Congress and, before that, the Nevada legislature, for his knowledge of parliamentary details.

A dimension of playfully grotesque humor is added to the story in the names, nominators or nominated, of the participators in the balloting. Five of the names are those of good friends of Twain's: Charles Langdon, his future brother-in-law; Daniel Slote and John A. Van Nostrand, companions on the Quaker City tour of Europe and the Near East; Samuel A. Bowen, a boyhood friend and steamboat pilot; and R. M. Howland. Other names are those of friends or acquaintances of Twain's from Missouri, Nevada, or Washington, D.C. John T. Morgan, for example, became an influential Democratic senator from Alabama.

1. *Relict:* another word for widow.

JOURNALISM IN TENNESSEE

Despite the title, Twain did not have any journalistic experience in Tennessee. But he did have a lot in Nevada and California, and some of it conformed to the vigorous and violent narrative of this story. Similarly satirical stories about mild editors in that rough-and-ready part of the Old West were written, among others, by Twain's western colleagues Ambrose Bierce and Joseph T. Goodman. The incongruity of murder and mayhem being committed by gentry in the name of high-mindedness is a phenomenon Twain pursued without humor in other works, for example, the feud between the Grangerfords and the Shepherdsons in chapter 18 of *Huckleberry Finn.*

1. *"old soldiers":* Discarded remnants of cigars and cigarettes.
2. *Nicholson pavement:* Wood blocks set upon a foundation of asphalt or packed sand.
3. *the fan-tods:* the fidgets.
4. *blacklegs:* swindling gamblers.

The Story of the Good Little Boy Who Did Not Prosper

Written five years after "The Story of the Bad Little Boy," and a counterpart of it, this tale continues Twain's ridicule of Sunday-school moral teachings. As with the earlier piece, this example of the humor of exaggeration also exemplifies Twain's serious purpose of approaching the truth by undermining falsehood.

How I Edited an Agricultural Paper Once

In its main effects, this story is easily appreciated for its choice comedy. The topic of ridiculous agricultural advice was further pursued by Twain in 1872 in chapter 70 of *Roughing It,* the gentle but hilarious double spoof of Horace Greeley's handwriting and his belief that he was an agricultural expert. A more serious turn is given to the story in its penultimate paragraph, when the narrator resigns with the seemingly absurd comment that it was "the first time I ever heard of a man's having to know anything in order to edit a newspaper." With that generalization, it becomes evident that Twain had the larger target of journalism in mind, and not just agricultural journalism.

Political Economy

This ironic tale has two readily identifiable morals: you still must pay attention to worldly affairs even if you prefer to devote yourself to abstract theory; and being overprepared is not necessarily a virtue. The supposed expertise of the narrator on the subject of political economy is called into question by his superficial grandiloquence and his inattention to practical details. Similarly, the expertise of the salesman on lightning rods is also phony, as shown by both his impressive but meaningless sales pitch and the empirical effects of his recommendations. As was the case with the story's direct ancestor, Artemus Ward's celebrated "Babes in the Woods" lecture, a good deal of its humor derives from the narrator always working up to address his professed topic but never actually saying anything about it.

1. coup d'oeil *and* coup d'état: An example of the salesman's glib and incorrect use of language, *coup d'oeil* means a quick glance, and *coup d'état* is a sudden use of force to effect a change of government. Ironically, although the sentence might conceivably relate to the narrator's topic of

political economy, it makes no sense applied to lightning rods; yet the narrator admires its showiness.

2. *dephlogistic:* Phlogiston was in ancient times believed to be the material essence of fire, but the notion was disproved and discarded by the development of modern chemistry. The salesman's use of this high-sounding but discredited term exposes his pitch as fraudulent.
3. *Fiat justitia . . . est.:* a gibberish of Latin and pseudo-Latin phrases.

A True Story, Repeated Word for Word as I Heard It

This is one of Twain's universally admired short works, particularly important as an indicator of his attitudes on race and slavery. Starting off in a seemingly comic and condescending mood, then changing quickly first to sentimentalism and next to shocking realism, the story at the end elevates Aunt Rachel to dignified and even heroic stature. Despite its claim in the title, Twain made extensive changes to the raw materials of the sketch and revised and polished it until it achieved not the literal word-for-word truth of dictation but the naked truth of slavery and the transcendent truth of the humanity of its victims.

1. *"Aunt Rachel":* That the name is in quotes is an indication that the protagonist was not literally rendered. The real-life model was ex-slave "Auntie" Mary Ann Cord, the cook of the Crane family of Elmira, New York. Twain's selection of Rachel for her fictional name was inspired, because for the first readers of this piece, a generation familiar with the Bible, the name would have evoked the apropos and moving verse from Jeremiah: "A voice was heard in Ramah, lamentation, *and* bitter weeping; Rachel weeping for her children refused to be comforted for her children, because they *were* not" (Jer. 31:15, King James).
2. *Misto C——:* a thinly disguised reference to Twain himself, as Mr. Clemens.

The Facts Concerning the Recent Carnival of Crime in Connecticut

Appearing relatively early in Twain's career, this tale is both very popular and sophisticated. At the literal level it is, of course, funny. At a deeper level it is a serious study of human nature and conscience. The story was almost certainly influenced by Edgar Allan Poe's "William Wilson," with which it has many affinities. Insofar as the conscience is "appointed by authority," it is an innate part of human nature. "Carnival of Crime" is thus an important statement by Twain of his ambivalence toward Calvinistic teachings. In this story humans are shown caught in a double-bind, lose-lose situation. Life can be constant torment with an active conscience, but without it people could quickly revert to their default nature of murderous impulses and damnable because unchecked behavior.

PUNCH, BROTHERS, PUNCH!

According to Louis Budd, the origin of this story, also known as "A Literary Nightmare," was a notice on a New York City trolley car: "The conductor, when he receives a fare, will immediately punch in the presence of the passenger." Two journalists turned the sentence into the very popular doggerel verse the story quotes.

Few readers of this amusing tale fail to find themselves unaffected by the hypnotic effect of the rhythmic jingle at its core. The story is therefore memorable, but it also might make readers aware of their susceptibility to becoming captivated, even by a nonsense rhyme. The story's conclusion achieves a wry and ironic dig at human nature when the narrator saves his friend's peace of mind by enabling him to transfer the curse of the unforgettable jingle to unsuspecting university students, and again when the narrator claims a noble motive when he warns readers of the jingle's spell—after he exposes them to it.

JIM BAKER'S BLUE-JAY YARN

Critics are divided over whether this yarn, which occupies part of chapter 2 and all of chapter 3 of the novel *A Tramp Abroad* (1880), can be legitimately separated from the novel as a stand-alone tale. No effort is being made here to resolve the issue, except to note that regardless of their stands on it, almost all critics recognize this as a superb humorous tale. Like "Jumping Frog," its source was a story Twain heard in the winter of 1864–65, when he was visiting miner friends in Calaveras County, California. Capitalizing on the oral origin of the story, Twain infused it with a double charm, the pleasure we get from the vernacular style of a master storyteller, and the story line itself. The "Blue-Jay Yarn" participates in the ancient tradition of the beast fable, which itself is often an indirect commentary on human beings. Part of the appeal of this story of talking birds and the lone, simple-hearted miner who claimed he could understand their language is that it raises, but leaves unresolved, the question of what is funny. Jays mightily enjoy the folly of one of their own kind, but the storyteller relates it as mere fact, and the owl from Nova Scotia misses the point. Another part of the story's appeal no doubt derives from its reinforcement in fresh western vernacular of Robert Burns's gentle but wryly ironic reflection that the best-laid plans of mice and men often go astray.

THE STOLEN WHITE ELEPHANT

While the detective story was still a new genre, Twain recognized its adaptability to his fondness for the antihero, and therefore to spoofing. Inspector Blunt is a progenitor of that later marvel of ineptitude, Jacques Clouseau (the Pink Panther). The escapades of Blunt and his force of inspired idiots, the straight-faced narration of the terminally credulous narrator, and the praise of all the newspapers but one combine to create a picture frequently found in Twain's works, of a society of fools. The police and journalists are only the most prominent features of this society; potential replacements are abundant. In this story, the satire is moderated by good humor, but almost every sentence contributes to building an edifice that is doomed to collapse.

1. *Siam had been in the wrong:* a veiled criticism of British imperialism. Great Britain's proper frontier was thousands of miles away from Siam.
2. *Jumbo:* the name of an elephant owned by P. T. Barnum.
3. *Doré Bibles:* Bibles illustrated by the famous nineteenth-century French artist Paul Gustave Doré.
4. *repeaters:* The newspaper article neglects to mention that it is illegal to vote more than once. Twain is satirizing both notorious election frauds and journalistic distortion of news.
5. *noble right of American citizens:* another example of distorted reporting. The newspaper neglects to mention that O'Donohue and McFlannigan, both first-day immigrants, were not citizens, and were therefore participating in another notorious election fraud.
6. *"We Never Sleep":* the motto of the famous Pinkerton Detective Agency. The motto is ridiculously inappropriate for Inspector Blunt's colleagues, who slept through the theft of a stove from their headquarters the previous winter, and through Jumbo's entrance into their headquarters, his suffering, and his death.

The McWilliamses and the Burglar Alarm

The third of three humorous stories Twain wrote about the hapless McWilliams family, this tale and the others have been generally interpreted as deriving from Twain's personal life. Some critics have regarded the stories as reflecting Twain's frustration with technology, some as revealing that marriage turned Twain into a milquetoast, and some as a rueful acknowledgment that family leads parents into paranoid worries.

The story, however, also has an aspect of social criticism. Where "The Stolen White Elephant" casually alludes to widespread election frauds, this story concentrates on such prevalence of burglary in genteel American society that an industry has been created to cope with it. The industry, however, is itself semifraudulent for its product, the burglar alarm, is too trouble-prone to be effective. So what McWilliams does not lose to burglars he loses to the burglar alarm company. Both burglars and victims seem to operate under a common understanding of accepted procedure: that is, once stolen, property becomes the burglar's and can thenceforth be redeemed at pawnbrokers' rates, subject to negotiation. Secure in this arrangement, burglars can aspire to emulate genteel manners, as is shown by the conversation between McWilliams and a burglar that is conducted in so high-minded a way and with such flowery language that the burglar expresses concern for the "hallowed conventionalities of our Christian civilization"—while retaining his loot. Twain's humor, therefore, verges on the sardonic as he mocks a society whose folly includes prizing convention above principle and being too refined for its own good.

1. *enlightening the heathen:* an allusion to the common practice of donating to missionary societies, a custom that Twain seldom lost an opportunity to criticize on two grounds: the heathen probably did not need to be converted, but the society from which the missionaries came did.

THE PRIVATE HISTORY OF A CAMPAIGN THAT FAILED

When the Civil War broke out, Mark Twain fled it. Exactly what went on in his life and mind to cause him to do this is one of the biggest mysteries in Twain biography, and "The Private History" is one of his few works that is relevant to this decision. It is not clear, however, whether the piece is truth or fiction, or, if a mixture, how much of it is truth and how much a retrospective attempt to create a favorable image of himself, an activity with which he was much concerned. An invitation from the *Century Magazine* to contribute to its series of "Battles and Leaders of the Civil War" gave Twain an opportunity to say something for the record. The result is a work of skillful craftsmanship.

Missouri had been a border state; it permitted slavery but did not secede. From the perspectives of this band of immature Confederate volunteers who lacked guidance and discipline, Twain captures the ambivalence—"confusion" is what he calls it—affecting a great many young men of military age on the issues of the looming conflict. At first the narrative is comic, as the adventures of the unsoldierly young would-be soldiers are reported in all their naïveté and foolishness, but the account of the ambush they laid for the stranger is one of the most poignant passages in Twain's writing. Then Twain masterfully takes the reader down from this dramatic climax to a humorous conclusion. His pacing is superb, as is his quick but smooth transition from one mood to another.

Twain's 1877 speech on the same subject is included in the appendix. Clearly, both accounts cannot be true. Whatever the historical truth, "The Private History" is most certainly a true representation of the humanitarian Twain who by the time of its composition had come to loathe war and the leaders and writers who deceived their audiences with romantic conceptions of it.

1. *Buena Vista and Molino del Ray:* These were U.S. victories in the Mexican War of 1847.
2. *about three months:* It was a common misconception of both sides that what became the Civil War would last only three months.
3. *a few hours of seeing him:* Twain stretches the truth here about his possible meeting with Grant. "Weeks" would have been more accurate than "hours."

EXTRACTS FROM ADAM'S DIARY

Under the guise of retelling the story of Adam and Eve in an entertaining way (he had long since achieved the reputation of a preeminent humorist), Twain wrote a story that was disarmingly funny on the surface but profoundly and subtly seditious of both the Bible and Christianity. The tale of Adam and Eve is one of the great stories of literature and the source of such major Christian doctrines as original sin, the Fall of Man, and the Fortunate Fall—the notion that the expulsion from Eden had a good aspect for humanity, because it gave humans a chance to earn Heaven, an infinitely better place than Eden. Instead of following the Bible account faithfully and writing humorous glosses on the text, as John Milton had written serious ones, Twain took a freer approach. He set aside most of the centuries of interpretive reasoning that led to Christian doctrine and wrote a new and mostly humanistic version of events that greatly reduced the role of God in the drama. In this new version, the difference of the sexes begins as comic contrast, transmutes into interdependence, and culminates as a love that is sufficient unto itself and feels no need of a Heaven.

1. *Niagara Falls:* This story was probably conceived after Twain was invited to write a humorous piece on Niagara Falls for a souvenir book for the 1893 Pan-American Exposition in Buffalo, New York. He incorporated the locale into his story with area place-names: Buffalo, nearby Tonawanda, and Lake Erie. In addition, Twain made use of the association of the falls and honeymooners, and the story can be read as an account not of a couple who began there in love but of a couple who found love there.
2. *The new creature names everything . . . protest:* In having Eve name everything, Twain departs from the biblical account (Gen. 2:20), which has Adam do the naming.
3. *set apart last November:* a puzzling statement, unless Twain was somehow aware that the Jewish calendar, which dates from Creation, begins in the fall. Adam, however, follows Christian practice in treating Sunday, the first day, as the day of rest, instead of the biblical seventh day.
4. *intended to eat each other:* Twain might have been familiar with biblical commentaries that addressed this ominous observation centuries before. For Twain, his own contribution about the buzzard (see page 123) would have been consonant with the Calvinist doctrine of predestination, a sign that Edenic bliss was not intended to last.
5. *goodness . . . spirit:* Many commentators have recognized the likeness of Eve to Livy, Twain's beloved wife and soul mate.

The Man That Corrupted Hadleyburg

This is one of Twain's finest and most powerful works, but it is only in part about the corrupting influence of money. Readers of this tale typically have two questions about it: What did Hadleyburg do to offend the passing stranger, and who was he? Neither question can be definitely answered, but some working speculations may be proposed. Hadleyburg is described as a rigidly and narrowly righteous town, smug, sanctimonious, coldly indifferent to strangers, and proud of itself. Pride goes before a fall, runs the proverb, and Christianity regards pride as the first of the seven deadly sins. Hadleyburg was set for a fall, yet we are told that it was "the *most* honest and upright town in *all* the region" (italics mine), so the average could not have been impressive. The mysterious stranger (a recurrence of that powerful and ominous motif in Twain's works) seems to have been no ordinary mortal. He had a great deal of money at his disposal; he wandered for a year at a time; he was bitter, malicious, and revengeful; his knowledge of the town was infernally intimate; and when he finally thought up a plan to *corrupt* (a Calvinist term) the entire town, "it lit up his whole head with an evil joy." The stranger, therefore, has more than a touch to him of the Tempter, and the illustration of him emphasizes his devilish looks: pointed chin, ears, and eyebrows, deep and glowing eyes, and an evil grin.

The town leaders, who all claimed to have offered the fictitious advice "Go and reform" when they believed lying would make them rich, in their condescending pride never even considered the need to take their own advice. The shallowness of the town's vaunted honesty is exposed when it changes its name after its embarrassment, as if that would alter its basic character or was even an honest action. In the story's final twist, the ironic juxtaposing of the town's earlier and later mottoes tells it all. The first one, quoting from the Lord's Prayer, boasts of how devout it is. The latter, however, effectively denies its Lord by rewording the humble prayer into a dare. Nothing was learned; nothing was taken to heart; nothing changed. Hadleyburg was corrupt at heart when the stranger arrived, and all he did was to make the town reveal its true character.

The story is intricately devised, and all the parts of it work together. It is ultimately a very bleak view of human nature, but that view is not new in Twain. Glimpses of it can be seen in many earlier works, especially the novels, but where he was usually at some pains to bury it deep in those works, at this time of his life he expressed his innermost feelings more freely.

1. Missionary Herald: Twain's scorn of most missionary activities can be deduced from his famous epigram: "Nothing so needs reforming as other people's habits."
2. *"that kind man who set his boat afloat upon the waters!"*: cf. Eccles. 11:1.
3. *nineteen principal citizens:* In relating this story to Twain's sojourn in Vienna, Cynthia Ozick persuasively argues a parallel between Hadleyburg's nineteen principal citizens and the vicious and prejudiced parliamentarians representing the nineteen national enclaves of Austria-Hungary.
4. *"Sam Lawson"*: a well-known, likeable character in two popular books by Harriet Beecher Stowe: *Oldtown Folks* (1869) and *Sam Lawson's Oldtown Fireside Stories.*
5. "*a virtue which has not been tested in the fire*": cf. Milton's *Areopagitica* (1644): "I cannot praise a fugitive and cloistered virtue, unexercised and un-

breathed, that never sallies out and sees her adversary, but slinks out of the race where that immortal garland is to be run for, not without lust and heat."

6. *"delights to honor":* cf. Esther 6:6.
7. *sold:* hoaxed.

THE $30,000 BEQUEST

Partly in the tradition of Dickens's *Great Expectations* (1861), "The $30,000 Bequest" is a moral warning of the corrosive effect of wealth, even just the prospect of wealth, on character, and how destructive it can be to essential happiness. Twain's distance from the Fosters is implied by the pervasive irony of the story that applies to the values of the Fosters, and to the pattern of reversal. Other important aspects of the story touch on its reversal of conventional sex roles in marriage, establish a correlation of romanticism and unreality, and, most alarmingly, expose the susceptibility of the human mind to living in a dream world. Twain had explored this tendency at length as early as *Roughing It* (1872), devoted most of *Connecticut Yankee* (1889) to it, and built heavily on it in "The Great Dark" and the *Mysterious Stranger* manuscripts he worked on in the last decade of his life.

1. *Saladin Foster:* The Foster family had a predilection for strange and somewhat ominous names, all associated with violence or tragedy. Saladin was a famous twelfth-century Muslim sultan who successfully led military campaigns against Western forces.
2. *Electra:* in Greek myth, the daughter of Clytemnestra and the sister of Orestes. Electra encouraged Orestes to slay their mother for having murdered their father.
3. *Clytemnestra:* In this story Clytemnestra is the daughter of Electra, a reversal of the relationship in the myths.
4. *Gwendolen:* possibly a reference to a character in Ambrose Philips's historical tragedy *The Briton* (1722).
5. *romance-tinge in the parental blood:* Twain had a lifelong antipathy to romanticism; this comment, therefore, implies disapproval.
6. *a curious and unsexing one:* The pet names, Sally and Aleck, would seem to reverse the sexes and the sexual relationship of the Fosters. Aleck, furthermore, is devoted to accumulating wealth, and Sally to spending it, another reversal of conventional expectations.
7. *reading romances . . . dreams:* The association between romanticism and dreams is made explicit here.
8. *stickful:* a unit of set type in a frame.
9. *pied:* Type matter spilled or thrown into disorder is "pied."
10. *W.C.T.U.:* Women's Christian Temperance Union.
11. *Rowton hotel:* a hotel for poor men, part of a chain first established by Lord Montague Rowton in England.

12. *the Woman with the Hatchet:* Carry Nation, a temperance activist, who attacked saloons with her hatchet.
13. *combining business with grief:* Irony is apparent by the obvious alteration of the familiar expression "combining business with pleasure."
14. *could have left us . . . increase:* In blaming his uncle, Sally argues ridiculously that he and Aleck would not have been tempted if more money had been promised in the bequest. Thus, even on his deathbed, he denies responsibility for his own actions.

Eve's Diary

Some idea of the complexity of Mark Twain can be glimpsed by reflecting that this largely humorous story was written just one year after the death of his beloved wife, Livy, and yet is also one of the most tender and touching tributes he ever wrote. It bears an obvious, parallel relationship to "Adam's Diary," written in 1893, and it continues some of the same ideas in that earlier work. It continues, for example, the subtle subversion of the Bible and Christianity by creating an alternative, largely secular and humanistic account of our first parents. It plays down the role of the Deity; instead it emphasizes the way Adam and Eve—and therefore man and woman—discover themselves, especially their differences, yet choose to blend into a unit. In contrast to the traditional view of Eve as primarily blameworthy for the Fall and as inferior to Adam, Twain's story highlights Eve's intellectual curiosity, her senses of wonder and delight, her sophistication and introspective capacity, and her loving ability to bring Adam into his full human potential. The Bible is silent about the death of Eve, but Twain's Adam is eloquent. Eve brought love into Adam's world, and while he had that, he desired nothing more.

1. *eternal vigilance is the price of supremacy:* a saying usually ascribed to Wendell Phillips, in an 1852 speech.

Captain Stormfield's Visit to Heaven

Instead of the familiar "Extracts from Captain Stormfield's Visit to Heaven" that was originally published in 1908–09, this anthology uses the expanded revision Twain finished in 1909 but did not publish in his lifetime, which was not available in complete form until Professors Howard G. Baetzhold and Joseph B. McCullough prepared and published it in 1995 under a shortened title. I am grateful to the University of California Press for permission to reprint their edition. This expanded version of the story (the familiar "Extracts" version takes up all of chapter 3 and most of chapter 4) enhances the story in terms of plot, theme, and characterization. The author's note explains the appropriateness of the word *visit* in the title. With tactful delicacy, the author hesitantly confesses in that note that Captain Stormfield's account of his voyage to Heaven might have been only a dream. In any case, it certainly is Twain's wistful dream.

"Captain Stormfield" shows Twain, long a self-declared determinist, still ruminating over the Bible, religion, and the possible truths that may lie behind them. God, the captain discovers, is infinitely kinder and more liberal than He has been pictured, and Heaven has also been badly misrepresented by preachers, especially those who insist that all varieties of human beings must conform to their notion of it. In this story, Heaven is instead infinitely accommodating, a perfect place. But the human race is a botched job—variety of "Moral Qualities" carried to excess—and the temporal discrepancy between heavenly and earthly time keeps prayers from being answered as humans wish and God intends. All human beings have thought at some time that, left to them, a better Creation could have been conceived, but in this story a commonsensical Twain undertakes to explain why *this* is not the best of all possible worlds, though the best of all possible gods may have intended it so.

1. *Devil's Race-Track:* a fictional region that figures in Twain's unfinished story "The Enchanted Sea Wilderness" (c. 1890).
2. *prejudice against Jews:* By the time he wrote this, Twain was a philosemite who had on a number of occasions publicly taken the side of Jews or written favorably about them.
3. *"almost thou persuadest me to pe a Ghristian":* a quote from Acts 26:28, King James.
4. *Encke's and Halley's comets:* comets named after two astronomers who discovered that what were thought to be different comets were instead different sightings of the same one, whose periodic appearances could be predicted.
5. *under weigh:* under way.
6. *manna and quails:* the food of the Israelites in the Sinai wilderness. See Exod. 16:13–15, King James.
7. *Moody and Sankey:* Dwight Lyman Moody and Ira David Sankey were popular American evangelists in the late nineteenth century.
8. *Talmage:* Thomas De Witt Talmage was a popular Brooklyn preacher whom Twain mistakenly believed had insulted working-class people by implying that their body odors would be offensive to cultured people of the upper class. Twain refused to be corrected about his belief and retained an animosity toward him.
9. *Job . . . Ham . . . Jeremiah:* all Old Testament figures. Job is the subject of the Book of Job; Ham is one of the three sons of Noah; Jeremiah is the prophet of the Book of Jeremiah.
10. *Bannercross Murderer:* an ironic allusion to Charles Peace, a convicted murderer from Bannercross, England, who "got religion" as he was awaiting execution by hanging. By implication, Heaven was easy, maybe even too easy, to get into.
11. *Captain Kidd:* a notorious seventeenth-century pirate. Twain probably did not share Sandy's acceptance and admiration of Kidd.

12. *Prince Gortschakoff:* an accomplished nineteenth-century Russian statesman.
13. *slush-boy:* the ship cook's assistant, whose job it was to clean up fat and grease spills.
14. *Ezekiel, Mahomet, Zoroaster:* Ezekiel was an Old Testament prophet (Book of Ezekiel); Mahomet was the founder of Islam; and Zoroaster, the founder of Zoroastrianism. Such variety, in addition to Homer, Buddha, and Confucius, as well as beings from other astronomical systems, emphasizes the nonexclusive character of Stormfield's Heaven.
15. *mudsill:* a building support placed at or below ground level. Hence, someone of low status.
16. *screw a glass into their eye:* In adjusting monocles to their eyes, wearers sometimes look as if they are screwing the glass into place.
17. *never had a chance to show it:* possibly an echo of Thomas Gray's widely known poem "Elegy Written in a Country Churchyard" (1751), which popularized the sentiment that many potentially great individuals, deprived of opportunity to demonstrate their talents, live and die in obscurity. See especially lines 53–60.
18. *'Gates Ajar' proportions:* Twain intended "Captain Stormfield" in part as a satire of a popular novel, Elizabeth Stuart Phelps's *The Gates Ajar* (1868), which conceived of a somewhat smaller Heaven than Twain did. Twain later described her book as having "imagined a mean little ten-cent heaven about the size of Rhode Island."
19. *procasturation:* Sandy has occasional trouble with big words. He means "procrastination."
20. *hypotheneuse:* Sandy means "hypothesis."

LETTER FROM THE RECORDING ANGEL

Also known as "Letter to the Earth," this piece, originally written in 1887 but left unpublished until 1946, is reprinted here with the gracious permission of HarperCollins Publishers although our text has accepted the corrections of the Mark Twain Papers edition. It tells its story through the epistolary device of a letter from the recording angel to a man, and the story's trenchant irony is kept understated until the last, power-packed sentence. Why it was not published in Twain's lifetime is not hard to guess. It is addressed to "Andrew Langdon, Coal Dealer," the cousin of his wife, Livy. Her father had also been a coal dealer, so it might have caused his wife pain if it had been published while she was living, and it would have made him, who was treated very generously by her father, look ungracious if he published it after Livy's death. Why he wrote it at all with a Langdon in mind is a question for which I know no answer. Biographical considerations aside, the hypocrisy of "Professional Christians" is clearly the target of the piece, along with the notion that those whom Calvinism termed the "elect" had special grace. Short though this story is, in it Twain's coruscating irony is unmistakable and potent.

1. *Andrew Langdon:* Some versions of the story use the name Abner Scofield.
2. *Wanamaker grade:* Twain despised John Wanamaker, the founder of a prestigious department store, for several reasons. He considered Wanamaker a hypocrite for supporting the Sunday-school movement while, at the same time, underpaying his female employees and thereby inducing some of them to resort to prostitution to maintain themselves. He also resented Wanamaker for selling one of his books below the publisher's list price.

The Great Dark

"The Great Dark" is an incomplete story, lacking a conclusion and containing some minor inconsistencies. It is included in this anthology because although unfinished it is one of the most powerful stories Twain ever undertook to write and constitutes an important part of his literary record. It was published for the first time and named by Bernard DeVoto in 1962 in *Letters from the Earth,* and a text slightly revised and corrected was edited by John S. Tuckey in 1967 for the Mark Twain Papers volume *Which Was the Dream? And Other Symbolic Writings of the Later Years,* which text this anthology follows. The story has rarely been reprinted since then, and we thank HarperCollins Publishers for permission to print it in this anthology.

Scholarship has linked this story to events in Twain's life and has identified some autobiographical elements in it. In his 16 August 1898 letter to William Dean Howells, Twain expressed his intention to make the first half or three quarters of the story comic. This intention notwithstanding, although there are comic passages in the story (particularly those about the disappearing coffee in Turner's cup), the story as a whole is far from comic. In notes he left about the story, Twain outlined its conclusion. After ten or fifteen years of aimless wandering in unremitting darkness, the ship on the drop of water that is its world comes into the reflected beam of light in the microscope that is observing it. The "great dark" turns to a hot, white glare that dries up the sea. A previous meeting of the ship with another lost vessel had resulted in the children of the captain and the protagonist Edwards being abducted as prisoners. Now that the water is gone, Edwards and the captain take a grueling trip over the dry seabed to that ship, only to find all aboard dead and their children's bodies mummified by the heat. The captain is maddened by grief. Meanwhile, back on their own ship, crew members get drunk and begin killing one another. Others, including Edwards's wife and other daughter, die of stress and grief. Then Edwards awakens from his dream, at home with his family. But now he regards them as dreams.

The most frightening part of this story deals with the Superintendent of Dreams, a mysterious-stranger figure. When Edwards orders him to end the dream immediately, the Superintendent replies, "The dream? *Are you quite sure it is a dream?*" The issue of dream versus reality is, in Twain's works, more than a matter of psychological perception. Twain had for some years contemplated a horrifying prospect, that existence is a fixed dream, that other dreams occur within the dream of life, and that there is no way to be absolutely certain what is a dream and what is reality. In an essay on *Connecticut Yankee,* I have discussed how Twain even contemplates in that novel that existence and linear history are hoaxes, that the same unchanging events are continuously being replayed in different temporal dimensions, and that existence is illusory, a matter of slipping from one of those dream dimensions into another.

Twain was fascinated by the telescope, as "Captain Stormfield" shows, and by the microscope, as this story makes clear. He was fascinated by the thought that just as humans can look down upon tiny organisms invisible to the naked eye that are huge and terrifying in their own dimension, so may we and everything of our world seem equally minute and inconsequential to larger and more sapient beings. In fact, Twain speculated that only God truly exists as an independent and infinite being, and that everything else, from microscopic organisms to human beings to astronomical systems, is merely particles in His arteries, of which He is largely unaware and to which He is indifferent. The very idea of infinity implied to Twain that finite humankind and its world and solar system are ultimately of trivial importance. "The Great Dark" illustrates that point by allegorically proposing that the ship is a symbol of the world, but a nightmare world that is a plaything of a superior but malicious being, a world that does not know where it is going and is always in the dark. This world, moreover, moves like a planet in an orbit around a sun of intense light and heat—really the focused beam of light of a microscope—which would be fatal to it if experienced directly. The manipulator of the microscope does not care about the tiny beings that inhabit the ship or the drop of water it floats on. From the perspective of this story, the captain's statement in his last speech that the ship "is in the hands of God" may be literally true, God being the manipulator of the microscope. But that fact does not imply a benevolent, personal, and caring God, and Twain does not find it a source of comfort. Much of his fiction is ultimately not humorous but, rather, honest speculation on what the human condition may be, speculation that disturbs him as well as his readers who follow his thought.

Although Twain is generally regarded as a humorous writer, that evaluation is based on his earlier works, a number of which are collected herein. No one, however, regards Twain's later works as humorous, and "The Great Dark" is a case in point. It has been shown that even the early works have serious aspects, and this story has some comic aspects; the differences are those of proportion and emphasis. As this and the next story demonstrate, however, Twain at bottom is a profoundly serious writer.

1. *19th of March:* the birthday of Twain's daughter Olivia Susan Clemens—Susy—who was born in 1872. Also the feast of Saint Joseph, the patron saint of happy deaths. Roman Catholics are familiar with this

date. Twain would have had many opportunities to learn about it, including from Katy Leary, a longtime servant of the family.

2. *Sable island:* a landmark island, about two hundred miles east of Halifax, Nova Scotia.
3. *jimjams:* nervous apprehensions; the jitters.
4. *the Empire Express:* a very fast express train of the New York Central Railroad system.
5. *The Washingtonian Movement... Father Matthew* [sic]: a temperance movement that began in 1840 and ultimately signed up hundreds of thousands who pledged total abstinence. Rev. (Father) Theobald Mathew, a Catholic priest, was one of its star speakers.
6. *give* him *down the banks:* a slang term for "chew out"; criticize angrily.
7. hadn't ever been a member!: Cap'n Jimmy experienced a kind of hoax that, in Calvinism, would be like failing to be elected despite having lived morally.
8. *"Gulf Stream's gone to the devil!":* Twain puts a carefully crafted and subtly ironic comment into the mouth of the unsuspecting mate. Turner is using only a figure of speech and is unaware of the Superintendent of Dreams and, of course, does not know that he has placed the ship where it cannot locate itself. What Turner figuratively calls the Devil is, therefore, the Superintendent of Dreams, who might as well be the Devil.
9. "*where the Gulf Stream twineth*": an ironic echo of Jim Fisk's famous sarcastic and enigmatic reply to a congressional committee's question about what happened to all the money lost by investors in his scheme to corner the gold market: "It has gone where the woodbine twineth"—that is, it's lost beyond recall.
10. *"Very good... imposing":* See the headnote for a discussion of this paragraph.
11. *We are strangely made:* The same comment Mrs. Richards makes in "Hadleyburg." This and the next two paragraphs reflect Twain's thoughts about the insubstantiality of existence. The word *disenchants* here and elsewhere has a literal force; Twain is proposing that our sense of reality is only a dream brought on by an enchantment.
12. *perfectly devilish:* Apparently a figure of speech, this phrase also has a literal force that with other such terms cumulatively suggest the implication that the entire experience, including the uncertainty of the dream status, takes place in Hell.
13. *"Captain Moreland":* an autobiographical detail. Captain *Morland* was the captain of the *Batavia,* the ship on which the Clemens family had voyaged years before.
14. "*Doctor John Brown*": another autobiographical element. Dr. Brown had been Livy's physician in Scotland in 1873 and subsequently became a

family friend. He was the author of the children's story *Rab and His Friends* (1859).

15. *Damnation!:* yet one more verbal hint that the literal meaning may be the true one.
16. *and presently none was left but me.:* "The Mad Passenger," printed for the first time in *Which Was the Dream?* (560–67), is a rejected part of "The Great Dark" that was intended to follow these words. It elaborates on the dreamlike nature of existence.
17. *"if she goes to hell!":* another unconsciously ironic statement by one of the ship's company. In a manner of speaking, the ship is already in Hell.

THE SECOND ADVENT

Twain's two greatest exasperations were God and the human race. He heretically believed in God as an omnipotent, omniscient, but not benevolent deity. Twain was a devoted family man, a good friend, and a mighty champion of the oppressed, but he regarded the race as a whole not only foolish and morally disappointing but literally damned. In this story, published only once before, by John S. Tuckey for the Mark Twain Papers volume *Fables of Man* (1972) and reprinted here by permission of the University of California Press, Twain satirizes both Christianity and human nature. He especially targets Christian beliefs in the virgin birth as being based on patently and unconvincingly flimsy evidence; and in special providences (benevolent acts of the deity out of the normal course of nature for individual human beings) as wild cards that would inevitably upset everything else. In regard to human nature, just as the citizens of Hadleyburg at the end of the story in effect abandon their Christianity out of pride and self-interest, so in "The Second Advent" do the citizens of Arkansas find that the interposition of the deity in their affairs causes such havoc that they in effect reject Jesus, legally restrict Christianity to a nominal form, and put an end to the second advent. There is humor in this story, but it is a grim humor. For Twain, most of the preachments about the goodness of God and the human race were adult equivalents of the Sunday-school tracts he satirized much earlier in his career.

1. *Black Jack:* an ironic name for a village associated with a holy miracle. In one sense of the term, blackjack is a card game used in gambling; in another, it is a flexible bludgeon used usually by criminals to knock out their victims.
2. *Greeley... Bennett... Beach:* three prominent nineteenth-century American journalists: Horace Greeley, owner and editor of the *New York Tribune;* James Gordon Bennett, owner and editor of the New York *Herald* and the *Evening Telegram;* and probably Alfred Ely Beach, editorial chair of the *Scientific American.*
3. *Talmage:* Rev. Thomas De Witt Talmage. See note 8, "Captain Stormfield's Visit to Heaven."

4. *"Lord, Thy will . . . be done"*: an alteration of a line from the Lord's Prayer. The change ironically reverses the humble acceptance of the original.
5. *thirty pieces of silver:* an ironic allusion to the thirty pieces of silver Judas was paid to betray Jesus (see Matt. 26:14–16). Also ironic in that, human nature being unchangeable and corrupt, history repeats itself.

Selected Bibliography

Baetzhold, Howard G., and Joseph B. McCullough, eds. *The Bible According to Mark Twain.* Athens: University of Georgia Press, 1995.

Berkove, Lawrence I. "Poe, Twain, and the Nature of Conscience." *ESQ* 46:4 (2000): 239–52.

———. "The Reality of the Dream: Structural and Thematic Unity in *A Connecticut Yankee.*" *Mark Twain Journal* 22:1 (spring 1984): 8–14.

———. "The Trickster God in *Roughing It.*" In *Trickster Lives: Culture and Myth in American Fiction.* Edited by Jeanne Campbell Reesman. (Repr. from *Thalia* 18:1 and 2 (1998).) Athens: University of Georgia Press, 2001.

Brodwin, Stanley. "Mark Twain's Theology: The Gods of a Brevet Presbyterian." *Cambridge Companion to Mark Twain.* Edited by Forrest G. Robinson. New York: Cambridge University Press, 1995.

Covici, Pascal, Jr. *Mark Twain's Humor: The Image of a World.* Dallas: Southern Methodist University Press, 1962.

Cummings, Sherwood. *Mark Twain and Science: Adventures of a Mind.* Baton Rouge: Louisiana State University Press, 1988.

Fatout, Paul. *Mark Twain Speaking.* Iowa City: University of Iowa Press, 1976.

Hayes, John Q. *Mark Twain and Religion: A Mirror of American Eclecticism.* Edited by Fred A. Rodewald. New York: Peter Lang, 1989.

Le Master, J. R., and James D. Wilson, eds. *The Mark Twain Encyclopedia.* New York: Garland, 1993.

Messent, Peter. *The Short Works of Mark Twain: A Critical Study.* Philadelphia: University of Pennsylvania Press, 2001.

Ozick, Cynthia. Introduction to *The Man That Corrupted Hadleyburg and Other Stories and Essays. The Oxford Mark Twain.* Edited by Shelley Fisher Fishkin. New York: Oxford University Press, 1996.

Quirk, Tom. *Mark Twain: A Study of the Short Fiction.* New York: Twayne, 1997.

Rasmussen, R. Kent. *Mark Twain A to Z.* New York: Facts on File, 1995.

Twain, Mark. *Collected Tales, Sketches, Speeches, & Essays.* 2 vols. Edited by Louis J. Budd. N.p.: Library of America, 1992.

———. *Early Tales & Sketches.* Vol. 2, 1864–1865. Edited by Edgar Marquess Branch and Robert H. Hirst. Berkeley: University of California Press, 1981.

———. "Extract from Captain Stormfield's Visit to Heaven." Introduction by Victor Doyno. Amherst, N.Y.: Prometheus Press, 2002.

———. *Fables of Man.* Edited by John S. Tuckey. Berkeley: University of California Press, 1972.

———. Introduction to *The New Guide of the Conversation in Portuguese and English, in Two Parts,* by Pedro Carolino. Boston: James R. Osgood, 1883.

———. *Letters from the Earth.* Edited by Bernard DeVoto. New York: Harper & Row, 1962.

———. *Which Was the Dream? And Other Symbolic Writings of the Later Years.* Edited by John S. Tuckey. Berkeley: University of California Press, 1967.

Wilson, James D. *A Reader's Guide to the Short Fiction of Mark Twain.* Boston: G. K. Hall, 1987.

———. "Religious and Aesthetic Vision in Mark Twain's Early Career." *Canadian Review of American Studies* 17:2 (summer 1986): 155–72.

About the Editor

Lawrence I. Berkove, Emeritus Professor of English at the University of Michigan–Dearborn, is a specialist in American literature of the nineteenth and early twentieth centuries. His journal publications are extensive, and recent book and monograph publications include *A Prescription for Adversity: The Moral Art of Ambrose Bierce* (2002), *Dan De Quille* (1999), and *Ethical Records of Twain and His Circle of Sagebrush Journalists* (1994).

Mark Twain has long been a particular interest of his, and he has published and lectured frequently on him both here and abroad.

A Note on the Type

The principal text of this Modern Library edition was set in a digitized version of Janson, a typeface that dates from about 1690 and was cut by Nicholas Kis, a Hungarian working in Amsterdam. The original matrices have survived and are held by the Stempel foundry in Germany. Hermann Zapf redesigned some of the weights and sizes for Stempel, basing his revisions on the original design.

Other Modern Library Paperback Classics
by Mark Twain

Adventures of Huckleberry Finn
INTRODUCTION BY GEORGE SAUNDERS
Reproduces the text of the 1885 first American edition
0-375-75737-6; trade paperback; 304 pp.

The Adventures of Tom Sawyer
INTRODUCTION BY FRANK CONROY
Reproduces the Mark Twain Project edition, the approved text of the Center for Scholarly Editions of the Modern Language Association
0-375-75681-7; trade paperback; 304 pp.

A Connecticut Yankee in King Arthur's Court
INTRODUCTION BY ROY BLOUNT, JR.
Reproduces the 1889 first American edition, with original illustrations by Daniel Carter Beard
0-375-75780-5; trade paperback; 512 pp.

The Innocents Abroad
INTRODUCTION BY JANE JACOBS
Reproduces the text of the 1869 first American edition
0-8129-6705-4; trade paperback; 560 pp.

The Prince and the Pauper
INTRODUCTION BY CHRISTOPHER PAUL CURTIS
Reproduces the text of the Mark Twain Project edition, the approved text of the Center for Scholarly Editions of the Modern Language Association
0-375-76112-8; trade paperback; 240 pp.

Pudd'nhead Wilson and Those Extraordinary Twins
INTRODUCTION BY RON POWERS
Reproduces the text and illustrations from the 1894 first American edition
Illustrations by F. M. Senior and C. H. Warren
0-8129-6622-8; trade paperback; 288 pp.

A Tramp Abroad
INTRODUCTION BY DAVE EGGERS
Reproduces the text and selected illustrations from the 1880 first American edition
0-8129-7003-9; trade paperback; 400 pp.